THE MISFIT

JAY ANN FOLEY

This is a work of fiction. Names, characters, businesses, places, events and incidents are either the products of the author's imagination or used in a fictitious manner. Any resemblance to actual persons, living or dead, or actual events is purely coincidental.

ISBN 978-1-7392403-0-1 (paperback)
ISBN 978-1-7392403-1-8 (ebook)

Cover illustrated and designed by Catherine Clarke Design

For Chris, Carole, Kay and Richard … with love, always

Mist rolls in quick on the Moor, so locals say.
Don't venture from the path if you don't know the way.
There's pixies and beasts and will-o'-the-wisps too,
So just be careful that they don't catch you.
For if they do you may never be found,
Within the treacherous and boggy ground.
And if you hear mischief heading your way,
Beware for the moor sprites may spirit you away.

1

Georgie's dreams lay in a broken, smouldering heap beneath her on the turf. She could visualise them fading away with the cloud of breath blasted out of her lungs into the cold air, as she curled instinctively into a protective ball. Flashing hooves missed her by mere centimetres, the roar of jockeys, the shuddering earth, the crack of tack, the snort of breath. Then, seconds later, silence. As if an army, clad in chainmail and mounted on chargers, had marched right over the top of her, then moved on. Georgie lay still, blades of grass poking up her nostrils. The going had officially been given as 'soft'.

'Ha,' she groaned.

It didn't feel soft beneath her battered bones and already flourishing bruises.

'You all right down there? Need any help?' A kindly face above an ambulance uniform peered down at her.

Georgie raised herself on her right elbow, smiling as best she could. 'I'm good thanks. Just winded, I think.'

'Take your time then.' Having checked he no longer had a casualty to deal with, the medic moved away to stand on tiptoes, keen not to miss the remainder of the race.

Georgie flopped back and closed her eyes as the ground-staff swarmed to fix the hurdle Dotty Day had flattened clumsily, before ejecting her jockey skywards. Reopening them moments later, the picture had not improved. That Dotty's owner's pretty pink silks were stained with mud and grass was the least of Georgie's worries. Bert was going to be furious … no, not furious, apoplectic at the sight of his favourite mare careering loose around the track, reins flapping, stirrups bouncing, more circus performer than thoroughbred.

'Mate, you'll need to shift before the three-thirty race,' one of the ground-staff called over. 'Unless you want to be flattened and I'm gonna give you my honest opinion, you're tiny enough. I'd motor if I were you.'

Heeding his words, Georgie rose with as much dignity as one could when covered in muck and five feet tall. Wincing, she scooped up the pieces of the dislodged silk cap cover, trampled and torn into the ground by the passing stampede, then undid the chinstrap, pulling the hat from her head. There was no point trying to fit the pieces of silk back over the bald shell of the skull cap.

As the tannoy announced the result of the three o'clock race in buoyant tones, the winning punters cheered, while the losers groaned. The race was over. Tidying her bobbed brown curls to try and improve her appearance, Georgie ducked under the white railings and slunk off. The ambulance crew and ground-staff had melted away, but she was so close to the grandstand it wasn't worth trying to cadge a lift back anyway.

Abandoned betting slips fluttered around her paper-thin boots as she crossed the concourse. Kicking out at them had no impact on her mood; all she gained was a stubbed big toe. Wafting smells of sizzling burgers and stodgy chips turned her stomach, but not half as much as the sight of Dotty Day, still hurtling around the course, ducking in and out of the horses making their way back in along the walkway. One jockey made a valiant attempt to grab hold of the mare's bridle as she passed, but Dotty dodged away. Georgie could see the tall slim figure of Jess running towards Dotty, who also spied her and skipped away back onto the course, prancing up it in the wrong direction towards the final hurdle.

'Get hold of her.'

A familiar voice thundered from nearby, as Bert Russell, Dotty's trainer and Georgie's boss, waved his arms in agitation. Limping on to the grass, his lopsided gait more pronounced as always when under pressure, he threw Georgie a look of loathing. Hoping to make amends and help clear up the mess she'd partly caused, Georgie set off after the stocky ex-jockey.

Closer now, Jess dived for the reins and managed to get a firm hold of them, despite being dragged momentarily off her feet as Dotty pulled onwards. A scuffle ensued but the mare had spent all her energy. With sides puffing like a bellows, she allowed the game to end and herself to be caught. As soon as he reached them, Bert ran his hands cautiously down the mare's mud-caked forelegs, while Jess pulled the reins over the horse's head, the sleeve of her waterproof jacket smeared with slime from Dotty's lips. Deftly she unbuckled the girth and removed Georgie's saddle, weight and number cloth one-handed.

'Glad to see you're all right,' she called over to Georgie with a half-smile. 'Here grab this lot, will you? Dotty's gonna knock me into next week if she keeps rubbing at me. I'm not a fence post.'

'Cheers.' Georgie retrieved her gear from her colleague's outstretched arm, leaving Jess free to rescue her long blonde ponytail from Dotty's encroaching teeth.

Hoping for a quick getaway to the weighing room, Georgie tucked the dangling girth neatly against her body and turned away.

'Not so fast.' Bert straightened up, his craggy face red from a combination of gravity and anger, the thread veins covering his pointed nose pulsating. 'What were you playing at, pushing the horse for an extra stride? Dotty would've cleared it fine if you hadn't interfered and fallen off.'

'I didn't ask her, she put the stride in. I wasn't ready for it.'

'Clearly you weren't, but you should have been. Can't believe I put up with you bleating on about trying over fences. A right mess you've —'

'Dad, don't have a go at Georgie. Remember it's her first go over hurdles. She'll improve,' Jess protested loyally, receiving a grateful glance from Georgie.

Ignoring his daughter, Bert chuntered on. 'As far as I'm concerned, there won't be a next time. You'll be raking the muck heap for the next six months, Georgie, so long as those owners don't interfere.' He rounded on Jess: 'Now get that horse washed off and put a rug on her. What a state, every inch of her covered in mud. Hurry up, before she gets a chill.'

'Don't get any perks being the trainer's daughter,' Jess grumbled as she led Dotty away, steam rising from the retreating mare's grey rump.

Georgie grimaced. As Bert well knew, several of the horses at Beech Tree Stables belonged to Dotty's owners and they had always been supportive of her, at least until now. True today had been a disaster, but top jockeys weren't formed overnight. She kept her distance as Bert clomped across the parade ring, whipping off his tweed flat cap and rubbing his head in frustration. He walked too close to the rear of a strapping brown thoroughbred, narrowly missing a viciously lashing hindleg. Georgie knew he would be muttering furiously under his breath.

With a sigh, she moved towards the weighing room, unnoticed by the crowd now dispersing from applauding the winning horse into the enclosure. Attention had switched to the next race, already Georgie's tumble was forgotten. Deep in thought, she reviewed whether she had messed up. Dotty had been jumping fluently, Georgie had begun to think they might be in with a chance. What had gone wrong? She would watch the replay later, try and figure it out. With the weighing room mere steps away, running footsteps from behind were followed by strong hands encircling Georgie's waist; her hair brushed by lips whispering in her ear.

'Poor you, Gee-Gee. Hitting the deck on your first try. Most unfortunate.'

Georgie turned to greet her boyfriend, dazzled by the sun reflecting from the gleaming trophy he held casually in one hand. 'Oh, hey, well done you. Another winner.' She worked on keeping the tone light and free from envy.

'Yeah, got to keep stacking them up if I want a shot at being champion this season … and I do.'

'Course you do, Sam.'

'Another one for the mantlepiece,' he boasted, tossing the silver cup in the air, then catching the elaborate handle one-fingered. 'But look at the state of you. You must've face planted spectacularly. Can't tell what's freckles and what's mud. Ha ha.'

Georgie rubbed at her face with gloves so dirty she wasn't sure whether she'd wiped mud off or merely made it worse.

'Thankfully Dotty's all right, as am I,' she said, slightly spitefully at Sam's lack of concern.

'You're fine, but listen and don't take this the wrong way, might be best to stay with the flat racing, eh? Safer for you. I keep telling you this over-the-sticks malarkey is a tough old game. Riding all winter in the rain and cold, it's not for the faint-hearted or the glamourous.'

Anger rose in Georgie, gushing up her throat. She bit back retorts about being well aware what Sam was talking about. She'd been in the sport ten years; she knew how it worked.

Hard graft and proving yourself was what got you results. Bristling, she opened her mouth but before she could reply:

'Excuse me?'

The voice which spoke wasn't Georgie's. She noticed with a start that a gaggle of smartly dressed ladies had sidled up to Sam. She ought to have been tipped off by their scent, a mixture of floral perfumes she could taste so strongly they must have been reapplied every hour. No chance of less being more where they were concerned, she thought, as the leader of the group, a brunette wearing a hat decorated in what looked to be peacock feathers, thrust a racecard and a Sharpie pen at Sam and simpered, 'Can we have your autograph?'

'Course you can. It'd be my pleasure,' beamed Sam. 'Oi, Gee-Gee. Here.'

Unexpectedly he threw the trophy at Georgie, who scrabbled to catch it, almost dropping her expensive leather saddle in the process. Humiliated she glared at him. He didn't notice.

'See you back at the car later, yeah.' Sam gave it as an instruction, not a question.

Deflated, Georgie nodded and walked away, glancing back once to find Sam asking for all their names. He oozed the confidence of one successful at what they did and aware of it, as he charmed the group with easy banter and signed the numerous racecards with a huge smile on his handsome face. Sam Christie, one of the top jump jockeys in the country, possessor of so much natural talent with the horses he was always in demand. Blessed with a lean frame, he never struggled with his weight. Not looking where she was going, Georgie tripped into the weighing room, swearing loudly. The Clerk of the Scales raised his eyebrows in her direction.

'Tough day?' he asked kindly.

'Yeah, you could say that.' As she trooped through to the changing room, Georgie was glad it was nearly over.

In the full-length mirror, she glimpsed the extent of the damage to her clothes. Had she stood behind a large vehicle while its wheels spun in wet, runny mud, she would have looked no different. Spattered from her boots to her breeches, her face resembling a failed attempt at camouflage, Georgie couldn't wait to get warm and dry.

She waited around until Sam had finished riding in the last race, then they walked together across a now deserted racecourse to the car park. Sam had ridden another winner and was buzzing.

'I'm starving. Let's stop at that pub up the road,' he suggested, revving the engine. He pulled out into a convoy of horseboxes trundling towards the exit. 'I can't see a thing around this lot.'

'It's OK, we're not in a hurry,' Georgie replied, fastening her seatbelt.

'My stomach is.'

Ironically, they found themselves tucked in behind the familiar blue horsebox of Beech Tree Stables with "Bert Russell – Racehorses In Transit" festooned in huge red lettering across the back.

'It's not only Bert's horses that are slow,' Sam growled, swinging out to check the coast was clear, then flooring the accelerator with impatience. As the sports car sprang to life, pushing Georgie back into her seat, she caught the disapproving look on regular driver Damien's face as they roared by.

A light drizzle was falling by the time they had travelled a few miles up the road and pulled into the gravelled car park of The Gossiping Nag. The ramshackle ancient pub looked from the outside to be falling apart, but inside was all cosy thick stone walls, low beams and few customers.

They were served soon after ordering. While picking at the limp lettuce of her prawn salad, Georgie tried not to covert

Sam's delicious looking steak and chips. He was almost finished when his phone sprang to life on the table. He answered through a mouth full of onion ring.

'Can't hear you that well, mate. Signal's patchy through these beams. Hold on a sec.' Gesturing to Georgie that he was going outside, Sam stood up.

Georgie watched him, as did the bar staff, as he strolled through the dining area. He paused in the porch, chatting intensely, his face breaking with laughter, oblivious to the appreciative looks he received from those around him. He was so good looking with his blonde hair, toned body and designer clothes. Being with Sam was part ego-boost and part ego-wrecker. Sure, he was flirty, but then he was subjected to a lot of attention and flirting didn't mean cheating. Georgie was reminded why horses had always been her first love. They were uncomplicated, loyal and always there to cheer you up or bring you down to earth if you got overconfident.

She swiped a few of Sam's chips, then picked up the bottle of Thousand Island dressing and smothered the lettuce until no green was visible. It wasn't likely she'd be needing to do a lightweight anytime soon anyway. She just hoped Bert wouldn't jock her off for too long. To be booked for rides you needed to be seen and not forgotten.

Sam reappeared and pushed his plate of cold food aside. 'That was Toasty, offering me a lift to Cheltenham at the weekend. Course I don't need one. Got the Porsche, haven't I?'

Georgie gazed at him, feeling both the usual jolt of irritation at the mention of Toasty, Sam's fellow jockey, best mate and all-round troublemaker, plus an inkling of dislike at her boyfriend's tone. She shook it away rapidly. What was she thinking? She'd had a bad day, was all.

Outside the drizzle had become a downpour. Tumbling into the low seat of the Porsche, Georgie's phone began to ring. She pulled it from her pocket with damp hands. The voice on the other end was bossy, well-spoken. Petra, the secretary at Beech Tree Stables, wasted no words on niceties, merely stated facts.

'Bert wants to speak with you first thing tomorrow at morning stables. Pop in before you start work.'

2

'Check the girth … no, not there … ah, go on then … ha ha.' Sam mumbled in his sleep and rolled over onto his stomach.

Already wide-awake preparing clever retorts for whatever Bert might say later, Georgie stretched out and pushed the button, cancelling the alarm. Gently she got out of bed and peeped through the curtains. Being five o'clock, it was still dark, the moon shedding timid light over the golf course opposite Georgie's cottage. Nothing stirred; even the keenest of golfers unwilling to venture out in the frost.

For a moment, Georgie contemplated calling in sick. She loved her job and had worked hard at Beech Tree over the decade since she joined the team aged eighteen. Though sometimes tempted by the trendier yards, loyalty would surely count in her favour. The odd mistake, the occasional fall, these were hazards of the job and an everyday occurrence for those employed in numerous racing stables up and down the country. She grinned at the memories of visiting the local course as a child. She'd always stood right on the rails, absorbing the uniqueness of the race; beating hooves moving the ground beneath her feet as half-ton thoroughbreds pounded the turf. Jockeys crying to each other for more room or to encourage their mounts, the creak of leather, the swish of a tail. She still loved the raw thrill of it all; it was dangerous and uncertain; you couldn't let your concentration lapse for a split second. The camaraderie and the elation when it all went right for you, that was the best. The horse and you working as one. There was nothing else to compare.

'What's up with you?' she whispered crossly to herself.

To be chased out of the career she loved by a stroppy Bert was unthinkable. She'd get to work earlier than usual and make a point.

Showered and stepping outside the en-suite bathroom snuggled in a fluffy dressing gown decorated with horseshoes, Georgie found the bedside lamps on and the bed empty, duvet thrown back by someone keen to start their day. Downstairs in the kitchen, Sam was singing Coldplay's 'Fix You' at full volume while he struggled with the temperamental toaster.

'All right?' Georgie asked from the doorway, fanning the air against the smell of burnt toast.

'Got to get going. That film crew from the *Racing News* are interviewing me on the gallops at six-thirty.'

'Oh, that's today, is it?' Georgie winced, having forgotten.

She was alone in that judging by the amount of aftershave fumigating the small country-style kitchen. Sam was obviously looking forward to his rendezvous with Gina West, the glamourous blonde presenter. Georgie was sure the former model could make early morning on Epsom Downs seem fashionable and stand out in comparison to the usually oddly dressed stable staff, who would have thrown on whatever was to hand.

'Laters.' Sam pecked her on the cheek, leaving a sticky smear of margarine, marmite and toast crumbs.

'Will I see you later?' she asked, following him into the hall while wiping her face with the sleeve of her dressing gown.

Flamingo-like, Sam wobbled on one leg, then the other, pulling on polished knee length riding boots, voice contorted by the piece of burnt toast clenched between his teeth. 'Nope. Gotta be back home in Lambourn tonight.'

'Oh.' Georgie was disappointed. 'It's Quiz Night at the Final Furlong. I thought we'd join the guys. It's usually a laugh.'

'Sorry, Gee-Gee. The *Racing News* gang are taking me out to dinner as a thank you for my time.'

'I didn't know that.'

As he scooped up keys and mobile from the hall table, Sam chuckled. 'Tut tut, Georgie Wright, jealousy is not an attractive trait.'

'I'm not remotely —' The front door slammed behind Sam, the wall shook, dislodging the mirror which slid precariously to the side yet remained intact. 'Jealous.'

Half an hour later, Georgie sat inside her ancient Peugeot, which was colder and damper than outside. She shivered as the windscreen demisted with the speed of a sloth, hoping the heater would eventually realise it was turned to maximum. A sliver of light was showing on the horizon. Patches of green began to appear amongst the silver carpet of grass on the front lawn of Rose Cottage. A square of light suddenly appeared in an upstairs window of Tulip Cottage, the only other home at the end of the unmade track where Rose Cottage was situated.

With enough visibility, Georgie revved the engine and the car clattered down the pothole strewn lane. The headlights picked out the gleaming white of stray golf balls buried in a verge of overgrown nettles, abandoned out of reach unless you fancied being stung.

Minutes later, Georgie's hopes of being first at work were dashed. The double gates of Beech Tree Stables were already propped open, an assortment of trucks and cars abandoned in the parking area with no consideration for maximising the space. Even at such an early hour the yard was busy. Lights were on, stable doors open with rugs thrown over the bottom halves, as the preparations for riding out began. The staff whistled cheerily and called out greetings as they mucked out, chucking pitchforks full of shavings and manure into rusty wheelbarrows.

Georgie kept to the shadows as she crept round the corner of the L-shaped yard, hoping to get to the barn and begin work without being spotted, hoping even more that Bert had calmed down and forgotten he wanted to see her. She had managed to get tools and a wheelbarrow together before her presence was given away by Luna, who barked a greeting, tail wagging frenziedly. As she tried to calm the dog down, she rued working with the world's friendliest border collie. It had its downsides as it summoned Briggsy, the Head Lad, who stuck his head out from behind one of the towering piles of hay bales. Wisps stuck to his grey curls, giving him the look of a scarecrow with his checked shirt and neckerchief.

'Morning, Georgie. Looking lovely as always. Um, Bert wants a word, told me to send you over to the office when I saw you.'

Feeling her shoulders slump with dismay, Georgie grumbled, 'Has he told everyone? Or did Petra? Oh, never mind, I'm sure he just wants to say a special good morning.'

'And when you're finished, bung some tack on Minotaur.' Briggsy ignored the sarcasm as he turned away and missed Georgie's flinch of surprise, causing her to drop the handles of the barrow.

'Minotaur?' Georgie's voice was barely audible as the clang echoed through the barn. 'I don't usually ride Minotaur.'

Being the meanest and scariest horse in the yard, just coaxing Minotaur up to the gallops without an equine punch-up was a struggle usually left in the capable hands of the strongest staff members.

'You heard right. There's been some changes to first lot this morning. I've swapped you and Nabil around. He's taking Golden Goose.'

Though disgruntled, Georgie didn't argue. You rode whichever horse's name appeared on the board alongside yours, whether you liked it or not. Today was definitely a not, she thought, reaching the office, tucked away in the far corner of the yard, backing onto the paddocks. Georgie eased the door open. Swamped in a khaki North Face padded jacket, Petra sat at a desk typing into a laptop with pink painted nails which matched the hairband in her shoulder-length brunette bob. A little electric heater glowing orange had no impact on the chill. Petra didn't speak, though her breath was visible as she moved her lips soundlessly re-reading whatever she had composed. She merely inclined with her head that Georgie should go through to Bert's separate office.

The room was awash with stacks of the *Racing Life* newspaper. Tucked up on the nearest tower, the ginger yard cat was snoring instead of mousing. Faded framed photos of various champions from over the years hung higgledy-piggledy on the walls, a battered filing cabinet, all four drawers stuck open, stood in the corner and Bert sat behind a desk hidden under mugs of cold tea and glasses of fizzy orange vitamin tablets. Georgie lowered herself into the opposite chair but before her jodhpur-clad bottom reached the threadbare cushion, Bert spoke without looking up.

'No need to sit. This won't take long.'

Georgie rose again, trying to contain her annoyance.

'We're both busy so I'll get straight to the point. Following yesterday's disaster, I have taken the decision to return you to yard duties for six months. You will ride three lots a day and undertake regular schooling sessions over the training hurdles with Briggsy. When Briggsy decides you are ready, we will consider giving you another go.'

'Six months?'

'Yes, that's what I said.'

'That's ridiculous. Such an overreaction. I'm an experienced rider. You can't revert to treating me as an apprentice. I'm not fresh out of the Racing School, you know.' It was all Georgie could do to refrain from kicking the desk. 'Put me back in a flat race then, but don't stop me racing altogether.'

'It's not open for discussion.' Bert looked up now and met Georgie's eyes with his bloodshot grey ones. He looked beyond tired, more worn out. The horses weren't performing well lately. From next door came the sound of Petra trying to placate another disillusioned owner who thought they'd bought a superstar but had yet to win a race. 'And I'll remind you it was me who took you on straight from said Racing School and have given you the chances you have so eagerly taken.'

Georgie breathed slowly, fighting the inclination to tell Bert she wasn't going to put up with it. Thoughts flooded her mind: how competitive the sport was, her age, competing with highly ambitious youngsters for few opportunities. If she stayed, she could win back the coveted ride on Golden Goose, entered for next year's Cheltenham Gold Cup. She felt too exhausted to argue. 'But if I do my bit, I keep the chance to ride Goosey?'

Bert avoided a direct answer, merely stating, 'Prove yourself.'

They stared at each other for a few seconds until Bert's mobile began to ring from beneath a pile of papers.

'I will,' Georgie uttered, striding out as he answered it.

Minotaur charged out of his stable with the bullishness of a boxer entering the ring, almost ripping Georgie's arm from its socket. He plunged, forelegs pumping, reminding Georgie of raised fists. Eyes wild, he glared around for a challenger, but the yard was empty. The other horses were already winding their way up to the gallops.

Both het up, Georgie fought the dark brown gelding, swearing at everything, from the low sun in her eyes to the pigeon which took off under Minotaur's nose, causing him to shy. Losing a stirrup, Georgie squirmed back into the saddle, trying to concentrate on the rough, hoof-pitted track which led from the stables, across the Downs to the fibresand gallop. By the time they caught up with the others, circling at the entrance to the gallop, Briggsy was shouting instructions about the morning's work.

'Give them a good workout but not too strenuous. Stay in single file and don't get up the arse of the horse in front, give yourselves plenty of room. It's not a race.'

'No fear of that. This lot have forgotten what a race is,' heckled one of the staff, to sniggering from the others.

'Right, for being cheeky, you can go first.' Briggsy pointed at Georgie. 'And you, keep at the rear.'

Nabil turned, giving Georgie a sympathetic smile. 'Don't take it personally. Bert and Briggsy are steamed up over the unexplained poor performances lately.'

'And they think the rest of us aren't?' Georgie reined back an impatient Minotaur who was tossing his head aggressively and pawing the ground.

Nabil shrugged and set Golden Goose off along the narrow strip of sand-coloured surface which snaked through the grass, marked by white railings.

Aware of Minotaur's lack of gallop's etiquette, Georgie distracted the horse as best she could, turning circles until eventually the last hindquarters had disappeared and it was their turn. The gelding set off calmly, happy to be on his way. Georgie kept him on a short rein. He arched his neck and snorted briskly, flecks of foam and airborne sand spattering his chest. Relaxing a little, Georgie released some rein. The sun was warming the day. Birds had woken and were chattering in the surrounding trees. The air filled with the smell of damp ground and warm horse. Bert and Briggsy stood halfway along the grass bank to the left, watching the action through binoculars. She'd show them, she thought, adjusting her pose. Just behind Bert, a tall slender blonde lady stood beside a cameraperson, who appeared to be filming the string of horses on the fibresand, while in the distance, a female voice was calling, 'Popkins, Popkins. Come on.'

What a lovely morning to be out riding a thoroughbred on the Downs, Georgie thought, humming to herself in time to the beat of Minotaur's hooves. The air had a fresh autumnal feel to it as it brushed her face.

The voice grew louder, now more urgent. 'Popkins, get back here at once. Bad dog, do as you're told.'

Georgie grinned. Popkins sounded in need of some dog obedience lessons.

The voice grew harder, alarmed. 'Popkins, no … Popkins, stop. Do not go under those rails. Don't you dare. Get here now.'

They coincided with a white fluffy something dashing onto the fibresand just ahead of Minotaur's forelegs. The horse was travelling much too fast to stop. Startled Minotaur took a huge leap over the dog. A jumble of legs, arms, reins and stirrups landed in a heap as the petrified dog shot out the other side and ran off into the trees. Georgie was still in the saddle, but only just. Minotaur took off, Georgie clinging to his neck, legs dangling down his sides. Unable to put her weight behind her, she had no control and could only sit helplessly as Minotaur raced upsides a startled lad on the horse in front. Desperately trying to regain the stirrups, which were banging against the saddle, urging the horse on, Georgie yelped, 'Move over, brakes have gone.'

In a flash they were past and gaining on the dapple-grey bottom ahead. They charged through the string of horses until the path was blocked by the gleaming chestnut hide of Golden Goose.

'Move over. Move over. I can't stop,' Georgie yelled in warning.

Nabil glanced around but too late. Minotaur sped up and barged through, easily shunting Golden Goose aside and through the plastic railing, which snapped under the horse's weight. Out the corner of her eye, Georgie saw Nabil tossed high out the saddle and Goosey tumble to the ground.

The leading horse moved hastily aside, giving Minotaur a clear path ahead. He gave three huge bucks, throwing Georgie up in the air in the style of a Jack-in-a-box. She landed on the sand with a thud. Hooves approached, then abruptly stopped.

'Blimey, Georgie, you OK?' a voice asked with concern.

Georgie sat up, then wanted to lay back down again. A frantic Bert was running towards Goosey, who was not yet upright. Besides the horse, Nabil was bent over, winded, hands on his knees. Briggsy was waving his arms at Minotaur, attempting to stop the runaway. It was chaos, all caused by a dog not on the lead. Yet Georgie feared it would be she, not Popkins, who would ultimately get the blame.

3

Slightly woozy, Georgie rose and shook herself. The string had caught up now and were huddled around, peering at her. Another trainer's horses out for exercise at the same time were backed up behind them. It was an equine traffic jam.

'What's the hold up?' someone yelled from the rear.

'We've got a person down,' called back one of Bert's staff.

'Can they get out the way? We've got work to do.'

'Sod off,' Bert's staff member replied.

'You wouldn't be that smart if we were in the Final Furlong and you had to say it to my face.'

Sensing more trouble brewing, Georgie ducked under the rails to let them by.

'Briggsy wants you,' one of the riders pointed out as they drew alongside.

Georgie glanced over to where Briggsy stood beside the Land Rover, beckoning her over. In the distance, Minotaur was galloping along the verge beside the road around the racecourse, headed towards the grandstand, tack flying. He charged through a string of racehorses coming up the road, scattering them in all directions. One of the riders made a brave attempt to grab his flapping reins with no chance of success.

Georgie puffed up the bank to where the Head Lad waited.

'You all right, Georgie?'

'Yep. Well, about as much as you can be when you've hit the deck.' Georgie rubbed her back.

Briggsy pulled open the passenger door. 'Hop in. We need to round up Minotaur before there's any more damage.'

'What about Goosey? From the glimpse I got, it could be serious.'

'Bert'll sort it. I've been told to get the loose horse and limit the carnage.'

Georgie removed her hat and stroked her forehead in dismay. 'Let's go then. Hopefully he'll run out of steam and pull himself up soon.'

'That won't be for some time. Minotaur stays at least three miles, remember.' Briggsy started the engine and sped away, past the camera operator loading gear into the back of a van. 'Hope you don't appear in the *Racing News* blooper section.'

Up ahead, Georgie watched a plucky early morning jogger try to flag down the horse, who skipped around them and proceeded on towards Tattenham Corner, a direction tricky for the Land Rover to get through.

'I'll go on foot and meet you by the grandstand,' suggested Georgie.

Briggsy pulled over, Georgie leaped out and stood aside as he set off for the main road.

Running in boots and a padded jacket, the majestic glass fronted buildings of the Duchess's Stand and the Queen's Stand on her right, Georgie was sweating. Her legs ached. Worse still, she could no longer see Minotaur, just a lot of white rails.

'The loose horse went that way,' a couple of elderly dog

walkers informed Georgie helpfully. Grunting her thanks, she lowered her head and sped up.

She reached the road and caught sight of Briggsy, who had parked up outside The Derby Arms pub and flashed the headlights to get her attention. She flung the passenger door open, telling him breathlessly, 'I've lost him.'

'He's gone downhill to the town centre. I saw him go by but couldn't stop quick enough.'

'Perhaps he fancied shopping,' Georgie joked, pulling the seatbelt and buckling up.

Traffic was building but even so Georgie thought it should be easy to spot seventeen hands of thoroughbred amongst the deserted shops. Instead, it took some time trawling through the town to find him, gazing in the window of a newsagents, drooling about Polo mints.

Briggsy bumped up on the pavement and switched on the hazard lights. Georgie jumped out and approached Minotaur slowly, fearful he would bolt again, but he seemed happy where he was, admiring his reflection in the glass.

'You'll have to lead him back. Look, your saddle's ruined.'

Georgie pulled the still intact reins over the gelding's head and gazed in dismay at the mangled remains of what had been a pricey leather racing saddle. One of the stirrups was missing and the rest was now held together by only a couple of taut stitches.

'Marvellous.'

Keen to move the Land Rover, which was partially blocking the traffic, Briggsy said, 'Be careful. See you back at the yard.'

As he drove off, Georgie raised a hand in acknowledgement and led the horse, sweating as much as she was, to the pedestrian crossing. As they waited for the green signal, the pair received some strange looks from the early morning commuters, used to seeing the horses on the Downs, not in the town.

It was a long walk up the hill. Hungry from his exercise, Minotaur attempted to desecrate every neatly trimmed hedge along the way. Georgie grew increasingly cross, until eventually he got the message, but not before dragging her backwards through a prickly holly bush bordering one of the front gardens, ripping her Puffa jacket.

They slunk into the yard. No one noticed. Bert, Petra, Briggsy and the entire staff were crowded around Golden Goose and a sombre faced vet. Georgie felt a surge of relief that Goosey was standing and obviously well enough to have walked back to the stables.

'Oh, thank goodness,' she cried.

The crowd turned, a sea of scowling faces. Georgie stopped, as the vet began to speak.

'Well, it's not as bad as it could have been but there's no chance of recovery by the Gold Cup next March. It'll take more than six months. These leg injuries are complicated. He'll likely race again, but not for some time. Best to send him away for rest and recuperation and hope he improves.' The vet turned to Bert. 'I'm sorry not to be more upbeat but one has to be realistic in these circumstances. He's a fine fellow. The priority is his welfare, not his future race entries.'

A murmur of agreement rippled through the staff, who loved their horses dearly.

A resigned Petra spoke up. 'I'd better inform Goose's owners. They'll be awfully disappointed.'

'I'll come with you, in case they want my opinion,' the vet offered.

As they walked away towards the office, Bert turned on Georgie. 'This is all your fault.'

'It was the dog's fault, not mine. That lady ought to have had it on a lead, as you're supposed to.'

'What dog?'

'The fluffy white menace that spooked Minotaur and triggered all this.'

'We didn't see a dog ... or a lady, for that matter,' said Nabil.

'Well, you wouldn't have, would you? You were all ahead of me.'

'No one came over afterwards to check if we were OK. I didn't see anyone on foot except the Boss and Briggsy,' chipped in a lad towards the back.

'She probably scarpered when she saw what had happened. She wasn't likely to volunteer her dog caused it. The dog, Popkins, disappeared in the trees. I expect she went after it, then made herself scarce.'

'I think you're making this up,' said Bert. 'There's signs telling people to keep dogs on leads and away from the gallops during racehorse exercise hours. You fell off and now you're trying to blame it on a non-existent dog.'

'I didn't spot no lady and no dog,' backed up someone else.

'Me neither, yet Georgie was directly behind me,' a different voice spoke.

'Yeah, who calls a dog Popkins anyway?' yelled another voice.

'The owner obviously approves of the name.' Georgie was starting to feel exasperated. Having got so hot earlier, she had cooled considerably. Every part of her ached. Minotaur was resting his head on her arm. She wanted to put the horse away and get a cup of tea, preferably a soothing chamomile one. 'And obviously I know all about the signs. I ride past them every day, same as you. Doesn't mean everyone follows the rules though.'

'This is the final straw. I'm placing you on yard duties for the foreseeable future. No riding out again until I can trust you. You could've brought Beech Tree into disrepute causing an accident. For the second time in two days, you've proved to be irresponsible,' erupted Bert.

'You're accusing me of lying?' Georgie was furious. 'That's totally out of order.'

'Two falls in two days is not acceptable,' thundered Bert.

No one moved to disagree nor did anyone back up Georgie's version of events.

Georgie saw red. 'All right then. I quit.'

In a dramatic gesture, she threw Minotaur's reins at Briggsy and began to unbuckle the remains of her saddle, fingers fumbling with fury.

'Wait, Georgie, think about it. Think it through,' Briggsy pleaded, quietly enough only she could hear.

'No, I quit. None of you believe me. The definition of an accident is something that happens unexpectedly and unintentionally. It can't be predicted and avoided. It wasn't my fault.'

'You can't just quit,' growled Bert.

'Yes, I can … see, I'm quitting.' Georgie slid the saddle off the horse's back.

'This is not a conversation for out here. Let's move into the office.' Bert's tone softened slightly, as it dawned on him Georgie wasn't bluffing.

'No, for the umpteenth time. I quit.' Georgie marched off to the tack room, girth buckle screeching along the ground behind her.

The stunned crowd watched her go.

While Georgie was throwing her meagre belongings together, Jess came into the tack room alone.

'You sure you won't change your mind?' she asked hopefully.

'Nope.' Georgie didn't stop what she was doing.

'Dad's stressed.' Jess placed a hand on Georgie's shoulder, trying to placate her friend.

'That's not an excuse. We've all got our own stresses and difficulties. It's not right to take it out on others, it just increases their stress and that's not fair.'

'You're right. He'll calm down. I'm not making excuses but dad's not in a good place. You know how it is, the horses aren't firing on all cylinders. Unlike some yards, we're not financed by any mega-rich owners. We can't afford to lose any of the horses and he's worried if they don't improve soon the owners will start taking them away. It's a huge responsibility.'

'I don't care.' Georgie hefted up the crate she'd filled. 'Bye, Jess. Hopefully we'll still see each other in the Final Furlong.'

Georgie crossed the normally rowdy but now deserted yard. Even the horses made no sound. They had all gone into hiding; the atmosphere one of shock.

She chucked the detritus of ten years in the boot of the car. It made a sorry sight, mostly a pile of mud-stained waterproof jackets, hats, gloves and a broken saddle. The boot clicked shut. Hovering nearby, Luna whined.

'Bye lovely Luna.' Georgie blew the collie a kiss.

She reversed and drove away, fighting the tears in her eyes. The end of an era and no idea what the next one would be.

As soon as she arrived home, Georgie hit the gin and tonic. She knew she shouldn't. What she should do was begin ringing around other trainers trying to secure some work, but she was too angry and befuddled to do anything except sooth her nerves with a drink. Who did these people think they were, she thundered, hurling ice cubes into the crystal glass with the force of hailstones? She would not be humiliated and called a liar in such a way.

Georgie's mobile rang and pinged with voicemails and

messages from Jess, Petra and Briggsy. She ignored them all. No one could make her feel better. The events of the last few days piled on top of her. She sat in an armchair and stared at the fire. The room grew warm, she was exhausted. Gradually she slipped into a sleep filled with dreams of being chased through a field of tall grass by a Great Dane called Popkins.

Georgie awoke to darkness and an annoying buzzing noise. Then a distorted face appeared at the latticed window. She screamed. The face disappeared. Seconds later the buzzing noise began again. Georgie realised it was the doorbell. She stretched as she approached the front door. To her surprise, it was seven o'clock in the evening and Briggsy was on the doorstep with a bunch of colourful flowers.

'For you.' He smiled shyly handing them over. 'I've been worried. Came to check on you.'

The obvious question popped into Georgie's head. 'How did you get my address?'

Briggsy flinched a little. 'Petra gave it to me. Actually, she didn't give it to me, I persuaded her to let me have it. Told her one of us ought to check up on you, to which she replied you were the one who walked out and were therefore no longer a concern of Beech Tree. Besides which, at your age you were perfectly capable of looking after yourself and she was only calling to tell you she'd forward on your P45.'

'Ah, delightful Petra. Always such a people person. Come in.' Georgie opened the door and led Briggsy through to the lounge, realising how stuffy it was. 'Can I get you a drink?'

'Oh, erm, just a Diet Coke please, if you've got one.'

'Sure.'

Minutes later, they sat with their drinks opposite each other a little awkwardly; work colleagues who had never really made it to friends.

'I'm fine,' reassured Georgie. 'Just need some time out to think things through.'

'Will you come back?'

'No.'

'Will you think about coming back?'

'No.'

'What will you do?'

'Don't know.' Georgie knew she resembled a petulant child, but her head hurt and she really didn't want to make plans in her current state of mind.

'I, erm … well, I might have a suggestion.'

'Oh.'

'A friend of mine from way back, Tom Pengelly. His dad's a farmer but he also has a small team of racehorses down in Cornwall. Er, Bodmin, actually. They're always short-staffed. Difficult to get people to move down there when they've got the likes of Lambourn and Newmarket to choose from, where the pay and nightlife are better. Anyway, I put the question to Tom, did they need anyone right now. They'd be happy to take you on temporarily, bridge the gap, sort of thing, while you sort yourself out.'

Georgie was taken aback at Briggsy's thoughtfulness but also by the fact that he assumed she'd move to Cornwall, even temporarily.

'But … I … that's in *Cornwall.*'

'Oh, silly me. Forgot to mention. It includes accommodation.' Briggsy clearly saw that as the clincher.

'Gosh but, you see, my life is here.'

'Yeah, I know that. But Fred, that's Tom's dad, he's one of the shrewdest judges of a horse I've ever met and I've known them most of my life. I spent my early years in Mullion, down on the south coast.'

'I never knew that.'

'Well, we've never really socialised much to get to know each other, have we? I wish we had.'

Georgie smiled wryly. 'Life's always been so busy. I've got the gift of time now though. I'll need it for job hunting.'

'Why don't you see this as a kind of working holiday? There's no opportunities in the yards around here. I'm always catching up with the other Head Lads. They're all fully staffed and got stable jockeys in situ.'

'Wow.' Georgie sat back.

She could barely believe she was having this conversation. How things had turned topsy-turvy in such a short space of time she couldn't fathom and yet something about Briggsy's offer was appealing. It solved the short-term problem. Meant she didn't have to worry about finances and how to pay the mortgage or become beholden to Sam by asking for a loan. Travelling far away, leaving it all behind, had a kind of romanticism, even though Georgie knew the reality likely wouldn't match up.

'I know, I know. It's a stupid idea.' Briggsy looked embarrassed. 'I just wanted to help.'

'You did.' Georgie surprised herself. 'I'll do it. Text me the details and when they want me to start and I'll be there.'

Georgie knew Sam had dinner with the *Racing News* crew that evening and would be up early the following morning for a flight to Edinburgh, followed by a full day of rides at Musselburgh. It was odds on he'd be out on the town after the dinner, enjoying being in the spotlight, regaling everyone with his tales and probably being provided with copious amounts of expensive Scotch malt whisky. He eventually returned her missed calls.

'Hey, Gee-Gee. How was your day?' Sam's speech was already slurred, the sounds of a busy bar in the background.

'Rather eventful actually. I'm moving.' Georgie had to shout to be heard above the din. 'To Cornwall.'

'Yeah, yeah, course you are. You're drunk, I can tell. You're talking nonsense. Now go to bed and sleep it off and stop making pathetic jokes to get attention.'

'No, Sam, I'm serious. I quit Bert's today and I've been offered temporary work in Cornwall. I've accepted it.'

'Right and I've been offered the part for the next James Bond.' Georgie could hear Sam's companions begin to hum the theme tune. It annoyed her that he wasn't keeping their conversation private. No doubt, he'd be rolling his eyes across the table at Gina. 'And guess what, I've accepted it too.'

There was much laughter. Speaking slowly to try and get through to her distracted boyfriend, Sam eventually understood and was sympathetic but told Georgie she would grow to regret quitting Beech Tree.

'You know, being freelance, it's incredibly competitive. You'd need an enormous amount of luck to get rides on good horses. Let's face it, most of the trainers and owners have dedicated jockeys who always get their pick of the best ones. Even if you could find yourself a good booking agent, there'd only be so much they could do. I hate to say it, but you've been cossetted at Bert's. It's tough out in the real world. I'm sure Bert'll have forgotten about this by Christmas. When he can't get enough staff on the rota, he'll be begging you to come back. Trust me.'

Georgie ended the call feeling angry again. She was sick of everyone telling her how she should feel, what she should do and whether she really had seen what she said she saw on the gallops. It was her time now. Bert had told her to prove herself and that was what she intended to do.

4

Before dawn a week later, Georgie was cramming the last of her possessions into a suitcase stuffed to the point of splitting. She'd dithered over what to take for the next few months, winter months at that, in the wilds of Cornwall. Scenes from Daphne du Maurier novels played through her mind as she folded jumpers and waterproofs, placing them in the case. She visualised acres of rough landscape, windswept and bleak and hardy sheep grazing in a downpour. She smiled as she pulled the zip closed. It was rather exciting if she ignored Sam's negativity and the bubbling uncertainty threatening to derail her.

'I will not give in,' she announced, though whether to herself or the groaning zip, she couldn't say.

Overnight, Jack Frost had danced across the front lawn, closely followed by a fox. Paw prints zig-zagged around the ornamental wishing well and the bird bath, then disappeared around the side of the cottage, in search of a wheelie bin with an unsecured lid. The moon was full, providing some light as Georgie loaded the suitcase into the boot, cramming it alongside cardboard boxes jingling with half the kitchen.

Doubtless, she didn't really need to take so much, yet she wanted to be prepared. Briggsy's brief text had merely provided the location and start date, not anything about the type of accommodation. Georgie feared it could turn out to be a damp caravan in a field, likely to be blown over by the first strong gale into a sea of mud. She hoped not.

As she slammed the boot, the front door of Tulip Cottage opened a fraction and an elderly lady in a purple velvet dressing gown placed a pretty silver tabby cat on the step. She glanced up at Georgie with a start.

'Oh, hello dear.'

'Morning, Mrs Knight.'

'You're up early, even for you.'

'Off to Cornwall for a while.'

'Oh, how lovely. You're keen, setting off at this time.'

'Actually, I'm stopping off on the way for lunch at my parent's home in Exminster.'

'How sweet. Well, don't worry. We'll keep an eye on the place for you, won't we, Chester?'

Chester seemed more interested in getting back in the warm but was prevented from doing so by Mrs Knight's boot slippers.

'Thank you. My friend has a spare key and will be dropping by a few times a week,' Georgie explained.

'Jolly good. Do have fun. Safe journey.'

The door closed, leaving a disgruntled Chester on the mat.

With the Peugeot eventually rumbling to life, setting off sluggishly under its full load, Georgie turned towards the motorway and the start of the many miles west.

The traffic was light as she whizzed along the main road past Stonehenge. Driving allowed plenty of thinking time, but Georgie kept the music turned up to fend off the voice which wanted to scold her, tell her she'd done everything wrong, that she ought to turn around and beg Bert for her old job back.

At the familiar roads around Exeter, Georgie's spirits lifted. Some of the tension of the past few weeks began to ease. Her shoulders dropped a little. A tentative wave of confidence arose. Being back in the area where she'd grown up reminded Georgie a job wasn't the be-all and end-all. She had travelled many paths, made many choices and could do so again. Beech Tree had been familiar and safe, but it had also led to her being taken for granted. She'd been the reliable one, the one who would stay and help, take on extra work and rarely grumbled. She needed a new routine and a challenge. Something to put the spark back into her life.

Pulling up on the drive, Georgie climbed stiffly from the car. The front door of her parents' thatched cottage was framed by hanging baskets of begonias still in bloom. The lawn was bordered by vibrant blue crocuses. A flock of blue tits swung from a feeder overflowing with seeds. A squirrel hopped around underneath, picking up any surplus food, while a speckled thrush flapped its wings as it bathed in a stone water feature. Georgie opened the gate in the railings, breathing in the scents of what must have been a mild autumn so far; everything still so bright and alive.

The dainty wooden door swung open, rattling the brass knocker of a horse's head and Georgie's mum stepped out to kiss her, looking the same as ever. Grey hair held off her face by a clip, blouse and flowery-patterned skirt hidden by an apron and a smudge of flour on her rosy cheeks. The smell of a cake almost ready in the oven wafted down the narrow hall, walls crammed with family photos.

'Hi darling, how are you?'

'Knackered,' Georgie replied truthfully.

'We were surprised when you called last night with your news, love.' Dad stepped out from behind and swooped for a hug. Glasses perched half-way down his nose, shirt untucked from casual chinos, a mass of wiry white hair; he still resembled the professor he used to be. 'Come on, your mum's got lunch ready. We know you can't stop long.'

Georgie followed them through the lounge and into the light warm conservatory.

'Charlie sends his love,' said Georgie's mum, as she placed a cheese salad in front of her daughter. 'He said to tell you the Cayman Islands are lovely and when are you going to visit?'

Georgie laughed, breaking a chunk of bread off the long stick. 'When I become an IT expert too and can live in exotic places.'

'You know your brother. All he ever wanted was to work with computers. Still, he's made a success of it. There's not many people lucky enough to do what they love every day and make a living out of it,' said Georgie's dad proudly. 'I remember when you were, what were you? About six years old. You both wanted to ride so much but poor Charlie, he was terrified of horses, even the smallest ones. He cried on a merry-go-round once. The opposite of you, who took to it straight away and here you are.'

'Yes, here I am,' nodded Georgie. 'I've often wondered whether some of us are born with horses in our soul.'

After lunch, Georgie went upstairs to her old bedroom where dusty rosettes were still taped in pride of place around the dressing table mirror. Georgie smiled as she brushed clean the ribbons of a red one, recalling the thrill of winning first place at the local riding school's annual gymkhana. Then she spotted the time on the Thelwell wall clock. She needed to be on her way.

As Georgie drove past the *Welcome to Cornwall* sign at the roadside, she gave a little cheer. The drive had been long, time was getting on and she now felt a mixture of curiosity and nerves at her impulsive decision to move to Pennhalow. From the scant information Briggsy had given her it sounded very much a family affair. She hoped to fit in with the Pengelly's and not be viewed as an outsider.

The sat nav on Georgie's mobile announced it was time to leave the main road just as dusk began rolling in. The road took a sharp bend under the dual carriageway, then over a cattle grid which threatened to finally dislodge an exhaust already battered by the unmade track back at Rose Cottage. The countryside became wilder as Georgie drove along a lane across a wide-open expanse of bleak heather covered moorland. Scattered piles of granite rose from the ground. The light turned a soft pink. It was beautiful in a desolate way. Georgie turned up the heater.

As the lane narrowed, the openness turned to banks of grassland either side. Driving carefully to avoid scraping the wing mirrors, apprehensive should something come the other way, especially a tractor, Georgie realised she hadn't seen a single building for miles. She must have gone wrong; programmed an incorrect postcode or Briggsy had mistyped it in his text. No one could be training racehorses out here. The awful thought that this could all be a spiteful prank by the staff at Beech Tree Stables crept into her mind. They were a renowned bunch of practical jokers. Just then the sat nav piped up again.

'In two hundred yards turn –'

It stopped, mid-instruction.

'Turn what? Turn what?'

The sat nav didn't reply.

Georgie pulled over in the entrance to a pitted pasture with a rusted gate hanging off its hinges. Her mobile had no signal. She could see the sign for the crossroads a hundred yards ahead. It was an old white wooden pole, with the arms snapped off. She tapped the steering wheel, summing up the situation. Pennhalow was either right or left. The odds were fifty-fifty. She'd had worse.

She gambled on taking the left turn up a track which wound, twisting and turning through a shallow ford, over an ancient stone humpback bridge and past a derelict outbuilding. There were no signs of life, even the fields contained no animals. Georgie had almost reached the point of accepting she would have to turn back, when suddenly the track opened into a tiny hamlet. There was a pub called the Smuggler's Barrels, obviously an old coaching inn, a tiny general store, which was set up in the cottage owner's front room and a weathered church the far side of an overgrown green. It was all very quaint and forgotten by time.

Georgie's phone beeped with a text from Sam, indicating the signal strength had picked up enough to check the map.

Georgie found she was only half a mile from Pennhalow, which was further on, up a road marked "Private – No Trespassing" by a hand painted wooden sign on one side and "Caution – Livestock" on the other. Georgie drove past sheep grazing the moorland beneath a crescent moon. The lack of streetlighting made the sky seem vast, especially on such a clear night.

It was a relief when finally a granite block with gold lettering sunk into a bank, almost concealed by undergrowth, announced she had arrived at Pennhalow. The entrance was grand but shabby; two stone pillars overrun with ivy and topped with boulders shaped in what could be shields. In the darkness it was difficult to make out much detail, other than a driveway which rounded a bend and spread into the courtyard of a manor house. It didn't resemble either a racing stables or a farm. As Georgie parked up, she began to doubt she was in the right place. Rapidly scanning Briggsy's text, it confirmed she was expected at Pennhalow. She left the car and didn't bother locking it. There was no one about. The house itself was dilapidated, but in a way that suggested it needed to be taken care of, rather than run-down. The Pengelly's must once have been wealthy landowners.

The house appeared unoccupied. No lights were on and the surroundings gave off an air of abandonment. Georgie rang the ornate bell. No one answered the door or called a welcome out a window. By chance she looked down. A piece of notepaper was tucked under the brown coir doormat. Georgie stooped to pick it up. By the light of the torch on her mobile, she read the large black handwriting, clearly hastily written, her name amended.

Hello Georgi~~na~~e

Sorry we can't be there to welcome you. Please follow the path around to the stables and ask for Tom.

Cheers.

Tom

A glance to the right confirmed there was no way through the thick, towering leylandii hedge. It would have to be left again, where Georgie discovered a gap running between the trees and the house marking the beginning of a path down the side of the manor. It was overgrown with weeds, broken paving slabs and the odd hoofprint in the dirt.

As she stepped around the rear of the house, Georgie triggered a bright security light, which revealed a lawn strewn with bare patches of mud and an ornamental circular fountain, long ago run dry. In its centre, a statue of a knight, made of chipped stone and spattered with bird droppings, held a sword aloft. Nearby was the skeletal frame of a partially erected marquee.

Georgie kept going to the far end, where a hedge was broken by a high wrought iron gate, through which wafted the familiar smells of livestock and she caught the clang of a bucket. On it was fixed a sign which originally read "Beware of the Terrier", but someone had scrubbed out the word "terrier" and replaced it with "staff", which also had a narrow line through it and in different handwriting had been added the word "donkey". Had it not been for the note with her name on, Georgie would have been certain this was all a mistake and high-tailed it back to Surrey.

Beyond was a stable yard with the lights on, illuminating a square of loose boxes, a small barn and a tack room, adjoined by a wide iron gate, secured with a heavy-duty padlock, beyond which Georgie could see nothing. It was a characterful and compact yard, unlike the more modern purpose-built ones. Mostly brick-built, a rusted weathervane of a cockerel which looked to have long ago stopped spinning, sat atop a tumbledown shed. Off to the side, a five-bar gate signalled the way to Pennhalow Farm. The dark shape of the outbuildings could be made out in the moonlight, a faint mooing coming from inside.

Georgie strode along one row, peering over doors at different coloured rumps poking out from underneath good quality rugs. The occupants chomped, noses deep in mangers, obviously well cared for. Georgie was pleased. There had to be someone about and at the last stable, she finally came across a person; a man of similar age to her. He was wrestling with a brown donkey. Neither man nor donkey appeared willing to budge. They froze as Georgie called from outside, 'Hi, I'm Georgie. Hopefully you're expecting me, otherwise it's going to be embarrassing trying to explain why I'm trespassing.'

The man looked round abruptly. The donkey seized the opportunity to stomp a tiny hoof on his foot.

5

'Found us all right then,' the man said, beaming smile below watering hazel eyes. 'You passed the first test!'

'I did. Although you're rather out in the sticks here, I thought I never would. Thanks for the note, without which I'd probably still be looking for you.'

'Yeah, I expect it's rather different to Surrey. Briggsy tells me you're after a change of scenery though. Sorry, left my manners on the muck heap. I'm Tom, Tom Pengelly. I'd shake your hand, but I'm rather busy being put in my place by Jackson.' He motioned towards the donkey with his eyebrows.

'Can I help?'

'Can you fix broken bones? I'm kidding. Jackson's not heavy enough to inflict real damage, but if you could shut the door, that'd be great. He never wants to be inside. Can't have him escaping again.'

'Again?' Georgie pushed the bottom half of the door closed and secured the top bolt.

'Yeah. Last time he was seen by a motorist trotting the wrong way up the dual carriageway. After he was identified by a fellow farmer, the police called at midnight asking me to collect him.'

'Oh dear.'

'Indeed. He's the best escape artist this side of the River Tamar. Our very own Houdini.' Tom rubbed the donkey's ears fondly. 'Donkeys. Trouble with a capital T.'

Tom limped over to Georgie as she unlocked the door, allowing him to slip through the gap. With a snort Jackson moved to the triangular manger in the corner and scoffed noisily. The stand-off was over.

Wiping his hands on his jeans before holding one out for Georgie to shake, gave her the opportunity to get a proper look. Soft hazel curls matched his eyes, tanned skin and the toned muscles of a physical worker. There was a carefreeness about him. He spoke with a West Country lilt.

'You must be pretty tired. I don't want to bombard you with details, so I'll show you around tomorrow. We keep the farm and stables separate and these days, dad tends to oversee the farm. I'm in charge of the yard which, I'm sure Briggsy explained, you'll be working in with me and the team.'

'No multi-tasking milking of cows required then?'

'Nope, just twenty horses, plus the donkey. Most of our chaps are slow enough to be overtaken by a fully loaded double-decker bus going uphill, but we love them all, the lazy rogues.'

'Do any of them know they're supposed to be a racehorse?'

As Tom led her over to a stable on the opposite side of the block, Georgie thought how refreshing it was to meet someone who seemed down to earth, easy going and lacking in ego.

'This boy here does.' Tom indicated Georgie look inside, where a black colt hidden under a thick red rug was housed. 'He's ditched every experienced rider from here to Land's End.'

Taking in the thoroughbred dozing against the back wall, wisps of hay stuck to his whiskers, Georgie could see he wasn't particularly big, standing what looked to be the average sixteen hands high. He turned his handsome head, revealing one white mark, a tiny teardrop shape between his nostrils, known as a snip, in a pose which reminded Georgie of the horse in the famous Stubbs's painting of Whistlejacket. He seemed placid.

'He doesn't look that type,' she observed.

'Trust me, he is. Got such exemplary breeding, his previous owners entered him in the Epsom Derby as a yearling. Yes, it's a shame, as he was to be our first ever Derby hopeful.'

'Was?'

'He's cantankerous. Thrown more people to the ground than an Olympic wrestler. We can't get anyone to ride him anymore. Got some speed plus super talented but all going to waste because of his attitude. I'm not sure what the future plans are right now for our Monty. Or The Misfit, to give him his proper name.'

'But surely there's something that will help?' Georgie asked, as they walked away.

'Guess we could contact the UK Stunt Riders Association or similar. In all seriousness though, I don't know. We bought him as a two-year-old. The previous owner was rich, paid his Derby entry fees. I can't see that happening now though. It's for three-year-olds only so it's next June or never.'

Georgie was troubled. 'Do you think something went wrong before he came here?'

'He came from a reputable yard, so I doubt it. Just never settled here. Good night chaps.' Tom switched off the lights. 'Come on, I'll show you to your digs. Don't worry, it's not a caravan. You're in the annexe.'

'Well, that is a relief.'

Tom chuckled as they crossed the lawn side by side. 'You'll meet the team tomorrow. They're a good crew. Hamish and Clemmy. Clem's all loved up with her fiancé, Noah. The wedding's in a few weeks and they're having the reception in a marquee here. My step-mum, Angie, is already getting it put up, which is a mistake. The first storm and we'll be picking bits of it out the hedge for weeks. But Angie's in a panic that we won't get one so it's here already. And this is you.'

At the far end of the manor house, Tom had stopped at a solid wooden door with a small diamond shaped pane of frosted glass. He handed Georgie a large brass key.

'Thanks.' She took it.

'I'll leave you to get your things and settle in. If you need anything, I'm in the manor. Just give me a bell.'

'You live there?' Georgie was pleased to learn she wouldn't be all alone at Pennhalow outside working hours.

'Yeah. Dad and Angie used to, but they have a bungalow in the town now, so I only live in a few rooms. It's been in our family for generations but costs a fortune to upkeep. A money pit. You fix one thing and another breaks straight after.'

'I can imagine.' A yawn escaped before Georgie could suppress it. 'Oh, I'm sorry. You're not boring me.'

'No worries. You get sorted out and I'll see you in the morning.'

The previous evening, Georgie had stepped into a tiny but clean living room with a sofa, flat screen television, circular dining table and two chairs. A large window overlooked the lawn and off the living room was a kitchen. A very narrow and rickety flight of stairs led to a landing with one bedroom and a bathroom which was modern, not decrepit, as Georgie had feared when she opened the door to find the delights of a power shower.

Now in daylight, Georgie drew back the bedroom curtains and gasped at the amazing view over the moors. Miles and miles of unspoilt countryside.

Eager to meet her new colleagues, Georgie was soon rushing across the lawn on a bright and chilly morning. A pair of blackbirds hopped around the grass and a robin perched on the marquee frame, singing loudly.

As she closed the gate behind her, to keep in the chickens pecking around the bottom of the muck heap, Georgie heard a brisk Scottish accent coming from one of the stables.

'Ouch get away you lump o'lard.'

A donkey brayed, followed by the sounds of a tussle taking place, then a bucket flew out onto the cobbles with a loud clatter. Seconds later, Jackson trotted after it, an expression of triumph on his face.

'Jackson,' the Scottish tone wailed again.

A man emerged, lanky legs flying in their brown and tartan two-tone jodhpurs, hurdled the bucket and raced the donkey to the padlocked gate. Opening it, he bowed, long black fringe flapping forward despite a generous dollop of gel. 'After you, Your Highness.'

Jackson slipped through and was gone, just as a girl with a tiny frame and pink hair, dressed in dungarees, emerged from the barn and called over, 'Hiya. You must be Georgie. I'm Clem and that idiot over there is Hamish.'

Georgie raised a hand in greeting.

'Welcome to Pennhalow,' greeted Hamish, 'Cornish for "end of the moors".'

'Always full of useless information that no one will ever need,' ribbed Clem.

Hamish ignored her and pointed to a high peak in the distance. 'And that over there, is Rough Tor. But be warned, it's a lot higher and further away than it looks. I don't recommend any solitary hikes on your day off, especially after what happened to the last one.'

'The last one?' asked Georgie, puzzled.

'The last one Fred employed. She was gone within two weeks. Kept moaning about it being too remote here and she didn't like the weather. Then she went trooping off across the moor and got lost. No phone signal. Took ages to find her. To be honest, we nearly gave up.'

'Stop scaring my new staff,' a stern voice spoke from behind and Georgie turned to the welcome sight of Tom.

Hamish shrugged. 'Just some friendly advice.'

'Actually, the advice I could do with is where's the best place to get a phone signal. It seems patchy here.'

'It is rather. Outside the Smuggler's Barrels in the village is the strongest,' replied Clem.

'Oh, I passed that on the way here. Sounds the perfect excuse to spend a lot of time in the pub,' joked Georgie.

'Right, enough chatting until break. Let's get these horses exercised,' instructed Tom. 'Hamish, you turn Monty out and then we'll get going. Georgie, I've put you down for Hazel. She's a sweet mare, you'll get on OK with her.'

'Yeah, except I can run faster than she can gallop,' muttered Hamish as he sloped off.

It took Georgie some time to find out where everything was. The cosy tack room was littered with grooming kits. A coarse haired Jack Russell, all white except for a brown patch over one eye and his ears, was chewing on a plastic curry comb. He rolled over on his back and extended a paw in greeting. Georgie bent down to briefly rub his tummy. The disc on his collar identified him as Boffy. Underneath a cabinet, whose surface was covered with bits of tack, horse rugs and blankets, jackets, boots and skull caps, was a collection of well chomped brushes. Saddles and bridles hung from pegs lining three of the walls and the familiar smells of saddle soap, hoof oil and worn leather filled the air. The far corner served as a kitchen, sectioned off for a fridge with a miniature table, housing a stained kettle and an assortment of chipped mugs, half opened packets of biscuits and cartons of milk.

Nosing next door, Georgie established the adjacent barn was where the hay, feed bins, bales of straw and wood shavings for the horses' bedding were stored.

She was tacking up Hazel, a dapple-grey mare with gorgeous eyes framed with luscious lashes, when she noticed Hamish struggling across the yard with Monty. She tightened the girth, then stepped outside.

'Shall I have a go?' she offered, as Hamish flicked the lead rein at the colt in frustration.

'Be my guest.' Hamish handed the lead rein to Georgie. 'He's destined for that field there.' He pointed to a gate and walked off.

Georgie stood still for a moment, leaving the lead rein loose. She didn't look at Monty. Minutes passed and neither of them moved. Monty took a step forward. Georgie didn't move. Monty stretched out his silky neck and nipped Georgie's sleeve. Still, she did not move. Eventually curiosity overtook the colt and he barged Georgie with his head. Slowly, talking softly all the time, she led him to the field, removed the headcollar quietly and watched with satisfaction as he dropped to the ground and began to roll, scrunching his back into the dirt while kicking his legs with delight.

'Well, well. It appears we've had a horse whisperer join us at last.'

The voice from behind was broad West Country. Georgie turned. A small, grey haired, weather-beaten man with Tom's hazel eyes, dressed in a tweed jacket and corduroys, had been watching her.

'You must be Fred. I'm Georgie.'

Fred took her hand with one calloused from years of manual work. Georgie sensed he was a no-nonsense type. 'Glad you're here. Clem'll be off on honeymoon after the wedding and we've plenty going on.'

'You put Monty out. Oh, well done,' Tom called over. 'He'll never budge an inch for me, he only just tolerates Hamish and Clem won't deal with him at all yet.'

'Glad to help,' replied Georgie with a smile.

She rode Hazel alongside Tom out through the gate, behind Clem and Hamish, who were bickering about something.

'Those two never stop,' explained Tom, 'but secretly they're fond of each other.'

The horses strode out with enthusiasm. A squirrel flitted noisily up a nearby tree, rustling the branches, causing a shower of autumn leaves to cascade down. Georgie tensed up but the horses were used to the creatures of the countryside and took no notice.

'Have you always lived and worked here?' she asked, brushing leaves off her thighs.

'On and off. I tried to make it as a jockey. Worked for a trainer near Newton Abbot but I couldn't make the weight. I'm naturally stocky. In the end, a life of saunas and eating little didn't appeal to me and I gave up five years ago. Heart-breaking at the time but now I'm glad. I'd never have made it. If you can't make the weight, there's always someone else who can.'

'Still a tough decision to make. I know the day I quit being a jockey I'll be devastated. Then again, I'm also hoping I'll know when it's time to go and not make a fool of myself trying to carry on.'

'I think you'll know. The important thing is to have a plan in place for what you'll do next. I was lucky. I had Pennhalow.'

'I suppose I've never thought about it before.'

'You don't need to yet. I'm not saying life's perfect. Living on the moor is tough and it can be lonely. My mum couldn't take to it, she never settled. That's why she left. She lives in New York now. Has done for years.'

'I'm sorry, I didn't know.' Georgie reined Hazel back as she broke into a jog.

'Briggsy said you needed a break. Listen, Clem's taking Split Trousers to Newton Abbot racecourse tomorrow. Why don't you go with her? Have a day at the races without the pressure. Enjoy yourself for a change. It'll be good for you.'

'Thanks, I'd like that and I'm sure Sam's riding there tomorrow. We could catch up at the same time.' Georgie felt enthused at the idea.

They rode through the hamlet, past the Smuggler's Barrels, the horses' hooves ringing on the tarmac, then turned up a track to the open moorland. Clem was now trying to push a cackling Hamish out the saddle.

'Oi, you two. Quit all that. Focus on what you're doing. This is where we canter,' shouted Tom, trying to restrain an already eager Guido. 'Just follow us. Keep it steady.'

Georgie gave a thumbs up and, as Guido took off, Hazel followed. The mare had a smooth canter and, although keen, didn't try to run away.

The terrain was undulating but the horses picked the safest route. They cantered past grazing sheep, who raised their heads to watch the horses go by. Hazel leaped effortlessly from bank to bank of a narrow stream with no loss of rhythm, until they pulled up by the rocky outcrop of a tor, the horses all blowing hard.

'Phew, good workout.' Tom seemed exhilarated, as if it was he who had just run at full pelt not his mount.

'Hazel is a dream. I'd buy her myself if only I could afford it.' Georgie stroked the mare's damp neck.

'If she goes any slower you can have her for free,' joked Hamish.

While the horses had a pick of the grass, Clem turned to Georgie. 'I hear you're joining me at the races tomorrow.' Georgie nodded that she was. 'Good. We can get away from those two and have a nice day.'

6

Georgie was in the middle of fastening the velcro straps of some protective travelling boots around Split Trousers' legs the next morning, when an aerated Fred charged into the yard.

'Those blighters have been rubbing themselves against my walls again and dislodging the stones.'

'Did any get out?' asked Tom.

'No, I counted and double-counted but we need to watch them. Can't have the sheep getting loose.'

'Perhaps we should move them to the other field? The one with the better fencing,' Tom suggested.

'I'll think on it, son.' Fred seemed to come back to the present and notice the bright red horsebox, which had arrived via the farm, being the only vehicular access to the rear of Pennhalow. 'Got everything under control, Clem?'

'Of course,' Clem called from inside the horsebox.

'Good. You're in charge today.'

'You're not coming, Fred?' Clem appeared at the top of the ramp and ejected a nosey Boffy, who trotted down the ramp and scuttled away.

'Got walls to fix.'

With Split Trousers ready to go, Georgie led him up the ramp and secured the bay gelding inside. She slid the window ajar, then stroked the horse's soft neck.

'You're all good to go.'

Unperturbed, Split Trousers proceeded to close his eyes for a doze. He was hardly raring to go, thought Georgie. Today was unlikely to be a winning day.

Between them, the hired horsebox's driver and Georgie secured the ramp.

'Don't come back a pair of losers,' Fred called over as Clem opened the cabin door.

'Don't call them that,' scolded Tom, throwing his hands in the air. 'Trousers isn't the easiest of rides, as you know. They'll all do their best.'

'Sorry. Have fun. Go team Pengelly.' Fred punched the air.

Georgie gave Tom a grin and then they were on their way, the driver squeezing the square-shaped vehicle down the single-track lane. Georgie gazed out at the field of cows on one side, the manor house hidden behind the hedge on the other, only the roof and chimneys visible.

Once they reached the main road, Clem produced a flask of tea and a packet of chocolate digestives.

'Here you go.' She handed Georgie a mug filled with strong tea and three biscuits. 'Breakfast.'

Georgie took them with a wry smile. It was hardly the healthiest start to the day. She didn't mind, being too excited at the prospect of surprising Sam to worry. Purposefully not sending him a message letting him know she'd be at Newton Abbot too gave her lovely, anticipatory, butterflies in her tummy, similar to the early days. Tender moments had to be snatched at various racecourses while, at Sam's insistence, they'd tried to keep their relationship out of the sporting press. Exchanging romantic, meaningful looks across the parade ring, private only to them, had been so exciting. To be honest, even once their secret was out, the press hadn't really been that interested. Sam was a name, but only within the sport itself. Still, after not seeing each other for a while and communicating only by text and the odd phone call, she knew he'd be thrilled to see her.

She finished her tea. Clem was chatting to the driver about whether to dye her hair blue for the wedding or keep it pink. Georgie smiled, resting her head and closed her eyes to the hum of the tyres on the road.

She woke up as they pulled into the racecourse's horsebox entrance and drove through to an area already scattered with horseboxes in various states of unloading.

As soon as the driver had helped lower the ramp, he loped off in search of a fry up with coffee.

'Urgh, I don't know how you got to sleep,' Clem complained, as she waited for Georgie to lead Split Trousers outside. 'That cabin stinks. I had to keep surreptitiously sniffing the perfume on my wrist, now all I can smell is a mixture of damp sheep and honeysuckle.'

'According to Tom, he's local, cheap and reliable,' Georgie informed her, keeping tight hold of the lead rein as Split Trousers leaped off the ramp, then tried to pick at a strip of grass. 'Does this horse even know he's at the races?'

'Probably not. Last time he ditched the jockey on the way to the start, did two circuits unaccompanied and was withdrawn.'

'Great.'

They walked off towards the racecourse stables in silence.

. . .

With their horse tucked up in his temporary stable, Clem went off to declare Split Trousers a confirmed runner. They agreed to meet up in the stable staff canteen. Georgie fidgeted in her chair, picking at a sandwich, keen to go find Sam, but with only the two of them she couldn't disappear until after Split Trousers had run in the second race. Clem reappeared and wolfed down a bacon sandwich, two bags of crips and a chocolate bar before glancing at her smart watch.

'Better go get Trousers ready,' she said.

Once their horse was prepared, Clem led him towards the parade ring, happy to be getting some steps in, while Georgie went over to the weighing room to collect the saddle and cloths. In the saddling boxes, Georgie secured the tack while Split Trousers snoozed and Clem chatted.

Georgie stood alone on the lawn in the centre of the parade ring watching Clem leading Split Trousers around the circular perimeter track. She made an eye-catching sight, dressed in dungarees and red patent Doc Martins, pink hair tucked under a red knitted bobble hat with a luminous yellow pom pom. Split Trousers looked well, mane and tail neatly plaited and hooves sparkling with freshly applied oil. He appeared to be still half asleep. Georgie sighed, eyes roving the jockeys now filing out from the weighing room, searching for Sam. He wasn't amongst them.

'All right then?' Roddy Love, the jockey booked for their runner, bounced over to Georgie with a grin, revealing several missing teeth. 'Packed my super speedy breeches this morning!'

'Great. I don't think our chap packed his.'

'Ah, you always need to watch the quiet ones.' Roddy winked. Beneath his skull cap, he had a kindly face.

The bell rang, the signal for jockeys to mount. Georgie gave Roddy a leg up into the saddle.

'Any instructions?' he called down.

'Er.' Georgie paused; she knew nothing about the horse. Was he a front runner? Should he be held up and come with a late run? 'Just go with the flow.'

Clem smirked as a cringing Georgie moved aside.

Minutes later, Georgie and Clem stood together in the chilly grandstand, huddled beside each other for warmth. They watched the horses canter to the start, Roddy taking his time. The field circled for a few minutes and then: 'They're under starter's orders,' boomed the commentator over the tannoy, 'and they're off.'

Roddy positioned himself in midfield, Split Trousers jumping fluently, ears pricked as he leaped confidently over the fences. For the first circuit the positions remained unaltered but halfway through the second circuit the leaders began to tire and drop back and suddenly Split Trousers was in contention, with only one horse to beat. Georgie couldn't take her eyes off Roddy's grey and pink silks. They ranged upside the leader, Roddy's body pumping rhythmically away in encouragement, elbows flapping like wings.

They jumped the second last fence in synchronisation, but Split Trousers took a huge leap and gained ground in the air, to land a length ahead.

'Come on, Trousers, you beauty,' roared Clem, vibrating Georgie's eardrums. 'Only one more … jump it … jump it …'

Georgie found herself caught up in the excitement as the pair approached the last. 'We're gonna win … we're gonna win,' she shrieked.

The last fence loomed. Split Trousers twisted in mid-air, flinging Roddy down his shoulder.

Clem's buoyancy deserted her. 'He's only gone and fallen off.'

However, out on the track, Roddy was performing acrobatics the circus would be proud of. Somehow, he had managed to claw his way back into the saddle and now, reins tangled, silks untucked, he was gaining on the leader. Georgie found herself clinging to Clem's arm. Split Trousers lowered his head, Roddy wobbled precariously, and they dashed past the finish post the most unlikely of winners. Georgie and Clem jumped up and down hugging each other in delight.

After all the excitement of being in the winner's enclosure and with Split Trousers resting in his stable before the journey home, Georgie left Clem replaying the entire race stride by stride over the phone to Tom and set off in search of Sam.

She found his friend Toasty loitering outside the jockeys' changing room, yellow and blue silks untucked over grubby breeches. He sniffed the air longingly, desperate to follow the tempting scent of fried onions wafting from a nearby burger van.

'I'm starving,' he groaned to anyone who would listen. 'Oh, hi, Georgie.'

'Hey, Toasty. How's it going so far?'

'One unseated, one second, one nowhere and the next one I could beat pedalling a bike …'

'Oh, bad luck. Is Sam inside?'

'Nah, he's round the corner, next to the weighing room.'

'OK, thanks.' Georgie made to leave but Toasty suddenly moved across her path, his freckled face frowning.

'Maybe come back later?' he suggested, pushing a hand through his scruffy red hair, then smoothing his goatee beard in agitation.

'Can't. I'm pushed for time.' Georgie ducked around him.

She found Sam deep in conversation with someone she recognised as Abi Ryman, the leading apprentice jockey. Fingers entwined they were laughing. Sam looked up in shock and quickly released Abi's hand.

'Gee-Gee. I had no idea you were here today.'

'Clearly.' Georgie stood frozen, eyebrows raised, as Abi dashed away.

'Just doing a bit of coaching, you know. Helping the up-and-coming talent.' Sam gave Georgie an unreciprocated hug.

'Of course. Ever keen to give back.' Georgie's tone oozed sarcasm.

'Oh, come on. Don't be like that. I was only demonstrating the required pressure on the reins. Abi said it was useful for building her skills.'

'Of course.'

'Buy you a coffee?' Sam wheedled.

'I need to be back at the horsebox in ten minutes.'

'Shame. Call you later?'

'OK.'

'So good to see you.' Sam planted a kiss on Georgie's lips. 'I'll make it down to Cornwall soon, promise.'

'Whenever you can fit it in. It'd be difficult for me to get to Lambourn. It's a bit far for a day off.'

'Yeah, I know. We'll make it work.'

'Really?'

'Sure. Just because you're in Bodmin for the time being, doesn't change anything. You know how I feel about you.' Sam took Georgie's hand and squeezed it gently.

Georgie's phone pinged with a text notification. 'That'll be Clemmy saying we've got to go.'

'Take care, Gee-Gee.'

Slightly placated, Georgie gave a brief wave and walked away.

The atmosphere back at Pennhalow was buoyant. The team were overjoyed with their first winner for months and Split Trousers was given a hero's welcome home. The gelding walked into his stable and fell asleep straightaway, unbothered by the fuss.

Clem took centre stage giving an action replay of Roddy's

riding at the last fence. Hamish, Tom and Fred's bellows of laughter only encouraged her to exaggerate more, until eventually it bore no resemblance to what Georgie had actually seen.

Georgie quietly unpacked the gear in the tack room, watched by Boffy, curled up in his basket with a chewy dinosaur dog toy he'd been given to try and spare the remaining curry combs.

'Good time?' asked Tom, poking his head round the door.

'Yeah, I guess.'

'You guess?' Tom repeated. 'You feeling all right?'

He came in and sat down, legs crossed, hands clasped.

'I don't know.' Georgie was reluctant to confide in a person she'd only known a few days. Her gut feeling about Tom was positive, but she barely knew him. Dissecting relationship issues was usually done over alcohol with trusted friends. Strangers gossiped, but friends would always support you and find the answers, if deemed necessary. 'Forget it. I'm bringing you down and I shouldn't be. This is a good day.'

'For the yard, yes. For you, I'm not so sure. Are you having regrets about coming here?'

'No, not at all. Please don't think it's that.' Before she could stop herself, Georgie had blurted out the saga with Sam.

'Hmmm. I agree it doesn't sound that good but it's probably a misunderstanding. Things are often not what they seem. Tell you what, a bunch of us are meeting at the Barrels for a few drinks and a quiz later. Why don't you join us?'

The silence that followed while Georgie considered Tom's offer was filled with the sound of Boffy's slurping.

'Thanks for the offer. It sounds a good night, but I don't think I'll be much company.'

'Come on, Georgie. It'll make you feel better. My mates are so annoying, you'll soon forget worrying about Sam. You'll be distracted by a feeling of misery at being stuck with them instead.'

Georgie laughed and relented. 'All right then.'

'Cool. We can walk down together. I'll call for you at seven.'

7

Settling on smart jeans and a black sparkly top, Georgie briefly considered wearing heels but, as going to the pub involved crossing the lawn and walking up the lane, she pulled on flat ankle boots with a diamante pattern instead. Applying a hint of mascara and lip gloss, she felt dressed up just enough not to have overdone it for an evening in the local pub.

Flashlights in hand, Georgie and Tom strolled up the lane, dodging puddles. A breeze had picked up, wafting Tom's aftershave Georgie's way. Sniffing the fresh, musky scent, she thought how much it suited him, as she tiptoed around the edge of a pool of water flowing down from the bank and almost completely covering their route. She picked her way carefully to avoid wet feet.

'Are you ready for this?' asked Tom, as he prepared to push open the heavy wooden door of the pub.

'Should I be?'

'They're all friendly but being so far off the beaten track it tends to be locals in here. Expect a bit of showing off. They'll be delighted to have a new face to beat in the quiz.'

'I need a drink already.'

Inside the Smuggler's Barrels was snug, with open fireplaces roaring behind iron grates and thick stone walls. Clever lighting gave the effect of being lit by lanterns, creating darkened nooks for hiding. Elongated shadows and low beamed ceilings led to an atmosphere of having gone back in time. Georgie could picture a band of smugglers in tricorn hats bursting through the door demanding a pint of ale. She guessed that was the point. Tonight, however, the pub was packed with locals, some of whom had brought their dogs. Spaniels and retrievers lay under tables, alert for any snippets of food dropped in their vicinity.

Fred was already seated at a corner table next to a petite lady with a short auburn bob, wearing a navy-blue Joules gilet. Absentmindedly, Tom reach for Georgie's hand and steered her through the throng. They took the two vacant chairs opposite.

'Hi, Georgie. I'm Angie, Fred's long-suffering wife,' the lady said, smiling kindly. 'Hope these two have been behaving themselves and made you feel welcome. You're a long way from home.'

'Absolutely. I'm settling in nicely.'

'Pleased to hear —'

Before Angie could finish, a ruddy faced man of about Fred's age approached the table, hands in the pockets of his tweed jacket. He addressed Fred. 'I hear tell you had a winner today, young man.'

'That I did, Cador. It's been a long time coming.'

'Well done.'

'Buy you a drink my friend?' offered Fred.

'No, thanks. I'm with my lot over there and they won't want me fraternising with a rival team. Actually, I came over to give you a warning.'

'A warning, you say.'

'Yes, to be on your guard. There's thievery afoot in the

area. Several of the farms have been hit. Old Ted lost a quad bike, Phil and Molly are missing two of their best bulls and I nearly lost my brand-new tractor. Only my faithful dogs saved the day and chased them away.'

'I'm sorry to hear that,' said Tom. 'We'll be extra careful with the locking up.'

'You do that,' agreed Cador. 'If we all keep an eye out for each other hopefully this will pass.'

Cador moved away and the mood of the table became gloomy.

'Stealing, out here?' Georgie expressed surprise.

'Yes, afraid so. Crime isn't just for towns and cities, you know. Now, who's having what?' Once he had the order, Tom went to fetch the drinks. They all watched as he joked with his mates up at the bar.

'Good to see Tom enjoying himself,' Angie said to Georgie. 'We do worry about him living up at the manor alone. He says he's fine but it's an isolated life for a young man. We're glad he'll have you around for a while.'

Georgie nodded. With Tom being a genuine and likeable person, she'd assumed he had a partner but didn't want to ask.

'Of course, it's not been easy since Julie left,' Angie confided, as if reading Georgie's mind. 'They were good friends, then it turned into more than that, but as so often happens, Julie was offered a good job up in Manchester. Well, she couldn't refuse. There was nothing down here the likes of what they were offering. They tried to keep it going but it fizzled out.'

'It can't have been easy,' Georgie agreed. 'It's going to be difficult to see much of my boyfriend while I'm here.'

Tom returned with a tray of miraculously intact drinks. 'Quiz starts in five minutes, so I'm told,' he said, handing Georgie a slimline gin and tonic. 'They think you're our secret weapon, Georgie.'

'They're going to be proved wrong,' Georgie insisted.

As the quiz began, Georgie learned she was now part of *Team Giddy-Up.* The evening was highly competitive, the banter lively. Tom's friends Francois and Joe were especially rowdy. Every time he scored a correct answer, Joe jumped up from his seat, waving toned, tattooed arms above his blonde curls in celebration. The more sophisticated Francois sipped red wine, brown eyes looking thoughtful beneath his dark fringe. Georgie surprised herself by answering some of the questions correctly and in the end *Team Giddy-Up* came second and won a bottle of Veuve Clicquot champagne, which Tom gave to Georgie.

'Maybe I'll drop around one evening for an after-work drink,' he suggested with a cheeky wink.

'Of course. Anytime,' Georgie replied, as they stepped outside.

The night had turned cold. Georgie pulled gloves out her pocket. Fred and Angie were getting into a taxi, having bid goodnight. Francois and Joe lurched out the door, crashing into Georgie and Tom, singing a tuneless rendition of 'Drunken Sailor'.

'Do you need a lift?' Fred called over to them.

'Nah, we'll walk,' Joe replied, gazing down at his feet as if trying to remember whether they were in the correct place. 'Ta though.'

Fred strode over and shepherded them towards the vehicle. 'Come on you two. It's far too late and dark to walk along these lanes. Besides, no one could take listening to that for long.'

Once the taxi had pulled away, Tom complained, 'My ear drums literally hurt.'

Georgie heard the landlord locking the pub door and an owl hooted from the trees over by the church. They walked in silence. Once back at the manor, Tom insisted on accompanying Georgie to the annexe door. The security light seemed extra bright after the darkness of the lane. On the periphery, a badger scurried under the hedge. The white material of the half-constructed marquee flapped in the wind like a ghost.

'You're welcome to come in. I've haven't got much in yet, but I can rustle up an instant coffee,' Georgie offered.

Tom hesitated, looking uncertain. 'Thanks for the offer. Another time, perhaps. It's been a long day.'

'It has. I must admit I'm exhausted. Thanks for inviting me though. I had a lovely evening.'

'My pleasure.' Tom smiled warmly. 'Glad you had fun.'

The clocks rolled back and November rolled in. Georgie had assumed sole responsibility for Monty. To begin with it didn't go well. Georgie would lead the colt halfway across the yard when he would rear up, half a ton of horse, forelegs spinning inches from her head. Afterwards, she always wore her skull cap when leading him out. Gradually, through patience and Georgie's calm demeanour while Monty threw his tantrums, a respect formed between them. The colt became less challenging. He seemed to take to her and waited, head over the stable door, for her to arrive each morning, greeting her with a friendly whinny. On Georgie's days off, Clem would step in, emulating Georgie in her dealings with the thoroughbred.

As Monty had improved, one morning Tom decided to have another go at riding him. Georgie tacked him up, struggling to secure the girth.

'He's put on weight gorging grass all day,' tutted Fred, stopping by the stable.

'My jodhpurs are the same after all those break time biscuits,' Georgie replied, head beneath the saddle flap.

'There, all done. Tom won't be able to blame the saddle slipping if he comes off.'

While Georgie gave Tom a leg up onto a restless Monty, Clem, Hamish and Fred gathered the other side of the gate into one of the farm's vacant fields.

'You've got an audience,' Georgie commented, leading them through.

Monty was crunching the bit, froth forming in the corners of his mouth. The whites of his eyes were showing. Despite the ominous signs, Tom instructed Georgie to let go and stay clear. By the time she'd joined the others, Monty was circling on the spot, in a pirouette of which a dressage horse would be proud. Hunched onboard in his body protector Tom resembled a tortoise, clinging on.

'Uh oh,' muttered Hamish.

Monty took off, bucking non-stop. Tom did his best, one arm waving in the air, trying to balance as a rodeo rider, but he was unseated before the pair had reached halfway across the field.

'Argh, that horse,' said Hamish. 'He only puts up with you two. If he was human, he'd be a right ladies' man.'

'Yeah, we're his favourites,' teased Clem.

Georgie set off in pursuit of the loose horse, passing a hobbling Tom. 'Better luck next time,' she commiserated.

'Not bloody likely.'

'We just need to give it more time and patience.'

Tom frowned. 'He shouldn't have been entered for the Derby. He's better suited to the Wild West.'

As she walked on, Georgie smiled to herself. She hadn't given up, not by a long shot. There was potential and there was hope. That was all she required.

. . .

Towards the end of the month, an increasingly distracted Clem, fretting about her upcoming wedding, accidentally shut the chickens in the feed store. They consumed copious amounts of expensive grain before being discovered by Fred and chased out.

Since Tom's failed attempt to exercise Monty, Georgie had progressed from leading the colt to his field every morning to putting a bridle on him and taking him out for walks. The day before, they had ventured out through the pillared gates and further up the lane. They had both enjoyed it and Georgie was planning to do the same again. She led Monty out into the yard and straightened his yellow, red and black striped exercise rug, which had slipped a little.

'Anyone seen dad?' asked Tom, looking around.

'Last sighted heading for the farm muttering about early retirement after Clem massively overfed the chickens,' Hamish informed him.

'Ah, perhaps I'll leave it then.' Tom turned away.

'I'm off —' Georgie got no further as Fred rushed into the yard, arms waving, shouting incoherently.

As he got closer, they could make out what he was saying. 'The sheep, they've broken through and are all over the moor. Quickly, help me round them up before we lose them.'

Tom sprang to life, sprinting to the barn to get the quad bike, Fred did an about-turn to grab the smallest tractor and Hamish ran, hoping his long stride would get him there quickest.

Without thinking, Georgie fastened the strap of her skull cap, whipped the rug off Monty and dropped the reins back over his head. She climbed on top of a pile of bales of bedding waiting to be stored in the barn and slipped her right leg over Monty's back. Gathering up the reins, she urged the colt forwards. He leapt into a canter and they shot through the open farm gate, around the barn and out into the field. At the far end, Georgie could see the sheep streaming over a broken gap in the stone wall. They were swifter and agiler than she had imagined, leaping high and darting away. She feared it was going to be as difficult as gathering up spilt peas.

'Come on, Monty,' she urged.

The colt's acceleration took her by surprise. Similar to Sam's Porsche, the jump to supersonic was instant. Monty dropped low, greyhound-like, as they galloped across the field, Georgie wrapping her legs tightly around the thoroughbred's body. With no saddle and no stirrups, it was an effort not to slide backwards. Georgie had never sat on a horse so fast. She could barely see and only knew they were jumping the wall when she felt the change in Monty's stance. They landed safely the other side. Swerving left, then right, all Georgie's gymkhana experience came back to her, as she began to try to contain the sheep.

Tom got to them first, straddling the quad bike as he bumped across the terrain. He gestured to Georgie that he would go round the opposite way to her. Georgie eased Monty back to a steady canter and raised a hand in acknowledgement.

Between them they managed to bring the sheep back together and steer them towards the adjacent field where a puffed-out Hamish was holding the gate open. All was going well, when suddenly three sheep seized the opportunity to breakaway and made a dash for the open moorland. Georgie was nearest, walking Monty on the outside of the herd.

'I'll go,' she shouted, unsure whether Tom could hear her through his helmet.

Tom was calling something in reply, but she couldn't understand him and looked to Hamish, who was midway between them.

'He's saying watch out for marshes and bogs,' Hamish yelled at the top of his voice.

Georgie spun Monty around and cantered after the runaways, who were fortunately sticking together.

'Marshes and bogs,' she chanted to herself reassuringly, though she had no idea how to identify either and therefore avoid being sucked into one.

She circled wide around the sheep, hoping to head them off. The flighty trio changing direction numerous times, a frustrated Georgie brought Monty to a halt and sat watching. The sheep stopped running.

'Oh, come on. Typical.'

She had Monty going nicely beneath her, ears pricked, when the colt ducked fiercely to the right, almost unseating her. She looked down. Stagnant water, almost hidden by the high grass, lay directly ahead of them.

'Good lad.' Georgie patted Monty's sweaty neck.

The sheep had stopped for a sneaky graze. They seemed to realise they'd be on their own if they kept up the game and capitulated to being nudged back to the farm, especially once they were close enough to hear Hamish rattling a feed bag. Tom rode out on the quad bike to escort them the last part.

Georgie rode away to where she had spotted a narrow stream of clear fresh water and loosened the reins. Monty lowered his head for a drink, swishing his muzzle and blowing out with a sneeze.

With the others gone, they walked back to Pennhalow alone at a steady pace. The tense muscles in Georgie's legs were seizing up. She stretched as best she could as they clattered into the yard, where four astonished faces, their jaws on the floor, stared back at her.

'You just —' began Hamish.

'Rode —' chipped in Clem.

'The unrideable,' finished Tom.

'Never in all my days,' summed up Fred.

Georgie glanced down at the thick black mane in front of

her, as it dawned on her which horse she was astride. 'I didn't think about it,' she admitted. 'I just needed a horse.'

'She just needed a horse,' repeated Fred incredulously.

Monty shuffled, throwing out a hindleg as Tom tossed the exercise rug over his hindquarters. 'What are you thinking, dad?'

'I'm thinking we're back in the running for next year's Derby and we've just found ourselves a jockey.'

Georgie could barely contain her excitement. The best she'd been hoping for was another chance over fences at Exeter or Newton Abbot or perhaps Wincanton or Taunton. Never had she imagined even being considered for a ride in the historic Derby, the Blue Riband of the turf, the most prestigious flat race. Champions bred champions and everyone in the sport wanted to win it.

Sitting in the annexe that evening, Georgie sent a flurry of messages but there was only one person she wanted to tell the most and that was Briggsy. After all, he was the one who had inadvertently led her to this chance. She called and Briggsy answered immediately. Georgie gabbled excitedly.

'You see, it's the perfect opportunity,' she summed up, 'to show Bert what I can do. To make him see he shouldn't have doubted me.'

There was a brief silence before Briggsy spoke. 'You're still angry about the whole Minotaur incident?'

'Not really. I've kind of moved on from that but I do want to prove myself. That's what Bert told me to do.'

'So, you're not planning to ask for your old job back?'

'No. I'm wanted here. Why return to a place I wasn't valued?'

'I guess I thought you might be feeling cut off by now. Be missing Beech Tree. You were here a long time.'

Georgie confessed she didn't feel that way and it was only after the call ended that it struck her Briggsy hadn't seemed very pleased. Perhaps, as Sam had predicted, they were short-staffed and he'd hoped to have her back to share the workload again.

8

Early on the Saturday morning of Clem's wedding, Georgie was woken by a combination of a flock of crows tap dancing on the roof above her bed and dazzling shafts of sunlight pouring through the crack in the curtains onto her pillow. Lying still, she watched dust motes twisting in the rays. Clem and Noah had chosen a dry day for their nuptials. Georgie was pleased for them.

She'd arranged to meet Tom out the front of the manor for the short walk to the church on the green. Georgie waited at the bottom of the steps by the front door, wrapping the long camel coat around her floral dress. Her feet were already feeling chilly in shoes. She wiggled her toes and, as the door opened, Georgie tried to peep inside. She was curious about the house itself. The annexe had clearly once been a part of it, perhaps the servant's quarters, now separated off. Tom stepped through wearing a navy-blue suit and black lace up brogues.

'You look very smart,' Georgie told him, leaning slightly to the right. She caught a glimpse of something moving in the hall before the door was slammed shut.

'Same to you. May I?' Tom offered his arm and Georgie slid her hand through.

Half-way along the lane they discovered the trickle of water had now grown and was covering the entire lane widthways. Georgie glanced down at her suede stilettos in dismay.

'I should have worn wellies and changed at the church.'

'Here, I'll give you a lift.'

Before Georgie could protest, Tom had swept her up and taken her over to the other side.

'I thought it was only the bride who was meant to be carried over the threshold on the day,' she joked.

Tom smiled, rather sadly, leading Georgie to wonder if she'd hit a nerve. Perhaps he had intended to propose to Julie. They didn't link arms for the remainder of their walk to the quaint, compact church, nestled amongst the trees, opposite the Smuggler's Barrels. It was a perfect venue for the intimate wedding Clem had, mostly, insisted she wanted, in between bouts of considering making enquiries at Truro cathedral.

Georgie and Tom entered through an arched doorway with a cascade of flora woven above. An aisle ran down the centre of the wooden pews, at the ends of which hung posies of flowers. Above the altar, the winter sun lit up an ornate stained-glass window. Protected for centuries from the renowned Cornish storms by thick stone walls, the air inside was chilly. Georgie shivered as they took their seats on the bride's side of the church. Tom waved to Finn, the landlord of the Smuggler's Barrels, who was sitting with Hamish and his partner, Craig. Georgie recognised Cador, whose wife was fussing about the white horse hairs stuck to his jacket.

Clem looked beautiful in a plain white satin dress with faux-fur bolero. She beamed and waved enthusiastically on her way down the aisle and did the same on her way out after the service, a handsome Noah by her side.

Georgie stepped outside onto the path which wound through the tiny cemetery of ancient lichen covered headstones. Angie joined her, as they watched the photographer trying to organise guests moving in all directions.

'Well, that was lovely,' commented Angie.

'It was,' agreed Georgie, 'although I can no longer feel my feet.'

'Me neither. Let's get in the car and turn the heater on.'

A shivering Tom and Fred joined them soon after.

Fortunately, the marquee was dotted with heaters, discreetly placed at regular intervals. Angie had done an amazing job organising everything. Round tables were set with pristine white tablecloths, golden candelabras and matching ornate chairs. Mini chandeliers with candle-shaped bulbs lit a soft green carpet, which gave way to a black and white tiled dance floor, a giant polished chessboard. A local disc jockey was assembling towers of multi-coloured lights and speakers.

After the speeches and meal, Fred and Angie disappeared to look after the animals. Despite protests from Georgie and Tom, who wanted to help, they insisted they could manage alone.

'Have a day off. Enjoy yourselves,' they chorused, as they left.

As dusk fell, solar powered lanterns twinkled to life. The disc jockey began playing the song for the couple's first dance. Then the guests hit the dance floor; Francois sweeping one of the bridesmaids up for a waltz while Hamish twirled energetically, his Campbell clan tartan kilt swirling above his hairy knees. Soon you couldn't see the tiles for the mass of stomping feet.

Georgie found herself sitting at a table now devoid of others. She was feeling rather self-conscious when Tom came and sat down beside her.

'Not dancing?' he asked.

'Perhaps after a few more of these.' Georgie waggled her flute of champagne in his face.

'Is that a hint?'

'Not remotely. I might head back to the annexe soon actually. I'm not feeling the rhythm tonight.'

They sat for a few minutes listening to the others singing along to 'Sweet Caroline', when Tom abruptly rose to his feet and reached for Georgie's hand. 'Come this way. I've got something to show you.'

Georgie allowed herself to be towed out of the marquee into the cold night air. There was no one else outside. Side by side, they walked around to the front of the manor and up the steps to the front door. Georgie noticed details she never had before. The pillars either side decorated with leaves, the royal blue paint that needed a recoat, the old-fashioned bronze bell she had rung when she'd first arrived.

'I know you're intrigued.' Tom produced a large skeleton key and clicked it in the lock. 'Welcome to Pennhalow Manor.'

Georgie stepped inside to damp air which intensified the cold. The décor was patchy with mould and the carpets worn, the underlay rucked up beneath, but in its prime it would have been stunning. Directly in front was a vast, ornate floor-to-ceiling mirror, speckled with age. As she admired the intricate silver border of swirling roses, Georgie realised what she had seen moving earlier in the hall was her own reflection. Tom was watching her with a faint smile.

They passed through from the vast square entrance hall under an archway, to a grand staircase. A door to the left led to a dining room set around a rectangular table and a lounge with marble fireplace, decorated with chiselled cherubs. Some of the furniture was covered with protective dust sheets. Georgie resisted an urge to pull them off, put a record on the gramophone and dance from room to room, as though at a grand ball back in the roaring nineteen-twenties.

Downstairs in the basement kitchen, unused pots and pans hung above the Aga. A wooden board mounted high up on the wall still contained the rows of servants' bells. This nod to a bygone era contrasted with the modern kettle, microwave and toaster Tom had installed for use.

Along the staircase and landing were displayed portraits of various characters.

'Are these all your relatives?' Georgie asked, studying them as she walked by.

Following her as he replied, Tom said, 'Some are. No hidden gems though, I'm afraid. Would've sold them to fund refurbishing this place if there were.'

'Have you checked the attic? That's where priceless heirlooms always seem to be hidden.'

'Yeah. And the cellar, before you ask.'

Georgie had stopped in front of a vast painting of a gentleman in military uniform. 'He looks stern.'

Tom caught up with her. 'Oh, that's dad's great-grandpa. He died on the Western Front in the First World War. I'm sure I was once told at the Battle of the Somme. Tragic.'

'And yet not an uncommon tale, I'm sure,' said Georgie sadly, running her fingers through the dust on the gilded frame.

'Many Cornish families lost loved ones during the Great War.'

'How many years have your family lived here?'

'Not sure how many generations. The number fluctuates depending on how many pints of ale dad's consumed in the Smuggler's Barrels.'

While admiring the stained-glass window which adorned the stairs, Georgie heard the opening bars of a jazz song drift up from below. Mystified, she followed the sound, which led to a library. Tom stood beside a gramophone, an empty record sleeve in his hand.

'I couldn't help it,' he said emotionally. 'With you here, it feels like the house wants to come alive again.'

Georgie crossed the room of floor-to-ceiling shelves full of leather-bound books. Softly, she took Tom's right hand and placed it on her lower back, the other she held in the classic ballroom position. They swayed gently on the spot.

'I hope you've found your rhythm now, Miss Wright,' whispered Tom.

With a whoop he pulled Georgie closer, then took off, dancing wildly around the ground floor to Fats Waller crooning 'Ain't Misbehavin'' at full volume. Georgie's hair spun, she circled under Tom's arm again and again until giddy. They danced up the stairs, in and out of the bedrooms. Laughing, they attempted the Charleston around an old cast iron free-standing bath, jazz hands waving, feet smearing the dirt from the white tiles.

'Now the tango,' cried Tom eagerly, as they pranced along the landing, exaggerating the drama of the dance.

Song after song, until they were breathless and dizzy. Georgie felt free, timeless. Lost in the moment, it could have been any year, any era.

And then the music stopped as the gramophone wound down. From downstairs a grandfather clock began to chime the hour. Georgie and Tom were standing very close together, the tips of their noses touching. Georgie could feel sweat clinging to her body beneath the silky material of her dress. Her heart was thumping and her feet, unused to heels, were aching. Time seemed to hold its breath. Anticipation crackled in the air. Tom tilted his head slightly. Georgie felt a shift within her, a change of mood. Then a mobile began to ring. Tom let her go and stepped away.

'That must be yours,' he said. 'Mine's switched off.'

It was such a mundane thing to say, for a second Georgie didn't register what was happening. 'Mine?'

'Your phone. Ringing in your bag. You left it downstairs.'

'Oh … right, of course.'

Georgie hurried down the staircase and rifled through her bag for the vibrating phone. Sam's name was flashing on the screen, along with a photo of the two of them which Georgie had assigned to his number.

'Hey.'

'Gee-Gee. What are you doing for New Year?'

'New Year … um, not sure yet, why?'

'My folks have booked a lodge up in Aberfeldy for Christmas. They're planning to stay through for a New Year party. There's plenty of room. You're invited.'

'Wow, that sounds … great.'

'You'll come?'

'I'll look into it. I'll need time off work and a flight to Scotland.'

'Do say you'll come. It'll be boring if you don't. A bunch of my dad's friends talking fishing and golf.'

'But you like golf, Sam,' Georgie pointed out.

'Yeah, but I don't want to talk about it,' snapped Sam. 'You can fly up after Christmas. Go on. Hogmanay's huge in Scotland and they've arranged fireworks. It'll be a night to remember for all the right reasons!'

Georgie laughed at Sam's enthusiasm. 'All right, leave it with me. I'll chat to Fred.'

'Cool. Let me know soon.'

She ended the call. Tom was standing on the stairs watching her. The front doorbell rang. Wordlessly, he jogged down the stairs, crossed the hall and opened the door. Angie was on the doorstep in a full-length duffel coat.

'Clem and Noah are leaving. Are you coming to see them off?'

'Sure.'

Georgie picked up her bag and followed Tom and Angie back to the marquee, where everyone had gathered to wave the couple off on their wedding night. A tipsy Clem was sobbing and telling each person how special they were to her. Noah was chatting to Fred. When they'd left to get their taxi and the guests began to depart, Georgie offered to start clearing up.

'Don't worry, the hire company do all that. Get yourself off to bed,' said Angie.

Back in the annexe, Georgie mulled over the manor house with its cold, unused rooms. Surely Tom didn't intend to live there alone long-term, she thought, as she pulled the duvet up and placed both feet on a hot water bottle. A fox cackled; the security lights flicked off. All was normal, yet Georgie felt different in a way she couldn't define.

9

Overnight on Sunday a storm roared in, bringing strong winds and belting rain. Zipping up a hooded waterproof jacket, Georgie stepped outside the annexe to find the marquee looking as though it had been bulldozed. Saturated grass squelched beneath her wellingtons.

Tom and Hamish were mucking out in silence, the usually upbeat atmosphere soured by conditions. Soggy chickens scampered about seeking somewhere dry to hide. Tom raised a hand in greeting from Fiddy's doorway. Georgie grimaced in response.

Once the morning's chores were completed, Georgie, Tom and Hamish hunkered down in the tack room. They clutched mugs of tea, while their sodden waterproofs dripped on the floor.

'Might as well have been standing in a waterfall,' groaned Tom, collapsing into a threadbare armchair.

'Must be stopping soon.' Hamish leaned around to peer out the door, then paused, custard cream halfway to his mouth. 'What is she doing here?'

Georgie stood on tiptoe to look through the grimy window and was surprised to see Clem clambering over the farm gate.

'Wind's too strong to open it,' Clem panted, diving into the tack room moments later and slamming the door.

'What are you doing here? Aren't you meant to be on your way to Jersey?' Georgie asked, as she sat on the arm of Tom's chair to make way for Clem.

Clem scowled. 'Flight's cancelled, can't get another one for ages. There's no way I'm getting on a ferry in this.'

'So, you came to work instead?' Hamish was incredulous.

'Yeah, so what?' Clem snapped, hurling a tea bag into a clean mug. 'I need to change my holiday dates,' she informed Tom in an infinitely softer tone. 'We're postponing the honeymoon until later in the year.'

Georgie and Tom exchanged a look, which conveyed concern. The current mood did not bode well for the bickering, which would be worse than ever. Clem reached for a rug to wrap around herself, but Boffy refused to budge from the pile.

'Dog was there first,' said Hamish smartly.

'I'm cold,' retorted Clem.

Rain smashed against the window, the roof moaned and the door trembled.

'Should've stayed at home then.' With a flourish, Hamish finished his biscuit, to be hit on the cheek by the remaining custard cream thrown by Clem.

Tom jumped to his feet. 'Time to get these horses exercised.'

'You're kidding, ride out in this?' Clem looked to Georgie for support.

Georgie shrugged.

'Yep, idle hands and all that. Only two must go out today. Fiddy and Jump For Joy are entered in races next week.

Georgie, go with them on Monty. He needs to mix with the others more, it'll do him good. Meantime, I'll go give dad a hand on the farm.'

Hamish took the lead on Joy. Georgie mounted Monty and Clem rode Fiddy. Although the rain had eased, coaxing highly-strung thoroughbreds past flapping sheets of marquee canvas was like riding the gauntlet of obstacles to spook at. Raindrops pattered on the horse's protective exercise sheets and formed droplets on the peaks of skull caps. The overhanging trees dripped on the trio.

To warm up, they trotted briskly through the hamlet, past the Smuggler's Barrels pub, shuttered against the elements so early in the day.

'What I wouldn't give to be sprawled in a chair beside the fire with a pint in my hand,' grumbled Hamish, looking longingly at the closed stout wooden entrance door.

'At least it's not torrential now,' Clem replied, just as a cloud burst directly overhead and an ocean's worth of cold water cascaded over them.

Monty tossed his head, shaking moisture from his ears.

'Maybe we should call it a day?' suggested Hamish hopefully.

'We'll give them a burst of sharp canter up that shorter track we don't use very often,' replied Georgie. 'Tom's instruction, not mine.'

'Marvellous,' muttered Clem, as the ringing of hooves on tarmac was replaced by the squelch of peaty ground.

Conditions were miserable, but the horses came first. Hamish urged Joy on along the narrow track. Monty jumped off keenly, Georgie trying to keep a good distance. The colt tucked his head in, neck arched. Georgie rose in her stirrups. The ground was pitted and uneven. Loose clumps of earth were thrown up by Joy's hooves. Georgie squinted. Monty snatched at the bit. It was an effort to hold him. He whisked his tail and bucked playfully.

Drizzle and a low-lying mist drifting in made visibility poor. Rounding a bend at speed, Georgie almost rode into the rear of a stationary Joy. Pulling back on the reins, she managed to bring Monty to a halt within a couple of strides, hind legs skidding underneath him. Hamish was nowhere in sight. A faint moaning emanated from the other side of a half-submerged tree branch which had fallen over the path, blocking the way. Georgie reached out for Joy's reins, but the gelding sprang away, then popped from a standstill over the log. Dismounting as Clem drew up behind, Georgie peered over the log. Hamish was sprawled on the path, his left arm at an unnatural angle.

'Argh, my arm's agony.' Hamish was pale and clearly in a lot of pain.

Georgie turned to Clem. 'Have you got your phone with you?'

'What? Er, nope, I left it in the tack room, so it didn't get soaked.'

Georgie unzipped her pocket, withdrew her phone and passed it to Clem. 'Call an ambulance. I'll go after Joy.'

Clem took the phone. 'Can't I go after Joy?'

'No. Call an ambulance.'

'But I —'

'Just do it. Then get the waterproof rug off Fiddy and put it over Hamish.'

Georgie glanced at Hamish, trembling with shock and cold, on the wet ground. 'We'll soon have help here,' she reassured him.

'I'm sorry, Georgie,' he muttered through gritted teeth, 'I didn't see the log until we were on top of it. Joy spooked and that was that.'

'Don't apologise. Stay put until medics arrive. Clem, will you get a move on.'

Georgie vaulted back into Monty's saddle, as Clem pressed keys on the phone. She tapped the colt's sides with mud-caked heels and they cantered away.

The mist now swirled around Monty's chest and, with no phone, Georgie wasn't keen to go off alone, but Joy's welfare could be in danger. They had to find him. Monty took the direction Joy had taken, through ground at times treacherous, picking his way around boggy patches waiting to lure the unobservant. A haunting cry echoed out of the shadows. Monty stopped abruptly, ears back, quivering. The sound trumpeted again, closer this time. With relief, Georgie spotted a deer stag, bellowing. The bellow ended in a series of barks. Georgie urged Monty onwards. They followed ground which rose to a rocky outcrop, then dropped down to a valley. As they descended, Monty whinnied loudly and a response came from below. Georgie let Monty lead her to Joy, huddled against an ancient stone wall, reins entangled in the branches of a gnarly, dead, windblown tree.

Struggling with both horses, Georgie pushed Monty aside while trying to free Joy. Her boots sank into soil, permanently soft from the gully trickling along the valley floor. Fingers, scratched and sore from the brittle bark, finally released the broken reins with a snap. Joy jerked his head back and snorted. Monty refused to stand still for Georgie to remount. The air felt sinister. Joy reared; Monty lashed out. Squashed between them, Georgie was pulled one way, then another.

'Need a hand there?'

Certain she had imagined the voice, Georgie ignored it, until a man she recognised reached for Joy's bridle, making soothing sounds. It was Cador.

'Oh, thank you.' Georgie gratefully let go of Joy so she

could clamber onto Monty's soaking saddle. Once she was settled, Cador handed the broken strips of Joy's reins over.

'Head straight back now. This weather is not done with us yet. I'm hoping it'll keep the thieves at bay.'

Before she could thank him again, the farmer was gone.

By the time Georgie turned the horses between the pillars at Pennhalow, the brewing storm had arrived. Thunder rumbled in the distance; the light faded to resemble dusk. The horses' manes and tails streamed water; their ears laid back in misery. Tom was pacing the drive, hunched into the hood of his anorak, face riven with concern.

'Thank goodness,' he cried when he spotted the bedraggled group. Rushing over, he eased Joy's reins from Georgie's frozen hand, then walked beside her. With relief, Georgie took her feet out of the stirrups, rotating cramped ankles.

'I've been worried stupid,' Tom said. 'Six of you went out and only Clem and Fiddy returned. She told me Hamish had been carted off in an ambulance and you'd chased after Joy. She'd no clue where you were.'

'Yep, that pretty much sums up my morning.' Georgie grimaced. 'Feels like I've been through a carwash. What's the diagnosis for Hamish?'

'Broken arm and torn ankle ligaments. Poor lad.'

'Yes, poor Hamish.' Georgie slid from Monty's back, stiff legged.

'Unfortunately, it means we'll be a person down. I need to ask … no, now's not the best time.'

Georgie stopped. Monty nudged her impatiently with his nose, keen to get to a dry stable and a full haynet. 'Ask what?'

Tom turned to face Georgie. He seemed stressed. 'If you'll stay, at least until after the Derby. I know this was a temporary thing for you but, well, even if I can secure a trainee straight out of the Racing School, they'll lack experience. Hamish will be out for weeks. Please don't feel you have to say yes. The ride on Monty in the Derby is yours regardless, Pengelly's always keep their word.'

Georgie tilted her head as though thinking but, in reality, her decision was already made. 'Sure, I'll stay. Honestly, I've done nothing to find anything else anyway, so you'd be doing me a favour too.'

Tom beamed delighted, but his expression turned to fury as they gazed around the yard. The donkey wasn't in the field where he was supposed to be, but in the barn helping himself to an unlimited supply of hay. Fiddy was outside, head and neck reaching over the door into Hazel's stable. The dapple-grey mare cowered at the back wall to avoid the unwelcome visitor. A bucket filled with expensive racehorse feed had spilled across the cobbles, a flock of pigeons pecking at it greedily. Clem was nowhere to be seen.

Tom gasped, then shouted, 'What the hell. Clem, where are you?'

Clem strolled out of the tack room, a half-eaten Twix in her hand. 'Yeah, what's up?'

Tom gestured the chaos in frustration.

'Oh, yeah, don't worry, I'll sort it,' she said, stuffing the remaining chocolate in her mouth and waving her arms at Jackson.

'I'm really glad you're staying,' Tom told Georgie, as Boffy charged out the barn, barking at the pigeons.

'You get 'em,' encouraged Clem, waving a broom at the departing flurry of grey feathers.

A luminous bolt of forked lightning cracked across a sky black with the weight of the rain which began to hurl down. Horses stirred restlessly in their stables. Jackson kicked his door with agitation. Georgie dashed for Monty's stable, sloshing through the grains of spilled feed now swirling in the rapidly growing puddles. Despite the troubles of the day, a grin was spread across her face.

A new staff member, Amiyah, arrived at the beginning of December, having successfully completed a course at the Racing School. Slender, with long dark hair and a lovely soft voice, Amiyah showed eagerness to put her newly acquired skills to work. Following their struggles to attract staff over the years, Fred and Tom were delighted.

Christmas Eve arrived accompanied by a thick layer of ice. Out in the fields, Georgie and Clem had to break through frozen crusts on the water troughs. As she chipped away, Georgie watched Fred and Tom emptying feed bags along the ground, followed by a stream of sheep eager for extra fodder to keep warm. Georgie envied the sheep their thick coats.

In the stables, the horses were tucked up under rugs and blankets. Even with layers of clothing and thermals, everyone was chilled to the bone by the time they gathered in the tack room at the end of the morning's work.

'I'm off to do my Christmas shopping,' Tom announced.

'It'll take him the rest of the day and we still get the same presents every year,' whispered Fred.

Georgie grinned, feeling relaxed and happy. Fred, Angie and Tom had said they would cover Christmas Day and Boxing Day as a thank you for all the team's hard work and Georgie had extra time off for her New Year visit to Sam in Scotland. Boffy jumped onto her lap, snuffling after the shortbread she was eating from the Christmas biscuit selection tin Clem had brought in days ago.

'Nope.' She plopped the Jack Russell on the floor. He trotted over to try Amiyah instead.

'Don't forget, Angie and I are having a Christmas get together this evening and you're all invited,' reminded Fred.

'Yeah, you'll have to put up with me being there too, but you can't have everything,' laughed Tom. 'I promise not to talk shop… much anyway.'

'Hamish text me yesterday to say he'd be there,' said Georgie, scrolling through her phone. 'Yes, here it is. Craig can be chauffeur as he's not working.'

'And it'll be a proper welcome to Amiyah,' chipped in Clem.

10

Fred and Angie's home was less of a bungalow, more a modern open plan barn conversion atop a hill on the outskirts of the moor. A real fir tree decorated with multi-coloured lights, red and white striped candy canes and little gold wrapped presents stood in front of the floor to ceiling arched windows in the lounge. Georgie imagined the view across unspoilt countryside would be fabulous in daylight.

Angie had set up a buffet table and a rosy-cheeked Fred, dressed in a Santa hat, was serving drinks. Everyone had taken the opportunity to dress up. Georgie was wearing a sparkly maroon shirt dress with knee length black boots. It was good to let her hair down after a tumultuous time. She was gazing at the tree's reflection in the window, listening to the chatter in the room, when Tom approached her.

'I guess you're excited about your New Year trip to the north,' he said.

Georgie laughed. 'You make it sound as though I'm off to Lapland to track down Santa with my wish list.'

'Well, if you do bump into him, I'm coveting a Ferrari and winning the Derby next year would be nice too.'

'Sure, I'll put in a word, just as long as you've been exceptionally good this year. Have you?'

'What?'

'Been exceptionally good this year?'

Tom shrugged and Georgie began to blush. She changed the subject. 'It will be nice to spend time with Sam. We've hardly seen each other. He's always off around the country chasing rides in his bid for champion jockey. It sometimes feels I'm a long way down his list of priorities.'

'I'm sure he's not doing it on purpose. His focus is probably elsewhere for the time being. He's a young man chasing career success. We've all been there.'

A fluffy white cat stared at them through the glass, the tree lights casting rainbow colours on its coat. Disinterested, it moved on.

'Do you really think we have a chance with Monty in the Derby?' Georgie asked, turning to face Tom earnestly. 'You know, a real genuine chance, not simply a case of let's have a go because we've nothing to lose.'

Taken aback, Tom thought for a minute before replying truthfully. 'Honestly, I don't know. Monty is fast, he stays the distance and he's well balanced. They're the qualities you need. But if you're asking me, do you think a bunch of misfits – pardon the pun – from the West Country could win the world's greatest horse-race, I'd say: why not?'

'Why not,' repeated Georgie, liking the positivity.

'It's funny how it creeps up on you, the realisation that you can't go on being a jockey forever. Although in my case it was more weight that crept up on me than age.' Tom sighed. 'You have to make the most of these opportunities when they come along. First or last, we'll never regret it.'

'It's all I ever wanted,' Georgie said. 'Since I was a child. I was ambitious but on reflection I got comfortable at Beech

Tree. I guess I thought everything would come to me, but it didn't.'

'It rarely does, still change is never easy, but nothing can be achieved without it.' Tom sipped his drink. 'And how did you and Sam meet?'

'We kept coming across each other at various racecourses, got chatting and exchanged numbers. That was a few years ago now —'

From close by, Angie clapped her hands, making them both jump.

'Time for charades,' she boomed.

'I was hoping she'd forgotten that idea,' muttered Tom. 'Dad and I tried to put her off.'

The evening was filled with laughter and games which became progressively sillier. Georgie was sorry when it was time to leave. As Craig manoeuvred a drunken Hamish into the passenger seat of their car, Clem, Noah and Amiyah waved from a taxi and Fred and Angie called goodnight, then disappeared indoors. Tom joined Georgie under the lantern on the front lawn. She jingled her keys.

'No drinking for me until I get to my parents in Exminster.'

'I've got the bonus of staying here tonight, no journey home.'

A smattering of snowflakes drifted down, sparkling in the glow of the light. Peace descended, broken only by the sound of distant carol singing.

'Merry Christmas, Georgie Wright. Drive carefully.' Tom leaned in and kissed Georgie on the cheek, then turned and, hands in the pockets of his jeans, walked back to the house.

Georgie climbed into her car and started the engine. Tom's kiss was a cocoon of warmth against the damp iciness. She'd always figured her next move would be to Lambourn or perhaps Middleham. Not for a second did she consider

Cornwall, a county not linked with the sport at all. Funny how you could lose yourself, she thought, then rediscover your purpose in the most unlikely of places.

It was a typical Wright family Christmas. Too much food and alcohol consumed and the only exercise walking to the kitchen to get more supplies. Bloated, Georgie raised herself from the sofa, thankful she had no race-riding commitments in the foreseeable future; she would never make the weight. She'd need to get fit again in the New Year, she thought, as she retreated to her room to video call Sam.

Sam was extremely drunk. Wearing a tartan deerstalker hat at a jaunty angle, he kept turning away to joke with people in the background who Georgie couldn't see. She began to wonder whether he even knew she was there. Wishing him a happy Christmas, she ended the call.

A flurry of Christmas messages pinged through to Georgie's phone during the day including one from Briggsy sending season's greetings and a sarcastic comment asking whether she was bored being stuck in the middle of nowhere yet. Jess told her all at Beech Tree stables sent their love, which Georgie didn't believe for one second. Tom sent a brief message from the Pengelly's. It looked to be a generic one sent to the staff.

With Christmas over, Georgie's parents dropped her off at Exeter Airport. It was raining torrentially as she walked into the terminal building in Devon and still was when she walked out at the other end of her journey in Edinburgh. She could have flown around the sky for an hour and landed back at the same spot. She would almost have believed she had but for the sight of Sam, leaning against his father's silver Range Rover in the car park. Georgie wheeled her suitcase towards him, a smile breaking out at seeing his familiar face again.

As Sam leaned into kiss Georgie briefly, the golf umbrella he was sheltering beneath tipped forwards, pouring huge droplets of cold rain over her. Unlike Sam, suitably attired in a wax jacket and green Le Chameau wellingtons, Georgie had only dress and shoes beneath a flimsy mac. She tried to ignore the shower of rain as it leaked down her lace collar and seeped into her ballet pumps.

'Hey, Gee-Gee.' Sam picked up the suitcase and threw it in the boot. 'Bloody awful weather. Convinced I've not seen proper daylight since I got here.'

'If it makes you feel any better, it's the same down south.' Georgie slid into the soft cream leather of the passenger seat.

'Snow would be preferable. I packed the snowboard.' Sam lit a cigarette and dropped the window a centimetre, to allow the smoke out, but not the rain in. 'Hope we can get outdoors soon. Clay pigeon shooting's booked and tomorrow's a surprise apparently.'

They left the city, headed for the Highlands. Through the spray, Georgie could make out little other than the road ahead. The combined sound of the wipers swishing rhythmically across the screen and Sam's voice grumbling about missing out on rides for days because his family had guilt tripped him into a holiday, made Georgie feel overwhelmed by tiredness. She longed to tell Sam about her adventures in Cornwall, her hopes and excitement for Monty, but he ignored her attempts to get a word in. She wondered if there was a smidge of jealousy lurking behind it all.

Tall trees and rolling hills, lush and green, swept by the passenger window. Sam ceased moaning and was now speaking to his booking agent through the car's Bluetooth speaker.

'I mean, I'm under pressure. Got masses of catching up to do now, Stu. Those rides you slotted in at Perth were good, but I'm lagging behind after only a few days off …'

Georgie zoned out. As the Range Rover sped along it startled deer grazing beside the road, who skittered away into the trees, bobbed tails swishing. Through a break in the clouds, Georgie spotted the pointed wings and long tail of a kestrel hovering gracefully, scanning for prey.

She dozed off, to be woken by the sound of Sam swearing. He was leaning out the window, his arm soaked within seconds as he punched a code into a keypad to open a pair of solid wooden gates. The gates automatically swung inwards to reveal a sweeping grey gravelled driveway.

The old stone former hunting lodge was tucked away in acres of dense woodland, surrounded by mature trees. Its tall chimneys and long vertical windows gave a light, airy feel at odds with the rather stern looking exterior. There were three wings and a turret, decorated inside with deep earthy reds, greens and browns. Framed hunting prints adorned the walls and in the drawing room a huge stuffed stag's head had been mounted above a fireplace, ablaze with a log fire. Double doors led to a back lawn the size of an average park. Georgie and Sam walked down to a stream, where a pair of liver-and-white springer spaniels were frolicking.

'Beckett. Bobbin,' Sam barked, as the dogs growled and chased each other through the water and out the other side, oblivious to how cold it must be. 'Pack that in.'

The dogs scampered back, skipping along at Sam's heels.

'They're cute,' said Georgie, stroking one of the spaniel's heads.

'Dad's dogs,' explained Sam, letting them into a boot room where they curled up in matching baskets. 'Everyone's in the drawing room. We'll meet them there.'

Gathered around the fire, to escape the chill pervading every room, were Sam's parents, his two brothers and their partners, plus a couple Georgie didn't recognise, accompanied by a red headed woman in her early twenties.

Sam's dad, tall, handsome and blonde, handed Georgie a tumbler of malt whisky. She really wanted a cup of tea but didn't feel she could ask for one. From the cheek kissing and welcomes all round, Georgie discovered the couple were old friends of Sam's parents. They introduced themselves as James and Brenda, also tall and grey haired and their daughter Rowena, who had clearly taken a shine to Sam. Georgie watched her vivid blue eyes follow him around the room, lips slightly parted, with a determined look.

Dinner that evening was in a grand dining room lit only by scattered candles held in elaborate pewter holders. Georgie took her place at a long mahogany table. The dim lighting made it difficult to see what she was eating. Although atmospheric, she wished someone would simply turn on the overhead lights. The conversation mostly revolved around Rowena, who appeared to be involved in fashion, although Georgie couldn't figure out exactly how. As Rowena waved her arms above her head, she gushed about names Georgie didn't recognise.

'Georgie, dear.' Georgie gazed down the table in surprise that Sam's mother had spoken to her. 'Sam tells us you resigned from Bert's on the spur of the moment and are now based in Cornwall.'

'Oh, yes, I did and I am. The thing is, it's all working out rather well because they have this amazing colt called The Misfit, who's entered in the Derby next June and they've asked —'

Georgie got no further for Rowena cut across her speaking at such volume it was impossible to ignore. 'Daddy's asked Sam to ride Hocus Pocus in next year's Grand National, haven't you, daddy?'

'Oh, how marvellous,' Sam's mother instantly forgot her conversation with Georgie.

'Yeah, it's fab. Got a good chance too. Probably be the favourite come the spring,' boasted Sam.

'And only the best jockey for the best horse,' winked Rowena, starting a rather absurd round of applause, which the others joined in.

Georgie placed her silver knife and fork on the bone china plate with a clatter. Sam turned and mouthed an apology; Georgie batted it away with a hand.

'They're your friends. They don't know me,' she said, as Sam apologised again while they followed the group across the hall towards the drawing room.

'That's just the way Rowie is. Rather competitive. She doesn't mean to be rude.'

'It's fine.'

Sam grabbed Georgie's arm. 'I'll make it up to you, Gee-Gee. There's a massive four poster bed in our room and I've been sleeping in it all alone. It's time to put that right.'

They disappeared off up the wide staircase. Before they'd even got through the door Sam's hands were all over Georgie. The sense of urgency was palpable as they kissed intensely.

11

Georgie woke early to the repetitive beat of rain battering the steamed-up windowpane and Sam slamming around in the bathroom. She burrowed down under the duvet, reluctant to leave the warm softness of the bed and greet such a miserable day. Sam's scowling face as he stomped out the adjoining bathroom, towel wrapped round his waist, gave her the impression she wasn't the only one.

'How about we stay in here all day?' she purred. 'Just the two of us. Making up for lost time.'

Sam appeared not to hear. 'A distillery tour … of all the stupid things to waste my time on.'

Georgie sat up. 'Is that where we're going today? The surprise?'

'Can you believe it?' Sam huffed, struggling with a tangled pair of jeans. 'I'm missing a day of rides at Newbury for a tour of a whisky distillery. I'm tempted to tell them to forget it.'

Georgie flopped back on the bed not keen on spending a day with Sam in a bad mood. 'Can we back out?'

'No. It's only us and Rowie. Can't leave her to go on her own.'

'Why did they only book the three of us?'

'Stop asking stupid questions, Gee-Gee. I don't know. Something about she wanted to go and there were only three spaces left. Hurry up. We're leaving in an hour.'

Sam hurled the bedroom door shut behind him. Georgie curled up and wondered if there was a way to avoid the day. Then she thought of the simpering looks Rowena gave Sam and got out of bed.

A group of people dressed in walking gear were clustered on the distillery forecourt. They watched as Georgie, Sam and Rowena exited the Range Rover, then followed them to the reception area, where a staff member checked their booking at the door, before greeting them.

'Welcome to Murray Park. The tour will begin momentarily.'

Sam's mobile rang. He moved away to answer. Georgie yawned.

'You could have stayed behind,' said Rowena, 'if you're bored.'

'I'm fine,' Georgie replied curtly.

A staff member who introduced himself as Lachlan was now giving an introductory talk. Georgie wasn't listening. She was watching Sam's body language as he paced the car park, phone to ear. By the time he returned, Lachlan was wrapping up:

'…and ends with the obligatory gift shop. Well, that's the plan anyway.'

The group laughed and a few applauded.

'Everything OK?' Georgie asked Sam.

'Fine. A mate wanting some advice.'

'A mate?'

'Yeah. A Mate … a buddy … a friend. Whatever you want

to call them. Blimey, Georgie, why do you always have to be so suspicious?' Sam stamped off to where Rowena stood near the front, leaving Georgie feeling stung.

Georgie kept to the rear of the tour as they moved through a museum area filled with information boards giving the chronological history of Murray's Best Whisky. Lachlan led them through the building from area to area, stopping at various pieces of spotless machinery, to explain malting, mashing, fermentation to distillation. Up the front, Rowena kept touching Sam's arm to get his attention, pointing out different parts of the machines.

'And finally, the piece de resistance,' Lachlan announced, pausing dramatically in a low-lit room filled with casks, his arms out wide. 'The all-important maturation.'

The group gazed around enthusiastically.

'Those closest to me might argue that I've never reached that point myself, but I am an expert on the process here at Murray's. We pour the spirit into oak casks to allow it to mature. This must be for a minimum of three years before it can legally be called a whisky here in Scotland. Did you know that approximately two percent of the spirit per year is lost through natural evaporation?' A gasp of surprise rippled through the room. 'We call it the Angel's Share. Lucky angels, eh? The rest of us mere mortals have to pay for it.'

Peals of hilarity bounced off the walls as they moved on through to the tasting area, a hall with vast windows and a bar. Patio doors stood open leading to a balcony sheltered by the overhang of the floor above, set with circular tables and chairs. A few people broke away to take photos of a gushing waterfall, causing a dash to check out a supposed otter sighting.

'Probably a log,' the staff member behind the bar said to Georgie, pausing in putting out clean glasses to shake his head.

'No otters to be found here then?'

'You'll spot the best wildlife if you sit quietly. Scares off everything when you make that much racket.'

The group trooped back inside and crowded around a table where the samples were now set out.

Lachlan tried to get everyone's attention over the murmuring and excitement. 'The flavour will be different depending on which region the whisky is from. Here in the Highlands, it tends to be fruity, malty and sweet. Whereas the whisky from Islay would be more peaty, salty and powerful. See if you can guess which whisky is which. Just try saying that when you've had one too many.'

Georgie stood alone, watching as Sam and Rowena compared tasters of the amber liquid, taking sips and laughing at their disagreements over which was nicest. Was Sam right? Did she read too much into innocent situations and always overreact? She began to doubt herself, although she could have sworn as Sam had slid his phone into a pocket, that the unlocked screen had shown the last caller was Abi.

New Year's Eve dawned bright and bitterly cold. Puddles froze. Georgie pulled back the red brocade curtains in the bedroom and was alarmed to discover ice had formed on the inside of the windows. She chipped away, trying to clear a patch with a nail, as Sam danced out of the bathroom singing, his mood the opposite of the previous day.

'I've had an email,' he beamed, swooping from behind and kissing Georgie's neck, 'letting me know I've been nominated for an award at next year's Jocks.'

Georgie turned to hug him. 'Congratulations. Er, what for?' She couldn't recall any recent events worthy of a nomination.

'Jump Ride of the Year for Laird's Lug at Musselburgh.'

'Brilliant, Sam! Well done.'

Georgie recalled the ride because she'd been there that day. Laird's Lug, the hot favourite, had blundered at the last fence leaving Sam clinging upside down underneath the horse's neck. Somehow, he'd managed to clamber back into the saddle and go on to win the race.

Sam let go of Georgie with a grin. 'It's at the Luxe on the Strand in London next February. You'll come as my guest?'

'Of course I will. I'd love that.' Georgie beamed, delighted. She'd never been to racing's equivalent of the Oscars before. It was a prestigious black-tie event. 'How exciting.'

After breakfast, everyone gathered outside for the clay pigeon shooting, which had been set up on the lawn. Georgie pulled her woolly hat down over her ears, rather bored watching Sam's brothers have a go. They missed more times than not.

Beckett and Bobbin, overexcited, chased each other in and out of people's legs until Sam's dad ran out of patience. 'I'm putting them back in the boot room.'

A freezing cold Georgie seized the opportunity. 'I'll take them for a walk. I don't mind missing my go.'

'Be sure to keep well clear then. Don't want you wandering into the firing line.'

Georgie promised to stroll in the opposite direction and, calling the dogs to her, they set off around the front of the lodge and through the woods away from the property. Bobbin, the younger dog, kept whirling on the spot, chasing his tail, then dashing ahead, to look back and check Georgie and Beckett were still with him.

Tramping along a trail through the damp bracken, the soles of Georgie's wellies sunk into the soil. Apart from the sporadic sounds of shooting, it was peaceful; the only noise Georgie's breath and the dogs panting. Warmed up, she began to enjoy the walk. Unsure where the boundary of the lodge ended within the dense woods, Georgie kept going as there seemed to be no other properties for miles.

As the terrain changed to a gentle sloping hill, Bobbin raced off into a thicket of trees growing particularly close together. Georgie stepped amongst the towering trunks, catching a glimpse of a pine marten as it scurried up a tree. Distinct rustling came from further ahead.

'Bobbin, come here at once,' she hissed.

As she approached, the outermost branches began to bend and shake but what emerged wasn't spaniel shaped. A tumble of red hair, followed by a giggling Rowena, accompanied by Sam, with jacket askew and mud on his jeans. The trio stopped simultaneously, then eyed each other warily. Engaging his natural charm, Sam spoke first.

'Everything all right, Gee-Gee?'

'I could ask you the same question. I've been walking for ages. What are you doing out here? Why aren't you at the shoot?'

Without missing a beat, Sam replied, 'Looking for you. It's lunch time and, as you say, you've been gone ages. We were getting concerned.'

'Yes, most concerned,' Rowena echoed.

Georgie glared from one to the other. 'As you can see, all good. I'll make my own way back.'

Georgie walked off, Beckett at her heels, as Bobbin reappeared carrying a large stick in his mouth, clearly pleased with himself. She stroked his head.

'Hold on a minute.' Sam hurried to catch up.

They stood facing each other. Georgie folded her arms.

'Aww, come on, you're being ridiculous,' pleaded Sam.

'I'll tell you what's ridiculous … your behaviour.'

Sam raised his arms, then dropped them in a gesture of futility. 'This is exactly what I was talking about yesterday.

You're always thinking the worst. I've known Rowie for years.'

Bobbin dropped his stick and growled.

'Even the dog's fed up with your excuses,' Georgie pointed out.

Sam scowled. 'Walk back on your own then if that's what you're determined to do. No rush. It's golf this afternoon and I don't expect you'll grace us with your presence for that either.'

Georgie refused to follow as Sam moved away. She wasn't sorry to be missing golf, in her opinion it ruined a good walk, but her visit was becoming marred by increasing distrust in her boyfriend.

Relations between Georgie and Sam remained as frosty as the weather. Sam insisted Georgie's overreaction was spoiling their time together. Georgie was loathe to argue about it in a house full of strangers who would no doubt be listening.

The Christie's had pulled out all the stops for a spectacular Hogmanay celebration. After a six-course dinner at a fine dining restaurant nearby, they returned to the lodge and gathered on the lawn for a bonfire and fireworks. A dazzling display of multi-coloured explosions lit up the clear night sky, as they reached for the stars. Sam stood behind Georgie, his arms wrapped around her, swaying gently.

'It's always been you,' he said softly in her ear. 'You know that.'

A fountain of red and gold sparks exploded overhead, then twinkled down to earth. Georgie's uncertainties overwhelmed her. She couldn't figure out whether it was her, or if Sam's apparent closeness to others was a cause for question. She placed her hands over Sam's, locked around her waist, then tilted her head back on his shoulder with a sigh.

'Sometimes it doesn't feel like it anymore,' she whispered, her words lost in the din of a rocket exploding above.

As the clock struck midnight, arms were linked for an impromptu, drunken version of Auld Lang Syne. Georgie was swept up by Sam's dad and found herself whirled around. Over to her left, Sam and Rowena were holding hands while doing the twist.

'Happy New Year.' Sam's dad beamed down at her. 'Let's hope it's a winning one, for you and Sam.'

Georgie smiled in return, but despite Sam's words and the beauty of the location, she didn't feel entirely happy.

The next morning, while the others slept off their hangovers, Georgie caught a train from Aberfeldy back to Edinburgh, then boarded a flight bound for Exeter. After the tensions of the last few days, she was returning home to some space and time of her own with a sense of relief.

12

Being back at Pennhalow was a breath of fresh air after the slightly stifling atmosphere of Georgie's New Year break.

'Hey, welcome back stranger,' Tom called cheerily. 'We missed you.'

'I missed you all too,' Georgie replied, peering over the door into Monty's stable.

The colt looked around from his haynet and neighed a greeting but didn't move towards the door.

'I see in Monty's world I still don't rate higher than food. He looks well.'

'Yeah, Clem's done a grand job but none of us dared to try riding him. How was Scotland?'

'Not too bad, thanks. The weather was dreadful though.'

'Ah well, come and have a cup of tea. We're working through the leftover biscuits. Perhaps then, you and I take Monty and Zippy out on a quiet hack, to try and stop them fizzing over. They've not done much lately.'

Later, Georgie and Tom waved off Clem and Amiyah who were heading for the open moor, then turned Monty and Zippy out through the farm gate. The ground had dried out under the pinkish rays of a weak winter sun. A troupe of sparrows were pecking leftovers from the ground, while the cows bellowed from inside the barn. Monty was fresh and, on his toes, shied at Fred on the tractor.

'We've got our work cut out,' said Tom, perched high on the back of Zippy. With a white blaze running the length of his face and four white socks which Georgie thought looked like leg warmers, the bay horse stood a hand higher than Monty.

Monty's ears flickered as they trotted along the tracks in single file, keeping to the edges of the fields, avoiding the open spaces. Monty relaxed and played with the bit. At a narrow path banked with trees, Tom suggested, 'Let's canter here. I'd be struggling to hold this monster back in the open.'

Frustrated at the sedate pace, Zippy shook his head and Tom did well to hold the gelding, whose muscles rippled with restrained power. Focused on keeping back and not losing control of her mount, Georgie was taken by surprise when a man stepped out from a concealed footpath crossing the track. Alarmed, the man leapt back as Georgie snatched at the reins, bringing Monty to a sudden halt.

'Goodness,' he stuttered, just as Georgie gasped: 'Sorry.'

'No, my mistake. I ought to have been more careful to check the coast was clear.' The man dusted down his cream corduroy trousers. Although his checked shooting jacket and binoculars blended in, Georgie noticed his polished brown loafers jarred with the rest of his outfit.

'Are you OK?' Georgie asked with concern, struggling to keep a dancing Monty clear.

'Yes, totally. What a handsome horse. Would you mind?' Without waiting for an answer, the man reached out and stroked Monty's nose. 'What's his name?'

'The Misfit, although we all call him Monty.'

'Hello, Monty.'

Sensing he had a fan and hoping for food, Monty dropped his usual haughtiness, pricked his ears and nudged at the man's jacket pockets. Georgie was astonished. 'He doesn't usually take to people easily.'

'I'm honoured,' the man said.

Hooves trotting back from up the track heralded the return of a stern-faced Tom and a sweating Zippy. 'What's going on?'

Georgie gave a brief explanation as the man gave a salute of a wave and disappeared back up the footpath. 'No harm done,' she summed up.

Tom's eyes roved over Monty. 'He's bleeding from his near fore.'

'What?' Georgie jumped off and crouched down to examine Monty's left front leg. 'We stopped so quickly he must have caught himself with his near hind hoof.'

Monty didn't seem in any distress as he peered round and down at her, curious what she was up to. Georgie parted the dark hairs to reveal a small cut through the skin, trickling blood.

'Trot him up ahead of me so I can see whether he's sound,' instructed Tom.

Georgie pulled the reins over Monty's head and led him cautiously past Zippy, who laid his ears flat back and bared his teeth but didn't attempt any violence. She encouraged Monty into a trot and jogged alongside him a short way up the track.

'He's not lame,' Tom shouted after her, 'but we need to get some antiseptic. It'll be a nightmare if it gets infected.'

Georgie vaulted back on and they turned the horses back towards Pennhalow.

'Seems strange. That man wasn't ideally dressed for winter moor walking, was he?' she said, 'and he disappeared pronto after nearly colliding with us.'

'Probably birdwatching. Perhaps there's been a reporting

of a rare something or other he simply must tick off his list. He has to be keen to go out voluntarily when it's freezing.'

Back at the yard, Georgie showed Fred Monty's injury. He wasn't overly concerned and once the wound had been cleaned and treated, they thought no more about it.

Mid-morning break the next day was interrupted by an angry Fred storming across the yard, waving that day's edition of the *Racing Life* in the air. Georgie was halfway through an apple, Clem was rubbing Boffy's tummy and Tom was thawing out next to the fire after scrubbing out the water troughs with Amiyah.

'I think I've got frostbite,' he complained, holding blue tinged fingers as close to the fan heater as possible, when Fred burst into the tack room.

'Spying,' Fred chuntered.

'What is?' Tom asked, trying to glimpse the crumpled newspaper.

Fred threw the *Racing Life* on the table. 'That person you bumped into yesterday must have been a journalist.'

'How so?' asked Georgie, picking up the paper and smoothing the pages. Tom, Clem and Amiyah peered over her shoulder and read:

READ ALL ABOUT IT - ELUSIVE MISFIT SPOTTED ON THE MOOR!

It's been a long time since Cornwall based trainer Fred Pengelly had a runner in a group race, never mind a Classic. Rumours have been rife he intends to run lightly raced colt The Misfit in this year's Derby. So far Mr Pengelly has steadfastly refused to provide any update other than to confirm the horse is still entered in the race.

Despite numerous attempts to obtain the current status of The Misfit, or Monty as he is known by stable staff, the team at Pennhalow have consistently provided a "no comment" response to all enquiries.

However, news reaches us from a far-flung corner of Bodmin Moor that the horse is alive and well and looking better than ever. An unnamed source said: 'I saw The Misfit out on the moor. He was galloping so fast it was as if he were flying.'

In another surprising turn of events, The Misfit was being ridden by Georgie Wright. Miss Wright used to be one of the stable jockeys at Bert Russell's Epsom based Beech Tree Stables but unexpectedly quit last year and disappeared off the radar. After a couple of years of lacklustre results, it was assumed she may have given up her career, such as it was, due to lack of rides.

While it seems most unlikely, we ask: could this elusive pair be on the verge of staging a comeback together?

'I wouldn't hold your breath,' commented the unnamed source. 'Neither of them has experience of the unique undulations of Epsom racecourse. They should stick to easier races if they want to win anything at all.'

Watch this space folks, you read it here first!

'How rude,' declared Clem.

Fred picked up a mug and poured water from the kettle, spilling most of it in his temper. 'Now we'll have every gallop-watcher, ante-post punter, Derby expert and nosey parker down here, trying to sniff out what's going on.'

'You're overreacting rather a lot there, dad. People aren't likely to travel down here simply to watch a horse exercise.' Tom folded up the paper.

'Mark my words, son, they will be. Would've been preferable to keep it all quiet, turn up at Epsom the rank outsiders with no expectation and no pressure.'

'But there is no pressure,' Clem pointed out. 'They're hardly saying we've got a chance. The opposite in fact. They've practically called Georgie worse than useless.'

'Thanks.' Georgie grimaced, throwing her apple core at the bin.

'Word gets out if a horse is going well at home,' muttered Fred. 'No talking to anyone, all of you. Understand?'

'Dad, be reasonable. You can't ask that,' Tom protested.

'About the horses, I mean. Answer no questions. It's our business.'

Fred left the room, fists clenched. Boffy crept out from hiding under the rugs.

Georgie turned to Tom. 'What do you make of it?'

'Dad's being oversensitive. It's one article on page seven. There'll be some interest sure, but nothing on a par with the big names and the top trainers. We'll be viewed as the joker in the race, the no hoper, which suits us.'

Georgie remained silent, focused on the paper, brow furrowed, as the others left to get on with their work. Nerves fluttered in her tummy as she read the article again. She turned to the front page and was startled to see a large colour photo of Abi Ryman, under a headline about her nomination for apprentice of the year at The Jocks. Clearly Sam's coaching was making a difference, Georgie thought as she took satisfaction in placing her mug of tea on top of Abi's face, obscuring it with a big wet ring.

The second surprise of the day came in the evening when Georgie received a message from Jess Russell saying she would be in Cornwall for a few days the following week and asking to meet up for a coffee. Buoyed by the thought of seeing a familiar face from her Beech Tree Stables days, Georgie replied confirming she'd love to see Jess.

As she jostled through Bodmin Town, headed for the café to meet Jess, Georgie realised she'd adjusted to the isolation of Pennhalow. Used to just leaving her car out the front of the manor, she'd got stressed about parking and was running late. Her phone pinged a message, no doubt Jess wondering where she was. She flew in the door, almost dropping her bag.

Jess was already seated with drinks and shortbread biscuits on the table before her. Despite her twinkling blue eyes and hair held neatly in a long ponytail, draped stylishly over her pink designer shirt clad shoulder, Georgie thought Jess looked tired.

'It's so good to see you and you look amazing,' exclaimed Jess as they hugged, the cups and saucers clanging as Georgie lent over the table.

'Must be all the fresh air. What are you up to down here, so far from Beech Tree?'

'Oh … catching up with relatives and checking out a horse dad was interested in buying.' Jess smiled but Georgie detected a hint of nerves behind the façade. 'It's a no for the horse.'

'Shame.' Georgie picked up one of the shortbreads, realising how hungry she was having skipped lunch.

'Actually, there is a purpose to me asking to meet up.'

Now we're getting to it, thought Georgie, nodding encouragement with her mouth full.

'Dad bumped into Gina West a few weeks ago and she told him, the footage from that morning on the gallops with Minotaur, well, it proves you told the truth. *Racing News* never showed it because of Golden Goose's injury. They only wanted footage of horses on the gallops to use as filler for their interview with Sam. But Gina said it's all there. The dog, a little white thing, spooked Minotaur.'

Taken aback that Gina would put herself out to defend Georgie's version of events, she assumed Sam must have told her what had happened. 'No one would believe me.'

'I know and that was wrong. I'm not excusing it, but everyone was upset over Golden Goose and they needed somewhere to put the blame.'

Georgie shrugged awkwardly. 'Thanks for telling me. I

mean, it makes no difference now, but I'm pleased Bert knows. He should have given me the benefit of the doubt.'

'I agree.' Jess paused, then plunged on. 'So … does this change anything? Will you consider coming back to Beech Tree?'

Georgie snapped the remainder of biscuit in half. 'Come back? Why would I?'

'I thought this Cornwall lark was temporary. Briggsy said it was. We need you. Experienced staff are hard to come by.'

'Has Bert sent you as some sort of emissary?' Georgie was puzzled. 'Does he even know you're here?'

Now Jess appeared awkward. 'Dad would take you back, I'm sure. We're short-staffed and besides Briggsy would persuade him. He never wanted you to go. He fought to try and get dad to call you and smooth it all over. But you know dad and his stubborn streak.'

Georgie turned to look out the window at the shoppers hurrying to get last minute purchases before the shops shut. It had grown dark. Streetlights had come to life. Back at Pennhalow, the team would be tucking the animals in for the night. She could visualise them, topping up water buckets, filling haynets, straightening rugs, scooping feed into mangers. She felt a glow of fondness.

'No, I'll not be going back,' she informed a disappointed Jess. 'Whether where I am turns out to be temporary and ends after the Derby or not, I don't belong at Beech Tree anymore. There are plenty of other places I can try.'

'I never had you down as a grudge holder,' said Jess with a hint of malice.

'I'm not,' replied Georgie. 'I've simply moved on.'

13

Feeling distracted, Georgie drove back to Pennhalow, wondering whether she should have burnt her bridges with Jess. The Pengelly's had given no guarantees for the future once Hamish was fit and back at work. They also now had Amiyah. If they no longer needed her, she would have to find an alternate yard to work for and hope they'd be prepared to let her ride some of their horses in races. There had been some truth in the *Racing Life* article. Georgie had been off the radar for some time, since the fall from Dotty Day. Perhaps she ought to ask Sam if his agent Stu would put out some feelers for her with potential yards.

As she crossed the lawn, Tom was walking up from the yard.

'Did you have a good time with your friend?' he asked.

'Yes thanks, it was good to catch up although Jess wanted to know if I'd go back. They're short-staffed.'

'What a cheek!' Tom looked alarmed. 'What did you say? I hope you told them where to go, in no uncertain terms.'

'I did tell them no.'

'You don't sound totally sure about it though.'

Georgie dug into the grass with her boot. 'It's unsettled me. I never thought of Bert's as still being part of my life.'

The security light flicked off, plunging them into darkness. Tilting back his head, Tom suddenly pointed to the sky. 'Look, a shooting star. You're supposed to wish on those.'

Georgie looked up, following Tom's direction, mesmerised as a trail of sparks arced across the clear night. 'Beautiful.'

When she looked back, Tom was gazing intensely at her. 'Absolutely.'

'I'd better go get something to eat.' Georgie turned towards the annexe. 'I've a stomach full of coffee and nothing soaking it up.'

'If you're hungry, I'm cooking the culinary delight of frozen pizza in the aga. Can I tempt you?'

Remembering the eggs on toast she'd planned, it took seconds for Georgie to admit she was starving and accept Tom's offer.

Snug in the warmth of the manor kitchen, eating slices of cheese and tomato pizza with a glass of wine, the radio playing in the background, Georgie felt content and sleepy. She listened as Tom chattered about plans for future races, until they fell into a companiable silence. At some point, Georgie nodded off for she woke with a start, slumped in the chair. Tom had laid a blanket over them both and was also asleep in the chair beside her. Carefully she slid out from underneath and tucked the blanket around him as best she could without disturbing him. The large grey skeleton clock on the wall read midnight.

Easing her handbag onto her shoulder, Georgie made to creep out, then hesitated.

'Hmmm.' Tom shifted but did not wake.

Georgie lent over and placed a soft kiss on Tom's smooth warm forehead.

'Goodnight,' she whispered, before tiptoeing away.

Outside the temperature had dropped considerably. A fox scampered around the fountain. It stopped to stare but didn't run away.

Georgie slept fitfully, dreaming she was locked in a cupboard with Sam outside. No matter how hard she banged on the door he couldn't hear her.

'What the —' Georgie's eyes fluttered as she rose from the dream, confused. It appeared to be daylight and the banging was real and outside. The bedroom was freezing.

Reaching out for the clock, the luminous numbers on the digital display said it was three o'clock in the morning. Puzzled at the light behind the curtains, Georgie got out of bed, pulled on a dressing gown, then peeped out the window. The security light was on and the banging was coming from the yard. A sound of one of the horses continuously kicking their door. Sooner than usual, the security light went off.

She had to give the ancient window a shove to open it, the warped wood not keen to give way. Flakes of paint fluttered away with her breath as she stuck her head out. Some sort of commotion was taking place in the yard. Recalling Tom's stories of Jackson's previous escapades, she picked up her mobile and tried his number. It diverted straight to voicemail. If he was still asleep in the chair, there would be no signal in the basement kitchen. With a resigned sigh, Georgie trooped downstairs and tried not to topple over as she pulled on wellies and a full-length padded coat.

She kept close to the manor rather than go diagonally across the lawn, it gave her a sense of protection. Her movement did not trigger the sensor and the security light remained inactive as she approached. Under her boots came the crunch of broken glass. The light was smashed. With no idea how that could have happened, Georgie pulled out her mobile, switching on the torch.

Half asleep and perplexed, she found the gate to the yard

fractionally open, the chain broken, the padlock missing. Beyond, the yard was dark, but the animals disturbed. Jackson brayed and booted the door again as if trying to break it down. From Zippy's stable came the crash of water buckets sent flying against a wall. A swish of hooves pacing through bedding could be heard from Monty.

'All right, settle down,' Georgie called, headed for the light switch outside the tack room.

Guido's head appeared, nostrils flaring, head shaking. Shadows loomed from imaginary bogey creatures in the corners.

'Try the lights, try the lights,' Georgie chanted, resisting the temptation to look over her shoulder, mind still fizzing about the broken lock.

She'd almost made it when she sensed movement from behind and footsteps coming from the direction of the muck heap, as though someone had been hiding there. As she turned, Georgie was shoved hard, as if by both hands. A figure ran for the farm gate, dropping a flashlight, which spun erratically, highlighting a person as they vaulted the gate. Georgie could only make out a pair of trainers and the hems of black trousers, before she crumpled winded to the ground.

Panting from shock and cold, she rose to all fours, sure her back was bruised. The flashlight had stopped spinning. A pair of green wellington clad feet walked into its circle of light, before it moved upwards as the light was lifted. Georgie scrabbled for her mobile, flung aside as she had fallen. It was out of reach.

'Who are you?' she shouted, trying to sound fearless, but her voice was just a squeak. She wished for something to defend herself with, but all the tools were secure in the barn.

'What the hell … Georgie.' A presence crouched beside her, bringing a waft of musky scent. Tom propped the flashlight on the ground so he could see. 'I heard something going on and came to check it out. I'm guessing you did the same. What's happened?'

'Tom,' she gasped, 'there was someone here. They attacked me, then ran for the farm.'

'Steady.' Tom helped Georgie upright. 'Did you bang your head when you fell?'

'No. I put out my hands. They broke my fall.'

'OK. Stay put and ring my dad. Tell him to get down here straightaway. I need to make sure the blighters aren't trying to steal the expensive stuff.' Unlocking the barn, Tom grabbed a shovel. 'Just in case.'

As Tom headed for the farm buildings, Georgie dialled Fred's number with shaking hands and spoke briefly to a sleepy Angie, before she hurried after him.

By the time she caught up, Tom was at the door of the storage barn where the machinery was kept. He tried the door. With a soft click it opened a fraction and they slipped inside to a high-ceilinged space; the air filled with the scent of oil. As though dumped at the end of a long day, various farm implements were parked haphazardly against the walls on either side. Shades of moonlight shone through the dusty skylights, casting eerie shapes on the floor. Tom motioned with a hand for Georgie to check down one side while he did the other. Feeling distinctly unnerved, Georgie backed against the wall and slunk like a cartoon villain from one tractor to another. When they met up again at the far end neither had spotted anyone.

'All clear, let's check the outbuildings.' breathed Tom.

They searched the barns and outbuildings. The cows, disturbed, shoved moist noses in Georgie and Tom's direction, long tongues drooling with expectation of an unexpected snack. Irritated lowing followed as they slid the door closed behind them.

Feed stores and bales were all still neatly stacked. In the

gateway, the only visible signs of an intruder, the single wheeled tracks gauged in the mud.

'Looks like they got away on a moped or scooter,' said Tom, highlighting the tyre tracks up the lane with the beam. 'They'll be long gone by now. Fortunately, they left empty handed.'

'What do you suppose they were after?' Georgie leant against the solid barn wall, seeking support.

'Who knows. Probably anything they could snatch easily, assuming there was only one of them.' Tom turned to look at Georgie. 'Hey, you're bleeding.'

He stepped close, reaching out to brush hair away from Georgie's forehead. Georgie's fingers sought the spot where Tom's were, their hands touched, briefly entwined. Georgie noticed Tom was still wearing the blue checked shirt with the sleeves rolled up, a little dark chest hair visible in the open collar. She felt undressed with only flimsy pyjamas beneath the coat. Tom shifted, Georgie swivelled towards him, then headlights bounced up the track.

Fred's pick-up truck stopped by them, the driver's window down. Tom explained what had taken place.

'Everything is accounted for. Georgie must have disturbed them early on,' Tom summed up.

Fred was furious. 'We'll have to up security, invest in stronger locks. They'll not be getting their hands on anything of mine.'

Unable to restrain herself, Georgie yawned. Tom noticed. 'It's the early hours, dad. I'll walk Georgie back, then keep watch.'

'If you're staying, I am too,' she protested.

'No, you need to get some sleep. Let's go.' Tom reached for Georgie's hand and led her back through the yard, to the annexe.

Bleary eyed after only a few hours' sleep, Georgie was

back at the stables on time the next morning. The pick-up truck was still parked in the farmyard, Fred fast asleep in the reclined driver's seat. Clem and Amiyah were filling buckets with feed, accompanied, to Georgie's surprise, by Hamish.

'You're back,' exclaimed Georgie, giving him a careful hug.

'Aye, on condition I only ride the quiet ones for a while. Doctor's orders.'

'Tom's gone off to buy new locks for all the gates. Fred stayed on guard all night, but he can't do that again,' said Clem, handing Georgie two buckets. 'He's reported it but as nothing was taken and you didn't see the perpetrator in any detail, there's nothing much that can be done.'

'Buy a rottweiler?' suggested Hamish, tongue in cheek.

'We have not missed your jokes.' Clem chucked the scoop at Hamish. 'Here, make yourself useful while the rest of us do some work.'

The days which followed were tense. At the end of each one, Fred would go around double-checking everything was locked up and Georgie noticed he would linger until much later, clearly concerned. The only event which pleased him was Georgie galloping Monty upsides Zippy and Tom. Despite Zippy's best efforts to remove Tom's arms from their sockets, Monty had raced ten lengths clear by the time Georgie eased him up.

'He's really well,' a red-faced and sweating Tom commented, as he caught up.

'Let's hope that doesn't get reported in tomorrow's papers,' grumbled Fred, eyes roving, checking the bushes for concealed spies wearing camouflage.

Georgie and Tom exchanged a grin.

'Not to worry, dad. I'm sure any reporters will be far more interested in the hot favourite, Polecat. He's odds on now, you know.'

'Jackson can run faster than any horse trained by Brewster Smith,' snapped Fred. With a swift pat of Monty's neck, he walked away.

'Still tetchy about the break-in, isn't he?' asked Georgie, as they let the horses have a pick of the grass.

'Yeah, there's that plus the fact that he and Brewster have never been able to stand each other.' Tom tugged on the reins, lifting Zippy's head. 'We'd better get these guys back and washed off.'

Georgie felt a mixture of emotions as she drove away from Pennhalow a few days later, signalling the start of her holiday. She was eager for a night of letting her hair down, drinking and dancing at The Jocks and it seemed ages since she'd last seen Sam. Still as she passed the Smuggler's Barrels and waved to the landlord Finn, balanced on a paint spattered wooden ladder cleaning the windows in a sleeveless t-shirt which showed off the large tattoo of a pirate on his bicep, she knew she was leaving a piece of herself behind.

14

It was late evening by the time Georgie made it back to Epsom. The traffic had been worse than she remembered and the air felt different, grittier, not as pure. She unloaded the car and waved to Mrs Knight, peeping through the net curtains of Tulip Cottage to check out who had drawn up.

Rose Cottage was cold and dusty. An enormous pile of unopened post balanced in a heap on the hall table. The cupboards were empty. After dumping her bags, Georgie drew the curtains. The kitchen light bulb wasn't working. As she moved from room to room, it occurred to Georgie she ought to have rented the place out. Perhaps that would have stopped the uninviting air, a sense of isolation more intense than Pennhalow ever had, magnified by the arrival of a message from Sam to say he couldn't stay over and would see her at the London hotel the next day. Her tummy rumbled. Comfort eating was the way forward, she decided. Placing an order on her mobile, she fetched keys and bag, then headed for the Final Furlong pub and a takeaway pizza.

The Final Furlong was crowded with what looked to be mostly stable staff. A group played pool, others lounged around watching football on a large television screen fixed to the wall. Queuing at the bar to collect her order, Georgie gazed around for a familiar face but didn't spot one. Distracted by scrolling through Instagram on her phone, she was startled by hands being placed over her eyes from behind as a voice asked, 'Guess who?'

She recognised it straightaway. 'Briggsy!'

Delighted she spun around to give her old colleague a hug, grateful for the support he had inadvertently provided finding her a place at Pennhalow.

Briggsy beamed. 'I knew you'd return. So … tell me, which trainer are you working for now then? I heard Titus Mitchell was looking for staff at his place on Tattenham Corner.'

'Oh … no, I'm only here briefly, checking my place. Then off to London for The Jocks, before going back to Bodmin.'

Briggsy's face dropped, crestfallen. 'You're still with the Pengelly's?'

'Yep.' Before Georgie could say any more, a pizza box was handed over. 'Better get going before this gets cold. Good to see you.'

Briggsy placed a hand on Georgie's forearm. 'Shame you're not here longer. Would've been nice to catch up.'

Georgie grinned. 'I'm dress shopping in town tomorrow. We could meet for a quick coffee.'

Briggsy shook his head. 'No can do. I'm taking Minotaur to Sandown.'

'Another time then,' Georgie said over her shoulder as she departed.

As usual, clothes shopping proved way more stressful than riding a highly-strung thoroughbred with a mind of its own. Everything Georgie tried either fitted her top half but not the bottom, or vice versa. Despairing, she began to wonder whether she could get away with a smart pair of jeans when she spotted a small boutique she'd never noticed before in a tucked away location. In the window was a full-length sapphire blue gown with a halter neck. Decorated with delicate sequins it sparkled under the lights.

Georgie tried it on. Surrounded by mirrors in the softly lit dressing room, the dress fitted perfectly. The shop assistant slipped a pair of matching high heeled sandals through the door. Georgie was delighted. Despite leaving it until the last minute, she had found her outfit.

Georgie's regular hairdresser tonged her hair into a perfect chignon. Now all she needed to do was keep it that way until the evening, no mean feat when she, plus her gear, had to travel to Central London on public transport. As the tube arrived with hurricane strength winds, she ducked back round off the platform with a squeal, to the bemused looks of fellow travellers. Strolling by her reflection in shop windows, she marvelled at the transformation only a professional hairdresser could achieve. Her usual mane of unbrushed tangles barely recognisable and, along with deep red nails, Georgie felt properly glamorous as she wheeled her travel case up to the iconic black and gold entrance of the Luxe on the Strand Hotel.

The smartly suited door attendant tipped his top hat as Georgie passed, making her glad she'd smartened up from her usual attire of jeans and Converse trainers. The hotel didn't seem a particularly casual kind of place, she thought. Passing through the revolving doors, with butterflies of anticipation at the thought of seeing Sam again after so much time apart, Georgie paused in the lobby. She checked which room Sam had text her the number of, then made for the lift.

A staff member was buffing the black and gold tiled floor to a brilliant shine, reflecting light from beautiful golden lamps affixed to the walls and ceilings. The lift travelled smoothly upwards, Georgie's image in the mirrors reassuring her not a hair was out of place.

The high-pitched squeak her case emitted as she towed it along plush carpeted corridors gave Georgie the giggles. She half-expected someone to shush her.

At door number five hundred and fifty-two, Georgie stopped and knocked. Seconds later, Sam opened the door and it was Georgie's turn to squeak, as her boyfriend lifted her off her feet and swept her into the room. Resplendent in a tuxedo minus the black tie, Sam handed Georgie a crystal flute of champagne. As she took a sip, she gazed around at the glamorous art deco décor. Doors to a tiny balcony stood open. She stepped outside and looked down into an interior courtyard. Sounds of traffic buzzed in the background, so different to the tranquillity of Pennhalow. Sam joined her, glass in hand which he lightly chinked against Georgie's in a toast.

'To Laird's Lug. May nearly falling off the clumsy old nag win me an award tonight.'

'Hear, hear,' Georgie sang, as she put her arms around Sam, feeling the familiarity of his embrace.

He pulled away, then produced a square box from his pocket. 'All right, Gee-Gee, I almost forgot. I've got something for you.'

Georgie impersonated her suitcase again, squeaking as she was handed the iconic Tiffany & Co blue box tied up with a ribbon. Opening it revealed an exquisite pair of gold drop earrings, set with diamonds and hearts.

'Oh my gosh, they are so perfect, I love them,' she gushed.

'That's good. I'm not an expert on earrings. The sales lady was rather helpful.' Sam smiled. He lifted Georgie into his arms and kissed her passionately. Georgie wrapped her legs around him as they stumbled back inside, following which the tux didn't last much longer and neither did Georgie's hair style.

Later, Georgie managed to salvage what she could of a now not-so-sleek chignon. She slid the new earrings in place, admiring them in the mirror of the grey marble bathroom. Sam called through that it was time to go. Holding hands, they made their way downstairs to the Blenheim Ballroom, where the award ceremony was taking place.

As soon as they entered the ballroom, Sam was mobbed by colleagues, leaving Georgie slightly pushed aside. With thanks, she accepted a glass of wine from a waiter carrying a silver tray. Across the room, Georgie's former boss Bert Russell was talking to his wife. Sensing her gaze on him, he turned and glowered. From the corner of Georgie's eye, a silver streak, light bouncing from it like a nineteen-seventies disco ball, rushed over. Abi Ryman in a sequined mini dress almost flattened them all.

'Abi's been nominated for Apprentice of the Year,' Sam said quickly, surreptitiously warning Georgie not to ruin the occasion by making a fuss.

'Sam, you look so smart,' Abi squealed. 'I owe you a drink for all your help. You got me nominated.'

'No, you did that.' Sam beamed proudly, then turning to Georgie with an apologetic look asked: 'Do you mind?'

Georgie gritted her teeth. 'Not at all.'

She watched them go, weaving through the clusters of guests gathered in the large rectangular room. Round tables for eight had been set up at regularly spaced intervals, facing a stage, backlit by a big screen with 'The Jocks' written in huge capitals and a spinning trophy whirling around. It made Georgie feel dizzy. She moved aside to the double-fronted doors, ornate arches framed with silk roses, besides which a seating plan was propped up on an A-Board. Each table was named after a famous racehorse. Georgie and Sam were seated on Frankel.

Georgie worked her way around the red and white balloon decorated tables, in the centre of which a photo of each racehorse had been placed in a silver horseshoe clasp atop a stand. The air was overpoweringly sweet with the scent of lighted candles, mixing with the various perfumes and aftershaves filling the room. The chairs were draped with white fabric covers, encircled with a red ribbon tied in a bow. Finding the table marked by a photo of a bay thoroughbred with a large white star on his face, Georgie sat down at her place card with relief. The room had filled up with hundreds of people, dressed in their finest, guffawing. Feeling conspicuous seated alone, Georgie flipped through the programme.

'Are you starving? You look eager for the food.'

Georgie looked up from reading about the various awards and nominees, into the broad smiling goatee bearded face of Toasty.

'Sam's been side-tracked. I thought I'd keep out the way.'

'Ah. I'll keep you company. I'm on your table anyway.' Toasty sat down two seats along. 'Never been one for these kinds of events but I had to support Sam, being one of his best buds. I hope he wins otherwise he'll be insufferable.'

It turned out most of Sam's jockey friends were on their table. The meal progressed with much merriment and glass topping up. Georgie was feeling light-headed by the time Jump Ride of the Year came around. She squinted at the replay of Laird's Lug's race at Musselburgh, as it was shown on the big screen. Sam's dexterity at managing to cling on when so far beyond the point of gravity was admirable. As the video came to an end, the room broke out in a wave of applause, cheers and whistles. Sam raised a hand in acknowledgement.

The evening's compère, Gina West of *Racing News*, practically hopped onto the stage in a red fishtail gown so tight it was impossible to walk. Dramatically she ripped open the envelope. The ballroom went quiet.

'And The Jock goes to … Sam Christie. Congratulations, Sam, I'm sure we'd all agree what an impressive ride that was.'

Sam gave Georgie a quick peck on the cheek, then made his way to the stage, giving numerous high fives as he passed various tables. Gina kissed him lightly on both cheeks, handed him the award, followed by a few questions about the race. Self-depreciating and amusing in his responses, Sam came into his own when the centre of attention and had the room charmed.

As soon as he returned and placed the trophy of a horse and jockey in full flight on the table, his mates dressed it in colourful streamers from party poppers, then posed for selfies.

With the awards over, The Yellow Submariners took to the stage. A Beatles tribute band, they began with 'Ticket to Ride'. With a cheer, racing folk who couldn't dance as well as they could ride, leapt to their feet. Sam pulled Georgie up to join the throng. They spun around beneath the flashing lights. By the time the song list reached 'Hey Jude' the dance floor was heaving with sticky bodies, ties and high heels long since removed. Arms were raised, hands joined above heads, swaying and chanting to the chorus. Georgie had been dancing with Toasty. She sought out Sam, keen to share the moment, but couldn't see him. Awkwardly, she left the dance floor and checked by the bar, but gave it a swerve when she spotted Bert and no Sam. The lobby only contained a few couples collecting coats from the cloakroom.

Back in the ballroom, Georgie kept to the perimeter,

assuming she'd find Sam chatting at one of the tables. In the shadows of the dazzlingly bright lights from the dance floor, she came up behind a couple of guests, who she recognised as fellow jockeys. She made to walk away but caught Sam's name in their conversation, as they were shouting to be overheard above the music.

'… and, of course, slimy Sam won Jump Ride of the Year. How predictable. Why everyone thinks the talentless guy is so good, I don't know. I got jocked off a certainty the other day because of him.'

'Yeah, he's a lucky guy but he never appreciates it,' replied the other. 'Georgie's looking hot tonight.'

'Sure is. Shame she doesn't know about her boyfriend and Abi Ryman. Then I might stand a chance.'

'He's always been a sly dog, has Sam. He's disappeared with Abi now to have a smoke.' The last sentence was said with tittering and quotation mark gestures in the air, insinuating Sam and Abi were up to something which didn't involve smoking.

Shocked, Georgie turned and walked quickly away, her head spinning. Surely what she had just heard was jealous gossip, she reassured herself. They'd probably realised she was there and were being spiteful. She needed to track down Sam and reassure herself. If he'd gone for a cigarette, he had to be outside. Georgie decided to start with the courtyard.

Through the glass panes of the external doors, she could clearly see Sam and Abi, standing close together, virtually pressed against each other. The jacket from Sam's tuxedo was draped over Abi's shoulders. Georgie watched as she leaned forward on tiptoe to whisper in Sam's ear, her lips so close to his skin, Georgie's fists clenched involuntarily. They threw their heads back, roaring with laughter, then Sam bent towards Abi and kissed her cheek. Georgie rocked back in horror at their intimate body language and fought her inclination to storm outside and start yelling. Aware she'd had a lot to drink, she feared this would backfire and she'd be made to look a fool in front of other familiar faces smoking nearby. She needed time to clear her head before confronting Sam. It wasn't the time or place to do it.

Staggering back to the Blenheim Ballroom, Georgie retrieved her jacket and the room key, then fled upstairs, taunted by the strains of 'Let It Be'.

15

Throwing her possessions back in her case, including her handbag, Georgie only kept her train ticket, keys and mobile phone in her coat. She dashed for the lift, inside which the flushed faced woman with the wild hair and smeared mascara, peach lipstick on her teeth, looking back from the mirror bore no trace of the pristine Georgie who had stepped into the lift full of hope earlier that evening

The alarmed door attendant moved quickly to clear the way as Georgie stampeded out the entrance, case squeaking noisily in her wake. Feeling sick, her agitated stomach churned the rich food she'd eaten. She attracted attention from groups of smokers outside the late-night clubs. Ignoring it, she ran by. Her shoes rubbed her feet, she considered kicking them off and throwing them in the nearest bin. Somehow, she made it through to Epsom, but it was the early hours of the morning by the time a taxi dropped her outside Rose Cottage. She ditched everything and fell into bed fully clothed.

When Georgie woke up in darkness, it was with a sore mouth and a banging headache. Struggling to recall where she was and what had happened, she just knew something major had occurred. It nagged at her brain as she read the bedside clock, which said eight o'clock. On the bedside table, her mobile screen was lighting up with silent notifications. Groggily, she picked it up. There were several missed calls, voicemails and messages from Sam asking where she was, why she'd rushed off and concerned about her welfare. The last message timed seven o'clock advised Sam was on his way to her home. It was then Georgie noticed the PM on the screen and realised it was eight o'clock in the evening. She'd slept through the whole day.

In a panic, with no desire to be faced with Sam in her current state, Georgie jumped off the bed. She would return to Cornwall straightaway. As she wasn't expected back for another day and Tom had the annexe key, Georgie called his number. Frustratingly, it diverted to voicemail, Pennhalow's lack of signal again. It didn't matter. She'd deal with it later. Wolfing down a hastily prepared sandwich and cup of tea, without even bothering to get changed, Georgie threw everything in the boot of the car and set off. There would be plenty of time to mull over the Sam situation on the long drive. She would speak to him when she was feeling better.

Georgie drove between the pillars and up the drive. Pennhalow was hiding in the lack of light and a drifting mist. She shut the engine off and checked the doors were locked. Alone, the sounds of the night seemed spooky, unnerving. A loud rustling in the leylandii hedge disturbed her. A mournful howl, followed by a screech, caused Georgie's heart to pound. Determinedly, she tilted back the driver's seat. She would endure sleeping in the car rather than wake Tom at three o'clock in the morning. Ten minutes later, Georgie knew it was no good. Frozen and uncomfortable, every time she closed her eyes, she opened them again, fearful what might be leering through the windscreen without her knowledge.

Enough,' she said to herself.

Georgie tried Tom's mobile and got his chirpy voicemail recording again. With no other option, she unlocked the car. Her heels sank into the damp earth of the drive. Whipping off her shoes, she carried them one handed, toes curling at the iciness of the stone steps beneath her feet. Tiptoeing up, Georgie rang the bell, then cringed. The sound of the peal seemed to echo for miles. Convinced she must have woken all the residents of Bodmin, she waited. Tom did not appear. Tilting her head, Georgie checked his car was parked in its usual spot. It was. She'd have to try again. As her hand reached out, the sound of a lock clicked and the door opened an inch.

'Tom,' Georgie murmured guiltily. 'It's me.'

Tom opened the door, his face unamused. Georgie noticed he held a sturdy wooden shepherd's crook in his hand.

'Georgie. It's stupid o'clock in the morning. Why aren't you still in London? And why are you wearing a ballgown?'

Overcome, physically and emotionally exhausted, teeth chattering non-stop, Georgie simply could not find the words to explain her predicament. The light of the hall showed up the dirt clinging to the hem of her gown. In her hand, the ruined shoes dripped gloopy mud on the step. A pathetic vision, she simply burst into tears.

'Oh, hey… don't worry. It's OK. You freaked me out. I thought you were an intruder.' Tom put an arm around Georgie and steered her inside, then relocked the door. 'Let's go through to the kitchen, it's always warm and you're practically blue. Don't go back to the annexe tonight.'

Sitting by the aga, a mug of hot chocolate in her hand, Georgie realised she was ravenous. The only thing she'd eaten since the meal at The Jocks had been a sandwich. Tom had gone off to find a blanket for the sofa, leaving an open packet of chocolate hob nob biscuits on the table. Greedily, Georgie crammed two in her mouth.

'Whoa, whoa, you don't want to be doing that,' Tom cried from the doorway, raising, then lowering his hands, palms forward, as though Georgie was a startled horse.

'Oh, yes, I do, more than absolutely anything,' she replied, spraying crumbs.

'Um, much as I'm not complaining about finding an attractive woman in a sexy dress on my doorstep in the middle of the night, I feel I ought to ask, is everything all right?'

Georgie burst into a garbled explanation of The Jocks, waving her arms exaggeratedly to emphasise her distress. Tom absentmindedly chomped a biscuit, listening sympathetically, until she ran out of steam.

'So, quick recap. What I'm hearing is you don't know for sure that Sam's been messing around with this Ali … Abi … whatever her name is, because you left rather than confront him.'

Georgie considered Tom's words. 'No … but … yes … but … well, I know what I saw. The evidence. I was hardly likely to wait about for a signed confession, was I?'

'From what you said, it wasn't a full-blown snog. Doesn't sound the height of passion.'

'Typical, take Sam's side,' Georgie huffed. 'You weren't there. They seemed so … so familiar and the body language was so…so…'

'Listen, I'm not taking sides and you need some sleep. The sofa's ready for you.'

Feeling ungrateful, Georgie apologised to Tom as she stood.

'Forget it. We've all had bad days. I'll see you at a more sociable time.'

Curled up on the sofa, wearing a t-shirt Tom had left in

a pile with the blanket and a spare pillow, Georgie felt restless and strangely disappointed that Tom had disappeared.

Georgie wandered down to the yard the next morning. Having messaged Sam to say she was OK but back in Cornwall, she didn't want to sit about waiting for a reply. Tom and Hamish were busy loading Guido into the horsebox for his race at Exeter in the afternoon. Seamus the farrier was whistling a tune he purported to be Snow Patrol's 'Chasing Cars'.

'If you say so,' tutted Clem, covering her ears. 'Thought I could hear cats arguing.'

Despite being bent over with Zippy's foreleg resting on his leather apron while the gelding nibbled his hair, Seamus spotted Georgie.

'Good morning,' he called out, a cloud of smoke rising as he pressed the shoe against Zippy's hoof.

'Oh, hello,' Georgie replied, casually lowering oversized sunglasses.

'Looking the worse for wear today,' Seamus tittered. 'I hear you were partying in London recently.'

'Seems ages ago already,' said Georgie. 'I'm supposed to be off today, but thought I'd help out.'

'Nonsense,' said Fred, leading Jackson out his stable. 'You're entitled to your holiday. Take yourself off for a nice stroll. Get some Cornish air through your pipes. Clem and I have everything covered.'

'We do,' called out Clem. 'Do us a favour and take the dog with you. Try and wear him out. He's driving us mad today, chasing the chickens.'

Georgie tracked down the Jack Russell halfway up the muck heap, barking at three chickens perched on the summit.

As she clipped a lead on his collar, she waved Tom and Hamish off. 'Good luck.'

Not knowing where she was going to go, just that it would be somewhere, Georgie drove until she reached the sea and a car park directly on the coastal path. Delighted to be in different surroundings, Boffy shot off snuffling through the thorny undergrowth until all that was visible were the points of his ears and the white tip of his tail.

They walked for miles, following a path which rose and dipped along the top of vertigo inducing cliffs. The land was barren, the shrubs bent horizontal by the fierce winds which blew in from the sea. Come the spring, the area would be transformed into a blooming carpet of sea pinks. Far below, Georgie could hear the sea cresting upwards, hurling spray against the ever-changing colours of the weathered granite. Gulls cried, rising from the abyss to spiral with ease above. Boffy barked at their harsh caws. They ignored him, just a little dot below their expansive horizon.

On a headland jutting out to sea were the ruins of what had once been a mine. Crumbling stone walls and a chimney towered over the landscape, a proud reminder of an industry that had once been thriving. Fascinated, Georgie walked around, following the trodden down grass, wary of the hidden mine shafts the locals had warned her about. Tucked away, a weather-beaten and faded but still readable board informed her the area had once been Wheal Crown. Intrigued, she climbed inside, carefully picking her way over the boulder strewn floor. Through an archway she could see the ocean and many hundreds of feet below, the sounds of waves spouting up what had once been the old mine shaft, now securely covered with a grate. With no one else around, the atmosphere was peaceful, yet oddly alive, as if the miners were still there, sitting eating their pasties, observing Georgie's curiosity with amusement.

Georgie found a simple wooden bench nearby and pulled out a flask of tea from her rucksack. Boffy trotted over to drink the water she set out for him, then curled up between her feet with a yawn.

'Guess this is more exercise than you've had in a while,' she said, tickling his ears. He snored in response.

For the first time in a long time, Georgie's mind stopped whirring about the unknown, the future, what may or may not happen. This land of myths and legends, of pixies, knights, mermaids, mining, hard work and heart break, had forced her to slow down. Treasure hunters, smugglers and pirates all held secrets concealed, never revealed. Did Sam have secrets too or was Tom's lenient view correct and it was another classic Georgie overreaction? If she was honest, Georgie was bothered why she didn't miss Sam more. He didn't seem to miss her desperately either. Perhaps they were just both so busy, wrapped up in their own lives. After all, it was a mature relationship that should stand up to a temporary separation.

Boffy woke up with a snuffle and returned to exploring. Georgie glanced at her watch. She'd eat her lunch and then retrace her steps. She didn't want to be walking back along the route they had taken in fading light.

Back at Pennhalow, Georgie popped down to the yard to see how the day had gone and found the mood boisterous. As the horsebox chugged through the gate, Hamish leaned out the cab window and announced that Guido had won his race by five lengths, following which the winning jockey Roddy Love had declared him a good prospect for the future.

The ramp clanged down and Tom led the gelding out. Spotting Fred, he called over, 'Guess who I bumped into today, dad.'

'Father Christmas,' Fred replied, keen to finish up for the day rather than play games.

'Correct. He told me he fancied a day at the races.

Seriously though, I met Heather. Heather Thompson. Remember, she was in my class at school.'

'Heather … Heather. Hold on, it's coming back to me. Does she have a twin brother?'

'She does. She was on a day out with friends. We had a nice chat and a laugh about the old days. Didn't have much time so we exchanged numbers to meet up again.'

'Ah, that's grand. Angie'll be pleased to hear that.'

Still nattering, Tom and Fred led Guido back to his stable, to remove the travelling gear and settle him in.

Georgie moved away, tripping over Boffy who had been following her around since they returned. She swore loudly.

'Are you OK?' asked Clem.

'Yeah, going to head back to the annexe.' Georgie bid farewell to Clem and Hamish and slipped through the gate and on up the lawn, trying to convince herself she was pleased for Tom. He was a nice person who deserved happiness. She shouldn't be churlish simply because her relationship was in a difficult patch.

16

March brought lighter mornings and evenings and, much to everyone's relief, milder weather. With winter nearing its end, grass in the fields was sparse. Georgie cursed as the wheel of the barrow full of hay she was pushing caught in a rut. Dragging it backwards, she took a run at it. With momentum she managed to free the wheel, leaving a trail of hay strewn behind her. The horses gobbled it greedily. She began shoving armfuls of hay in the feeder tub as Tom appeared.

'You'd think they never get fed.' Georgie paused, hands on hips. 'I didn't get to the feeder before they were stuffing their faces.'

Tom laughed. 'Yeah, they're such gluttons.'

'I can manage this, Tom, if you want to make a start on cleaning the tack.'

'Actually, I came to give you a message from dad,' Tom replied, lending a hand anyway. 'He said, can you meet him in the Barrels at one o'clock.'

Georgie froze, midway between barrow and feeder, wisps of hay whipping away in the wind. 'Why? What for?'

'I don't know, he asked me to ask you. That was all.'

'I don't know why Fred's being so cryptic,' Georgie complained.

'Perhaps he just wants to buy you a drink.' Tom shrugged his shoulders. 'Anyway, mustn't dally. I've got saddles to clean and numnahs to wash. Lucky me.'

'Yeah but —' Georgie called after Tom, but he was already striding away. Annoyed, she lobbed a bunch of hay at his back.

'Now, now,' he shouted over his shoulder.

'Tell me what's going on then.'

Tom's response was to jog away with a chuckle.

As Georgie pushed through the door into the fuggy, steak pie scented bar of the Smuggler's Barrels she thought how out of kilter it was to be entering the pub at lunchtime, when she'd only been during the evenings before. Her stomach contracted with hunger as Finn carried a delicious looking plate of scampi and chips past her.

'Smells good,' she sighed.

'Perhaps Fred'll treat you,' Finn teased.

Georgie took a seat at the round table in the alcove where Fred was waiting. He'd already bought their drinks.

'I'm intrigued,' Georgie informed him.

Fred wasted no time, launching straight in. 'We need to make a decision about The Misfit and the Derby. My inclination is that, with further work, it's a go, however I've asked a good friend of mine for her opinion. She's coming tomorrow to watch Monty workout. I need you to get the best performance you can out of him.'

'Of course. Absolutely. Who's your friend?'

'Lucinda Fox-Beckerington.'

Georgie sat up straighter. 'Lucinda F-B, the former champion three-day event rider?'

'That's right. What Lucinda doesn't know about horses, no

one else knows either. I trust her judgement above anyone else.'

Georgie understood the importance of being sure Monty had a live chance in the Derby, otherwise the time and expense would be wasted. They had to be realistic over a race of such calibre, in front of a worldwide audience. Making fools of themselves wasn't an option.

'I'm ready,' Georgie confirmed.

'I don't believe you are.'

Georgie was taken aback by Fred's reply. Tonic water spurted from her mouth and nose. A puddle seeped across the table. As she apologised, Finn dashed over with a cloth to wipe up the mess. Fred sat motionless.

'In what way am I not ready?' Georgie tried not to come across as petulant, as she looked Fred in the eye.

A shaft of sunlight shot through the opaque window and fell upon Fred. Georgie noticed lines running across his face, deepening between eyebrows dotted with grey. He looked weary. Georgie wondered how old he was, beneath the lively exterior.

'You're young and enjoying yourself. That's fair enough, but if you're serious you need to pause it for a few months. Get yourself fit for the race. I need a jockey who's focused. It's no use Monty being at his peak if you run out of puff in the final furlong and can't see it through.'

Vanity made Georgie want to protest but she knew Fred was right. Scoffing biscuits at break time and pottering around on the moor did not get you fit enough to compete. It was a long time since she'd ridden in a race. She knew the truth was she would struggle.

'I'm one hundred percent dedicated.'

'Good, that's what I want to hear. I like you, Georgie, you're part of the team, but I won't hesitate to book an alternative for Monty if necessary, even if I have to superglue them to the saddle. This could be my last shot before I put myself out to pasture and Tom takes over.'

'Nonsense. You'll go on for years yet, Fred,' Georgie insisted. 'As for me, I'll start today.'

Fred rotated his half-empty glass between well-worn hands, resting his forearms on the table. 'No need. Let's give it the weekend. Wait and see what Lucinda says.'

It was an agitated Georgie who made her way across the lawn in the early morning. She'd not slept, due to a combination of a terse exchange of messages with Sam the evening before and the prospect of being judged by Lucinda. No experienced person relished putting themselves up for criticism and Georgie was no exception. If this was the day Monty decided he no longer liked her the best, she could be out of Pennhalow. Having her future resting in the colt's fickle hooves put her in a bad temper. She needed to snap out of it.

Her feelings were not helped by the sight of a relaxed Lucinda leaning against the tack room wall, drinking tea and joking with Tom.

'Here's Georgie. Let me introduce you,' he beamed.

Lucinda was in her late fifties, sinewy, with a crinkled face and a bob of wispy silver blonde hair. Georgie's fingers crackled beneath the pressure of her firm grip. She nearly winced.

'Always an idea to check out the competition beforehand,' Lucinda stated, eyes twinkling as she squeezed harder on Georgie's fingers.

'I wasn't aware that's what I was,' Georgie squeaked.

'Cindy's joshing with you,' explained Tom, 'she's riding out with you, on Beanie. Says she'll get a better feel for Monty that way.'

'Quite right. Far better to be in amongst the action.'

Lucinda clapped her hands briskly. 'Let's get this show on the road.'

Georgie tacked Monty up with fingers shaking, partly from nerves, the rest resentment at Lucinda's forthright manner. Clem legged her up into the saddle with a grimace that indicated she too wasn't amused by the interloper.

'Whatever you do, please don't let her win, otherwise we'll never hear the last of it from her … or Fred. You should have heard him earlier, simpering away. He truly believes the sun shines out her arse,' said Clem sotto voce.

Despite the tension, Georgie giggled and gave Clem a discreet salute, then steered the colt to where Amiyah was holding the gate open ready.

To Georgie's embarrassment, Monty decided today would be the day to show off. He snatched the reins, tossed his head, snorted and pranced. He bumped into Beanie, reared at a squirrel and threw a wobbly about having to go by a petrified jogger, who lost their earphones diving into a bush to avoid the horse.

'Sit quiet. He'll soon get it out of his system,' said Lucinda.

Georgie bristled at being told what to do. She wasn't some learner taking instruction. Her hands clenched on the reins, causing Monty to lunge forward in protest. Beanie's tail swished in warning as Monty flew into his hindquarters. Georgie was on the brink of tears. It was all going wrong. She was going to throw away an opportunity she may never get again.

Lucinda turned in the saddle and gave a smile. 'I guess you see me as a smug high achiever, here to make you look bad.'

Georgie bit her lip. 'Not at all.'

'Good. Fred's been a true friend of mine for decades. I

want you to show that horse off as a priceless jewel. He's a bit of a rough diamond but he's got potential.'

'You think?' Georgie stroked Monty's arched neck.

'I know.'

They had reached the flat open ground. Away in the distance, Georgie could make out the glint of sunlight on Fred's binoculars. She relaxed. After all, if she couldn't learn from the best, who could she learn from. Years ago, she would have given all the coins in her piggy bank for a one-to-one with Lucinda Fox-Beckerington.

'Hup!' Without warning, Lucinda nudged Beanie with her heels and they were gone.

Taken unawares, Georgie's reins were too long and Monty stood, distracted by the sound of a faraway tractor. Digging his hooves in, head turned to the right, he refused to move. Shortening her reins, Georgie urged her mount forwards to no avail.

'Are you kidding?' she yelled.

Monty's ears flattened. He took two steps back.

'Get going.'

He pawed the ground.

'Move it … Oops.'

It was as if somebody had suddenly plugged Monty in. He came alive. Crouching low, tucking herself down into the colt's body, Georgie poised, merging as one, balanced and still. The patchy ground didn't trouble Monty, his hooves barely touched it. With the grey rump of Beanie as his target, Monty stuck his neck out and found another level. Georgie caught Lucinda's shocked expression as they charged alongside and then flew by. Her mouth was full of mane, her eyes full of water and her heart full of love for the plucky colt running free beneath her. She could barely pull him up. They were well past Fred before she managed to regain control and circle back.

Lucinda was leaning down over Beanie's withers deep in conversation with Fred, who had removed his flat cap and was scrunching it in his hands. Georgie stopped close by. She couldn't hear what they were saying. Monty lowered his head, still blowing. It seemed ages before Fred turned and acknowledged her.

'Best lay off those biscuits, Georgie. We're going for it.'

Lucinda whooped, startling Beanie. 'The Epsom Derby, guys. What a thrill. Better dig in those coffers Fred and pay the entry fee for the next stage.'

Georgie's stomach heaved; it was really happening. She'd naively got on a ride with no idea what lay ahead. It could be Derby glory, or she could end up labelled part of a pair of misfits who'd misfired. In the unforgiving competitiveness of sport, her career could soar or sink.

As evening fell, Georgie hummed along to the radio while she prepared a rather measly looking salad for dinner. A splodge of French dressing ought to liven it up, she decided, squeezing a large blob on the plate. Simultaneously there was a knock on the door.

'Um, two seconds,' she called out, hoping it wasn't Fred come to check up on her healthy eating habits. Just in case, she shoved the plate in a cupboard, vowing not to mention the sauce.

As she clicked the lock, it occurred to Georgie that Tom might have decided to drop by to finally open the bottle of Veuve Clicquot. Perhaps she ought to have anticipated he'd want to celebrate the Pengelly's first runner in a Classic race and put the bottle on ice. Never mind, they could chat and she'd rustle up some snacks while they waited for it to chill. The visitor was crouched down, but the top of the head she looked upon wasn't the hazel curls of Tom, rather the blonde hair of Sam. He stood up, lifting a plant in an elaborate terracotta pot.

'Gee-Gee.' He greeted her as though his arrival was planned. 'Brought you a present.'

He heaved the enormous whatever it was inside, dumping it in a corner of the living room as soon as he could.

'Sam, what, er, what are you doing here?' Georgie wondered how he'd found her.

'Surprise!' Sam raised his arms above his head, then collapsed dramatically on the sofa. 'Blimey, it was difficult to find you.'

'How did you find me?' Georgie perched on the edge of a cushion, still processing Sam's appearance.

'Got the details from Briggsy … eventually. Took me ages to persuade him though. Don't get why he's so secretive.'

'So, what are you doing here and why didn't you let me know you were coming?'

'I'm whisking you away for a romantic weekend a deux.'

'Wait a sec —'

'And before you say you can't because you're working, I've cleared it all with Fred. He's fine about it. Agreed that it'd do you good to have a splurge before you get down to the serious business of Derby prep.'

Georgie sat back, stunned. This was not how she had expected her Friday night to pan out.

'Get a move on, Gee-Gee. Go and get packed,' Sam ordered, waving his arms as though he were shooing one of the chickens up the stairs. 'Dinner's booked at eight.'

Georgie rose to her feet. 'We're not going far then?'

Sam rolled his eyes back. 'How many times must I use the word surprise before you stop asking ludicrous questions and get a move on?'

Half an hour later, Georgie, towing her hastily filled case and Sam, walked around the front of the manor, where the mud-splattered Porsche was dumped skewwhiff in the middle of the drive. As Sam unlocked the car, the front door of the manor opened. In the beam of bright light from the interior, stepped out a lady wearing a claret-coloured jersey dress and knee length black boots. Swishing waist length blonde hair, she turned and spoke to someone over her shoulder as she fastened her coat. Seconds later, Tom appeared behind her. Aware they weren't alone, he glanced over and caught Georgie's eye.

'Evening,' he called across, awkwardly.

Sam took control. 'Unless I'm mistaken you must be Tom.' He marched over, hand outstretched.

Georgie watched as Tom and Sam shook hands. One dark haired and stocky, the other fair haired and whippet-like. Seeing them together for the first time, she felt strangely conflicted, but was jolted as Tom introduced his companion as Heather.

'We're off out for dinner,' sang Heather, in a singsong tone. 'Tons to catch up on. Literally years.'

A brief silence ensued, as all four waited for one of the others to speak.

'Have a lovely …' Georgie and Tom spoke in unison.

'… time,' finished Tom, with a tiny smile.

'Yeah, hope you two lovebirds enjoy yourselves,' Sam jollied. 'Ta-ta then.'

He placed a hand on Georgie's back and propelled her towards the Porsche. She did not look back.

17

While she waited for Sam to programme the sat nav, Georgie watched the taillights of Tom's Golf disappear up the drive.

'Don't expect it'll help much. I had to stop for directions at three other farms to find this place. None of them had even heard of Penny-farthings,' Sam informed her, pressing buttons with a flourish.

Georgie laughed. 'Probably because it's called Pennhalow.'

'Whatever. I've no clue what's possessed you to stick it out here.' Sam fired the engine and spun the steering wheel, in a huff. 'Never seen a place less likely to have a Derby prospect.'

'Image isn't all there is to it,' Georgie snapped defensively.

'As long as they're not making a fool of you with their wild fantasies just because they've got one horse who's faster than a cow.'

'Don't be so judgmental.' Furious, Georgie reached out and turned the music up, attempting to cut the conversation off.

Sam turned it down again using the control on the steering wheel, before responding in softer tones. 'I'm only trying to help out here. You know I've always got your back.'

Georgie sighed and sat in silence.

The directions seemed to make no sense, sending them off down lanes so narrow and overgrown by trees they resembled tunnels, as Sam swore continuously. At one point Georgie feared they were stuck, as the tyres swished through a brook. Eventually, they crunched up a squiggly gravelled drive. Sam braked adjacent to the entrance of a large building, uplighters on its façade giving it a gothic vibe. Numerous windows were unlit. It looked uninhabited. No one came outside to welcome them or offered to park the car. Georgie doubted they were at the right place but, fearful of stoking another argument, said nothing.

Carrying their bags, they entered through a porch guarded by a pair of stone gargoyles, into a dimly lit reception, dominated by a chandelier designed as stag's antlers. Suits of armour stood to attention beneath an oil painting of a stately gentleman surrounded by hounds, which filled an entire wall. Under his life-like haughty stare, Georgie got chills.

'Is there anyone here?' she whispered, just as Sam hit the bell on the reception desk with the palm of his hand. A loud ping followed to which no one responded. 'It seems deserted and rather creepy.'

'Great start, Gee-Gee, you describing my efforts as creepy,' Sam hissed.

'Well, where is everyone?'

'They took payment. They knew we were coming.'

A man in uniform popped through a door concealed in the panelling behind reception. 'Apologies. We've been expecting you. I have your key here. It's the suite right at the top of the tower. Magnificent views.'

Sam accepted the key with a forced smile. They rode up in a creaky, old-fashioned lift.

'How did you hear about this place?' Georgie asked, as the lift juddered to a stop.

'Rowie recommended it, in conversation at New Year.'

The suite took up the entire top floor. A king size bed had been strewn with rose petals, scented candles flickered in glass orb shaped bowls, though couldn't quite diminish the fusty smell. Logs spattered behind the protective grate of a fireplace as tall as Georgie and the neck of a bottle of champagne rose above the rim of an ice bucket, sitting between two crystal glasses.

Georgie and Sam faced each other, completely alone for the first time in ages, unhindered by family or friends.

'You look gorgeous and that dress is beautiful. All I want to do is peel it off you.' Sam glanced at his watch with a sly grin. 'We've got time before dinner.'

They kissed, wrapped in each other's embrace. Sam's hands worked their way down the numerous buttons on the back of Georgie's dress, releasing each one in turn from the loop of material it was threaded through. His fingers moved deftly from one to the next, never seeming to reach the end. Georgie began to giggle.

'Blimey, Gee-Gee, how many buttons are there on this thing? I'm getting repetitive strain injury.'

Georgie erupted into hysterical laughter; the romance of the moment lost to merriment. Sam joined in. He spun Georgie around and they laughed in unison. Then Sam's face turned serious.

'To hell with taking the dress off,' he growled.

Lifting Georgie up, he pulled the layers of floating chiffon above her hips. She wrapped her legs around him as he carried her to the bed, where they celebrated their reunion beneath the tapestry of a Victorian lady in a high-necked gown, who had probably never seen anything like it.

The next morning they enjoyed a leisurely swim in the hotel's pool before breakfast in a restaurant empty except for them. Georgie ordered the full English, wolfing it down with toast and butter. Sam watched with wide eyes, as he ate muesli and yoghurt.

'What?' Georgie asked, between forkfuls of scrambled egg.

'Nothing … apart from, I thought you were healthy eating from now on.'

'I am. This is my last blowout before that starts.'

Sam smirked, reaching over the table for Georgie's hand.

'You enjoy yourself, while it lasts.'

Afterwards, they strolled, gloved hands entwined and rosy cheeked, across the lawn, down to a rolling landscaped garden. Trimmed hedges were interlaid with statues of cherubs playing trumpets, a boar and a lion poised ready to strike, tail mid-swish, paws raised. A pond strewn with vibrant green lily pads was home to a muscular Poseidon, trident raised. They crossed a dainty arched wooden bridge and on along a gravel path, to the entrance of a maze.

'Come on,' encouraged Sam.

Pulling Georgie by the arm, he moved towards the towering dense yew hedges.

She resisted. 'Should we? There isn't anyone else around, not even a gardener. What if we get lost and can't find a way out?'

'I can think of much worse things than being stuck in a maze with you.' Sam swivelled on his heels innocently.

Georgie pointed above to grey clouds moving in. 'The sky's looking dodgy.'

'Be more adventurous, Gee-Gee. The whole point is you get lost and wander hopelessly, but there's always a way out. Let's go.'

'Oh, all right then but you'll have to catch me.' Georgie sprinted past Sam, taking a sharp left, followed by a quick right.

Neither turned into a dead end. Georgie could hear Sam's footsteps pounding not far behind. She switched one way and then another, legs flying along the enclosed pathways, laughing out loud as Sam cursed from the other side of the hedge that ran between them. She lost all sense of direction, the only signs she wasn't revisiting the same route over again, little stone carved creatures located in the dead ends. She found a squirrel, a rabbit, a hedgehog and a fox, never seeing the same one twice.

By a fluke, she ended up in the centre, marked by a lichen covered urn on a plinth, spouting a dreary dried-up display of twigs and shrivelled leaves and a broken bench. Georgie had expected a more impressive reward for those who reached the centre.

Sam arrived, panting, a few minutes later.

'You win,' he puffed, 'like you always do.'

'What's my prize?'

Sam held his arms out wide from his sides and rotated around slowly on the spot in a circle. 'Me?'

'Well … that's the best kind of prize.' Georgie sashayed towards him.

Sam's mobile began to play in his pocket. 'Sorry, Gee-Gee.' He moved aside, out of the centre, to answer.

Georgie waited, unable to make out any of what he was saying.

He returned, placing his phone on the rickety arm of the bench. 'Where were we, before we got interrupted? Ah yes.'

Grabbing Georgie, he kissed her on the nose, pushing her back up against the chilly limestone surface of the urn, inserting his legs between hers, with a groan. A tiny bird flittered out the bush, chirping, before diving back to shelter as the first raindrop hit the ground with a splash. Within seconds, it was pelting down.

'Run, we'll get soaked.' Sam skedaddled, pulling his hood up as he went.

Georgie spotted the mobile still on the bench. 'Wait, Sam, you forgot your phone.'

Sam was already out of earshot. His phone's screen was getting wet. Georgie snatched it up and dried it on her sleeve, her actions causing the wallpaper to light up. As she put it in her jacket, she indulged herself in a smile at the photo of her and Sam, their hands both wrapped around Sam's The Jocks award, the flash from the camera reflecting off her silver dress. Hold on, Georgie thought, raising the phone to inspect closer. Her gown hadn't been silver, it had been sapphire blue. She also didn't recall having her photo taken with the award. Ignoring the rain, she pressed the button to wake the screen and recognised Abi Ryman immediately. In the background, the Blenheim Ballroom looked empty, meaning it was likely to have been taken at the end of the evening. Realisation dawned. Sam hadn't been worried and searching for Georgie after she left, or certainly not for long. He'd been larking about taking photos with Abi.

As if aware of the impact on Georgie, the phone emitted the sound of a cork popping and a message arrived. Blinking water from her eyelashes, Georgie saw the sender was Abi. She read aloud the part she could see before it cut off:

'Only a couple more days and then it's over …'

Disbelief turned to disappointment. She pushed the phone away and trudged back to the hotel.

Sam was in the room. He'd changed into a tracksuit and was warming himself by the fire, his sodden jeans steaming over the back of a chair.

'You're slow. Looks like Fred has a valid point. You need to work on your fitness if it takes you that long to run back here.'

Georgie placed the phone on a chair between them. 'You left your phone. Interesting choice of background.'

All the romance disintegrated, plummeting the room with its curled up rose petals on the floor, into feeling tacky. Above

Sam, Georgie noticed a huge cobweb strung across the ceiling. Wallpaper was peeling in the corner and the window frame was leaking.

'What are you going on about?' Sam seized up the phone and glared at it. 'Oh, that, that's nothing. After you did a flit at The Jocks, Abi and I were messing about. She dared me to make that my background photo. I did it for a joke and forgot to change it back. I was pretty drunk by then. Overdid the celebrating.'

'But that was ages ago. You're always on your phone, yet you never noticed?'

'My phone's just that, a phone. I'm not fussed whether the wallpaper's recent or the ringtone's OK. It's a means to get hold of me, it doesn't define who's important to me.'

'And what about the message Abi just sent?' Georgie grabbed a dressing gown from the bed and wrapped it around her wet clothes.

'You fled The Jocks like Cinderella and now you're manipulating it to be my fault. I won an award, I was happy, having the best time. It was my evening and you missed out on the end of a fab night. The band did 'Twist and Shout' and we all danced around the trophies on the stage. Well … all except the guy on the drums obviously.'

'Ringo Starr.'

'What?'

'It was Ringo Starr who played the drums for the Beatles.' Georgie was waffling, confused. She needed to get to the point. 'I saw you with Abi in the courtyard and I heard rumours about the two of you.'

Sam sighed, rubbing the side of his face, exasperated. 'I've been helping Abi with her career. She asked me to be her mentor and I agreed. She's got real potential. As for rumours, you know the weighing room can be a hotbed of gossip. Doesn't mean any of it's true.'

Georgie could feel herself wavering. She sat down on the end of the bed, as Sam ploughed on.

'Don't forget, you were once like that. When I first met you, you'd have done anything, gone anywhere for a spare ride to boost your career. And you were always asking the experienced jockeys for advice. Abi's young and determined. There's nothing wrong with that.'

'Surely she could have found a mentor at the yard where she's based. Wouldn't that have been more convenient anyway?' Georgie knew the answer without receiving it.

Abi would have flattered Sam, told him she was a fan, cooed over his talent. And Sam would have lapped it up. He lived to be admired.

Underneath the window, rainwater was now overflowing the sill and trickling down the wall in teardrops. Georgie knew Sam was fond of her, as she was of him, but it was no longer enough to be fitted in as and when. They both deserved better. She could offer to leave Pennhalow, sell Rose Cottage and move to Lambourn, but she would lose the ride on Monty. Besides, she wanted to stay. She was enjoying her work again, feeling valued, her opinions respected. Giving it all up would only cause resentment.

Sam was pacing in front of the fire. 'You know, Gee-Gee, no matter what I do, you're never satisfied. I'm attracted to Abi; I'm not denying it. She's fun and she gets what I'm about. Is that what you want me to say?'

'No.' Georgie's reply was honest, but a tiny part of her had expected to hear that.

She finally admitted to herself that she did have feelings, strong feelings, for Tom and there'd been moments when she'd sensed they might be reciprocated.

'Let's cool it off for a while, eh? Then you can focus on the Derby and I can push for champion jockey, without all this,' Sam moved to stand in front of Georgie, his arms windmilling, 'to add to the pressure. I don't want to choose and neither of us should have to.'

Georgie shunted along, allowing Sam to sit beside her. 'Perhaps it'd be for the best,' she agreed sadly. 'My head's spinning. I don't know what to believe.'

Sam kissed her on the cheek. 'OK then. I'll drop you back at Penny-farthings. There'll be better times for us ahead.'

18

Alone in the annexe, Georgie's mind flitted between disbelief and uncertainty. She felt she'd been taken for a fool agreeing to separate so amicably, especially without proof Sam had been unfaithful. She feared it would have ended eventually anyway, with bitterness and accusations. The truth was the relationship had been floundering for some time. Feeling sluggish, she considered going back to bed. No, she told herself firmly, she would not retreat, she would tidy up.

With the kitchen cleaned and the festering salad, hidden in the cupboard when Sam arrived, thrown away, Georgie felt better and compelled to go for a run. The new fitness regime could start there and then, she thought as she hurried to change into trainers and workout gear. With dusk not far away, she'd stay local. Securing earphones and selecting an energetic song list, she set off down the drive, turned right along the lane, then climbed a stile leading to the open moor.

She soon discovered running on such an unforgiving surface was more of a challenge than anticipated. Georgie's feet caught in numerous hidden dips and rough hillocks of grass, as she puffed her way uphill. Clambering over a crumbling stone wall, then bunny hopping over a trickle of a stream besides an ancient weeping willow, Georgie was fearing collapse by the time she circled round to the Smuggler's Barrels. Finn was by the door, watering a trio of new hanging baskets with a hose.

'Looking good,' stammered Georgie.

'Wish I could say the same for you,' Finn teased. 'I got ketchup sachets paler than your face.'

Glad of the excuse to stop, Georgie leaned over and rested her hands on her knees, while sweat dripped from her nose and chin. 'Got to keep fit for when I'm back race-riding. I promised Fred.'

'Ha!' Finn scoffed. 'Hark at Fred Pengelly. I'd wager he hasn't broken into a run since his school days. Don't put up with it.'

'It's OK. I needed to do it, for my sake.'

'If you go out alone at this time of day again, get that waster Tom to go with you. It's almost dark. Actually, I'll walk you back myself, if you can hold on —' Finn ceased talking as a voice from inside the pub shouted about a beer pump. 'Darn, I'm needed here. Head straight back though. Cador was only saying last night there's more reports of unsavoury characters lurking around and Francois told me a heap of rubbish was fly-tipped near old Ted's.'

'I will,' Georgie promised. 'See you soon.'

Unnerved by Finn's talk of lurking dangers, Georgie sprinted the section of lane, until she reached the pillars. With the drop in temperature as evening fell, Georgie hurried up the drive, not wanting to get a chill. Thinking about a hot shower and a drink, she didn't notice Tom washing his car's windscreen, until he called a greeting. The sight of him gave her a spark of warmth. She would do it, she decided. She would ask him out, somewhere low key, perhaps the cinema or a meal someplace different to the Barrels. Clem always raved about The Burrowing Badger, another local pub out on the moor.

'Hi,' she replied, 'got a minute?'

'Sure, just clearing up the mess. Went to Charlestown earlier and the seagulls got my car. Absolutely peppered it from bonnet to boot. Bet Ross Poldark never had that problem.'

'Probably not, but to be fair he didn't have a car.'

'Good point. How was your weekend?'

'Um …' Distracted by Tom's biceps in rolled up shirt sleeves, Georgie sought the words. 'It was —'

'Must have been good getting to spend time together at last.' Tom stepped back then spotted a patch he'd missed and began buffing the glass again.

'Not exactly. I mean —'

'I've heard mixed reviews about the place dad said Sam had booked though.'

'Yeah, it wasn't —'

'Still, I bet it was good to get away.'

'Tom, I wanted to —'

'Well, Heather and I had a great time, laughing, reminiscing, good fun. She's setting up a reunion of our year through Facebook. Such a stroke of luck bumping into each other again. Can't wait to see her on Friday. Though, sorry, Georgie, you were saying something.'

'Oh, um, you're going out again?' Georgie breathed. 'It doesn't matter. Nothing important.'

Tom threw the cloth into a bucket and picked it up. 'Cool. See you in the morning, wide awake and full of beans. Dad'll be pleased you've made a start on your fitness training.'

He strolled off, whistling merrily, leaving Georgie full of words unspoken.

. . .

The only way forward was through, Georgie decided. Over the next few weeks, she immersed herself in preparations for the Derby. Though still three months away from the race, every day which wasn't a day off, she took Monty out. In all weathers, they roamed the moor, cantering up tors and trotting alongside streams, Georgie always on the alert for bogs and marshes.

Concurrently, lambing season had been in full swing, the farm busy with extra helpers lending a hand. Fred hadn't been involved in the yard as much, so Tom had stepped in, bouncing around with arrangements for runners in races and keeping everything ticking over. With the team so busy, personal chat wasn't a priority and it was Hamish who suggested a night at the Smuggler's Barrels was required.

Everyone piled in the pub, salivating at the thought of home cooked pie washed down with a beer. As Georgie took her seat at the end of the table, the door opened and Heather burst in, full of smiles and kisses for Tom. Georgie chucked the healthy eating menu aside and ordered battered fish and chips and a Pimm's.

Seated beside her, Hamish nudged Georgie playfully. 'All right there?'

'Yeah. Never better.'

'Do I detect a note of sarcasm hidden in those words?' Hamish raised one eyebrow.

'Not at all. Why would there be?' Georgie avoided looking at Hamish and further along the table where Heather was stroking Tom's arm.

'Well, I hope you don't mind me mentioning it but when I took Split Trousers to Chepstow the other day, I noticed Sam Christie getting rather cosy with that apprentice who's always all over the papers, Abi Ryman. Discretion was not a word they are familiar with, me thinks.'

Unsure how to respond, Georgie gazed down, studying the humorous cartoon farm animals gambolling on her placemat.

Hamish took Georgie's reticence for upset and, blushing, began to apologise. 'Forget I said anything. I shouldn't have done. It's none of my business. Probably a misunderstanding on my part. I blame my new contact lenses —'

'Hamish,' Georgie interrupted, 'it's fine. Sam and I agreed on a time out.'

'Oh, I hadn't heard.' Hamish lied unconvincingly.

'Good job I'm not going to make you promise you hadn't.'

'Thank goodness.' Hamish fanned himself with his hand. 'It's all over racing that they're an item apparently. You're my friend, I wouldn't want you to be hurt.'

Georgie placed her hand lightly on Hamish's. 'And you're a good person but it's OK. I can take care of myself.'

Despite her anger at Sam's recent behaviour, it still stung Georgie to know he had moved on already, if he hadn't before they split up, which she suspected might have been the case. She spent the remainder of the evening smiling through a feeling of detachment from those around her.

Early one Sunday, Georgie woke to pattering on the bedroom windowpane. Assuming it was rain, when she opened the curtains, it was a surprise to see light snow spiralling in the wind. Being Tom and Amiyah's day off, Georgie made her way over to the yard early to get started on the chores. Pulling her woolly hat over her ears against the biting cold, she unlocked the gate and did a double take, trying to work out what was amiss. Or rather, what was missing, for the farm gate was gone and where it usually stood was a gaping hole. Georgie's eyes roved over a scene which didn't make sense. Secured the night before, the chickens were everywhere, the wooden ramp to their coop smashed away, as was most of the door. Jackson was halfway between the yard and the outbuildings, chomping on the verge. Guido, rug askew, was peering confused out his stable, while Hazel kept tossing her head, snorting, then cavorting around her stable in ever decreasing circles.

'What the …'

Unsure where to start, Georgie decided securing the gate would be a good place. She found it dangling from its remaining hinge, crushed beyond use, the 'Pennhalow Farm' sign broken to pieces of splintered wood. Georgie kicked them uselessly with her wellie, trying to decipher what had happened. There were miniature hoofprints all over the place, sliced into the larger planks and sunk into the ground. With thoughts as disarrayed as the muckheap, Georgie set to sorting out the mess.

Making soothing noises, she approached Hazel. The mare's speckled grey neck was patched with sweat. Georgie managed to secure a handful of forelock to try and steady Hazel and keep her still, when the gate from the manor lawn creaked open and Hamish stepped through, looking half-asleep. His eyes swivelled around, then widened in amazement.

'Oh, my days, Georgie, what have you done? Fred's going to blow a gasket.'

'Was like this when I got here,' Georgie panted, steering Hazel backwards so she could get inside to straighten the mare's rugs. 'No idea what's going on, but I suspect we don't need to look far for the culprit.'

Georgie pointed to where Jackson was now gobbling up the cows' hay, much to their annoyance.

'I assume you mean Jackson, not Clem,' said Hamish.

For cycling up the track past the farm was Clem. She did a doubletake when she spotted the donkey and was even more puzzled when she realised the gate was missing.

'What's up?' she asked, propping her bike against the wall. 'And why are you two standing there like gaping idiots while Jackson's at an all-you-can-eat buffet?'

'Chaos this morning,' Georgie explained. 'It looks as though Jackson must have got out, wound the others up because he was loose and they weren't, then kicked down the gate to get to the good grass.'

The trio's eyes took in the smashed remains, which looked more likely to have been driven over by a tank than a diminutive donkey.

'That's a lot of damage for Jackson's tiny hooves.' Clem voiced what they were all thinking. 'I mean, he must have taken a run at it.'

'I'd better call Fred,' Hamish sighed, shaking his head. 'The gate will need replacing today. He won't be best pleased to have to pay Sunday rates to get it fixed.'

'I'm surprised there's no other damage,' observed Clem. 'I figured you were going to say someone must have broken in.'

They looked at each other askance, then Hamish sprang away, calling, 'You two check the tack room, I'll take the barn.'

As they neared the door, Georgie half expected to find it shattered with the lock broken and the tack missing, but it was exactly as they'd left it the day before. Hamish reappeared and reported the barn, filled to the ceiling with expensive feed and bedding, was also untouched. The shadow of Fred suddenly loomed in the doorway, his face puce. Clem picked up a headcollar and said she'd catch the donkey, Hamish replied he'd put Guido and Hazel out in the fields to let off steam. They disappeared, abandoning Georgie to the onslaught.

'I assume there's an explanation for all this,' Fred growled.

'Well, I don't have one,' replied Georgie, picking up the kettle. 'I'll make some drinks.'

'Have we been robbed?'

'Nothing's missing. Everything's here, just one destroyed gate, an escaped donkey and somehow the chickens got out too. We've got it under control. Most likely Jackson's behind it. If we had CCTV, we could've seen what he got up to … though that really would be a case of closing the door after the horse has bolted.'

'I'll not splash out for cameras because of one ruddy donkey.' Fred banged his fist on the door frame in annoyance. 'Right now, I need to make some calls about the gate. Who knows if anyone'll be prepared to come out on a Sunday.'

Georgie and Clem retreated to the barn to prepare the breakfasts.

'Perhaps it was joyriders who didn't know the gate was there and didn't brake in time,' suggested Clem.

'Who then got out the car to unlock a donkey's stable and a chicken coop for the fun of it? No chance, they would have legged it.'

They walked outside carrying buckets filled with feed.

'On the positive side, at least it's stopped snowing,' said Clem.

Georgie tipped buckets into mangers, puzzling over how Jackson had got out. They'd always known he had a knack for undoing the top bolt with his teeth, but she was certain she'd secured the lower bolt last night. She could recall kicking over the latch with her foot, hearing the metallic clunk as it slid into the bracket. Split Trousers nudged her out the way, keen to get to his food. She moved aside, stroking the gelding's neck, listening to the soft swish of his lips sweeping up the grain. Taking in a deep breath, the comfortingly familiar scents of hay, warm horse and the sweetness of molasses, filled Georgie's nose. After such a tense start to the day, she could feel herself beginning to relax. Clem's sudden screaming made them both jump, the horse's front hooves crushing Georgie's toes. Freeing herself, she limped outside to the sight of Clem collapsed over the bottom door of one of the stables. Feed trickled out the bowl dangling from her fingers. The chickens flocked to peck at it until they were chased off by Boffy.

'It's Monty,' she wailed. 'He's gone.'

19

'What are you talking about … gone?' snapped Fred, marching over, temper flaring. 'I can feel myself ageing by the minute with you lot today.'

Being closer, Georgie got there first. She stood in the doorway of an empty stable. The straw bedding was fluffed up, water buckets untouched, a half-eaten haynet on the back wall. The only thing missing was the black colt who usually resided there.

'It makes no sense,' she muttered.

'Well … where's the bloody horse?' demanded Fred, turning on Georgie for an answer she didn't possess.

'I don't know. I wasn't aware he wasn't here.'

'The door was locked and the bolts secure,' rallied Clem. 'I'd opened them before I realised. I thought Monty was in the corner at the back, waiting by his manger.'

'You must be mistaken,' said Georgie. 'The door must have been pushed to but not locked.'

'I'm not wrong. The bolts shoot backwards from halfway every time and I nearly always trap my fingers. They were definitely done up.'

Georgie stepped onto the straw-free area immediately inside the doorway, searching for clues. 'He couldn't have climbed through the gap.'

'Nor has he been beamed up.' Fred kicked straw into the air, disturbing a nosey chicken. 'When you two have finished playing detective, we've got a horse to track down. Clem, you must be wrong. Monty's obviously got out on the moor. Ring everyone you can think of who can join a search.'

As Fred yanked his phone from his trouser pocket, ripping the material in his haste, Clem insisted, 'I'm not mistaken, Georgie. The door was locked, otherwise I'd have noticed sooner something was up.'

Georgie considered the likelihood of Jackson being able to undo the lower bolts of the doors. It seemed impossible, as was the suggestion that somehow Monty had taught himself how to reach out and undo both top and bottom bolts from the inside, then close and lock them again on the outside before running off. She'd certainly never heard of a horse being clever enough to cover its own tracks and was beginning to feel uneasy. Nothing had been stolen, but now she thought about it, the damage seemed extensive for one mischievous donkey. There was no more time to ponder, as Fred shouted over for Georgie to get on her phone and round up some help. Before doing so, she hurried after Clem.

'Wait up.'

At Georgie's call, Clem turned around, her eyes were tearful. She wiped her nose with a sniff. 'No one believes me, but I know those bolts were done up.'

'I agree with you. Something's not right. I can't quite figure it out either but for now let's help with the search and see what transpires.'

'Those bolts were —'

'Look, I'm saying I believe you,' Georgie insisted, 'but

arguing with Fred isn't going to get us anywhere. Come on, make some calls. It'll do us both good to have a focus.'

Within an hour, Amiyah was on site, closely followed by Tom, who had stayed at Heather's overnight. His friend Francois, dressed in a yellow fluorescent jacket and carrying a compass, arrived with Joe, who'd brought along a tubby West Highland terrier in a little tweed coat, called Nugget. Georgie suspected long walks were not Nugget's forte.

'Clem, Hamish, you stay put. Finish up the mucking out and deal with the gate guy when he gets here. I've managed to persuade him to come today for double his usual rates,' ordered Fred. 'Cador is checking his land. Joe, you take the quad bike, Amiyah and Francois can go on foot, I'll use the tractor. Georgie, Tom, I want you to tack up Emerald and Zippy. Follow the old Smuggler's route. Monty will stick to the paths where he can and that's a well-known one.'

Hurriedly, Georgie slipped on Emerald's bridle, then secured a waterproof sheet beneath the chestnut's saddle, not trusting a sky still heavy with cloud.

Picking up on the tension, the horses were skittish. Emerald's back arched beneath Georgie as she coaxed him out through the gate to the moor. He didn't want to go and kept turning sideways so the gap was too narrow to fit through. Also reluctant, Zippy half-reared, spinning round, trying to remain in the yard. Tom's face was set with stress.

Eventually they managed to set hooves on the moor.

'What's up with them?' asked Georgie. 'We don't usually have any trouble getting them out for exercise.'

'They're upset and the weather's closing in. They sense it.' With clenched jaw, Tom's hands held the reins so tightly Zippy tossed his head with frustration.

In the distance, Georgie could see the quad bike roaring across the ground, the tractor chugging in its wake. A yellow blob moving the opposite way revealed the route Francois and

Amiyah were taking. Tom and Zippy did an about turn, following a trail which formed the third point of a triangular area Fred had mapped out. Georgie followed, trotting along a path both picturesque and desolate. When she looked over her shoulder, the reassuring sight of Pennhalow and the others had already disappeared. A couple of snowflakes twirled downwards, spattering Emerald's waterproof.

'Keep your eyes peeled at all times,' said Tom, as the trail widened, allowing Georgie to draw alongside him. 'Monty could be anywhere, but I'd be surprised if he's gone far.'

They rode on, Emerald clinking his bit, Tom restraining Zippy when the bay surged into a jog. They spotted herds of cattle and a lone buzzard, which followed them for a while, snooping on their progress, then swooped away. Clusters of moorland ponies raised their heads from grazing and trotted away warily, the wind catching in their thick manes and tails. Zippy and Emerald didn't settle, they fretted constantly the further they travelled from Pennhalow. The wind was growing in strength and the sporadic snowflakes had now increased in volume to be heavy enough for Georgie to comment it was snowing.

Hunched into his thick Puffa jacket, Tom grunted in reply. His words had not proved prophetic. They had covered enough ground to have reached the rectangular monument of tall standing stones marking the remains of King Arthur's Hall with no sign of either Monty or any proof he had been there.

'Let's hope the others are having more luck,' said Georgie, eyes searching the prickly bushes, hoping to spot a torn piece of red rug or similar. Anything to prove Monty had passed that way.

As though it had heard her, Tom's phone began to ring, making Zippy shy so violently Tom was almost unseated. Across the open ground, the wind screeched. Tom could barely hear and indicated they tuck the horses into a sheltered hillock. With a finger in the opposite ear, Tom was managing to hold a conversation although Georgie couldn't make out what was being said. Clearly from Tom's grimacing expression and the length of time he was speaking, it wasn't a call to say Monty had been found. They would be pushing on. It made Georgie anxious. The horses were upset. Zippy's ears were flat against his skull, his disquiet radiating. Emerald swung his rump against the growing gale, the strength of which pummelled Georgie's back. Tom ended the call.

'They've got nothing,' he said, expressionlessly. 'Finn's joined in but no joy. My guess is Monty will hole up because of this.'

He held up his right-hand, fingers splayed, to indicate the weather, just as a gust lifted the corners of the horses' waterproof sheets. Only the straps running under their tails kept them from blowing away.

As Georgie fought to flatten the sheet back over Emerald's hindquarters, she said, 'Tom, it would be sensible for us to head back.'

'Back's further away than forward. We keep on.'

Georgie made to protest but Tom had already swung Zippy up the hillock, back on to the trail, his horse stumbling on the uneven ground strewn with hidden rocks, the tips of which were turning white. The snow was starting to settle. Georgie could imagine on a good day this would be one of the best riding routes in the country, but it had begun to feel hostile, as though the moor itself was coming to life and was in a bad mood.

The trail dropped downwards and became deeply churned with patches of pooled muddy water congealed in the dips. Georgie did her best to encourage Emerald around the edges, scared when her mount sank up to his hocks and had to free himself. The worn path they had been following appeared to peter out. Water ran off Georgie's waterproof jacket and trousers and stung her face with icy spears. Cold, tired and hungry, she could sense that, even beneath the protection of his sheet. Emerald was also getting chilled. Although no expert on survival, Georgie knew the situation was turning precarious. This time she didn't hold back and, to her relief, Tom agreed.

'I know … I know. Zippy's struggling too. Try to stick to the firmer ground if you can.' Georgie could hear the strain in Tom's voice reflecting her own fear.

'We need to find shelter and get ourselves and the horses out of this,' Georgie shouted.

'I know that,' Tom yelled back. 'I was raised on the moor. Do you think I'm stupid?'

'I never said that. Stop putting words in my mouth I didn't say.' Georgie turned on Tom but could only see the blurred outline of him. Zippy's white socks were obscured by the rapidly falling snow. It made him appear as a ghost, hovering above the ground.

'Great, so now it's all my fault. In case you hadn't noticed, Georgie, we're in a whiteout.'

'Really? And here was I thinking what a beautiful summer's day.'

Emerald suddenly stumbled badly, thrusting Georgie forwards out of the saddle. She slid back and patted his soaked neck, pacifying him. Disturbed that his head carriage had become unusually low, his demeanour that of a marathon runner unsure how much longer they could continue, she called, 'Seriously Tom, we need to …'

Tom reined back abruptly and raised his hand for Georgie to do the same. She pulled Emerald alongside, feeling his hooves sink into the sludge.

'Tom —'

'Shush,' Tom interrupted. 'Can you hear that?'

Georgie strained her ears but could only hear the howl of the wind and the plop of the snowy drops landing on the peak of her skull cap to slide down her already numb cheeks.

'No, I can't hear anything except the wind tunnelling through my ears and freezing my brain —'

'Shush.'

'*Stop* shushing me. You asked me a question and I answered.'

She got no further as both horses leapt sideways into the air; Emerald's jump so extreme he crashed into Zippy. Both horse's ears were pricked so intently their tips were almost touching. And then Georgie did hear, the faint sound of music coming from the right.

'It's The Burrowing Badger. Follow me.' Tom urged Zippy into a trot, the fastest he dared go in the poor conditions. Without any encouragement, Emerald took off, sticking close to the bigger horse.

'You want to go to the pub?' Georgie was incredulous. 'We need to get back to Pennhalow and warm up, not get a gin and tonic.'

'Just follow me,' Tom snapped. 'Isla will look after us.'

They trotted on; the horses glad to be on the move. Georgie's hands and feet had lost all feeling. It took all her concentration to keep rising out of the saddle in time with the two-beat gait. They had been riding for so long she felt welded to her horse.

Tom stood high in his stirrups, raised his right arm and waved it around his head, whirling an invisible lasso, whooping at full volume. Looking straight ahead, Georgie understood why as a patch of mist and snow cleared to reveal in the distance a pub. A large solid building, squatting in the centre of a cobbled courtyard. Every window was lit with a warm yellow light and Georgie imagined she could see the glow of a real log fire.

'Come on, Georgie, nearly there,' Tom beamed.

Reaching the lane, they slowed to a crawl. Zippy skidded as they walked through an open gateway into a car park, filled with abandoned cars and vans, unable to go any further through the high drifts of snow accumulating everywhere. Despite being only mid-afternoon, it was growing dark, the sign of worse still to come.

'Let's go that way.' Tom indicated the courtyard out front.

A board on top of a tall signpost was billowing backwards and forwards with a shriek, making the painting of a badger emerging from its burrow appear as though it were on a swing.

The horses' metal shoes couldn't get any traction on cobblestones slick with slush. Emerald lost his hind legs out from under him, sinking low on his haunches to keep his balance. Zippy tumbled sideways, narrowly missing a collision with a wooden picnic bench hidden under inches of snow. Legs wobbling in an impression of Bambi, he managed to stop himself in time.

'We need to get off now before they fall,' said a shaken Tom.

Georgie's legs gave way as she touched the ground. Tom reached out to assist, placing a supportive arm around her waist. The door to the bar opened and a lady in tan snow boots put up an umbrella as she stepped outside.

'Hello, Isla,' greeted Tom, with a wry grin.

'Oh, Tom. You poor darlings,' she cried. 'What were you doing out in this?'

'We lost a horse,' replied Tom.

'What? No! There should be three of you?' Isla's hand covered her mouth with a gasp. 'I'm disappointed at Fred allowing this to happen. Angie will not be happy with him.'

'Sorry, didn't explain that well. We lost a horse this

morning. Georgie and I went out looking for it, then the weather turned.'

'You're not the only ones to get caught. Many other folks are stuck here. You'll not get back today. The roads are blocked with ice and fallen trees.'

Georgie slumped against Tom, asking plaintively, 'What will we do?'

Isla jumped in. 'We've a barn out back. Take the horses round there and settle them in. Then come and find me in the bar. In the meantime, Tom, I'll give your father a call and a piece of my mind.'

'Thank you.' Georgie smiled gratefully. 'We'd be totally stuck without you.'

They led the horses back the way they'd come, then turned in around the rear of the pub where they found an ancient barn, protected by the building from the worst of the elements. Solid beams, pitted and worn, held a lantern giving enough light for Georgie to see a couple of old wooden stalls where the horses could rest. Emerald cantered through the door, pulling Georgie with him, desperate to be out of the powerful wind and snow. Georgie struggled to undo the buckles and straps on the tack, fingers throbbing painfully as they came back to life. One of the bar staff brought some old tea towels for them to rub the horses down with and dry off the worst. Tom found a couple of buckets for water, which he placed one in each stall.

'There. They're safe now and so are we,' he said, as he flicked off the lantern.

20

Fortunately, one of the vans trapped in the car park belonged to a local feed merchant, who kindly offered to provide food for the horses. Georgie and Tom accepted gratefully and, before battening down the hatches for the night, ventured back outside. Darkness had fallen and the snow had turned to sleet. Emerald was dozing when Georgie lurched into the barn carrying a sack of feed. He neighed a welcome, while Zippy banged his door with an eager hoof. Georgie and Tom were happy to be able to leave the horses content, warm and munching. They would be fine overnight, for the barn was cosy and secure.

'They'll probably have a better night than us,' joked Tom as they dashed across to the pub.

Isla had rustled up piping hot chicken soup and thick wedges of granary bread which Georgie dived on appreciatively, while Tom called Fred. His face was grim when he returned to the table, pulling out a chair opposite Georgie.

'They called off the search when the weather got worse. Dad says they'll be back out at dawn as long as it's safe.'

'No one found anything then?' Georgie asked hopefully.

'No, nothing. And with the weather this bad ...' Tom dunked bread in his bowl. 'Well, let's just hope it encourages Monty home and he's waiting at the gates tomorrow morning.'

Georgie found herself no longer hungry. Once Tom had eaten, they moved through to a bar filled with stranded travellers, all with their own tale to tell of being caught unawares by the sudden onslaught of the blizzard.

'It was supposed to be rain. That's what the forecast said ... heavy rain,' a flush faced elderly gentleman kept repeating to anyone who'd listen. 'Sixty odd years I've lived on the moor, man and boy. Never not made it home before.'

He didn't seem too distressed as he picked up another in a lengthy line of pint glasses filled to the brim with ale.

In an atmosphere of bonhomie with a sense of all being in it together, Georgie and Tom drew up chairs to join the huddle around the fire. The conversation soon turned to the visitors who'd been blown in on horseback.

'What an adventure you've had,' commented a friendly lady with curly grey hair.

'Hmmm, something like that,' Tom replied.

'And you say you lost a horse?' asked her companion.

'Yes, earlier today. We were trying to find him,' Georgie added.

'Ah, he'll turn up. They always return once they're hungry. Same as kids!'

Watching the flames, Georgie's eyes were closing. Now dry and warm, her bones ached with tiredness, her muscles sore from so many hours in the saddle. Tom offered to brave the elements for a final check on Emerald and Zippy. Georgie yawned her thanks.

By eleven o'clock, the others began to disperse. Isla apologised that all the rooms had been nabbed by the earlier arrivals, as she handed Georgie pillows and bedding for her and Tom to camp by the fire. Georgie replied that it didn't matter for they were most grateful to have a place to spend the night and wait out the storm.

Curled up on the floor, wrapped in a duvet with her head resting on a soft pillow, Georgie was on the brink of much needed sleep when Tom's voice came out of the shadows.

'Georgie?'

'Uh-huh.'

'Can I ask you something?'

'Uh-huh.'

'I hope you don't mind me asking though … perhaps I ought not to.'

'Tom, just go ahead and ask will you before I nod off.'

There was a brief pause during which Georgie assumed Tom had changed his mind, then: 'Do you think you and Sam will get married one day?'

Georgie laughed uproariously, the sound akin to a bark, echoing in the now empty bar area. 'I'd have to say that's highly unlikely seeing as we're no longer together.'

She sensed rather than saw Tom shoot upright. 'I'm really sorry. I didn't know. I'd never have asked such a stupid question if I had.'

'You couldn't have known. I didn't tell anyone. Hamish knows, but only because he figured it out after seeing Sam and Abi together.'

'*The* Abi … Abi from The Jocks? The one you suspected Sam was messing around with?'

'The one and only, very same Abi.' Georgie hated the note of bitterness in her voice.

'Wow. And I told you not to be suspicious, when all along …'

'Perhaps … or perhaps not. Sam denied it, of course, but he always was a bit of an enigma, right from the beginning. I never really knew where I stood with him.' Georgie still hadn't made up her mind whether Sam had told the truth. It all seemed irrelevant now anyway. She'd heard nothing from him and didn't expect to. They were gone from each other's lives.

'Do you mind being single again?'

'I've not had any time to find out. It's been full on ever since I set foot in Pennhalow. You know, you really ought to consider renaming the place. Never mind all this end of the moor stuff, how about non-stop adventures or expect the unexpected. Much more suitable, in my opinion.'

Tom laughed as he laid down again. 'I admit it does seem like that's the case, but we had years of not much going on at all. That's partly why we bought Monty a few months before you joined us. To liven the yard up, bring in some potential. We seem to have overshot the mark with that. It's been all go ever since.'

'Is Monty gone forever?' Georgie asked quietly, almost not wanting an answer.

'Absolutely not. We'll find him. It'll all work out, it always does.'

Georgie listened to Tom shuffling around, getting comfortable.

'Does it though?' she asked softly. 'Feels to me as if life just keeps on throwing obstacles at you to see how much you can take. You must go on finding ways over them, around them, through them but what if one day you can't anymore? What then?'

But Tom was already asleep, no doubt having pleasant dreams of future happy days spent with Heather.

Georgie, however, dreamed she was lost on the moor in a ferocious blizzard. Sam was a little way ahead and she kept calling out to him to save her, but he wouldn't let go of Abi's hand. They kept looking back and laughing at her, then running away. A tinkling noise was in her ear, she tried to bat it away, then woke to Tom sitting beside her, holding out a cup of tea, the teaspoon rattling on the saucer.

'Good morning,' he chirped, chin sporting a hint of dark stubble.

'Thanks. Yikes, I'm stiff.' Georgie winced upright.

'A day in the saddle followed by a night on the floor does that to you,' teased Tom. 'It's a magic brew though.'

Georgie took the saucer. 'Is that because you didn't make it?'

'Very funny. Wait until you see breakfast.'

'The horses.' Georgie started, slopping tea on the duvet.

'They're fine. I've checked them and fed them. No harm done following yesterday, thank goodness.'

It felt peculiar resting on the floor of the deserted bar in the half-light. Georgie could see the outline of beer pumps and rows of glasses. The fire was almost out. She huddled near Tom to keep warm, the duvet tucked around them both.

'Here's breakfast,' said Tom, producing two packets of Bourbon biscuits.

'Breakfast in bed and my favourites too. You are a gem.' Georgie pulled open the wrapper. 'And you're good company in dire circumstances.'

Tom feigned embarrassment, nudging Georgie with his shoulder. She missed her mouth, the rectangular biscuit almost going up her nostril, making her laugh.

'You have the best laugh. It's a mixture of innocent and dirty. I love it,' said Tom. 'And it was one of the first things I noticed about you. It's quite distinctive.'

Georgie became aware of Tom's proximity, as she crunched biscuit.

'You do have a beautiful smile, Georgie.'

'Why, thank you. Yours isn't half bad either. You know, when you smile your whole face beams. It's catching, I find I have to smile too.' The words were out of Georgie's mouth before she'd realised she was going to say them. 'It's the nicest part of my morning, seeing that smile every day.'

Tom's head leaned in closer. Georgie noticed how long and dark his eyelashes were and the little lines at the corners of his eyes. They were inches apart, Georgie's hand gripping the cup, heat searing her palm. Her heart was hammering, her brain waving its arms frantically to get her attention. She ignored it as Tom raised his hand, fingers moving towards her lips.

'You've got crumbs round your mouth,' he chuckled, brushing them away.

Georgie watched as the teeny pieces of biscuit floated onto the duvet.

'Well, good morning campers.' Isla's chirpy tones filled the room.

Tom and Georgie pulled apart. A look flashed across Tom's face so fast Georgie couldn't catch its meaning.

'I bring good news. It's four degrees outside so the snow's melting and travel reports say the roads are being cleared. You should be good to be on your way. Don't go before having some breakfast though. Our Chef's full English is not to be missed. We're serving in the dining area when you're ready. No rush.'

Tom walked over to the window alcove while Georgie folded away the bedding.

'It's amazing how it can change so fast,' he said, taking in the patches of earthy cobbles already revealed amongst the layer of smooth white. 'Last night it's apocalyptic, yet by lunchtime today it'll be a grey slushy mess. Are you ready? I'm ravenous.'

Being stuffed full of bacon, eggs, fried bread, tomato and mushrooms, Georgie could barely haul herself into the saddle.

'I'm not giving you a leg up after seeing you stuff your face with all that,' stated Tom, 'here, use that low wall, over there.'

Georgie's smooth soled jodhpur boots had no grip. Precariously, she stood on the wall, balancing herself against Emerald, who decided to step away at the crucial moment, leaving Georgie to pivot and roll onto his back. Emerald snorted in disgust, blowing snow dust off the ledge of stones.

'That was stylish,' Tom sniggered.

Georgie pulled a face. 'It's never easy when you're short. Still at least I'm not riding in a race tomorrow. I'd probably break the scales.'

They rode out past drivers scraping the slushy mess from their vehicles and called out thank you to the feed merchant who had helped them. He waved and wished them a safe ride home. The sign, which had been almost blown off its hinges when they'd arrived, now hung lifeless, the badger watching over the flurry of activity from his frame.

As they reached the trail, the horses' hooves squelched with each step, the bulk of snow rapidly turning to water. Tom led the way carefully, trying to avoid the worst areas. A weak sun had risen. Against its glare from the snow, Georgie scoured the ground for any sign of a black horse, knowing Monty would be easy to spot. She saw nothing, except distant peaks still swathed in whiteness. The trail was deeply boggy. She stuck to the exact route Tom took, following Zippy's hoofprints, wary of the badly saturated, hazardous areas. The air was fresh, cold and dry. Georgie tried to keep her thoughts away from how Monty would have fared overnight. Thoroughbreds weren't as robust as the clusters of hardy moorland ponies, scratching around on the ground for grass. She fervently hoped they would arrive back to find he'd come home.

21

The foursome clattered into the yard at Pennhalow, clothes and waterproof sheets askew, otherwise none the worse for their ordeal. Angie rushed out of the tack room, hands wringing with anxiety.

'You're back. I'm so relieved,' she cried. 'We've been worried stupid.'

'And Monty?' Georgie asked hopefully.

Angie's perky smile vanished as she shook her head slowly. 'No sign, but don't fret. Some of our helpers had to return to work today but Hamish and Finn are out, along with Heather, who's taken a day off to search with Cador. Fred's rung round all the locals he's got numbers for and they've promised to check their land. We're doing everything we can. I'm sure it won't be long until Monty's located.'

As Georgie dismounted, she noticed the top bolt of Jackson's stable now had a lobster clasp keyring through the loop to prevent it being lifted and opened from inside. The donkey's creamy coloured muzzle was poking over the door in protest. He brayed a welcome to Emerald and Zippy.

Fred joined Angie in the yard. He looked exhausted, dishevelled and concerned. 'All right, son? Georgie?'

Georgie and Tom babbled away about their adventure and the kindness of the staff at The Burrowing Badger, talking over each other in their rush to tell the tale.

'You've done well,' said Angie, with a sly glance at Fred. 'Fred should never have let you go that far with the weather as uncertain as it was yesterday.'

'How was I supposed to know it would be the worst weather we've had for ages? Just because Isla's wound you up, don't be getting at me. Besides, try telling Tom what to do once he's made his mind up.'

Clem dumped the wheelbarrow she was pushing towards the muck heap and joined the conversation. 'Hey you two. So glad you're safe. While you were gone, we've been trying to come up with more ways to find Monty. Amiyah and I have put it out on our Twitter feeds to alert people to the fact he's missing.'

'He's bound to be sheltering on someone's land, near their outbuildings, or even in them if they're open. The fierce weather will have driven him to that,' nodded Fred.

'So, we thought if we spread the word on social media then whoever finds him will know to contact us.' Clem bounced on the spot, proud of herself.

'Yes, those two had the bright idea that some twits might help us find the horse,' added Fred.

'Tweets, dad. They're called tweets, not twits.' Tom gazed skywards in exasperation.

'I don't care what they are as long as they find my missing horse —'

'We've had a few questionable responses so far,' Clem interrupted Fred.

'Yeah, with sightings as ludicrous as Glasgow!' Amiyah called out.

'Are you sure it's a good idea to advertise we've lost a racehorse and a Derby contender at that? Won't that make us look careless?' worried Tom. 'If an owner's considering sending us their horse, they might rethink in the circumstances.'

'You come up with a better plan then,' snapped Clem, bristling.

'Yeah, I don't hear you suggesting anything,' rallied Amiyah.

Angie clapped her hands briskly. 'Time for a cuppa. We're all in need of one.'

Georgie sipped her tea, Boffy snoozing on her lap, cocooned from the voices babbling around her. She hadn't returned to the news she'd wanted. Monty was still nowhere to be found. Privately she agreed with Tom about social media. She didn't feel it was the best means of dealing with the situation. Still, it probably wouldn't draw much interest. Pennhalow wasn't a famous racing establishment, few people had even heard of it. They'd probably receive a few more spurious sightings of Monty miles away and then it would fizzle out.

Over the next few days, a sombre hush descended on the yard. Even the animals sensed it. The horses became lethargic where usually they were frisky. Boffy gave up chasing chickens and kept a vigil by the gate to the moor, his nose pressed through the bars. Everyone went through the actions of day-to-day routine but without the usual frivolity and banter. Always the empty stable lingered, a seeping wound festering because no one knew how to stitch it back together. Georgie overheard Hamish and Amiyah whispering in the barn about how much longer they could go on believing Monty would still turn up.

'Surely someone would have spotted him by now,' said Hamish, as Georgie stiffened outside the door. 'He's sixteen hands of pure-bred thoroughbred. He's not going to blend in anywhere around here. Even the most unknowledgeable of ramblers would notice something as odd as that, especially if he's still wearing a bright red rug. No one's going to mistake him for part of a native herd.'

It frightened Georgie that in her head she could only agree.

On the Wednesday morning, the third day after Monty's disappearance, Fred called an impromptu meeting in the tack room. The team gathered, expressions downcast. Amiyah handed out drinks and biscuits, which remained untouched. Boffy snuck into his basket and curled up whining.

'As much as it pains me to say this,' Fred began, 'we may have to accept the likelihood that Monty has perished. I had a chat with our usual vet earlier and she stated it's a strong possibility a thoroughbred couldn't survive exposure to the inclement weather and lack of quality food and care. I would ask that you all remain optimistic, but we've reached a point where we also need to become realistic.'

No one spoke. Devastated Georgie realised she no longer cared about the Derby. It was only a race. All she cared about was the colt. She wanted him back. It was Clem who recovered first.

'This is bullshit,' she stormed. 'I've never agreed that Monty ran away. That stable door was locked, top and bottom, and I'm going to keep repeating it until one of you finally believes me. Unless Monty sprouted wings, he should still be here.'

'It's impossible,' Hamish said firmly. 'Monty doesn't trust strangers. He's still quirky with everyone he knows here, except you and Georgie. Nobody could have spirited him away against his will. You can't force a horse to do what it doesn't want to do.'

'You've forgotten what the gate guy said.' Clem turned to the others. 'He said he's been in the business decades and he'd never seen a donkey cause that much damage. He didn't buy it.'

'Clem, we've been over this time and time again,' sighed Tom.

Clem threw her mug to the floor and ran outside, smashing the door closed behind her.

'I'm posting another alert on Twitter,' said Amiyah, tapping her phone screen, 'and this time I'm including a photo. That ought to grab people's attention. There … hashtag missing Monty.'

She put her phone away with a flourish.

Georgie could sense Tom was biting his tongue.

For the rest of the day the sun shone, the birds sang and the cute lambs frolicked in the fields. Georgie didn't notice. She went to bed feeling sad and numb.

Georgie overslept. She woke with a jolt. The display on the digital alarm clock was flashing midnight. Grabbing her watch from the bedside table, Georgie found it was six o'clock in the morning. The power must have briefly dropped out in the night. Swearing grumpily, she dressed hastily, not bothering to open the curtains. In the semi-darkness she tripped over the edge of the dangling duvet, nearly head-butting the wall. With no time to spare, she stuffed her phone in her pocket and grabbed a slice of dry bread from the kitchen. She was cramming it in her mouth sideways as she opened the annexe door. An explosion of noise accompanied by flashing lights greeted her.

'Eh?' she babbled, slimy half-chewed bread on her tongue.

All at once a cacophony of voices shouted to get her attention. A furry boom microphone was thrust in her face.

'Eh?' Georgie shaded her eyes to find she was hemmed in by a crowd gathered in a semi-circle around the building.

'Is it true The Misfit has run away?' asked the microphone holder, setting off a flurry of questions.

'Is your Derby dream over before it ever began?'

'Has he been eaten by the Beast of Bodmin? They've always said there's an escaped big cat loose on the moor. I've seen the photos.'

Directly in front of Georgie stood two girls dressed in jodhpurs and hooded sweatshirts. 'We'll help you search. We love horses,' they sang.

Caught in the spotlight, it was like being at a film premiere; everyone wanting Georgie to say something profound, but she was rendered speechless. Her only viable option was to flee.

'Please, excuse me. Make way.' Georgie pushed her way through and, once out the other side, ran for the manor house, dropping a crust in her haste.

Behind her she could hear the stampede of the crowd following.

She took the steps two at a time and rang the bell for so long and with such force it made her ears ring. The door opened a fraction, Tom's arm snaked out, grabbed hold of Georgie and tugged her inside. She saw the lights were on, the curtains still drawn, as she followed Tom to the kitchen.

'Something very weird is happening outside,' she told him.

Tom picked up a mug off the table, took a gulp of coffee, then shoved an open laptop towards her. 'This'll explain it better than I can.'

Georgie sat down and shook the mouse to get rid of the screensaver. An internet page was open at Twitter.

'But Pennhalow's not on social media,' she said confused.

'Pennhalow wasn't on social media,' Tom corrected, 'but hashtag missing Monty has been trending for hours and now the entire world has descended on us. Or so it feels.'

Georgie tipped her chair back. 'Yikes. There goes our plan to turn up at Epsom the unknown outsiders.'

'Yeah … that's not quite what my dad said. He's on his way over with Angie. Told me to stay indoors and not say anything until he gets here.'

'What about the horses? Morning stables?'

'Clem, Hamish and Amiyah have locked themselves in the yard so they can get on. It's a mess.'

Georgie and Tom sat waiting, the ticking of the clock extra loud. Scrolling through her phone Georgie found messages from her parents, friends and even one from Sam, asking what was going on. She couldn't begin to fathom how to reply. What felt ages later, Fred and Angie burst into the kitchen.

Fred was waving a crumpled piece of paper scrawled with blue ink as he said, 'I've prepared a statement. I'll read it out to them, then they can all clear off.'

'Let's hear it,' said Tom, folding his arms.

Fred cleared his throat: 'This is an official statement from Mr Fred Pengelly. A recent unfortunate incident led to one of the racehorses in our team, The Misfit, departing the premises unaccompanied. A full search is underway with the assistance of our wonderful community of friends and neighbours. We anticipate reaching a positive conclusion very soon. Thank you for your interest, however the welfare of our animals is a top priority at Pennhalow, therefore we would ask that you leave the premises. We would not wish them upset by further distractions.'

Clearly it wasn't written by a PR company, thought Georgie, but it would do. Before she or Tom could respond, Fred's mobile sprang to life. Angie answered.

'Hold on please,' she said, then turned to Fred. 'It's Cador wanting to know why a bunch of people are tramping all over his land. Apparently, his dogs are going berserk and his pigs have just chased someone into a ditch.'

'Ah, to hell with it all,' stormed Fred. 'I wish I'd never bought the damn horse. No wonder he was a bargain price. They were probably laughing all the way to the bank, glad to have solved the problem I've lumbered myself with.'

'That's social media for you, dad,' said Tom. 'Once you're on it, people assume they know you.'

'I'm not on it,' Fred roared.

'Go and read out your statement,' soothed Angie.

Fred stood on the top step and gave his speech, then did his best to answer questions. It was all rather awkward and, as Tom had feared, wasn't the sort of publicity they would have wanted. No matter how Fred phrased it, there was no obvious explanation for why Monty still hadn't been found. If they couldn't easily explain it themselves, Georgie wasn't surprised they couldn't easily explain it to others.

Once the crowd had finally dispersed, Georgie and Tom were able to get to the yard unhindered to join the rest of the team. They walked down the lawn, now a churned sea of mud.

'At least it was only the local press and some curious bystanders, a handful of whom probably did mean well,' said Tom.

'Plus, one believer in the Beast of Bodmin and one psychic, who told me Monty's located near water. They know because they can hear waves.' Georgie clicked the latch and Tom followed her into the yard.

'Really? Not Dozmary Pool then?'

Boffy lurched over with an excited bark, jumping up to greet Georgie. She stroked his ears. 'Dozy what?'

'Dozmary Pool. It's a lake on the moor, supposedly where King Arthur received Excalibur from the Lady of the Lake.'

'Ah, no. They definitely mentioned waves not swords.'

'We won't be following up that lead in a hurry then.'

Later Georgie was sweeping the yard when shouts could be heard from the farm. She tracked Tom, who scrambled to check out what was going on.

'This is private property,' Fred was yelling up the track. 'P-r-i-v-a-t-e —'

'Calm down, dad,' barked Tom. 'Seamus is on holiday. It's the stand-in farrier.'

'Oh, sorry.' Fred was forced to spend the next few minutes profusely apologising for his short fuse.

Clem and Amiyah got on with their work, making sure not to come up with any further ideas for finding missing Monty.

22

The next morning Gina West, dressed in over-the-knee stiletto boots and black skinny jeans, turned up with a *Racing News* film crew. Taking onboard Fred's angry rumblings about private property, they set up against the pillars, blocking access to the front entrance of the manor. Midway through a piece to camera, Gina's hair ruffling in the breeze as she gesticulated up the driveway, Lucinda Fox-Beckerington drew up in a red sports convertible. Finding her path blocked, she leant on the horn continuously, much to Gina's chagrin.

'Do you mind?' Gina snapped, then to the crew: 'We'll have to do that again.'

'Get out of my way,' Lucinda snarled.

The ensuing argument could be heard in the yard and it was a furious Lucinda who barrelled through the gate minutes later. Fortified with tea and croissants, she set out determinedly to the moor, announcing she would return with The Misfit or not at all, because she was not going to fail. Hours later, she reappeared, to report not a single trace was found. Her misery was compounded by having left the roof down on the car, while unexpected showers rolled through.

Georgie wasn't too pleased either at being accosted by Gina as she rode Guido out for a trot up the lane. It seemed to her as though Gina almost enjoyed suggesting Georgie had never stood any chance in the Derby in the first place so, by not turning up, would simply fail earlier than she otherwise would have done.

Fortunately, the news didn't make the front pages and any damage appeared to be limited when Fred was contacted by the owner of a horse trained in Newmarket which they wished to transfer to Pennhalow. Georgie volunteered to be the one to travel back with the newcomer. Although she'd have to get the train from Cornwall to Suffolk, secretly she was glad to miss Heather's upcoming fancy dress birthday party.

Setting off on the long trek from Bodmin through London, then onto Cambridge and finally the place known as the home of British horse-racing, Georgie took a seat by the window. She popped in her ear buds as the train pulled out of Bodmin Parkway and watched as fields and villages gave way to towns. Her thoughts turned to Monty and how it could be that he had seemingly vanished into thin air. Legends abounded regarding the moor, but it was unusual for a hungry horse not to have returned home by now. Riding the colt was closest to sailing through the air. Georgie longed to be greeted by Monty's silky head and tuneful whinny in the mornings again. That harm could have befallen him was unthinkable. She fought images of the thoroughbred battling to escape from a bog. Instead, she recalled Tom's positivity on the night they had spent at The Burrowing Badger that it would all turn out OK. She smiled. Somehow Tom always made her feel better. She was fond of him and, if honest with herself, disappointed that Heather had scuppered any possibilities brewing between them, but as Tom and Heather's relationship seemed to be going well, Georgie had put aside her feelings.

As the train travelled onwards, Georgie dozed. When she

woke, the station signs informed her she'd reached the suburbs of London. Thinking back, the last time she'd been in the city was for The Jocks. Since that night, it felt as though her life had changed as many times as she would be changing trains.

Newmarket's station was only a short walk from the High Street, where Angie had booked Georgie into a room above a pub called The Mare and Foal. It was late afternoon when Georgie went in search of the old brick building with shuttered windows and two tall chimneys which her phone showed was her destination. With her holdall weighing heavy on her shoulder, she was pleased it didn't look a long walk. The large gold lettering across the façade, plus a sign depicting a pretty Palomino mare with suckling foal, could not be missed. She pulled open the mahogany and frosted glass paned door. Inside the décor was modelled on a wooden schooner, dark wood and low lighting, narrow alcoves and a bar area. Georgie half expected the floor to start swaying, while her nose sniffed appreciatively at the delicious waft of frying food coming from the kitchens. After checking in, Georgie's priority would be getting something substantial to eat.

Venturing downstairs from the comfy eaves room where she dumped her gear, Georgie discovered in her absence the bar had filled up with what seemed to be all the stable staff in Suffolk. Numerous speakers emitted loud music while a group played pool at a corner table. Opposite where she stood, a dodgy drunken game of darts was underway and a couple of lads were attempting to balance full pint glasses on their heads for a bet. Georgie made her way to the bar. Recognising her, a few grinning faces offered to buy her a drink. Politely Georgie declined, keen to keep to herself.

She was demolishing a burger at a tucked away table when a diminutive figure came and stood before her.

'Georgie Wright,' said an American accent. 'It's some time since we've seen you in this part of the world.'

Georgie looked up mid-bite, taking in the slight frame, grey designer t-shirt and dark blue jeans, unable to conceal bulging muscles. Tanned forearms and a wrist sporting a gold Rolex, mother-of-pearl dial beset with diamonds catching the light, as the man pulled up a chair.

'Hello Zane.' Georgie instantly recognised Zane Powers. She'd often bumped into the current champion jockey of flat racing at various racecourses over the years and knew he lived by Newmarket Heath. 'Only a flying visit. I'm collecting a horse tomorrow.'

'Ah, that explains why you're so far from where you're currently calling home.' Zane tipped his head, brown eyes wide. 'Not running away, I hope. I read you've had a mishap.'

'You could call it that.' Georgie pretended to slap Zane's hand as he swiped an onion ring from her plate. 'Or you could call it a total mystery and an unprecedented disaster.'

Zane chortled. 'The Misfit will be found. I'll wager he's been picked up by some unsuspecting equestrian who knows nothing about racing, hasn't realised he's missing and is probably wondering at their good fortune to now possess the fastest horse in the riding school. They'll be salivating at the thought of all the red rosettes they'll be scooping up at the annual gymkhana.'

It was Georgie's turn to laugh at the image of Monty participating in the egg and spoon race alongside the dinky ponies. 'You make it sound simple.'

'Life is simple. We complicate it. But let me tell you this.' Zane leaned over the table towards Georgie, who felt drawn to lean in too, her scarf dipping in the ketchup. 'A competitive spirit is intrinsic to the sport. You try, you fall, you try again. I admire that. It's how champions are made and you, Georgie, have that in you. So don't fret. I'll be seeing you in the starting stalls at Epsom.'

'You're riding Brewster Smith's Polecat aren't you?' Georgie recalled reading in the *Racing Life* that Brewster had booked Zane for the Derby favourite.

'I am.' Zane stood and pinched another onion ring. 'These do taste good.'

'I wouldn't know … you've eaten most of them.'

'All the best to you.' Zane moved away.

When Georgie had finished and requested the bill, she was informed Zane had already paid it.

Walking around to the stables in the morning to collect the new horse, Georgie was struck again by how flat Newmarket Heath was, especially having become accustomed to the undulations of Bodmin Moor. Despite it being so early, the gallops buzzed with activity as strings of thoroughbreds, some consisting of more than forty horses, went about their daily exercise. Georgie drank it all in, as always excited to be in the very epicentre of the sport. Black, brown, grey, chestnut and bay hides, the bright bobble-topped silks of the skull caps, exercise sheets decorated with the initials of various training yards, all joining together, in a colourful parade. With its meticulously maintained gallops, stable yards as luxurious as five-star hotels and thoroughbreds shining like million-pound gems while costing as much, if you weren't horse mad, it wasn't the place for you.

Checking the time, Georgie decided she could afford a brief detour, unable to resist stepping out from the trees to pause and admire a row of horses trotting by, replying to the chorus of greetings from the riders. A striking chestnut bringing up the rear frothed at the mouth, flecks of foam spattering its leather bib martingale, as it pranced with impatience at being reined in.

'Unless my eyes deceive me, that looks like Gee-Gee,' the rider said.

Tilting back her head, Georgie looked upwards directly into the eyes of Sam. 'You don't often come up here to ride out,' she commented in surprise.

'Likewise. Given up on the plodders of Cornwall and moved back to the centre, have you?'

'Nope, collecting a new plodder for the team today, actually.'

Sam's horse swung its hindquarters clockwise. Georgie leaped clear to avoid being knocked over.

'Steady, Cartier.' Sam soothed the horse with a pat. 'I'm test driving my father's newest purchase. This one's in training with Brewster. Cost a fortune at the sales. Sired by Gold Rush so ought to be worth every penny.'

'Lovely.' Georgie knew the stallion well. A champion father of champions whose offspring did not come cheap.

'You look well, Gee-Gee. It's been a while. Let's do drinks soon.'

'What about your burning desire to be champion jockey?' Georgie shifted, keen to leave.

'I do have other burning desires, you know.'

'Yeah … well … from what I've heard, I'm sure Abi can deal with those. See you around.'

As Georgie turned to go, Sam suddenly lunged sideways and grabbed her shoulder roughly. Leering, his face snarling, he spat, 'Just because you met a bunch of bumpkins who can't even keep a horse in its stable, doesn't mean you're better than everyone else. You think you're special. Truth is, the only reason the Pengelly's asked you to ride The Misfit was no one else would. They didn't want to be humiliated in public, unlike you.'

'Sam, let go.' Georgie tried to free herself. 'I'm not here to argue.'

'I'm not arguing, just telling you the reality. It's not the fairy tale you dream of. Bert tried to give you what you wanted, but it was never enough. You know, sometimes you can be so bloody stubborn. That's why you end up in these types of situations, but you can't even see it. If you'd backed down with Bert and apologised over Minotaur, you'd still be at Beech Tree, but you always have to dig your heels in.'

'You can't comment because you didn't see anything that day and Bert's now fully aware what really happened. He should apologise to me. Besides, what exactly has my career got to do with you?' Georgie lashed out, hurt by Sam's insinuations.

'Your career is over. You haven't been seen on a racecourse for months and people soon forget in this game, especially if you're not riding winners while lounging in some backwater —'

'Where they appreciate me,' Georgie interjected. 'And, for the record, I used to have to plead with Bert for opportunities. You knew that.'

'Did it ever occur to you why you never got them?'

Georgie wrenched herself out of Sam's grasp. 'A combination of Bert being a belligerent boss and me outstaying my welcome, getting too comfortable.'

Sam looked at Georgie with pity. 'Wake up, Gee-Gee, it's never going to happen. It never was, even before you misplaced your horse. You're about as likely to ride in the Derby as I am to marry Abi. Yeah, about that, guess what? It was all true. Every rumour.'

Pulling down tinted goggles, Sam snapped the elastic round his skull cap with a sneer. Tapping the horse's sides, he cantered off, spraying Georgie with dust.

Brushing herself down, Georgie jogged away, shaken by

the confrontation, but consoled that once again her instinct was usually correct. It reinforced her gut feeling about The Misfit. That, if only she could find him, they would prove themselves together. A pair of rejects who would never fit in but possessed hidden depths yet undiscovered. They only needed the chance to prove it. She'd never wanted it more.

By the time Georgie arrived at the stables, she was late. The hired horsebox driver was already loading a dark brown mare with the assistance of two staff. Rosey Posey was a dainty horse, who looked as though one puff of wind might lift her off her hooves, but she was good natured and walked up the ramp without fuss.

'Hop in the front,' the driver said to Georgie while he secured the side door. 'We've a long road ahead.'

As they drove by, Georgie gazed out the window at the toy sized racehorses moving along the distant gallops. One of them was probably Sam, on Cartier, making it all look incredibly easy, as was his knack. Time to bring the curtain down on that one, she decided, turning away. She knew her sadness was rooted in nostalgia, not love.

23

On her return to Pennhalow, Georgie was amused to discover Rosey Posey wasn't the only new feature.

Leaning on the bottom door, she watched as the mare pawed at her bedding, then got down for a back scratching roll. Kicking her elegant legs, Rosey snorted with glee, before rising to her feet and pulling at a fresh haynet. Georgie moved out the way, while Tom placed a full water bucket in the corner of the stable, patting the mare's hindquarters gently before he left.

Shaking excess water from his hands, he said, 'She seems a nice sort.'

'Yeah. Nice and relaxed.' Satisfied Rosey was going to be OK overnight, Georgie stretched. 'I could do with a relaxing bath myself.'

'Oh, um. Can you pop in the manor beforehand?' Tom looked uncomfortable.

'Why?'

'Heather was disappointed you had to miss her party. She came up with the suggestion for drinks and nibbles straight after work today. Everyone's invited and she's put a lot of effort into it. It won't take long, but you'd be doing me a favour if you could drop in. Otherwise, I'll have to polish off two plates of sausage rolls.'

'Oh … go on then. You've persuaded me.' Georgie elbowed Tom playfully as they strolled over to the manor. 'Has Heather moved in then?'

Tom didn't reply immediately, leading Georgie to wonder whether he'd heard her question, when he spoke. 'No. She's … well, let's just say it's —'

'Tom … what's that over by the pillars? Are those new?'

They had reached the drive and Georgie pointed to the end where two lights were flashing to attract their attention. A vehicle had arrived but been stopped by a pair of statuesque gates, which had been erected between the pillars.

'What? Oh. Those. Yeah, it boiled down to a choice between gates or dad losing his voice bawling people out for trespassing on his private property. He called the last ones interfering busybodies. Gates are obedient and less hassle. Worth every penny in the long run. Let's go see who that is.'

A green Land Rover was waiting, engine running. The window wound creakily down and Cador stuck his head out.

'Hold on there, give us a second,' called Tom.

Georgie took one gate and Tom the other. They pulled them back out the way. The steel was heavy. Georgie was glad to drop her half while Cador drove through. By the time they'd caught up with him, Cador was exiting the vehicle as Fred came out the front door, cocktail stick of cheese and pineapple in hand. Georgie heard him greet their visitor.

'All right, Cador, my friend. What brings you here on this fine evening? You know you're always welcome.'

Cador looked solemn. Georgie heard herself gasp out loud. One hand cupped the side of her face; she barely registered Tom take hold of her other one, his fingers meshing with hers. If it was bad news the farmer brought with him, Georgie didn't want to hear it.

'There's something you need to see, all of you,' Cador said as he shook Fred's hand. 'Do you have a tablet?'

Fred looked confused. 'You got a headache then?'

Tom shunted his dad aside gently. 'I've got a laptop indoors. This way.'

They went inside, Georgie feeling as baffled as Fred looked. Congregating in the kitchen where the others were already enjoying wine, Tom shifted a creamy gateau to one side to make way for the laptop. Heather's demeanour suggested she was not amused about the interruption and even less so when Tom ignored her request to be careful not to knock anything off the table.

Georgie stood against the aga intrigued as Tom and Cador put their heads together, talking in muffled voices, trying to transfer something Cador had saved on his phone. Unimpressed Fred heaped crisps onto a plate and began shovelling them into his mouth.

'OK, it's ready,' Tom announced.

They positioned themselves around the screen. Georgie found she was looking at what appeared to be black and white footage of a gateway, fence and a partial section of the lane Cador's farm was situated off.

'This is at the entrance to my farm,' explained Cador. 'Note the date and time.'

Following Cador's calloused finger to the bottom corner, Georgie saw the date matched the day they found Monty was missing, the time one o'clock in the morning. Nothing was happening. A bat whizzed across the camera lens, a deer trotted up the lane, stopped once, checked over its shoulder, then lolloped away. They kept watching as the minutes ticked by and then, from nowhere, coming out the darkness, a four-by-four towing a horse trailer crawled into the picture, moving right to left.

'Hey up,' said Fred, leaning closer. 'Who's that?'

'Pictures too grainy to make out any useful details such as a registration number. However, you don't have to be a genius to know a vehicle travelling by in that direction can only end up in one place —'

Tom cut in before Cador could finish. 'Pennhalow Farm's gate.'

'You can't go any further, it's a no through road,' agreed Hamish. 'Single track.'

'Could they've been lost?' suggested Amiyah, 'and accidentally destroyed the gate while trying to turn around.'

'Keep watching. Can you fast forward?' Cador asked Tom

Tom sped through the film until the vehicle reappeared, this time travelling left to right. A collective hum rippled through the kitchen, for they had all seen it. Swaying in the left-hand section of the previously empty trailer was the unmistakable arc of a horse's rump.

'All those times I've gone by the camera on the gate and I never thought to ask you, Cador,' Fred sounded amazed.

'None of us did,' said Amiyah, 'because we weren't suspicious of anything.'

'I was,' said Clem angrily.

'How come you found this now?' Tom asked Cador, his eyes glued to the screen.

'My son usually deletes the recordings regularly, otherwise we end up with no space, he tells me. I asked him to have a look at the date Monty went missing before he got rid of it, not expecting anything at all. It was more for my own peace of mind that I'd done all I could.'

'Surely this is an April Fool?' demanded Tom, referring to the date. 'It's not funny, it's unkind.'

'Alas not. You didn't lose a horse, you were robbed.'

Cador's sad eyes roved from one to the other of the shocked faces surrounding him.

'I knew it,' thundered Clem, knocking a bottle of fizzy apple juice flying. 'It didn't add up at the time and here's the evidence why.'

'We owe you an apology, Clem,' said Tom, 'we didn't listen.'

With a huff, Clem sat down and crossed her legs, one foot swinging in agitation, while she chomped on a slice of fruit cake.

Deep in thought, Georgie realised what was bugging her. 'We know one thing for sure.'

'What's that?' frowned Hamish.

'Whoever took Monty is familiar with horses. Only someone who was used to being around them regularly would make the mistake of relocking the stable door. It's a force of habit.'

'Georgie's right, you know,' agreed Fred. 'We all do it automatically. You leave a stable, you lock the door behind you.'

'We have to report this now,' said Tom. 'Can we keep this video, Cador?'

'It's yours. I only hope it's of help.'

'Come on, dad. Let's report this in person.' Tom grabbed his jacket from the back of his chair.

'Won't you have something to eat and drink before you go?' Heather's voice was sharp, as she indicated the spread she'd prepared.

'There's no time for that,' Tom snapped, irritated.

Not long after Tom and Fred left, the others dispersed, leaving Heather to pack away an abundance of untouched food.

Back in the annexe Georgie ran a deep bubble bath and lay in the warm water, emotionally drained. She couldn't figure out who would take Monty and why. There had to be a motive, but one wasn't obvious. Whoever it was couldn't run Monty in the Derby. They didn't have the required documentation and besides it would hardly go unnoticed if the colt turned up at the racecourse. He didn't have any huge value as a breeding stallion, for that only usually came after big race successes and Monty didn't have any of those to his name. His pedigree was classy but that didn't guarantee any offspring would be talented. His previous owners were exceedingly wealthy. There was no reason for them to snatch Monty back. If they'd wanted him, it would simply be a case of offering the Pengelly's a sum too good to refuse. No, there was a piece missing and Georgie couldn't find it, yet without it they couldn't find Monty.

A mood of intense despondency descended on the yard. The knowledge that someone somewhere meant Pennhalow harm made everyone tense and tetchy. Fred and Tom's frustration that reporting the theft had left them with a reference number and little else did not improve the situation. As the days passed with no follow up or clues from Cador's CCTV footage and no leads forthcoming, things got worse. Riding out, Georgie wondered whether unseen eyes were watching them, especially once Fred insisted that no one was to ride alone, for fear of further attempts to take the horses. He also booked a local company to install CCTV at various places around the yard and farm. The drilling did not help everyone's nerves. Watching the workers packing away the gear in their truck, Fred shook his head with tears in his eyes.

'Tragic. This was always such a friendly, close-knit community.'

'I'm sure it's not locals.' Tom tried to reassure his father.

'Could be anyone,' said Clem morosely.

'I'm going to go and recount my cows again. Make sure no one's nicking them.' Fred sloped away.

Boffy barked at the chickens, who ignored him. He increased the volume.

'I need a drink,' sighed Hamish.

'We all do,' said Georgie.

Seamus pulled up, music blaring from the van's speakers.

'You're all looking very glum. Tell you what though, I've got the exact thing. Some shiny new shoes'll cheer you up.' The farrier lugged tools out of the van's back doors with a smile.

'Nah, won't work. You don't do our size,' quipped Hamish.

A glimmer of hope was offered the next day when Fred was called to inform him a report had been received of an unusual black horse in a field out by Polperro. The person who called in, a caravan park owner, stated they'd never seen the horse there before and, knowing of the appeals about Monty, decided to act.

A request was made for someone to head over and check it out immediately. With Tom and Amiyah away at the races with Jump For Joy and Fred up to his eyes in paperwork, Georgie offered to go. Hamish volunteered to join her, leaving an unhappy Clem to hold the fort. Promising to call as soon as they knew anything, Georgie's Peugeot reluctantly agreed to start. She tapped on the steering wheel with impatience while Hamish shut the gates, then folded himself back into the passenger seat. With his long legs, even with the seat right back, his knees were almost around his ears.

While Hamish read out instructions using the map on his phone, Georgie crunched the gears in her anxiety to get there quickly. The country lanes meant adopting a slower pace than she would have liked. She wanted so much to find Monty and put it all behind them.

'If it is Monty, it could all turn out to be an innocent case of mistaken identity. A walker coming across a loose horse and shoving it in the nearest field. My friend did that with a cow once. Said it was ambling along a footpath towards him when he was out for an evening walk, so he opened the gate and put it back in with the other cows. Problem solved,' mused Hamish, as Georgie indicated left into the parking area of the caravan site.

'But how does that explain the horse trailer? What would that be doing out and about in the early hours of the morning?' Georgie locked the car and looked around for signage to the office.

'Hmmm, I see what you're saying. Perhaps he tried to break free, which made them panic and release him. Our horses aren't used to travelling in that kind of old-style trailer with the opening above the ramp. Usually, they're enclosed in the swish bigger horseboxes, which are much smoother. I can imagine that would've been swinging about all over the place and draughty. Brrr!'

Georgie was barely listening as she pushed open the glass panelled door into the office. An automatic buzzer sounded, summoning a lady from out the back. They had obviously interrupted her cleaning, for she carried a bucket filled with dusters, cans of polish and rubber gloves. Georgie apologised and explained who they were and why they were there.

'Not to worry. I've got more staff on at the moment. Coming into our busy tourist time, you see.'

She motioned for them to follow as she set off, speedy in jeans and trainers, along a winding a route through numerous caravans and a meadow pitched with tents, at the bottom of which a post and rail fenced paddock contained grazing horses. From a distance, Georgie strained her eyes trying to work out if it was Monty.

'I noticed, you see, that a different horse was out there. Then my daughter mentioned seeing on Twitter about a missing racehorse, a black one. Well, this horse is black with a white mark here.' She touched the end of her nose.

At the description Georgie felt a surge of possibility. Hamish clearly did also, for he sped up, covering the remaining ground in two huge strides, then climbed up on the bottom rail. Georgie joined him and called over to the horses, a few of whom raised their heads and glanced over.

'They're used to people, living next to a busy holiday park. I doubt they'll come over,' the lady said apologetically.

'There's no need anyway,' Georgie replied heavily. 'I can tell from here that's not our horse.'

For the black horse in the field, although a handsome Irish Draught of about the same height as Monty, was definitely not a thoroughbred.

The walk back to the car seemed to take forever. Hamish had a heated discussion over the phone with Clem about time wasters. Georgie could hear Clem's irritation at Hamish's lack of gratitude for people who were trying to help them. The argument lasted the duration of the drive back to Pennhalow.

24

Over the following weeks, the only positives were Jump For Joy winning his race and Hazel finishing a respectable third in a competitive field at Sandown Park. Despite this Tom returned to Pennhalow in a foul temper each time. Although they were managing to keep their suspicions that Monty had been stolen under wraps, Tom still found himself questioned everywhere by the racing press, keen to run a story on whether the colt would participate in the Derby.

'It's just gossip to them,' he complained fiercely to Georgie in the barn one evening. 'Whereas it's our lives, our business at stake and most importantly the welfare of our horse.'

'We have to get a break soon,' soothed Georgie, pushing Boffy off a feed bag so she could open it. 'We mustn't give up.'

'We've got no leads.' Tom threw the scoop down and picked up the bag Georgie had opened, tipping the contents into the large metal bin. 'Why take him if you don't want anything in return?'

'I don't get it either.' Georgie shut the lid. 'Every other day we get contacted by someone who's seen Monty in a field somewhere. Yesterday he was being used for pony trekking in the Yorkshire Dales and he's not even a pony.'

'There must be a way of finding a clue.' Tom picked up a bucket, absentmindedly spilling some on Boffy's head.

It was ten o'clock that night when fierce knocking on the annexe door woke Georgie from snoozing on the sofa. On the doorstep, Tom's face was manic, his hair messy, what looked to be dried soup on his chin, as if he'd been preoccupied while eating.

'Come with me,' was all he said.

Slipping on trainers, Georgie followed Tom to the manor, then upstairs to a bedroom. Curtains closed; a bedside lamp provided the only light. An electric heater wafted warm air into the room. Sitting on top of a hurriedly thrown back duvet, besides a bowl stained with tomato soup and the remains of a bread roll, was the laptop.

'Since we got the CCTV footage, I've been trying to decipher the writing,' explained Tom, sitting lengthways on the bed. Georgie sat beside him, tucking her hands beneath her thighs, only inches from Tom's jean clad ones. 'See here.'

Georgie unfurled over Tom's legs to get close to the screen. He had enlarged a small square metal sign screwed to the back of the trailer. Georgie could only guess how he'd managed to spot it; you'd need a magnifying glass.

'Pisky Equipment Hire,' she read.

'Exactly. Whoever it was hired the trailer from them.'

'I admit it's quite a find, Tom, but the company's not going to hand over personal information to us.'

'Maybe not, but they will to the investigation.'

'But that'll take ages, won't it? They'd have to request paperwork and, if Pisky Equipment Hire aren't willing to provide it, it could take months to go through the process. The Derby's only weeks away now. It'll be over by then and we'll still have no Monty.'

Tom laid back against the pile of pillows with a sassy grin. Georgie fought the urge to roll on top of him. This was not the moment to declare her desires, besides which Heather was still on the scene.

'I thought the same and that's why we're going to find out for ourselves.'

'We?' Georgie's forefinger swung from herself to Tom and back again.

'Yep. We.'

'How so?'

Tom swept up the laptop and tapped the keys, then turned it so Georgie could see. A webpage was open for Pisky Equipment Hire. A rolling banner was scrolling across the top of the page. Georgie read out the words as they went by: 'We welcome clients old and new to our annual open day. Come along and check out our exciting new buys. We guarantee you won't be disappointed. Cream teas and coffees available. See you there!'

Tom took the laptop back and put it on the bedside table, then took both Georgie's hands in his.

'One of the big problems these days is that people don't listen. They're too busy talking or typing or swiping. But listening is exactly what we're going to do. Who knows what we could find out, especially if the opportunity for a bit of snooping presents itself.'

Hesitant, Georgie wasn't sure it was a sensible or even useful plan, however it was currently their only one. Comforted by Tom's hands encasing hers, she agreed.

'Fabulous. I've got a good feeling about this … but look at the time. I'd better let you go and get some sleep.'

As Tom released Georgie's hands, the thought that she'd rather stay there flashed through her mind but remained unspoken. It was not good, she told herself, to have become so fond of Tom. Once all the drama was over, she would need to get a wider social life. Hankering after the unavailable never ended well.

Saturday afternoon found Georgie sitting in the passenger seat of Tom's Golf, as he drove to Pisky Equipment Hire's base on the outskirts of Cornwall's county town of Truro. They'd made an effort to smarten up from their usual work attire, Tom in a white shirt and black chinos plus a baseball cap, Georgie in smart jeans and a denim jacket. In the footwell a lipstick was rolling against Georgie's booted feet. She bent down to retrieve it, then held it up between thumb and forefinger. A circular sticker on the bottom of the gold casing indicated the colour matched Heather's usual coral pink one.

'What shall I do with this?'

Tom's eyes momentarily glanced over then back to the road. 'Just chuck it somewhere … in the bin, for all I care.'

Sensing a scathing tone beneath his words, Georgie flung the lipstick on the back seat and said no more.

It was a beautiful sunny day, not one Georgie would wish to spend on an industrial estate. She would rather be sitting outside the annexe, enjoying the warmth, than standing about on Pisky Equipment Hire's enormous forecourt. Only a handful of others had arrived so far making it difficult to blend in and Georgie found herself having to feign interest in a yellow digger.

'This one's strong and versatile,' explained the staff member, patting the solid yellow machine, a type of mini crane. 'What sort of jobs did you have in mind for it?'

'Er …'

Tom came to Georgie's rescue. 'Actually, it was more horse trailers that we're seeking today. I believe you hire those out too?'

'We certainly do. There's a good selection located round

the back.' The staff member indicated the hanger-style building which housed the offices.

'Is there a lot of demand for them?' Tom asked.

'Absolutely. We cater for all sorts. Even half day hire. It's a lot cheaper than buying your own if you don't require regular usage. Why don't you take a peek and come back to me with any questions.' Keen to move on to a couple hovering nearby, the staff member turned aside.

'Do you find mostly locals book them?' Georgie asked, trying to sound casual.

'Requests come from all over the place really.'

Having not gushed over the digger, it was clear they were being dismissed.

'Let's go and check them out,' said Tom.

'This is pointless,' Georgie moaned, as they made their way to the trailer storage area. 'We're not going to find out anything. We don't even know the colour of the trailer we're after. It was impossible to tell.'

Less than a minute later, Georgie was proved right. For, all along the perimeter fence, slotted in at angles, were about twenty trailers, all the same style as the one in the CCTV video, all decorated the same and all spotlessly clean.

Georgie raised her hands in a gesture of frustration. 'Marvellous.'

'Ah ha.' Tom winked chirpily. 'Clearly you didn't see what I saw.'

'Please do tell me it's a gigantic neon flashing arrow floating in the sky above the one we want stating "this one".' Georgie couldn't refrain from sarcasm, even though she knew it was unfair. Tom was doing his best.

'You're a bundle of laughs today, Georgie.' Tom placed his hands on Georgie's shoulders and steered her towards the building. 'Door's open. See? They're serving the coffee and cream teas from the staff canteen. Let's snoop.'

Not allowing Georgie time to react, Tom propelled her over the doorstep into a narrow corridor. A handmade sign had been pinned to the wall advising the canteen was on the second floor. They climbed a flight of stairs, then on through a set of double doors to another corridor. From their right came the clink of china and chattering voices. Bathrooms were located directly in front of them.

'Go ahead, I'll catch you up,' said Tom.

Georgie entered a cafeteria whose walls had been decorated with soothing scenes overlaid by motivational quotes. The smell of baking wafted over the scattered square tables, some already occupied. A queue had formed at a long rectangular table against the wall, which was set with large hot water urns, cups, saucers and clingfilm covered plates of scones with pots of jam and cream. They looked delicious. Georgie was drooling as she picked up a tray.

'Psst!' Tom's head poked around the door.

Pretending she hadn't heard him, Georgie placed her tray on the table.

'Georgie.'

Huffing loudly, Georgie turned and mouthed, 'What?'

'I've found something. We need to go the other way.' Tom mimed walking his fingers through the air to demonstrate. 'Follow me.'

Dumping the tray back on the pile with a thump, Georgie joined Tom back out in the corridor.

'This had better be worth leaving those scones for,' she grumbled.

Right at the far end, Tom stopped and tapped the glass sign affixed to the final door before the fire exit. 'Order forms,' he read out to Georgie, pushing down on the doorknob.

The latch clicked; it wasn't locked. They moved forward, bumping into each other.

'Sorry,' muttered Tom. 'You first.'

'No, after you.'

'I insist.'

As they slid through, Tom blew out a breath. Inside resembled more bunker than room. With no windows, it was exceptionally dark. Tom switched on his mobile's torch. Georgie blinked, as he swung the beam around, highlighting a row of four metallic grey towers of drawers.

'Filing cabinets.' Tom tried the nearest one.

The drawers would not budge. It was locked.

Georgie pulled on the drawers of the next three to no avail. 'They're all locked.'

'I've an idea.' Tom patted his pocket, then produced a hoof pick. 'I forgot to put this back before we left. It's been digging in me the whole time.'

While Georgie shone the torch so he could see, Tom inserted the hoof pick and began twisting and thrusting.

Watching, Georgie observed, 'I didn't know you could undo locks in that way.'

'Neither did I. I'm totally winging it.'

'Do you think you could wing it making slightly less noise?'

'Nope.'

Time ticked by with only the sound of metal scraping metal.

'Ah ha.' The cabinet emitted a thunk. 'Georgie, you take the top two and I'll search the bottom two.'

Inserting her fingers into the plastic groove on the top drawer's edge, Georgie drew it towards her. It rolled out gently on the runners. Crouched below, Tom couldn't get the bottom drawer to open.

'I've come across these before. You can only open one drawer at a time,' Georgie told him.

Tom refrained from tugging further on the bottom drawer and straightened up. 'What have you got?'

A row of hanging files were revealed, each labelled with a handwritten tab.

'These are months,' observed Georgie. 'Look there's April.'

The suspension file was rammed with sheets of paper, each of which appeared to be an order form.

'I hope they're in date order,' said Tom wryly.

Georgie didn't get the chance to respond for a sudden sound surged up the corridor. Footsteps approached growing progressively louder.

'Uh oh.' Tom shut off the torch.

'What do we do?' Georgie panicked.

Tom held his finger against Georgie's lips as voices sounded close by.

'I thought I heard something from down this end,' said one.

'Can't have,' replied the other. 'I made sure all these doors were secure before we opened up. Only one unlocked is the fire exit.'

Tom manoeuvred Georgie to the corner furthest from the door. Pressed against each other, breathing deeply, they waited.

Georgie felt Tom's mouth against her neck, as he bent his head to whisper. 'If they come in here, we'll have to pretend we sneaked in for a quickie. They'd be too embarrassed to chastise us. You might need to fluff your hair and undo a button though.'

'What? A likely story. No one would feel the urge to do that at a farm equipment open day!' Georgie hissed back.

'Maybe we're in the can't-keep-our-hands-off-each-other phase. We couldn't help ourselves. Overcome with lust amongst the tractors.'

Georgie couldn't contain it; she snorted a suppressed laugh. 'Could be the title of a budget romantic film.'

'Shush,' warned Tom.

The door was opened. A sliver of light beamed into the room. In the shadows, Georgie and Tom remained frozen as freshly carved ice statues.

'Must have missed this one out,' the voice said as it shut the door again. 'I haven't got the key with me. I'll have to go get it.'

As soon as the coast was clear, Georgie and Tom raced away, taking the stairs two at a time in their haste.

Once safely back in the car, Tom whooped with relief. 'Woo wee. Close call.'

'Too close,' agreed Georgie. 'My heart's still racing so fast my smart watch thinks I'm doing a workout.'

She wouldn't admit, even to herself, this was mostly due to her being briefly so intimately close to Tom that his aftershave was infused on her shirt.

25

Georgie's mood became withdrawn and sullen. After such a promising start, she felt as if nothing good would happen again. The limitless possibilities of the future had fizzled before her eyes. Pisky Equipment Hire weren't advertising any further open days and without one they could hardly go back and break into the hangar, when the bunker room of filing cabinets was bound to be secure again. It had clearly been mistakenly left open.

Everything was out of sync, Georgie mused, as a chunk of digestive biscuit she had been dunking broke off and sank into her tea, becoming a mushy mess at the bottom of the mug. Monty was lost, possibly forever. Any participation in the Derby now looked a non-starter. With no horse there could be no race and no chance to prove herself. Georgie was also aware she'd allowed herself to grow too fond of Tom, developing a full-blown crush which couldn't be sated. To top it off, Sam and Abi had just announced their engagement in a flurry of publicity. The front page of the day's edition of the *Racing Life* contained a colour photo of the pair cooing over a whooper of a diamond ring.

'Hope she remembers to remove that before she weighs out, otherwise she'll be putting up overweight every time,' said Hamish, examining the paper during mid-morning break. 'The stone's almost as big as her head.'

'Let's see,' said Amiyah.

Hamish held the paper up for inspection.

'Never mind those two posers, what's that about Brewster?' asked Clem, pointing to the photo opposite of a broad-shouldered man with grey hair and a moustache, snapped in a serious pose, binoculars at the ready. 'Give us it here.'

Whisking it out of her reach, Hamish asked, 'This bit, under the headline "Cat in Pole position"?' He speed read the article, eyes darting to and fro. 'He's going on about how unbeatable Polecat is. Says there's no point anyone else turning up at Epsom because the Derby's effectively theirs already. One way to keep the competition at bay, I guess. He's shrewd.'

'Or overconfident,' suggested Amiyah.

'More like arrogant,' said Georgie. 'Anyway, with us gone, one less for him to worry about beating.'

'Who says we're gone?' asked Tom sharply. 'Dad spends nearly all day every day making calls and chasing updates. He's tenacious. I know he won't stop until Monty is found.'

'If only we had a motive … you know, some hint as to why whoever snatched Monty took him. Without that we're clueless.' Hamish put the *Racing Life* down with a sigh.

'A disgruntled punter?' Amiyah looked to the others for a reaction to her theory. 'Lost money on a race and wanted revenge.'

'Unlikely.' Tom instantly dismissed the idea. 'Yeah, you might get a mouthful from a person who's had a losing bet on one of your horses the next time you're at the races. But to cook up an elaborate kidnap plot, commit all that time and expense, no. They'd vent their frustration in other, easier ways.'

'Could be to do with an ante-post bet,' suggested Georgie. 'A wager to win a fortune. Whoever stood to lose if Monty wins might want him gone.'

'Nah, can't see it myself.' Hamish looked unconvinced. 'No one would bet on Monty at this stage. If they did, they'd have more money than sense and wouldn't be bothered about losing it. He's an unknown inexperienced colt who's likely to boil over before he reaches the start.'

'He could have been taken abroad by now,' worried Clem. 'Then we'll never find him.'

'Again, unlikely.' Tom vigorously disagreed. 'For what purpose? That's our missing link.'

'Missing horse. Missing link. Anyone sensing a theme here?' Hamish grumbled. 'I was looking forward to the Derby. I've never been to Epsom before.'

Clem bristled. 'Fred promised me I was taking Monty, seeing as he prefers me to you.'

Quietly Georgie left the tack room and the arguing behind, seeking peace in the barn. A roosting chicken squatted on a bale above her head, clucking occasionally, as she untangled nets and stuffed them full of hay. They could debate until doomsday. If the answers were there, they would have found them. It was a mystery and an unsolvable one at that, no matter what Tom might say. As if summoned by her thoughts, his voice drifted in from the open doorway.

'You all right?'

Georgie carried on working as she replied. 'Fine. All good.'

'This news about Sam. It can't be easy for you. Another blow at a time when you need a break. Plus, I've never seen anyone use haynets as punchbags before.'

Pausing, Georgie sat back on her knees. 'Better out than in

and all that. Clem and Hamish's squabbling gets tiresome sometimes.'

'I'm with you on that.' Tom sat on the bale below the chicken, who clucked a warning.

'I very much doubt he'll marry her,' said Georgie. 'He's not the type. Mostly it's all for show.'

'He should have appreciated you more.'

'We've all been guilty of that. It's human nature, isn't it? The value of someone only becomes apparent once they're gone. Good luck to them though … right, I'm all done.'

Georgie had one foot outside the barn before Tom spoke again.

'There's a Thai restaurant in Bodmin which recently reopened with new owners. I thought I'd check it out later. Fancy joining me?'

Georgie didn't need to consider for long, it beat a Saturday evening of sulking in the annexe. 'Sounds good. Thanks.'

To cheer herself up, Georgie decided on a glamorous look for the meal out. As she checked out the black scoop necked dress and suede knee high boots in a full-length mirror, it occurred to her she didn't know the dress code for the evening and didn't care. If the others were all in jeans, it wouldn't bother her.

Tom was waiting by his Golf.

'Are the others meeting us there?' Georgie asked, as they set off.

'The others? Argh, these gates are fast becoming the bane of my life. I told dad we should've got remote control ones.' Tom jumped out the car, leaving the door open, the warning alert beeping continuously.

Watching him deal with the gates, while being careful to keep his smart blazer and chinos clean, Georgie smiled. By the time he got back in the car, he seemed to have forgotten Georgie's question. She didn't mind. A relaxing night out was required and whoever was there, they'd all have a good time.

The Thai was a small candle-lit restaurant. Georgie and Tom were shown to an intimate table for two, tucked in a corner.

'Oh, I thought this was a team night out,' Georgie commented as she placed the napkin over her lap.

Tom's face turned pensive. 'None of them could make it. They all had plans already. You don't mind, do you?'

'No, of course not. Does Heather though? I would've thought she'd want to be here.'

Tom fiddled with the menu, guzzled some water and knocked over a vase containing a single dried flower before replying. 'She's, um, we're not together anymore.'

Georgie arranged her face accordingly. 'I'm sorry. I just assumed …'

'We'll keep in contact as friends. We do go way back but it turns out all we had in common were our school days and you can only reminisce about them so many times. When Heather began telling me the same Sports Day story for the third time, I realised we were going around in circles. Our current lives aren't compatible.'

'In what way?' Georgie asked intrigued, as she'd always sensed Heather was keen on Tom.

'Heather's not a fan of horses … or sheep … or cows. Plus, she's frightened of donkeys since she was chased by one as a child. She wanted me to stay at hers all the time, whereas I have a commitment to Pennhalow. We're a pair. One doesn't come without the other. You know the demands of looking after animals. They must come before everything else. They're reliant on you. This is my life, it's not exchangeable.'

'I totally understand. It's probably why most of my relationships have been with others involved in the sport.'

'Exactly. Dad and I have always had an understanding that I'll take over eventually. Heather wasn't flexible on that. She'll be OK though. Francois went to the reunion she organised and said she's back in contact with another old school chum.'

'How about we just have a nice evening with no talk of ex-partners,' proposed Georgie.

Tom raised his glass. 'Cheers to that.'

Stuffed full of delicious food, there was a debate about whether to have dessert. Deciding they couldn't resist, they ordered. While they waited, Georgie showed Tom some of the photos on her phone from her time at Beech Tree. It was like reviewing someone else's life. Georgie could scarcely believe it had been ten years of hers. The good times, the bad times, numerous colleagues who'd been and gone, various horses she'd become attached to, then bid farewell as their owners moved them on to other trainers or retired them to pastures new.

'I look awfully young in some of these.' Georgie laughed, flipping through the album. 'Yikes, my hairstyles … did I not possess a mirror?'

'Give us a look,' begged Tom, taking the phone while Georgie cringed. 'This one's the worst … or best, depending on how you look at it.'

Georgie spluttered on her drink. 'No, the next one beats it by miles.'

Georgie sparkled at the memories the photos evoked: one a shot of Georgie cuddling Molly's Mermaid, one of her all-time favourites, the other a group of staff with their arms around each other's waists, waggling their left legs in the air, Georgie in the middle of the row. She could no longer recollect why they'd adopted that pose, except that they'd been in hysterics about it at the time.

'Did you cut your own hair with clippers while using a

washing up bowl as a template?' Tom had the sense to duck out the way of the scrunched-up napkin Georgie hurled at him.

Amid a good-natured debate about it, the attendant brought their puddings, placing them on the mats.

'We require another opinion,' declared a rather drunk Georgie, turning to the attendant. 'Please may we have yours? Which hairstyle is the ghastliest?'

'Whichever one of us is the loser pays the bill,' Tom advised, holding up the phone for examination, sliding between photos for comparison.

'I can't choose. You'll have to go halves,' said the attendant tactfully, preparing to give back the phone, then, 'How funny. Well, they say it's a small world.'

Georgie and Tom shared a bewildered glance.

The attendant placed the phone on the table, indicating the group photo. 'I recognise this one.'

Georgie half rose from her chair, leaning over so she could see the screen. 'That was taken years ago though and not locally.'

'That's as maybe but this person was here recently. I remember vividly because it was late and we were just about to close. I was literally locking the door, when they burst through in a state. Got stuck in the car park round the back.'

'Yeah, but how can you be sure it's definitely the same person as in the photo?' asked Tom doubtfully.

'We went to assist. They'd got lost and were in a hurry. Tried to turn round in the road and reversed a horse trailer under the barrier, got it wedged. Hadn't realised the height restriction. It wasn't their trailer, you see, they weren't used to it. Had only hired it for a day or two. By some miracle we managed to work it free.'

'Yet it can't be …' Georgie tailed off.

'But that's —' said Tom.

'Yes, that's —' echoed Georgie.

'Briggsy.' They finished each other's sentence.

As Tom drove back to Pennhalow, Georgie sobered up rapidly. Neither said a word, yet the spectre of the unspoken permeated the car uncomfortably. Georgie glanced in the wing mirror, half expecting the face of the proverbial elephant squished into the back seat, to be looking back at her. A barrier lay between them, an invisible trunk unrolled. Such an enjoyable evening, which had been bordering on romantic at times, had nosedived, along with their moods.

Stepping out the car, Tom suggested, 'You'd better come in. I need a drink.'

He led Georgie not to the kitchen, but the library. Unbidden, Georgie sat in one of the creased leather armchairs, positioned either side of the table containing the gramophone, waiting while Tom opened a cabinet and poured whisky into two glasses. He gave one to Georgie, the cut glass crystal cool in her clammy hands. The smell made her queasy. She didn't want any more alcohol.

'It's a coincidence,' said Tom, dropping into the chair opposite in a puff of dust, 'and nothing more. Briggsy's one of my oldest friends. Monty's disappearance will be nothing to do with him.'

'But we ought to ask him, just the same,' Georgie retaliated. 'You have to admit it's a bizarre story.'

'The attendant is mistaken. You can't tell anything from a small photo on a phone screen. Purportedly, he only saw Briggsy the once, it was night. He would have been focused on solving the problem and getting home, probably tired after a shift at the restaurant. We leave this here.'

Georgie traced the swirls on the frayed paisley rug with her eyes, trying to stay calm. She understood Tom's desire to stand up for his friend but if he was so convinced there was an innocuous explanation, there was no reason not to ask about it. Beneath the tapered light shade, a bulb went out with a pop. At once, all the other lights followed suit, leaving only the moon shining through the slats of the window shutters.

'It's tripped the fuse box,' sighed Tom. 'And it's in the cellar.'

'We should follow it up.' Georgie drummed fingers into the arm of the chair to emphasise her point.

'Yeah, I'll go flip the switch back.'

'That wasn't what I meant. I was referring to there being no explanation I can come up with for Briggsy driving a trailer down here.'

'Says who? He could've been out on Beech Tree business.'

'Damien's Bert's regular horsebox driver.'

'Perhaps Damien was required elsewhere.'

'There are no racecourses in Cornwall, Tom.' Riled, Georgie placed the glass on the table and stood. 'I know Briggsy's your friend, but Monty's my horse and I'm not prepared to leave any stone unturned in my efforts to find him.'

Tom reacted with anger, leaping out the chair to square up to Georgie. 'No,' he shouted, 'you forget, Monty's our horse, a Pengelly horse. Not yours. You are not to accuse one of my friends of stealing. I won't allow you.'

'Allow me! You won't allow me!' Georgie was incredulous. 'Uh-uh, you can't do that. Mates or not, Briggsy needs to explain what he was doing.'

'It wasn't Briggsy.' Tom walked out the room with such force, the books on the shelves shook, causing one to fall to the floor, pages flopping open. 'It's mistaken identity.'

'You're putting feelings ahead of what could be facts.' Georgie stepped over the book, hurrying after him. 'And for Monty's sake we need to know which is which.'

Tom stopped so suddenly in the hall, Georgie ran into the back of him. He didn't flinch. Instead, he pulled open the doors of a cabinet, then turned, gripping a powerful torch. Once switched on, they stood exposed in the spotlight, Georgie torn between stubbornness and subordination. Tom gave her no choice.

'You should go, Georgie.'

26

Georgie fled back to the annexe, hands shaking with anger and upset. She had to hold her elbow steady to get the key in the lock. Once inside, she unzipped her boots and chucked them on the sofa, then gave the terracotta pot Sam had given her a kicking. As her toes crunched, she yelped in pain, hopping on one foot. It hurt so much she swapped over, with little difference, they both hurt equally. Though she knew she ought to go to bed, fired up with adrenaline there was little chance of sleep. Somehow, she had to persuade Tom to speak to Briggsy, to ease the disquiet in her gut. Briggsy's personality had always hinted at depths unknown. Georgie put it down to him being a private person, who never gave much away. She needed reassurance and could only get that from finishing her conversation with Tom, whether he liked it or not.

Boot slippers were all she could stand on her feet, their soft soles soundless as she re-entered the manor.

'Tom?' she called.

The house was in darkness. Deciding Tom must still be in the cellar, which was likely to be off the kitchen, Georgie shuffled her way there, the weak beam of her travel torch not much use. A draft funnelled through the room from a narrow door propped open, causing the dangling saucepans to chime. Its wooden arched entrance blended so neatly with the cupboards; Georgie had never noticed it before.

The drop to the first stair was deep, gaping like the black hole of a mine entrance, causing Georgie to waver. She could wait. Perhaps get the kettle filled and two mugs ready for when the electricity was back on. They could have a civilised chat over a cup of tea. She waited. Time passed. Tom didn't appear. Georgie reconsidered. It could do no harm to check it out to the bottom of the stairs and no further. There was hardly likely to be any ghostly smugglers lurking down there. Wishing she hadn't had that thought, Georgie took a big step, careful to place her foot lightly.

'Who'd put a fuse box down here?' she muttered, brushing away a spider in mid-descent before it could land in her hair.

Descending timidly down the steep flight, keen to meet Tom coming the other way, Georgie was met at the bottom by a tunnel, not the vast expanse of open area she was expecting. It ran both ways. She peered up it. It looked stable. Solid walls curving up in an arch. She could stand upright although the roof brushed her head. Tentatively she took a few strides, reassuring herself she could turn back any time.

The tunnel curved gently, then continued in what could be a straight line, although it was hard to be sure. Georgie heard whistling, reverberating, impossible to tell from which direction.

'Is that you, Tom?' she bawled, immediately berating herself, for of course it was Tom. No one else would be down here. Would they?

The whistling ceased. It seemed as if the silence that followed was listening. Georgie was compelled to run, backwards. She knew she wasn't alone, she had to go. Afraid she might run towards rather than from whatever it was, she dithered. A fizzing noise filled her ears and then yellow light sprung from nowhere. Georgie screamed. Seconds later, footsteps came running from beyond and Tom, his face haggard, approached.

'What are you doing coming down here, Georgie? I could have locked you in, you fool.'

'I came to find you.' Georgie was gasping.

'I was in the cellar.'

'But I'm in the cellar and you weren't here.'

'If you'd gone left instead of right, you'd be in the cellar. These are the old tunnels. We never go down these.' Tom pointed to the light concealed in the roof. 'I'm amazed that bulb works at —'

Before he could finish the light went off again. Georgie and Tom could no longer see each other.

'That fuse box is testing my patience tonight.' Tom shifted, unintentionally stepping on top of Georgie's tender feet.

'Ouch,' Georgie wailed, the sound exaggerated as it bounced off the walls.

'I need to say something.' Tom moved closer to Georgie.

'I think you've just broken my feet. Can it wait?'

'No, it cannot.' Tom's voice was gruff.

Georgie became aware of Tom standing very close. Despite not seeing his face, his intention was clear. Georgie could feel the intensity. The easy-going vibe had vanished. Georgie took a step and stumbled, now their chests were touching. The bulb blinked a couple of times, then lit up. Georgie quivered at the look which passed between them; loaded with a recognition they both wanted the same thing. They gave themselves over to the moment.

They kissed with the fervour of feelings long restrained, wrapped in each other's arms. Georgie felt like a smuggler who'd finally gotten their hands on the treasure and wasn't letting go. She didn't know if it was the start of something or a passionate spur of the moment act, neither did she care. It felt right, it felt good and she wanted it more than anything.

They broke apart and grinned at each other shyly.

'You've no idea how long I've wanted to do that,' Tom whispered tenderly. 'I've felt this way for a long time.'

His hands caressed Georgie's hair. She moved hers down his arms, feeling the muscles beneath the softness of his skin. They kissed again, then Tom led Georgie back up to the kitchen.

Pressing her up against the closed door of the cellar, the smooth chilled wood against her back, Tom apologised. 'I'm sorry I got so upset earlier. It's wrong of me to take it out on other people, especially you. You're right. We do need to ask Briggsy. I'll call him in the morning.'

Georgie smiled coyly. 'We've got plenty of time until then.'

Sunday was a day off for both Georgie and Tom. They luxuriated in a lie in, followed by a leisurely breakfast. While Tom cooked scrambled eggs, Georgie sat at the kitchen table examining her multicoloured toes, bruises spawning in a variety of shapes and shades.

'On the positive side, they're not broken,' she said, as Tom placed her plate next to a mug of coffee. 'Last time they were this bad they'd been trampled on by a horse.'

Squeezing ketchup on his eggs, Tom grinned. 'That's what you get if you go exploring in slippers.'

'Anything else hurt my feet.' Georgie changed the subject. 'Do you have a plan for Briggsy?'

'I'll keep it casual. Say I'd heard tell he was in the area and was disappointed he didn't call me up to meet for a drink. We haven't seen each other for ages. If he asks how I know I'll tell the truth minus mentioning the trailer.'

Georgie found she couldn't settle. She loaded the

dishwasher, wiped the kitchen surfaces and hoovered the entire ground floor, much to Tom's embarrassment.

'Been meaning to do that properly for years,' he admitted, as she emptied the overflowing vacuum cleaner bin for the third time, before opening all the windows.

The air was fresh and warm, scented with flowers and filled with the sound of contented cows lowing, along with the odd bark as Boffy played on the lawn.

Finally, it was midday and Tom decided the best time to catch Briggsy after morning stables. Sitting on the clean sofa, Georgie tucked her legs up and chewed her fingers, while Tom called. To her surprise, within seconds he disconnected.

'Did you allow enough time for him to answer?'

'No need to. The number's unobtainable.' Tom placed his phone on a cushion.

Georgie scooped it up, comparing the number she had saved in her phone with the one Tom had called. They matched.

'You're sure Briggsy didn't message you with a new number at some point?'

'I'd have saved it straight away.' Tom scratched his head, unsure what to do next. 'Can you call the yard and ask for him?'

Georgie scrunched up her face. 'I'd get Petra though. She's the gatekeeper. I won't get to Briggsy unless I can get by her.'

'That's no good then.'

The bell at the front door rang. While Tom answered it, Georgie considered their options until Francois bounded into the room.

'Came to see how you're doing and if there's any update on The Misfit … and to scrounge some lunch … wait a minute, what's changed?' Francois took a breath and looked around. 'This place is spotless.'

'Thanks to Georgie and you're out of luck, mate. My

cupboard is empty. Georgie ate the last of my eggs and bread this morning.'

'Dropped by bright and early for breakfast, eh?' Francois sniggered. 'All down to the Barrels then, my treat.'

Over roast dinners, Tom casually checked with Francois what number he had for Briggsy. It turned out to be the same one.

'Can't get through on that,' Tom told Francois.

'Knowing Briggsy he's overlooked letting us know he's swapped numbers, then he'll berate us for not messaging him … I'll get the drinks in.'

'I'll go up to Surrey,' Georgie told Tom while Francois was up at the bar. 'Next week. I'm owed a few days off.'

Tom's face stiffened with unconcealed alarm, which he managed to shift into a neutral expression. 'I don't know.'

'Not for confrontation. Just to drop by socially.' Sensing Tom's reservation, Georgie left it a moment, finishing a Yorkshire pudding. 'It's the best way.'

Georgie spent long portions of the midweek journey back to Epsom sitting in traffic with the myriad of tourists heading to and from the West Country. Cornwall's wintertime hibernation had ended with an influx of holidaymakers heading for beaches, surfing, attractions and coastal paths.

Having expected her next visit to Rose Cottage to be in the heady days leading up to the Derby, it was somewhat of a let-down to be once again snaking in and out of the potholes beside the golf course in the current situation. Certain they would be discounting Briggsy of any involvement and keen not to destroy a friendship, Tom sent messages of encouragement, tinged with caution. Georgie understood Tom's reticence. To avoid false accusations, they'd made a pact to keep their investigations to themselves.

Dawn was breaking on a misty morning across Epsom Downs when Georgie pulled into her usual parking spot at

Beech Tree Stables the next day. Everything appeared unchanged and familiar, even Luna as she bounded over, threading her sinewy body through Georgie's legs. At the yard, time had stood still, making it feel alien to be back. Georgie no longer belonged. She wondered if she ever had, if any part of the insecure, angry Georgie who'd left here all that time ago, still lingered. Although precious, the past could not be morphed into the present or the future. It was as unreachable as the former version of herself, the one who'd been laughing in the photo which triggered her return. The one who had transformed into someone else.

Thudding hooves from the paddock adjacent to the car park broke into Georgie's thoughts. A glossy chestnut galloped over the lush grass, squealing and plunging, tail in the air, to an emergency stop against the railing. Head thrust outwards, the thoroughbred neighed shrilly, striking the turf, seeking attention. Georgie recognised him immediately. The speck of white between his eyes, as though he had been dabbed by the tip of a paintbrush, then the artist changed their mind and painted one white sock on his off foreleg instead. He was a near perfect canvas.

'Hello, Golden Goose.'

Georgie held her palm out flat. Goosey flapped his lips over her skin, his whiskers tickling.

A Jeep pulled up, blocking Georgie's Peugeot in. Nabil exited, carrying cans of fizzy drink and chocolate bars.

'Replenishing the breaktime tuck shop with healthy snacks then,' Georgie called over teasingly.

'You know us so well.' Nabil approached. 'Here, have a Mars bar.'

'It's a tad early for me, thanks.'

Nabil feigned shock. 'Ah, Georgie, you've changed. You always beat everyone to the chocolate stash.'

'I still could, if I'd done any work to get an appetite.'

'That can be arranged. I've taken over mucking out your horses, as well as mine. Feel free to lend a hand.' Goosey barged Nabil's arm with his nose. 'None for you lad. Not for horses, these.'

Georgie stroked Goosey's neck. 'He looks incredible. How come he's back so soon?'

'Turned out the injury was superficial. It healed in next to no time. Now he's jumping out his skin. Bert says we only need keep him ticking over for Cheltenham next year.' Nabil dropped a can of lemonade. As he crouched down to pick it up, he added, 'Guess we're all a little guilty of overreacting that day.'

'Yeah, I guess we are.'

Each was spared the discomfort of the moment by the arrival of Bert's daughter, Jess.

'Well, well, if it isn't Georgie Wright, back with a twinkle in her eyes.' Jess threw her arms around Georgie in welcome. 'What brings you here? I thought you were done with us.'

Dredging up what she hoped would be an award-winning performance, Georgie nonchalantly explained she was in the area for a few days and felt the urge to drop in and greet her former chums. They seemed to accept it, so she plunged on with the big question.

'Is Briggsy around? I'd love to say hi while I'm here.'

Nabil thrust the supplies at Jess and said urgently, 'I'll move my car.'

With eyebrows raised, Georgie looked to Jess with a shrug.

'Briggsy's not here. He requested a sabbatical some time ago, on the basis of exhaustion. Said he needed an extended break. As he's been a loyal team member for years it was authorised, although no one's heard from him since. We hope he's OK.' Jess stroked Goosey's cheek distractedly. 'Can I pass on a message when he eventually makes contact? It'll be a while yet, as he's not due back for months.'

Georgie started. 'No need, thanks. As I say, I'm only passing by.'

Moments later, Georgie reversed out her spot to allow Nabil to park his Jeep in her place, although waving and smiling, her mind whirred. On the one hand, Briggsy could have disconnected his phone to get away from it all completely but why not keep some contact going? It sounded as though he intended to return to Beech Tree in due course. Surely the odd message to keep in touch with your employer was a sensible idea, especially when your job was being kept open for you. For the time being, where on earth was Beech Tree's Head Lad hiding?

27

Georgie and Tom kept the mysterious appearance then disappearance of Briggsy to themselves until after the weekend, when carrying two secrets became too big a burden.

After evening stables, while the team were zipping up bodywarmers against the evening temperature drop and debating whose turn it was to take Guido racing the next day, Tom mentioned that he and Georgie were seeing each other. Although early days, both knew they were serious about making it work and it was only a matter of time before one of the others twigged or stumbled across them snogging in the barn.

Clem clapped her hands ecstatically. 'I knew it,' she proclaimed. 'I sensed the spark from the off. I thought to myself, it's only a matter of when.'

'How come Psychic Clem can't locate our missing horse as well then?' asked Hamish.

Clem raised herself, preparing to vent, as the surrounding faces which had been beaming only moments earlier, fell. None of them needed tarot cards or a crystal ball to predict a fierce argument was brewing. Tom clasped Georgie's hand

and pulled her out the door, stating, 'We need to catch dad before he leaves.'

They ran full pelt over to the farm, where Fred was holding the driver's door open for Boffy to hop inside the pick-up truck.

'Dad … wait,' Tom panted.

Misunderstanding Tom's purpose, Fred turned with a wide smile. 'It's lovely news, son. Angie'll be delighted, as am I.'

'Oh … yeah … it's … thrilled —'

Georgie butted in. 'We have some information, other information, we wanted to share with you.'

'It's more of an inkling than actual information, dad, but we need your advice.'

'Let's be hearing it.' Fred wandered into the barn. Georgie and Tom followed, while Boffy vacated the truck and joined them.

They sat on upturned buckets and Fred listened attentively as Tom relayed the situation. A field mouse skipped out from under a pile of swept up muck, before diving straight back in again at the sight of Boffy, who barked and was shushed by Tom. As Fred digested all he had been told, Georgie listened to the sounds of a cuckoo calling over on the moor and the squeak of Clem's bike as she pedalled homeward, fuelled by her clash with Hamish.

'I don't know,' Fred said. 'Briggsy's always been a dependable bloke. I can't see any logical reason for him to be involved at all. Being a Head Lad's hard work in a tough industry and he's not the youngster he was. It's highly likely he would want a rest. I would if I did his job.'

'I accept that, yet we can't get in touch with him.' Tom reached out, brushing the tips of Georgie's fingers reassuringly.

'His phone could be broken. You know, in years gone by, you couldn't call someone unless they were at home by their landline.' Fred wagged his head in consternation. 'Such high expectations these days that people are reachable every minute of the day.'

Amiyah dropped by, rucksack on her shoulders, long hair swinging in a ponytail, to inform them she'd locked up and shut the chickens in overnight.

As she bid them farewell, Fred thanked her, then stood and stretched his back, hands on his sides. 'Briggsy could even be away. Last I heard his folks moved to Portugal. I haven't met them since the final parents' evening at your school, Tom, but they're definitely not in Lanivet anymore.'

'They've not lived there for years.' Tom got up and stacked his bucket in Fred's, then added Georgie's. As she handed it to him, he sighed, 'We tried, Georgie. Gave it our best shot.'

Georgie moved off to retrieve Boffy, who was sniffing at the gate to the field.

'Give me time to think it through,' Fred said. 'I'll mull over —'

Georgie stopped mid stride. 'Wait … that's it … mull.'

She picked up Boffy and carried him over to the pick-up truck, passing him through to Fred, who was agitating to get home in time for his dinner or face the wrath of Angie.

Then Georgie and Tom walked up the lawn, pausing at the fountain. A robin was perched on the knight's helmet. Inside the basin was dry, the rain having stayed away for days.

'Briggsy told me he spent his early years in Mullion,' she said.

Tom sat on the fountain's rim and patted beside him. Georgie sat too. The sun was setting. Puffs of cloud decorated the sky, below which the sheep grazed, coats glowing in the pretty orange light.

'He may well have done before he moved Bodmin way. But, Georgie, Mullion's a village down on the Lizard Peninsula. We can't go knocking on every door asking whether

Briggsy's there. I know it's not what we want, but we have to be patient and let the investigation take its course.'

Georgie laid her head on Tom's shoulder, while a flock of crows flew noisily over, heading for their overnight lodgings. She knew Tom would feel some relief at dropping the whole tenuous link to Briggsy. He had never been comfortable with it and fully expected his friend to return from Portugal and confirm he'd never been near the Thai restaurant in Bodmin. If she wanted to continue sleuthing, Georgie would have to do it alone.

Georgie's next day off was a warm and sunny May Day Bank Holiday and she was alone. Tom and Hamish were away on an overnight trip to Ripon Racecourse, where Rosey Posey was entered for her inaugural run. Ensuring no one was around to ask after her plans, Georgie put on sunglasses and, leaving the annexe, hurried to her car.

It being the best beach weather of the year so far, the roads were busy and it took longer than the predicted hour and a half until Georgie arrived at her destination, a peninsula which formed the most Southerly part of Britain, known as the Lizard. Stopping to allow a pair of horse-riders to cross the road as she drove through the parade of shops and pubs that made up the village of Mullion, Georgie thought how charming the area was. Passing a church and picturesque buildings, the road led onwards to farmland. With no clear route, Georgie found space to park near an ancient walled harbour at Mullion Cove.

After the time spent confined in a hot car, the breeze catching wisps of Georgie's hair refreshed her skin as she walked out on the sea wall, overlooking the water. The tide was in. Gulls circled the jagged offshore rocks. A sailing yacht was anchored outside the protection of the harbour. Inside the sturdy walls, little fishing boats rolled on the gentle swell. A spaniel yapped as it played in the shallows, paddling alongside its ice cream eating owner. Flummoxed, Georgie didn't know where to start. When Tom had mentioned a village, she had envisioned a handful of cottages and a pub, easy to check out in a short time. Instead, she was in a sprawling landscape of numerous fields, farms and outbuildings.

Taking some steps up to a hotel, she joined the coastal path. With nothing else to guide her, she walked and walked, responding politely to the greetings of passers-by. To her left, the sea, to her right fields of farmland, some containing livestock, none the friendly neigh of a horse.

Stopping at a café for lunch, Georgie reached the conclusion that Tom had been correct. It was a fruitless search. She could march all the way to Land's End if she kept going long enough, spend days exploring, yet achieve nothing more than getting sunburnt on an exposed headland. Already her forearms had turned light pink. She might even have misheard Briggsy. The map showed a place up the coast called Polurrian. There were probably many others with similar sounding names, scattered over the entire county. Requesting the bill, Georgie took the decision to return to Pennhalow and say nothing of her visit. It would only lead to an I-told-you-so moment.

Driving a different route out, passing detached houses set back from the lane, their boundaries made of trimmed high hedges and tall stone walls, she daydreamed about relaxing in a vast garden. Pictured herself sipping a Pimm's under shady trees, while overlooking the sea, wearing a floaty dress and a straw hat with a matching-coloured band. The property names conjured images of garden parties and evenings spent socialising with friends amongst sparkling solar lanterns. Maybe she could persuade Tom and Fred that they could hold something on the lawn at Pennhalow Manor. They could have a marquee similar to Clem's wedding reception, bring everyone together again, ease the tensions of the weeks gone by. She read the names aloud: 'Cove Cottage, Tree Tops, ooh, looks a nice villa that one, Hillside House, very swish, Rambler's Retreat, stylish, Frogmore Farm, Farquharson Lodge ...'

Georgie slammed the brakes so hard it was fortunate the lane was quiet with no one behind, for they would have run into the back of her. A memory had flooded into her brain, hazy but with enough clarity for Georgie to remember a break time at Beech Tree Stables when the discussion had turned to middle names. Everyone had been divulging theirs. Mostly they were average names, such as Georgie's was Jayne, but they'd all had fun at Briggsy's expense, for his was unusual and unexpected. He'd told them in all seriousness that it was Farquharson, after his grandfather, who had also named his house after himself, a house Briggsy visited often as a child. Days of merciless ribbing had followed, to the point where Georgie suspected Briggsy must have regretted not making up an alternative, more common name such as Dave.

Pulling over to the kerb, Georgie closed her eyes. She could picture them all as though watching a film, slouching in various chairs, booted feet resting over the arms, chipped mugs in hand, snacks half-eaten. Most of the faces were vague now, only a few remained crystal clear in the replay, after all, years had passed. Opening her eyes, the memory vanished, as though at the end of the reel. She returned to staring through a dusty windscreen at a lane with well-maintained verges and a lady walking a Pekinese on a sparkly purple lead past a set of stately gates.

She was being ridiculous. It was a bigger long shot than strapping a bridle and saddle on Jackson and running him in the Derby instead of The Misfit. She ought to start the engine, drive away and stop the absurd notion that Briggsy was some type of horse stealing mastermind. She was desperate to find clues, which was impairing her reasoning. Yet, Georgie knew she wasn't leaving. One hundred percent she was going to give it a go. She meant no harm, intended no damage and if she was in the wrong place, she would simply apologise and leave.

Locking the car, Georgie crossed the road assertively, aware she mustn't appear furtive. Hadn't she read once the best place to hide was in the open … or something along those lines. Despite the presence of an intercom sunk into the mortar, the wooden gates weren't locked. They were too high for Georgie to see over, as she turned the circular handle. The latch lifted and she eased her way through. An expanse of brick paved drive, a stylish country mansion and manicured lawns, with contrasting stripes so symmetrical the gardener must have used a ruler, sprawled before her. A car port housed an Aston Martin convertible, while an electric blue feathered peacock lay beneath a palm tree. Combined with the heat of the sun, it was like passing through a portal to abroad.

'Um, hello,' Georgie used a stage whisper.

The peacock honked and, rising, flared its tail with a rattle.

Georgie moved fast, around the side of the house, following a path of steppingstones, careful to avoid the grass, a sprinkler and the peacock. All the windows were shut, no signs of activity or, to Georgie's relief, dogs. A table and eight chairs were set up on the patio outside French doors. Certain she was not in a place of Briggsy's childhood, for it oozed monied owners, she thought to leave. There could be concealed cameras in one of the numerous palm trees dotted along the border of a lawn which dipped out of sight. If they were linked to mobile phones and she was spotted, she could be questioned any moment. What instinct compelled Georgie to keep going forwards, she could not say. She crested the lawn. On the other side, the ground levelled out and upon it was a block of three stables, a tool shed, a square paddock and an outdoor schooling arena with dressage markers attached to the post and rail fencing. Over one of the stable doors, a black head was observing Georgie. The neigh of greeting was the same one she had heard many times before, the one she missed each morning.

'Monty!'

She ran down the slope, legs buckling. Monty rapped the door with a hoof. In the adjoining stable the dun-coloured head of a Highland pony appeared above a half door with a nameplate reading Tootles. Georgie rubbed Monty's neck, her eyes scanning his body inside the stable. Although the light was dim compared to the brightness outside, the colt appeared to have been well looked after. Georgie performed a jig of joy, then ceased. She could be in danger if found here. She must return to the car at once and inform Fred. Before she could move away, she heard a voice.

'Hello, Georgie.'

28

Georgie recognised the voice even before looking around to face who had spoken. She had heard it most days for years. Worked alongside it, laughed with it, argued with it, cried with it, celebrated with it, poured her heart out to it, even got drunk with it.

'Jess.' Georgie's confusion was immeasurable. 'I … I don't understand.'

Jess Russell appeared dazed, as stunned as Georgie. Her hair was in a single plait. She was wearing jeans, wellies and a sleeveless top. All appeared normal yet was anything but.

'You have to let me explain,' she pleaded.

'Oh, please do. Explain away.' Georgie crossed her arms. 'I'm all ears.'

'Briggsy called me. Told me he'd done something stupid and didn't know what to do. He asked me to meet him. Gave me this address. That was yesterday.'

'And where is he?' Georgie moved her body to form a shield between her former colleague and Monty. Her fingers loitered over the phone in her front pocket.

'I don't know. I've been waiting over an hour. Took me half a day to get here. The traffic …'

'This is my horse. He was taken without permission from the Pengelly's farm weeks ago. Did you know that?' Georgie asked with unrestrained anger.

'No. Georgie, I swear I know nothing about all this. I'm as baffled as you are.'

Warily, Georgie agreed to accompany Jess and take a seat at the patio furniture, where she agreed to give it half an hour. If Briggsy hadn't shown up by then, she was calling Fred to involve him. It turned out they only need wait for fifteen minutes, when a perspiring Briggsy jogged up the path. On spotting Georgie sitting the other end of the table from Jess, it appeared he might be sick. Both Georgie and Jess began bombarding him with questions. To their astonishment, Briggsy broke down.

'I made a mistake,' he wailed. 'Thought if I did this, everything would fall apart for you and you'd return, Georgie. Beg for your job back. I missed you so much. I always —'

'Always what?' asked Jess horrified.

'Always had feelings for Georgie. I never acted on them because … there was Sam, in the way with his good looks and his money and his stellar career.' Briggsy almost spat with disdain.

'So why am I here?' Jess queried. 'This has nothing to do with me. Why have you involved me in this mess you've made?'

'I was going to ask you how to get me out of this mess.' Briggsy pushed his fingers through his hair. 'See if you could figure out a way to return the horse. We've been pals a long time. I knew I could trust you.'

Georgie was finding it difficult to absorb what she was hearing. 'But you never said anything. We barely knew each other socially. Why would you try and destroy my life in this way? I never did anything bad to you.'

'I just wanted you to come back. I couldn't figure out any other way. Tom often told me about the donkey escaping all the time. I knew I could make it appear he was to blame. So, I took the Derby horse but stupidly I relocked the stable door without thinking. I only realised when I got here what I'd done and it was too late and too risky to go back. I never told anyone about this place, Georgie, how did you know?'

Georgie briefly explained, Briggsy and Jess absorbing every word.

Briggsy laughed ironically. 'And I thought this was the safest place to hide. I've never told anyone I inherited it. The only people who ever visit are the caretaker and my niece who keeps her pony here, while I keep it ticking over for my retirement. All I had to do was make up a story about looking after The Misfit for a friend. I called him Figaro.'

Attracted by the commotion, the peacock strutted up to Briggsy, who shooed him off. Affronted he moved to the other end of the patio, head tilted, as though listening.

'But, Briggsy, I don't get it. If you care about someone, don't you want them to be happy?' asked Jess, shifting her chair further away from the curious bird.

'Yes, but you want them to be happy with you, not some egocentric jockey who never cared about anyone else,' Briggsy wailed. 'I watched it all, you know. Yet who cares … I can't deal with this.'

He stomped away, lighting a cigarette. Jess sidled up to Georgie. 'Is there any way you can explain to the Pengelly's about the extenuating circumstances?'

'What circumstances? Briggsy broke into their farm and stole a racehorse, throwing us all into a state of perpetual worry —'

'I get that, I do, but Briggsy's not the first and he certainly won't be the last, to be driven by love into a foolish act. The colt is fine and you heard him say he intended to return the horse.'

'It's not my call, Jess.'

'How about if I promised my father and I will get Briggsy any support he needs? We'll vouch for him. He's not a bad person. He admits he realised the error of his actions almost immediately but was clearly trapped. With hindsight, he moped for weeks after you left. None of us realised what the cause was. We assumed it was linked to him requesting an extended break.'

'He's old enough to know better.' Georgie stopped talking as Briggsy returned from pacing the lawn.

'Georgie, I'm sorry.' Briggsy appeared contrite. 'If only I'd come clean about my feelings rather than arranging for you to come down here. I thought you'd be bored and scurry back to Epsom. I should never have interfered.'

Georgie had heard enough. She stood and pulled out her phone. 'My priority is to let the Pengelly's know their horse is safe and well —'

'Of course he is,' Briggsy cried. 'I love horses. I'd never have hurt him. I knew I'd been an idiot and I meant to return him but by then you'd put all that new security in, so I couldn't.'

'You've been more than an idiot,' said Jess despairingly. 'You should have sent an anonymous note and left the horse somewhere they could collect him. Sorry, Georgie, harsh I know, but Beech Tree is going to lose one of the best Head Lads in the business because of you. My father will be gutted. Briggsy's integral to the place.'

Georgie looked from Briggsy to Jess wondering how she could have misjudged them so badly. Were people really that duplicitous, she thought sadly. Were friends always in disguise, revealing their true colours only when they stood to lose or gain. Ten years she'd worked with Briggsy never once realising how he felt. Did that make her self-absorbed, career obsessed or stupid. She'd always assumed most people viewed her as the plain girl with freckles who spent most of her time in jodhpurs and a Puffa jacket, hay stuck to her hair. Game for a laugh but hardly a knockout. Could you really be in love with someone from afar or was it always lust mistaken for deeper passions? As she stepped away to call Fred, Georgie's head throbbed with it all.

Even over the phone, Fred's reaction was so ferocious it scared the pigeons out of the trees. They flapped away in all directions. Conversation over, Georgie returned to Jess and Briggsy, who were sitting mournfully at the table, ignoring each other.

'Fred's arranging for a horsebox to collect The Misfit as soon as he can get one,' Georgie told Briggsy. 'I've managed to convince him to inform the investigation the horse has been found in good health and we don't wish to take it any further. I cannot, however, speak for Tom who views you as one of his oldest and closest friends.'

With a cry of relief, Jess jumped up and enveloped Georgie in a one-sided hug. 'Thank you.' Then, turning to Briggsy: 'I suggest once you're sorted here you return to Beech Tree and get your head down. No more crazy stunts.'

A few hours after Jess had departed, Georgie opened the gates of Farquharson Lodge to allow the same horsebox which had taken her to Newton Abbot all those months ago onto the drive. She hoped it didn't still smell of damp sheep. Beside the familiar driver, Fred sat ashen faced. He carefully lowered himself from the cab, arms full of protective travelling gear for Monty.

'What a pickle we find ourselves in,' he stated.

'That's an understatement. Here, let me help carry those.'

Together they made their way to the stables.

'I've yet to tell Tom. It'll be difficult for him to accept this has all been caused by a friend.' Fred stood in the stable doorway, allowing Georgie to prepare Monty. 'Where is Briggsy now?'

With Monty's forelegs encased in the thickly padded boots so he resembled an ice hockey goalie, Georgie moved to his hindlegs. Facing away from Fred, her voice was muffled. 'I advised him to keep out the way. My guess is he's hiding in the house somewhere.'

'Probably for the best. I don't want to see him.' Fred pulled the door wide to give Georgie room to lead the colt outside.

Back at the horsebox, a young girl with brunette plaits and a hoodie decorated with a Thelwell cartoon was peeking up the lowered ramp. When she heard Monty's hooves on the bricks, she stepped away.

'Is Figaro leaving today?' she asked Georgie.

'Yes, he's coming home.'

'Tootles will miss him. They enjoyed playing in the field with each other.' She stroked Monty's neck. He prodded her gently with his nose. Georgie could see the orange tip of a carrot in the pocket of her hoodie.

'I'm sure Mon … Figaro … will miss Tootles back.'

'He was going to be my dressage horse. When I'm older, I'm going to the Olympics.' The girl said it with such certainty, Georgie smiled. 'I'll need a horse as big as Figaro then, because Tootles won't grow anymore.'

Georgie led Monty forwards. 'Figaro needs to get back to his owners now. They've been missing him lots. If you keep practising, I know you'll find your perfect partner soon.'

The girl skipped away, leaving Georgie to secure the ramp. She pulled her car keys out the pocket of her jeans. Fred was already in the cab with the window wound down. When she got near enough, the smell of damp sheep hit Georgie's nostrils.

'See you back home,' she said.

Fred nodded. 'Good work, Georgie. Your persistence has paid off.'

'It often does.'

As she closed the gates from the lane, careful to avert her eyes from the windows in case Briggsy was looking out, Georgie sighed. Her delight at having Monty back was levelled out by her sadness at Briggsy's behaviour. She knew she wasn't responsible or to blame. There were no winners in this episode.

By the time she arrived back outside Pennhalow Manor, Georgie's mobile had registered fifteen missed calls from Tom. Clearly Fred had broken the news.

The Misfit's return made the front page of the morning's edition of the *Racing Life*. The article reported the thoroughbred had been looked after properly, having been mistakenly kept by a well-intentioned unnamed person.

'Full steam ahead then,' yawned Hamish, plonking the paper on the tack room floor. 'Fred's kept up all the necessary entries and things. We're Epsom bound in a few weeks.'

'Well, I am,' Clem reminded everyone. 'You and Amiyah will need to stay here to look after the others.'

'I meant the Royal we.' Hamish yawned again, wider this time.

A surly Tom brooded in the corner chair. Georgie knew he was devastated on both counts. That his friend could take such drastic action at all and especially against Pennhalow. It had proved a difficult conversation with Georgie being purposefully vague about Briggsy's motivation, making it more about being short-staffed and desperate, than feelings for her. One day, the former friends may reconnect but for now Tom swore the friendship was over for ever. Time healed most things, though not all.

Fred's head appeared round the doorway with the cheery update that the vet had just departed after declaring Monty in sound health.

'Fitness is our biggest challenge,' Fred directed this at Georgie. 'In the timescale we've got, he needs to do some proper work. I'll join you today.'

While Georgie waited by the gate, relishing the familiar feeling of Monty fidgeting beneath her, Fred heaved himself into the saddle of Jigsaw, the oldest, calmest of the Pennhalow horses.

'I'll leave the fast stuff to you,' he said, lowering his stirrups to cowboy length.

An early morning low-lying mist shrouded the horses' legs. The grey Jigsaw moved ghost-like through the swirls, ignoring Monty, who jogged alongside like an impatient teenager held back by the slower pace of a dawdling grandparent. Georgie smiled fondly at Jigsaw's floppy ears as he plodded on unperturbed.

At a stretch of relatively flat grassland littered with rocky outcrops, Fred turned to Georgie with a nod.

'Give him a good fast canter up to Cador's place there.'

Far away, Georgie could distinguish a stone wall running horizontally across the horizon, on the other side of which the roof of a tractor's cab with its huge wing mirrors was visible chuffing back and forth. She barely touched Monty's sides with her legs. He required no urging as he transitioned from walk straight into canter, strides eating up the ground. Between his tipped ears, Georgie's view of the moor was blurred as it hurtled by. Monty leapt over small piles of rocks. Georgie tried to keep him on a tight rein, not wanting Monty to run flat out. Neck arched the colt bucked in protest. Georgie sat back, arms aching.

Catching sight of the tractor, Monty performed the equine version of an emergency stop, then reared up to full height, hind legs quivering. Georgie leaned forwards, handfuls of mane entangled in her fingers, fearing falling backwards and being crushed.

As Monty's hooves reconnected with the ground, Georgie soothed him. Blowing fiercely, flecks of foam sprouting from his mouth, he chewed the bit furiously, but didn't attempt to bolt.

Fred cantered to them, Jigsaw puffing with the effort of trying to catch up. His eyes appraising, Georgie could tell the cogs of Fred's brain were turning at a million miles an hour.

'Nothing wrong with the fella or his condition. Which leaves us only one obstacle to hurdle.'

'Which is?'

'He's no experience round Epsom racecourse and I know just the person who can help us resolve that.'

As they rode away, both returning Cador's wave of hello, Georgie wondered who that could be.

29

With only weeks to go until the first Saturday in June, the official day for the Derby to take place every year, Georgie focused all her energy on Monty. The colt grew stronger, his muscle definition improved, as did his stamina. Hills were no effort for him. He soared every obstacle in his way. He loved to run; speed throbbed through his veins. Through trial and error, Georgie had learned that with coaxing and gentle handling, Monty's confidence soared. None of the other horses could keep up with his fearsome pace as he raced across the moor, leaving moorland ponies awed in his wake.

At the beginning of Derby week, Georgie walked into the yard to the sound of raised voices. Fred and Tom were having a row. She stopped outside the barn with a frown. It was unusual to hear them disagree, normally they got on so well.

'I'm telling you to give it some thought,' Fred thundered.

'And I'm telling you, you let him off too lightly. He stole our horse and now he's trying to be mates again. He's not forgiven for what he put us through.' Georgie knew from the tremor in Tom's voice, though the words were strong it pained him to say them.

'When you get to my age, son, you learn we're all flawed in our own ways.'

'You don't kidnap a thoroughbred because you fancy somebody and didn't get what you wanted. You ask them out or send them a message or buy them flowers —'

'You need to switch your focus to the race. It's days away. I can't have you distracted by this Briggsy nonsense. If you can't let it go, Hamish will go to Epsom and you stay here.'

Tom had somehow found out about Briggsy's feelings for Georgie. Cringing, she signalled to Amiyah, who'd just arrived, to keep clear. There was no time to ponder on this turn of events for the barn door opened with tremendous gusto, missing Georgie's nose by centimetres.

'We travel up on Wednesday,' Fred snarled at her, 'be ready for then. The *Racing News* is holding a pre-Derby press conference on Friday morning. They're requesting you take part. Our recent saga has stirred up interest and you're the only female jockey. If you win, you'll be the first ever.'

Chickens came clucking out the barn, as though driven outside. Georgie watched them waddling about, directionless. During Monty's enforced absence, she'd felt the same and had to dampen any thoughts about the Derby. Now her brain flooded with the enormity of it. A female jockey had never ridden the winner, only a few had competed in the race at all. Could she be a trailblazer, lighting the way for others? She ought to prepare, there might be questions about that at the conference. She didn't want to be viewed as the comedy element. She feared she'd not been disciplined enough. What if too much eating and not enough running had made her vulnerable. Not only was her career on the line, but the Pengelly's standing in the sport was too and, with that, the staff they supported.

Keeping these feelings to herself, she asked, 'Why are we

travelling up so early in the week if the conference isn't until Friday?'

Fred's shoulders rose in a shifty manner. 'You're needed Wednesday night. I'm saying no more.'

He scuttled away to avoid further questions, garnering a glare from Georgie and a downturn of the mouth from Amiyah. Georgie entered the barn, where Tom stood in the middle of a semi-circle of overfilled feed buckets, clearly not paying attention to what he'd been doing. He met Georgie's eyes, she noticed his were unreadable.

'Hey.'

'I'll take these and get started, shall I?' Georgie picked up as many buckets as she could manage.

'Will you move back into Rose Cottage?' Tom asked, seeming not to have heard her.

'While I'm up in Surrey, yes.' Georgie frowned. 'After all, it's senseless me paying for a hotel.'

Tom sagged down onto a bale of hay, as if the energy had drained out of him. 'And will you come back?'

'I don't understand what you mean.' Georgie's arms were straining under the weight of the heavy buckets.

'I only ever asked you to stay until the Derby. That was our deal. We've never talked about what happens afterwards.'

At that moment, Amiyah took two steps into the barn. Sensing she'd interrupted a private chat, she relieved Georgie of the buckets and scooted away, leaving them alone again.

'I'm not sure if you noticed, but there's been rather a lot to contend with lately.' Georgie smiled. Tom didn't. 'Honestly, I've been so preoccupied with race preparations, I can't think beyond them. I … I really want to ask you something.'

'Sure. Fire away.'

'Do you think I should still ride in the Derby?'

Tom's jaw dropped. 'Don't be ridiculous. Absolutely you must still ride. Why would you even consider not doing so?'

'I'm really grateful, honestly, I am. It's just, it's all becoming real now and, well, rather scary. I've never been chosen for an opportunity like this before. Never. Always been the back-up. You know how it is. Oh, Georgie's all right for a rainy day at Lingfield but the richest horse race in the country … nah. What if I don't have the skills and mess up Monty's chances? I can't do that to him. He deserves a jockey who can give him everything.'

'Monty already has the best jockey he ever could have in you,' Tom said softly. 'No one else understands the horse the way you do. Don't allow doubt to cloud your judgement or steal your confidence. You're brave and you can ride with the best of them.'

'But what if … well, the reality rarely matches the dream, does it?'

'Hey, I don't know about that,' Tom said cheekily, 'in my experience the reality is way better than the dream.'

'If I make a mess of it in front of all those people, it'll never be forgotten. They'll say they knew all along I wasn't capable.'

Tom clasped his hands together and lent back, giving time to Georgie's concerns. 'The way I see it is, whatever career you've chosen; the bottom line remains the same. How much are you willing to sacrifice to try and make it? What are you prepared to lose for the chance? Say it all goes wrong, so what? The worst you've done is damage your reputation and that's hardly terminal.'

Georgie considered, before laughing ironically. 'Not that I've much of a reputation to damage. I'm not a sought-after jockey. More often one who's overlooked for rides.'

'Then there's your answer. You should ride. The only thing stopping you, is you. Don't let your decency become your downfall, Georgie. Don't you want to know? Don't you want to try? If I was in your shoes, wild horses wouldn't keep me away, if you'll pardon the pun.'

Georgie reached out and wrapped her fingers around Tom's hands, squeezing them fondly. 'Promise me you'll come to Epsom. I don't know if I can do it if you're not there. You've been such a huge support to me.'

Tom leaned across, kissing Georgie on the lips. 'Of course. I'll be there, in my top hat and tails, waving a banner supporting Team Misfit.'

'We are a team, aren't we? Although, I can't imagine Fred all scrubbed up,' Georgie giggled.

'And later?'

'Later … we can get as close as you want,' Georgie teased, rubbing her foot up and down Tom's leg.

She knew she had avoided Tom's question about their future.

Wednesday dawned with a cloudless sky, the sun's heat scorching the moor. Boffy lazed in the shade of the hedge, panting. Under a tree out in the field, Guido and Jigsaw stood side by side, nose to tail, scratching each other's backs with their teeth. Flies were becoming a nuisance. Clem sprayed the tack room with repellent. Tails swished, heads shook vigorously, hands waved about, attempting to keep them at bay.

Upstairs in the annexe, Georgie folded her racing breeches and laid them in the case, then zipped up her wash bag. She was ready.

Outside the manor, Clem was leading Monty into the usual horsebox, not looking best pleased at the prospect of many hours spent in the stinky cab. Georgie knew she had to relinquish care of Monty for the time being into Clem's capable hands.

'Ta-ra then,' Clem called, as Georgie, Tom, Fred, Hamish and Amiyah gathered to see them off. 'Don't miss me too much, you guys staying here.'

'We won't,' muttered Hamish, smarting over being left out.

He brightened up as the horsebox rolled slowly up the drive, galloping along beside it, thrusting his arms back and forth as though riding a finish, playing as a child astride an invisible pony, while giving a running commentary: 'And they're off. Around Tattenham Corner they come. And it's a tight knit field heading into the straight. Coming into the final furlong and it's The Misfit in the lead … The Misfit romping home. What a win for team Pengelly and a big pay day to boot.'

With that he swooped off, arms outstretched, imitating an aeroplane, diving all over the drive. A cheering Amiyah joined in, laughing and spinning, as she wove around him. Georgie looked on with a smile. These people, who not so long ago had been strangers, were important to her, their support and friendship mattered. She could not allow herself to let them down.

As the horsebox drove out of sight, Fred's pick up turned in through the pillars.

'Time for me to leave,' Georgie said.

Tom lifted her case into the car, before taking both her hands and swaying them as he spoke. 'I've got to stay here until Friday night, keep an eye on everything. Until then remember to believe in yourself. No crises, especially over the press conference. If they try and rile you, bat it away.'

Fred tooted the horn, keen to be on the way.

'Love you,' Georgie blurted, planting a kiss on Tom's lips.

'I love you more, Georgie Wright. Don't you ever forget it.'

Their fingers remained in contact through the open window until Georgie turned left into the lane and, following the mud splattered rear of Fred's truck, waved until she could no longer see Tom, Hamish and Amiyah, who were closing the gates behind them.

Fred had arranged for Monty to be stabled at a close friend's smallholding, tucked away near to the racecourse. Determined to retain secrecy, no one outside those immediately involved was to be told of Monty's location. Fred wanted Monty to remain in a bubble of calm, with no press getting wind of his whereabouts.

'They'll get to see the horse on the day and not before,' he insisted. 'Don't want him wound up by the carnival beforehand.'

Not long after arriving at Rose Cottage, Georgie was intrigued to receive a phone call from Angie asking her to meet Fred there at nine o'clock that night. No further information was divulged, other than the address and a request to ensure she took her skull cap. Feeling this cloak and dagger stuff was unnecessary drama, after all, the attention would be on the favourites, not them, Georgie was making beans on toast when the doorbell rang. Leaving her food steaming on the worktop, Georgie unlocked and opened the door. There was no one there, but a gigantic bunch of flowers had been placed on the step.

Georgie could see the rear lights of the delivery van driving off, as she gathered up the beautiful bouquet of yellow roses and white freesias nestled among eucalyptus. A small card was attached. Assuming it was from Tom, she didn't open the envelope, instead arranging the flowers in a couple of vases, which she placed in the lounge. Their fresh scent masked the slightly stale smell the cottage had accrued, from being shut up for so many months. Picking up her phone to message Tom a thank you, she thought to check what had been written first and was taken aback to find only two words and a single kiss on a plain white piece of card: *Good Luck x.*

It was clear whoever had ordered the flowers wished to be anonymous leaving Georgie no way of thanking them. The possibility they were from Sam crossed her mind. She wasn't going to try and find out. It would be too fraught with potential misunderstandings and embarrassing if he wasn't the mystery sender.

By the time she needed to depart, Georgie was overwhelmed with tiredness from the drive and cross about Fred's vagueness. Snatching up her skull cap, as she secured the front door, she decided if he'd got hold of one of those racehorse simulators and wanted her to ride a virtual Derby on it, she'd tell him where to go. She could come up with no other explanation for Fred wanting her to troop over so late in the day.

30

Monty's temporary home was an offshoot of a local riding stables. At a fork in the lengthy driveway, Georgie turned left as instructed, which took her away from the main stable area, where the headlights picked out an assortment of pony shapes grazing in the paddocks, to a house, opposite which was an American-style barn. Before Georgie had even switched off the engine, one of a pair of double doors on the barn slid back and Fred's face popped out.

'You're here,' he said excitedly, stating the obvious.

It was now fully dark and Georgie's tolerance levels had plummeted. 'What's this all about, Fred? I've driven halfway up the country today and you're —'

'Stop being a sourpuss and put on your hat.'

Grouchily, Georgie followed Fred into a brightly lit barn with loose boxes running down each side of a spotless passageway, with not a strand of straw visible. It was all varnished wood and silver metal grills. Georgie found it sterile, especially when compared with the slightly dilapidated charm of Pennhalow. The loose boxes were vacant except for one, which contained a tacked-up Monty.

He gave a shrill neigh, ears up, eyes alert, as pumped up as Fred.

Georgie rounded on Fred, askance.

'You two are off on a jaunt along the track,' he explained.

Massaging tired eyes, Georgie said, 'I feel it only fair to point out it's late, dark and … what are you on about?'

Fred led Monty out into the passage, his black coat glistening under the lights, while pulling the stirrup irons down the short leathers. 'A leg stretch up the racecourse. Nothing too strenuous after the long trip. Steady canter over a mile will do it.'

'The racecourse is closed.' Georgie could barely refrain from shouting. 'It's gone nine o'clock at night, not in the morning.'

'Exactly … look lively.' Fred indicated Georgie get onboard. 'I'll give you a leg up.'

Concerned all the stress had pushed Fred over the edge, Georgie tried to take the reins. 'Here, I'll put Monty away.'

To her surprise, Fred gently smacked her hand. 'He's not going away. It's all set up. You need to try out the course. I've got permission. Here, you'll need this.' Fred handed over a bright orange sleeveless high visibility vest, with "Caution" in reflective white capitals blazoned over the back.

Georgie was tempted to inform Fred the only thing she needed to be cautious of was his preposterous idea, yet she clipped the strap of her skull cap under her chin, bent her left leg at the knee and allowed Fred to boost her into the saddle. Monty's hooves clopped in the cavernous space as Fred led the colt outside, a hand on his rein near the bit.

'The course has undulations with a camber, so you'll need to make sure Monty doesn't lean to one side. It's downhill round Tattenham Corner and along the home straight, then starts to climb about a furlong before the finish.'

Feeling surreal as they made their way down the drive,

Monty breaking into a trot at times, Georgie tried to get into the best frame of mind for what was to come. Her breath hissed through gritted teeth, as they waited to cross onto the Downs, getting strange looks from drivers, not expecting to see a horse standing at the side of the road in the middle of the night.

'This'll shake the press off our tail,' crowed Fred, 'they won't be gallops watching at this time.'

'No, they've got more sense,' Georgie muttered. 'Shame we haven't.'

Lined up by what Fred insisted was the eight-furlong pole, Georgie looked ahead at the strip of turf, the white of the rails extra bright in the moonlight. She gulped.

'Fred, my gut's warning me this isn't wise. Wouldn't it be better to do this in daylight? I'm sure the press won't be remotely bothered about us.'

Monty was spinning round Fred, who hadn't let go of his bridle. Georgie still had time to bail out. She was beginning to get dizzy.

'Trust your horse, Georgie. He won't let you down.'

Before she could object, Fred released his grip. With a half rear, Monty tried to run off, delighted to be back on a racecourse and eager to go. Georgie leaned back, using all her strength to restrain him.

'Hold him. Steady as you go,' Fred shouted.

'I'll give you fu —'

Fred heard no more, for they were gone.

Two furlongs flew by with Georgie trying to tuck in by the rails. In the stillness, the sounds of Georgie's panting and Monty's snorting were amplified. Locked in a tug of war, expending energy against each other, Georgie was scared, certain Monty would stumble on the downhill turn, ejecting her into the ground. If she got hurt, it would be over for her. She would have to watch someone else take her place. Fear was making her cautious. Panic spread its wings. Monty would not listen to her calls to settle down.

On the cusp of hyperventilating, Fred's advice to trust her horse repeated in Georgie's mind. She took the chance on releasing a fraction of rein. Monty's pace, so fast as to be riding through a whirlwind, slowed. In front, the unspoiled expanse of grass beckoned, swathed in silver. As they cantered on, unobserved except for two eerily empty grandstands, Georgie sensed the ghosts of Derby winners from the past beside them. Did they relive their finest hour night after night? As they passed the winning post, Georgie eased the colt back. He was still full of running. She thought Fred might rebuke her for allowing him to go too fast, instead he was beaming.

'Handled that fine, then?' he asked. 'Stayed nicely balanced?'

Georgie confirmed Monty had done well with a nod of her head. She couldn't speak. She needed a drink.

A straggly line of young riders on ponies from the riding stables was wending their way down the driveway as Georgie arrived the following morning. She pulled over to the side, allowing them plenty of space to go by and returned the flurry of thank yous with a smile. The girl bringing up the rear was getting instruction in keeping her heels down and two boys in the middle were messing around pushing each other sideways, while their patient mounts plodded on. A Shetland pony on a lead rein was snatching mouthfuls of the long grass verge, munching as he went, while his rider clung on to the pommel of the saddle.

The day was already warm, with the hint of turning into a scorcher. The breeze through the open car window carried the tang of freshly applied hoof oil from the ponies' shiny hooves.

'Lovely day for it,' the lady heading up the procession said to Georgie as she drew up. 'Thanks for waiting.'

Once they'd all gone by, Georgie carried on, seeing the barn in daylight this time. In the gap between the half open doors, a ginger kitten was playing with a piece of baler twine, letting it blow away then chasing after it, claws out. A wren was taking advantage of the cat's attention being elsewhere to dip down for a drink in a saucer of water. Other than that, all was empty, with no one around.

Georgie strode into the barn, making her way to Monty's loose box. She found him lying down in his stable, flat out on his side, legs stretched out straight and crossed at the hocks. Coated with shavings from his bed, his mane and tail were splayed, as though he'd been rolling. As he raised his head and glanced at Georgie with a whicker of greeting, she was glad to find him relaxed and comfortable despite the strange surroundings. He began to rise to his hooves.

'Hey, don't get up, you need your rest,' she told him. 'You've got a big occasion coming up. A mile and a half to gallop soon.'

Monty didn't take Georgie's advice – she found horses rarely did. After shaking himself free of most of the shavings, he stuck out his head to nuzzle her face, while she rubbed the white mark on his nose fondly.

Clem's voice boomed into the barn. It sounded as though she were scolding someone. 'Yes, but still, you could have forewarned me. There is such an invention as the telephone, you know.'

'And here was I, assuming you'd appreciate a surprise.'

Georgie started at the sound of the other speaker.

'Oh, up yours. Fred said I'm in charge while we're here so don't you dare start trying to take over.'

'Wouldn't dream of it, Clementine. You're the boss.'

Certain now, Georgie sprinted down the barn, bursting

outside where Tom was grinning at a wound-up Clem who was holding a broom in such a way, she was clearly considering whacking him with it. Georgie leaped into Tom's arms with a shriek of delight. Clem turned away with a tut of disgust and began sweeping the already spotless ground.

Almost lost for words, Georgie gabbled, 'What … you said you weren't coming until tomorrow.'

'Changed my mind when I heard what you were up to. Clandestine gallops in the middle of the night. Whatever next? I thought I'd better get here and keep an eye on you.'

Georgie slid down Tom's body until her feet were back on the floor. 'It was all your dad's fault.'

'Yeah, he told me. He's in the kitchen, wanting to talk tactics over breakfast.' Tom took Georgie's hand, then sought out Clem, who was tickling the kitten's tummy. 'You coming, Clem?'

'Not yet. I'm busy working. Bring me a bacon sandwich please, Georgie?'

Promising she would, Georgie entered through a back door into a kitchen filled with the smell of frying bacon, toast and cinnamon. Fred was seated at a farmhouse table, wiping up cooked tomatoes from his plate with a piece of bread and butter. Beside him the *Racing News* lay open at a two-page article which, from the headline, seemed to Georgie to be all about Brewster Smith, boasting again.

They ate food prepared by their host, Fred's friend, Wendy, a kindly grey-haired lady wearing an apron over jodhpurs and a baggy jersey. Georgie was chewing on her last mouthful of beans, wishing there was more, when Fred produced a spiral bound notebook, filled with capital lettered writing, squiggles, arrows and doodles of stick horses and jockeys.

'I've been studying the other Derby runners,' he stated, placing a pair of round rimless glasses on his nose. 'I'm as certain as I can be that Polecat will go off fast from the stalls. Brewster's a glory chaser, he'll want Zane to make all, pillar to post. It'll appeal to his vanity if none of the others can get near them. Some of them will fall into the trap of trying to go with Polecat from the start. Flippity Flop definitely will. Bide your time, Georgie. Don't chase. There's a way to go. Use the distance wisely —'

'She should be in a handy position coming round Tattenham Corner, though, dad.' Tom's interruption received a glare from Fred.

'I'm getting to that. You're correct, son. Don't be lagging behind at that point, Georgie. Once they're in the straight, the others will kick on for the finish and you'll be left behind with too much ground to make up. Here.'

Fred slid the notebook over to allow Georgie to see the different scenarios he had sketched out. They all involved Monty being towards the rear, until the downward curve of Tattenham Corner, then moving through to be up near the front by the final run in. Georgie knew the reality of the race would pan out very differently from anything that could be presupposed. Fifteen thoroughbreds all running at approximately forty miles an hour meant split second decision making.

'Don't get boxed in on the rail either,' said Tom. 'You'll never get out in time.'

Her head swimming, Georgie finished her tea. 'Perhaps I'll walk the course after the press conference tomorrow.'

Fred thought this an excellent suggestion. 'For today though, take Monty out for a walkabout. Have an easy time. Just mooch over the Downs. Tom can go with you. Wendy's got a spare mount for him.'

Tom's mount turned out to be a skewbald cob called Patches, with brown and white splodges, feathery fetlocks, the longest mane Georgie had ever seen and only two speeds: plod and plod slower. He and Monty were such a mismatched pair, Georgie couldn't resist laughing.

'It's the only time I'm ever taller than you,' she teased, looking down at Tom, whose legs were stretched out around the cob's rotund belly.

'I'm working harder than him,' Tom puffed, urging Patches into a lumbering trot, which lasted only a few strides.

Monty was taking in all the sights, jig-jogging, finding excuses to leap about. Keeping off the road, they trotted around the edge of the golf course, busy on such a nice day, with its views over the skyline of London. A running club group jogged by them with a wave. Off in the distance, riders in a string of local racehorses heading for the gallops, shouted greetings. Georgie was just thinking how perfect it all was when movement in the bushes to her right caught her eye. Seconds later they were ambushed by a runaway electric golf trolley rattling out from amongst the foliage. Patches merely looked at it, then took a chunk out the bush. Monty freaked out, rearing up, as the cart's owner, in plus fours, burst onto the path behind him.

'Apologies,' the trolley's owner called, setting off in pursuit of his equipment once more, leaving Georgie clinging to Monty's mane, praying for a safe return to four hooves.

Monty lowered his body partway to earth, then abruptly rose again, catching Georgie off guard, his skull bone slamming into her nose. Gasping with pain, Georgie felt the ooze of blood dripping on her upper lip.

31

Wendy rustled up some ice cubes in a tea towel which Georgie held against her pain filled nose, while Clem made jokes about a punch up. Fred stewed.

'One day to go and this happens,' he snapped, 'could you two not have been more careful?'

'It's no biggie, dad,' Tom replied. 'Just one of those minor scrapes you get with horses, as you well know.'

Georgie rushed to back up Tom. 'I'm OK. Nothing's broken. Bruised and sore but not serious.'

The kitten jumped onto Georgie's lap, paws batting a loose thread on the towel. Tom and Fred were muttering in the corner of the kitchen, then they stepped outside. Georgie gave Clem a questioning look; she shrugged her shoulders. They listened to the sounds of an argument. Neither could make out the words. Tom reappeared, clearly furious.

'This had nothing to do with me, Georgie,' was all he would say.

'What?' Georgie asked alarmed.

Tom refused to elaborate, appearing preoccupied as he hunted through the fridge for some cold drinks.

There followed fifteen minutes of tense silence until Fred reappeared and wiped his feet on the doormat.

'I said there was no blame,' he stated, 'however, Georgie, I insist the Racecourse Medical Officer give you an all clear before the Derby.'

'What? No!' Georgie was aghast. 'There's no need for that.'

'And I say there is. I have a duty of care for ensuring the safety of you, Monty and indirectly all the other horses and jockeys in the race. If I allowed you to go ahead, I would be neglecting that. I must be one hundred percent happy you are fit and well enough to participate.'

'It's illogical. I wasn't knocked out or even knocked off Monty. If my nose hadn't bled, you wouldn't even be aware it had happened.'

'Exactly. What if the doctor doesn't pass her fit to ride? We won't have a jockey anymore,' raised Tom.

'But they will pass me fit to ride because there's nothing wrong with me. I'll go see the doctor right now, sort it out.' Georgie hurled the tea towel down, ice cubes scattering on the floor. She didn't like Fred's hesitation before answering, it made her fearful she was about to hear news she didn't want.

'I made a call to Matty Murray —'

'Matty Murray! Bloody hell, dad. That guy couldn't ride a child's tricycle. He's useless and he doesn't know his left from his right. Probably go the wrong way around the course. We may as well let Monty go on his own, he'd stand a better chance. Matty's so heavy-handed. We've said before he's got anvils for hands and that's the last thing a sensitive —'

Fred's voice increased to a shout. 'That's unnecessary. I get what you're saying but there's no one else. All the other jockeys are booked up. Matty's the only one without a ride who is prepared to step in, if necessary, at such short notice.'

'There's a reason why Matty is the only one available,' grumbled Tom.

Georgie closed her eyes in desperation, hoping she could somehow will the last few hours into not having happened, but when she opened them again her nose was still throbbing. 'I'm confused.'

'Matty agreed he'll take the ride only if you can't,' confirmed Fred. 'I've promised him nothing.'

'Yeah, because Pengelly's always keep their word, don't they, dad?' Tom said it with such venom, they were all taken aback. 'As Georgie said, let's get this over with.' Tom produced car keys from his pocket. 'Tell me where the doctor is and we'll go this minute.'

A can of fizzy drink opened with a hiss. Georgie had forgotten Clem was also in the room and had been staying out of the discussion. 'Surely you can't see the medical person until the day. They're only there when there's a race meeting going on.'

'Precisely.' Fred smiled, as though pleased Clem got it.

'Great. You've just loaded a ton of additional pre-race stress onto Georgie for no reason and she has to wait until Saturday before she gets an answer.' Tom reached out for Georgie's hand. 'Unfair.'

Uncomfortably stuck in the middle, Georgie pushed back her chair, intending to try and soothe the situation, but Fred fully indulged his anger.

'I'll tell you what would be unfair. Allowing Georgie to go ahead. What if she's actually taken a harder bump to her face than we realised? If she had a funny turn in the race and fell off, leaving Monty loose, how would you feel then, son?'

Georgie and Clem stared from Tom to Fred, who were both bristling and breathing hard, then back again.

'I'll do it,' Georgie relented. 'If Matty gets the ride, Monty still gets to race.'

'If you're side-lined, Matty won't remain in the saddle long enough for Monty to race. He'll probably barely make it out the parade ring before he hits the deck. Monty won't tolerate it. Mark my words.' With that, Tom left the kitchen, ending the discussion.

With a brief goodbye, Georgie went outside to where Tom was waiting by his car.

'I'll follow you home,' was all he said.

With Tom being in Rose Cottage, it was as though Georgie's two separate lives had collided. A headache was blossoming behind her eyes, her nose showing signs of the bruising yet to come through. As they carried their drinks through the lounge, out into the garden, Tom commented on the flowers Georgie had received.

'I've no idea who they're from,' she confessed, showing him the card.

Sitting on the swing seat, protected from the sun's fierceness by the canopy, Tom seemed unusually absorbed by his phone, typing speedily and responding instantly each time the message alert pinged. Georgie was on the verge of saying something when Tom swigged the dregs of his drink, then announced he had to pop out.

She filled the time he was gone trying to find the right outfit for the press conference. Jeans seemed too casual, a dress not really suitable, skirt and blouse too business-like and capri pants with sandals too much beach gear. Eventually she settled on a black trouser suit and kitten heeled boots, finished with a grey chiffon scarf printed with old style racehorse drawings. It was the best she could rustle up without resorting to silks and breeches.

Georgie was cooking pasta when Tom returned. She served the food while refraining from asking where he'd been, but he told her without prompting.

'Briggsy won't be sending you flowers again.'

Dropping the spoon with a clatter, Georgie was shocked. 'How did you guess they were from him?'

'It's always been his style, overwhelming a love interest with gifts and flowers … and I recognised his writing,' Tom finished sheepishly.

'But I thought that was all over and done with.' Georgie poured herself an extra slosh of wine, figuring she needed it.

'He's been pestering me to meet up and chat things through, so I knew for him it wasn't. It is now though. He understands where we are.'

'And your friendship?'

'Who knows. Time will have to work that one out.'

The *Racing News* team had booked the Final Furlong for the press conference. Being Ladies Day, when the fillies equivalent of the Derby called the Oaks, was run, the Downs were already busy as Georgie made her way to the pub. Traffic was building, bringing a plethora of dressed up racegoers eager for their day of entertainment.

The pub doors were locked. Georgie waited outside until she was greeted by a runner from the production company, who led her to the area where the press conference was to take place. Curtains had been draped in front of the bar, where a long table had been set up, overlooking rows of single chairs. To Georgie's fevered mind, there seemed to be a lot of chairs. She'd been anticipating a relatively small gathering.

The make-up artist was dismayed by the appearance of Georgie's nose.

'We'll have to cover that up,' she tutted.

A minute later Georgie emerged with watering eyes from an excess of face powder.

Nerves were making Georgie sweat. The artist's handiwork wouldn't last long, she thought, as a loud voice filled the room, followed by Zane Powers swaggering from behind the curtain in the pose of a cowboy in a bad western film.

'Georgie, great to see you.' He air-kissed her freshly buffed cheeks. 'Here to represent the underdog in this year's race, I understand. Fred the farmer going for the big one.' The tone was playful, but the underlying spitefulness hit its mark. He could be charming but now she was a direct competitor, all had changed. The make-up artist was oblivious, fluttering her eyelash extensions in his direction.

'We are indeed and in it to win it, as they say.'

'Sure thing, sure thing.' Zane grinned while smoothing dark over-gelled hair from his tanned forehead. He turned to the make-up artist, gave a megawatt smile, and said, 'Are you the one whose job it is to make me even more beautiful?'

With a light film of pink lipstick applied, Georgie's time in the chair had come to an end. Gathering up her bag, she moved aside for Zane to take her place. Fred was standing looking out the window, hands in pockets, chewing gum. She walked over to him and together they watched a helicopter coming into land.

'That's one way to beat the traffic,' Fred observed wryly. 'Some wealthy names involved both days.'

'Yep, so I wouldn't expect much interest in us farmers.' Georgie could see the couple now emerging from the craft were struggling to keep their hats in place.

'Is that what we are then?' chuckled Fred, turning away from the window. 'We'll have to let Monty do the talking … would you believe it? How does that television presenter manage to get herself involved in everything?'

For striding into the room, dressed in a coral pink trouser suit and matching shoes while holding a microphone, was Gina West.

'I guess her face fits,' Georgie whispered, as Gina

introduced herself, then gave a brief run through of the format.

Conveniently, Fred had been placed at one end of the table and Brewster at the other. Georgie was next to Fred, then four other jockeys and trainers sandwiched in-between. Georgie took her seat, clasping her hands in front of her. None of the others acknowledged her or Fred, they sat in uncomfortable silence, akin to guests at the world's unhappiest wedding.

Once the room had filled up with journalists, Gina gave an introductory spiel, then video footage of the Derby contenders in their previous races was played on a large screen television. As The Misfit hadn't run in a race for a long time, they used old film. He looked such a different horse. It really brought home to Georgie how much Monty had changed over the months, improving in confidence from exercising often on the rough terrain of the moor. She fidgeted, wondering when she'd be able to escape.

Eventually Gina opened proceedings to questions from the audience, the majority of which were directed at Zane and Brewster, as jockey and trainer of the favourite. They delighted in repeating how superior Polecat was to any other racehorse that had ever graced the turf. Considering the long and prestigious history of the race it came across to Georgie as arrogant and she could sense Fred itching to interrupt. As he could not without appearing rude, he settled for drawing random shapes on the note paper instead, ripping through it with the force on his pen. Georgie's attention was drifting when a question was directed at her by a small man in a brown suit.

'How does it feel to be riding the rank outsider in this year's race?' he asked.

Georgie took a sip of water, while processing a catalogue of witty remarks, none of which seemed appropriate. 'The

Misfit doesn't know he's the outsider and he's not going to run slower because he is. We're here because we believe our horse is equal to any of the others.'

Down the table, Brewster gave a derisive snort and Zane a barely audible laugh.

Without realising she was lighting a touchpaper, Gina piped up: 'Brewster, you have a response to that?'

'What? Well, I was merely reflecting on how competing in a Classic horse-race is different from rounding up sheep. I mean, they're poles apart. One might be tempted to ask why the Pengelly's have bothered coming all this way at all.'

Fred was halfway out his chair while Georgie placed a restraining hand on his forearm, frantically signalling with her eyes it was not worth rising to the bait.

'Brewster's got a point. Surely lack of experience in both horse and jockey is a distinct disadvantage,' shouted a hack from the back of the room, of whom Georgie could see only a thick mop of grey hair.

'Georgie's ridden in many races throughout her career. I have absolute faith she's the best choice,' Fred retorted. 'Unless, of course, you know better. I've only been training thirty years. What would I know?'

'Very little, judging by the fact you've entered two total losers.' Brewster's sarcastic words ended the laughter which had previously filled the room.

This time there was no stopping him. Fred was up and barrelling towards Brewster, with Georgie and Zane, arms outstretched, trying to keep them apart.

'You want to have a dig, do it to my face,' Fred was screeching.

'Go back to your cows, Pengelly, and take your donkey with you before you embarrass yourself.' Brewster was trying to jab at Fred around Zane's side. 'It's high time you retired.'

'You've always been an ego maniac, Smith.' Fred was skipping on the spot like a boxer. 'I'll show you.'

'Gentlemen … please. This is a civilised event.' Gina tried to diffuse the situation. 'Please, retake your seats and treat each other respectfully.'

'These clowns shouldn't have been allowed to enter the race at all,' yelled Brewster, practically lifting Zane off his feet. 'It's an insult. They're not fit to be seen alongside Polecat.'

'I repeat … respectfully.' Gina was sounding alarmed, with good reason for Fred grabbed his glass of water and threw the contents towards Brewster. The arc of liquid, complete with ice cubes and a slice of lime, sailed through the air, completely missing Brewster, soaking Georgie instead.

In retaliation, Brewster threw a pen. It snagged by its tip in the curtain. The journalists had begun to vacate the room, keen to avoid getting embroiled in the fracas.

'You won't be feeling so smug tomorrow,' Fred jeered, as reinforcements moved in from the crew. 'There's no such thing as a certainty in this game.'

'Got a trojan horse then, have you, Pengelly?' sneered Brewster. 'That's the only way you'd stand any chance. You ought to be point-to-pointing. That's your level. You and your amateur jockey.'

'Enough!' Zane roared so loud everyone froze. 'This juvenile behaviour ends here.'

'No. It ends at the winning post.' Brewster yanked free of Zane's grip. 'And Georgie hasn't got the talent to achieve it.'

He slammed out the door.

32

Desperately in need of both distraction from the strain, which was increasing by the hour and the sun to dry her clothes, Georgie swapped boots for trainers. With racing due to begin soon, she did not have a lot of time spare to walk the course. She cut across the Downs to the mile and a half start. Several jockeys were out walking between furlong poles, hands clasped behind their backs, testing out various scenarios and searching for the best ground.

Alone, Georgie paced the route Fred had drawn on the notepad. From the start, the course rose to the first corner, before heading downhill, sweeping around, into the straight, where there was a camber down towards the inside rail and a rise to the finish. Keeping both balance and momentum was going to be tricky and Georgie was glad of the distraction when Matty Murray approached her.

'All right there, Georgie? Doing your homework?' he asked, with no malice.

Georgie walked over and stood beside him, trying not to be daunted by the growing crowds gathering both in the grandstands and out in the centre of the course. Matty was relaxed, hands in pockets, a grey baker boy style cap covering his strawberry blonde curls. An old pro, he'd ridden the Derby course many times on a variety of horses. It held no demons for him.

'Thought I should. I've ridden it just the once in the dark, so basically blindfold. Monty's the best. I fear it'll be me who messes it all up. If I pass the medical of course, otherwise he'll be in your safe hands instead.'

Matty placed a hand lightly on Georgie's shoulder in a gesture of reassurance. 'I predict you'll be in the saddle tomorrow and rightly so. You and that horse are a team. You've done all the prep and deserve to be here.'

'Thanks, Matty,' Georgie said gratefully, 'although it feels as if not many agree with you. Brewster didn't have a good word to say about me.'

They had reached the winning post. Georgie spotted a racecourse official located nearby gesticulating to them to get off the course, indicating a gap in the railings. They ducked through, allowing the official to shut it behind them, just as the runners for the first race stepped onto the turf and cantered by on their way to the start. Georgie admired their gleaming coats and envied the shine of the jockeys' boots; hers never seemed to come out as good, despite copious elbow grease. They waited by a row of marquees until it was clear to walk over the crossing to the grandstand side, picking their way through the excited crowds, some fanning themselves with racecards to cool down.

'Come over here a sec.' Matty tucked in between the colourful flowerbeds decorating the boundary of the parade ring and the statue of the racehorse, Generous, a Derby winner of the past. 'Listen, I've been a jockey for a long time now. Crikey, I'm so old I remember Shergar! I know no other life. You haven't asked for my advice, but I'm going to give it to you. What other people think or say is irrelevant. It's their issue. Most of them are office jockeys who've never sat on a horse in their life and have no clue how tough it is. They love you when you win and blame you when you lose. Take no notice.'

Georgie stepped aside to make room for a racegoer who wanted a photo by the statue. The runners for the second race were beginning to enter the parade ring, all plaited manes and tails and pent-up energy.

'I appreciate your advice. Perhaps I'm being touchy, but I wish I didn't feel as though the vibe is people want us to fail.'

'Do *you* want to fail?' Matty asked directly.

'No, absolutely not. I want to win.'

'Then what else is there to worry about?'

'The medical.'

'Ah, that's merely a formality. Forget all about it. Ride your race as though the Four Horsemen of the Apocalypse are on your arse because, trust me, they will be. There's only one Derby and everybody wants to win it and if you do, Georgie Wright, you'll forever be inscribed in the record books and no one can deny you that.'

Matty kissed Georgie's hand flamboyantly, then left.

Guessing she ought to get an update on Fred's blood pressure after the shambles in the Final Furlong, she played a voicemail Tom had left earlier, letting her know he was taking Fred to collect Angie from the station and then on somewhere for lunch and a chill out. Georgie considered returning to Rose Cottage but the thought of pacing from room to room alone, alarming herself with scenarios ranging from triumph to falling off at the starting stalls, held no appeal. She contemplated calling Tom and suggesting she meet them at the lunch venue. Her fingers paused over the screen of her mobile, hovering above Tom's number. She was about to press the icon to connect, when something stopped her. A different calling: it wasn't human company she sought; it was equine. She wanted to see Monty.

Knowing Clem would have moved Monty to the racecourse stables by now, Georgie left the grandstand complex behind, along a path which took her away from the hubbub of the races, past a pub and a hotel, to the gates. A security guard scrutinised her pass, not willing to take any chances so close to the big race. As he allowed Georgie access, he spoke.

'Good luck for tomorrow, Miss Wright. My little girl's pony mad. Always racing around the garden on a pretend pony, ruining my lawn. She'll be cheering you on, riding every stride on the arm of the sofa. It's jockeys like you that are making anything seem possible for the girls who follow.'

Georgie thanked him, feeling quite choked with emotion. She had become insular in her thinking about the race, she decided, as she passed rows of stables, some empty, some occupied. The stable staff gave her friendly greetings and waves, some wishing her all the best. She had never seen herself as an inspiration before, she was simply doing her job. Yet if she took a different angle, perhaps she was paving the way for future generations to participate in the big races too. Her career had been modelled on the successful riders she'd admired and wanted to copy as a child. Her bedroom walls had been plastered, not with the latest pop sensation, but posters of showjumpers, three-day eventers and jockeys. Was the whole picture much bigger than she'd realised, she pondered, reaching Monty's stable and folding her arms on the bottom half of the door. She watched the colt tugging hungrily at his haynet, astounded by how much he was taking all these changes in his stride.

'Hey buddy, get a good sleep tonight. You're going to need all your energy tomorrow. It's a big day, the biggest ever for you and me …'

Georgie stumbled over the sudden thought it could yet be Monty and Matty. Monty ambled over and pushed his nose against her fondly with a little snort. She stroked his face reassuringly. All she could do was her best to keep them both calm in the midst of the whirlwind that tomorrow would bring. They had each other; they did not need anything more.

With a tuneless whistling, Clem hopped over to Georgie, all pink sticking up hair, red converse trainers, dungarees and bubbling over with gossip.

'I heard it was almost fisticuffs at the press conference. Everyone's talking about it. Fred and Brewster trading insults.'

Georgie wasn't surprised to learn word had got around. 'It wasn't nearly as entertaining as it sounds. Besides I got drenched. Good job no punches were thrown as Fred's aim is terrible.'

Clem clutched her stomach in amusement, causing the thoroughbred in the adjacent stable to whinny in reply. 'I'm talking horse,' she laughed. 'A group of us staying in the hostel tonight are going over to the pub later. You should come too. Then you can tell us all about it. Give us an action replay.'

'I can't. My parents have arrived and we'll be having takeaway.' Georgie gave Monty a final pat, as the colt, bored with his visitors, withdrew to his haynet.

That night Georgie's dreams were filled with insurmountable obstacles which Monty kept clambering over until exhausted he couldn't any longer. As he took off bravely, Georgie thought they would clear the towering hedge of solid yew blocking their way but then he fell backwards and she found herself falling … falling … down into a deep ditch. As they both lay stricken at the bottom, Briggsy shovelled dirt on top of them, pure nastiness etched on his face.

Georgie woke trembling in the early hours. Tom did not

stir beside her. She lay still relishing the calm. Later the buzz of helicopters would fill the air, the crowd would build, the tannoy would spring to life and by nightfall it would all be done and dusted. Another name would be assigned to history. Would it be hers? Could it be hers? For sure, Monty had the talent and the will, but the day would be on a scale neither of them had experienced before.

The morning's papers contained sports pull-out sections filled with news and information on the race, which Georgie's parents were pouring over when she came downstairs. She didn't feel up to eating anything; her stress levels rising with every minute ticking closer to the appointment with the Racecourse Medical Officer. Having no control over the outcome, Georgie had reached the point when she just wanted to get it over with, one way or another. She would not allow thoughts of being denied the ride, for if that were to happen, she would not be able to stay and watch Monty and Matty compete in the race that should have been hers. Equally to leave would be impossibly painful. She hoped not to be forced to decide.

While her mum fussed with the net veil of her chic pillbox hat in front of the mirror, Georgie picked up the *Racing Life* and scanned their pre-race opinion of Monty's chances. It was dismal reading. The top tipster was of the opinion Monty could have started yesterday and still be pipped to the post by Polecat. Regretting ever opening the paper, Georgie poured coffee. Her dad reached across the table to squeeze her hand.

'All right, love?' he whispered.

'Er, not really. I'm so nervous. Can't seem to get my head around the fact the day is finally here.'

'You'll be fine. More than fine, you'll be amazing. Do try and enjoy it as much as you can because, whatever happens, this is once-in-a-lifetime stuff. Savour every moment so you can tell your kids.'

Georgie grinned a little manically. Thinking further ahead than the next few hours would blow her mind, let alone visualising the possibility of a future Georgie married with a family. It was as though all the versions of herself Georgie had ever been were funnelling into the one moment at four o'clock that afternoon and the Georgie who came out the other side would be different again. In victory or defeat she would be changed by the experience.

A traffic alert flashed on Georgie's phone. 'I have to get going. Don't want to get caught in a jam.'

Georgie's parents and Tom were joined by Mr and Mrs Knight to wave her off. Tom unravelled a homemade banner with "Good Luck, Georgie and Monty" painted in cherry red letters, pushing the cane sticks into the dried earth of the front lawn with difficulty. Chester stalked over and rising on his back legs stuck his claws into the material, shredding it in half. Georgie was grateful for the distraction this caused as she tried to conceal her trembling hands while loading her saddle and a holdall containing her racing breeches, body protector, skull cap, lightweight riding boots and other paraphernalia onto the back seat. With a honk of the horn, she was on her way, which actually felt better than sitting waiting. She pulled out into a convoy of open-top double-decker buses but didn't follow them to the centre of the course, instead pulling off into the car parking area reserved for trainers and jockeys.

She almost blanked Fred, in a black morning suit with a top hat, as well as Angie, in a floaty mauve chiffon dress with matching wrap and feathered fascinator, having not recognised them as they stood beside a Ford Kia chatting to Matty Murray. They called her over.

'All set?' Fred asked.

'Of course she is,' stated Matty with a thumbs up. 'She looks fighting fit to me. Must've caught that off you, Fred, practically turning the Final Furlong into a brawl.'

'Ah, shut up,' Fred said, though not unkindly, the tightness in his face relaxing briefly into a smile.

The foursome started to walk towards the Lester Piggott gates, Matty chattering away. 'We're all sick of Brewster's constant crowing. It's not surprising your buttons got pushed. Imagine the gloating if Polecat wins.'

They stopped to show their documents at the entrance, then walked into a racecourse alive with activity. Helicopters swooped overhead, security staff and police with sniffer dogs patrolled the concourse, bookies were setting up their pitches and hospitality staff dressed in smart uniforms dashed in and out of the grandstands laden with flowers or pushing trolleys stacked with china and gleaming silver cutlery. Gina West was posing on the steps of the Queen's Stand in towering platform shoes and a tight yellow dress. She seemed to be interviewing Brewster for the *Racing News* morning show, although appeared unable to get a word in edgeways, judging by the microphone constantly next to Brewster's chin. Each time she tried to swing it back to speak, Brewster launched into another speech. Fred glowered and was quickly diverted by Angie, desperate to avoid a showdown which might culminate in Fred being ejected from the racecourse and missing the day.

As it was early in the day, the weighing room was calm and half-empty, with only a couple of jockeys who were preparing to jog around the course before racing. Georgie sat alone, breathing deeply, counting down the minutes, too superstitious to unpack her gear. To have to repack everything unused would destroy her. If she failed the medical, she would not be able to stay and watch the race but the thought of abandoning her parents when they had travelled so far to support her made her feel guilty. She would probably end up crouched underneath their table in the restaurant trying to block everything out with her fingers in her ears and her teeth clenched around a breadstick.

At the appointed time, Georgie's legs carried her to the Medical Room on autopilot. Her mind retreated inside to protect itself, as if she walked beside the real Georgie in an out-of-body experience, curiously wondering what would happen to the version who felt sick and dizzy as its hand reached out to knock on the door. For the first time in Georgie's adult life her entire future rested on a decision about to be made by someone else.

The doctor called, 'Enter.'

33

Georgie pushed down the handle and stepped over the threshold to whatever her fate would be.

'So, you took a bump to the face recently,' the doctor read from his notes, then looked up over half-moon glasses directly at Georgie, taking her in. 'Gosh, yes that's a shiner you've got there and no mistake.'

'It looks bad but it's not even painful now,' Georgie rushed to explain. 'I didn't pass out or anything. Didn't even feel dizzy. I have told Fred Pengelly all this.'

'Well, let's be checking you out before we make any diagnosis.'

Standing and moving out from behind the desk, the doctor checked Georgie over thoroughly, prodding here and testing there. Georgie answered the questions truthfully in a voice that never wavered. Her nose felt fine. Now that the bruising had come out it was simply in the ugly phase.

At the end of the consultation the doctor reclined in his chair and tapped his fingers against each other, deep in thought. Georgie sat motionless, too afraid to try and chivvy him along.

'Hmmm … it's a physically tough race even for jockeys at their peak. Takes a lot of effort to compete at this level.'

Georgie held her breath.

'If you were to experience any symptoms of dizziness or faintness during the race you would be at risk of severe harm, as potentially would those around you.'

He paused. Still Georgie barely breathed.

'It's a difficult call to make. I don't want to prevent you from riding today, but I must consider the potential for serious complications were you to overexert yourself. Ultimately, we must ensure all who take part have the best chance of finishing the race in the condition they started it.'

Slowly Georgie let out a breath as her heart sank into her boots. It looked as though Matty would be taking the ride after all. She focused on her hands, neatly folded in her lap, trying to appear professional. The doctor had a job to do, she understood that. She just wished Fred had let it go. She loved Monty and would never forgive herself if he came to any harm because of her. That said, she was more than fit and well enough to ride. The tricky part was how to convince the doctor, who was riffling through some papers while inexplicably appearing to suppress a grin.

'There's nothing wrong with you whatsoever, Miss Wright. You have a bruise which, when compared to some of the monsters I've seen over the years, is relatively minor.'

Georgie's mouth dropped open as she took in the monumental news. 'Oh, thank you so, so much.'

Practically dislocating the doctor's arm with her frenetic shaking of his hand, she tried not to whoop with joy.

'It only remains for me to call Mr Pengelly and give him a proper telling off for putting you through the stress of this appointment for nothing. All the very best. I hope both you and The Misfit come back safe and sound. Have a good race.'

Georgie was utterly dazed as she stepped outside, her

mood soaring between utter elation and sheer terror. Not looking where she was going, she bumped into someone in her path.

'I'm so sor —' she began, lifting her eyes to find herself gazing into a familiar and welcome face beneath a grey top hat. 'Tom! I'm so happy you're here.'

'So … come on … the suspense is unbearable. Tell me fast.' Tom hopped on the spot with agitation.

'The doctor said all good. I'm going to ride in the Derby.' Georgie let the words go with glee, raising her arms in the air triumphantly, until her knees went weak and she stumbled. 'Oh my God, I'm going to ride in the Derby. In front of millions of people.'

Tom's embrace held her steady. He picked her up, spinning until Georgie's feet left the ground and swung through the air.

'I can't believe I'm doing this,' she gasped, feet reconnecting with the ground.

'You are! You really are!' reiterated Tom. 'And I'll be here always. Win or lose, you're amazing, Georgie. I hope this is your opportunity to prove it to everyone, once and for all.'

Georgie threw her arms around Tom's broad solidness, knocking the top hat to the ground and kissed him deeply, unperturbed by the wolf whistles and shouts of 'get a room you guys' from the floods of racegoers now filling the grandstand.

'Bloody stop all that soppy stuff,' a recognisable voice bawled out.

They turned around, delighted to see Fred.

'You'll never guess —' Georgie began.

'Yes, I'm a buffoon, Georgie, for which I apologise. I shouldn't have taken my fears out on you. That doctor gave me a well-deserved earful over the phone. No doubt, I'll also get a rollicking from Angie when she tracks me down and I can only hide for so long.'

'No harm done… in the end,' said Tom pointedly, dusting off his hat and putting it back on his head.

The air crackled with the sound of the tannoy announcing the start of the first race.

'The clock's ticking. Better get ready, Georgie,' said Fred,

Georgie jumped to it with a smart salute. 'Absolutely boss.'

Tom held her back with a hand on her waist and whispered, 'Give it everything you've got. Go create history. We're all behind you.'

Georgie pushed her way back towards the weighing room through an ever-expanding crowd beginning to buzz with expectation. Bookies called out the odds as she fought a path through the throng of excited racegoers clutching their racecards. She wove her way through uninterrupted, until she heard someone calling out her name repeatedly. Georgie chose to ignore it, certain it would be a racegoer who had recognised her and wanted to chat about Monty's chances. She knew it was best not to say too much. Horses were horses. You could never predict a result. But the caller was extremely persistent. She could tell from the increased volume of their voice that they were gaining on her, as she ducked around a gathering of ladies, dressed in their finest attire, sipping from champagne flutes. The sanctuary of the weighing room was in her sights, when someone seized her arm.

'Georgie, love, hold on a sec, we can't keep up with you…' huffed Georgie's dad as he drew red-faced and sweating upsides her.

Tottering in his wake in her heels, Georgie's mum clung to her hat.

'Well now,' she panted, 'if Monty runs as fast as you, we'll see you in the winner's enclosure.'

'We heard from Fred you got the all clear at the medical.'

Georgie's dad gave a thumbs up. 'We love you, keep safe.' He hugged her tightly.

'We'll see you after the race,' added Georgie's mum. 'Take care out there and whatever happens you've achieved so much. We're very proud of both you and Monty.'

'Aren't you coming in the parade ring?' Georgie asked.

'No, we agreed we wouldn't. You'll need to focus and we'd only be in the way. Fred told us it gets really crowded. Besides your dad's hungry.'

'Starving,' Georgie's dad chipped in.

To a flurry of hugs and kisses Georgie left them trying to work out how to get to the restaurant and dashed into the comparative peace of the weighing room. The bustle and pageantry of outside cut off.

Georgie tried to relax while the other jockeys came and went, dressed in different silks for each race, until it was time to get ready. She wondered how Monty was coping with the parade ring and hoped Clem was managing to keep him calm. She could hear the roar of the crowd as the races were underway. She'd never heard anything to match it. Her hands quivered as she struggled with fastening the buttons of the black silks decorated with white cross belts over her body protector, then pulled the matching silk over her skull cap.

Once she'd weighed out correctly and handed saddle, weight cloth and number cloth to Fred to take over to the pre-race saddling boxes, Georgie felt a sense of release. The only obstacles remaining in her path were the physical ones out on the turf. A cluster of jockeys had gathered around the television, watching the horses converge in the parade ring. She joined them. The stable staff were keeping the horses spaced well apart. Flippity Flop, a sturdy bay, reared up, almost escaping the girl leading him, who did well to hold on. Georgie spotted Monty easily, for Clem's pink hair was difficult to miss. She was wearing a jacket with the race sponsor's name and "The Misfit" displayed on the back and black suit trousers with jodhpur boots. As the camera closed in on them, Georgie got a good view of Monty looking picture-perfect with his plaited mane and tail and Clem had applied some decorative diamond shaped quarter marks on his rear. Georgie watched Fred arrive and signal to Clem to lead Monty into one of the saddling boxes. He reached out a restraining hand to steady the horse, who tossed his head and jogged.

It was a beautiful day with few clouds, the sun was warm but fortunately not as overbearingly hot as it had been. Georgie squinted as she tucked in at the rear of the group filing out of the weighing room. Notes from a brass band playing out on the course could be heard.

'Flippin' heck, wish they'd play something more soothing,' muttered the jockey ahead of her. 'My ride's already boiled over. He's just a blob of sweat.'

'I'm sure they'll finish in a minute,' Georgie replied, as a microphone was thrust out of the crowds gathered on either side, right under her nose.

'You're live on the *Racing Right Now* channel,' a disembodied voice announced from whoever was at the other end of the arm now blocking her way. 'How does it feel to be the only female rider in today's race? What about being the rank outsiders? Do you think there's less pressure on you because there's less expectation?'

Georgie stuttered, 'I haven't given it any thought. I'm focused on the job in hand right now so excuse me.'

She did not pause any longer for there was no time. She was stepping onto the pristine grass in the centre of the parade ring, searching for Fred and Tom. Neither was speaking. Tom tapped his foot nervously and Georgie had never seen Fred so pale. He looked spaced out as he chewed at his fingernails and studied the field of amassed equines.

'Remember what we planned the other day. Don't go off too fast, conserve as much energy as possible, be in a handy position by the straight, keep him balanced, save some reserves for the uphill finish.' Fred barely drew breath as his rapid-fire instructions were almost lost in the melee. The bell rang and the jockeys and horses matched up in a crazy game of find-your-partner, made more challenging by the constantly moving pairs.

They dodged across the parade ring, careful to keep a distance from the thoroughbreds now getting overexcited and kicking out. Georgie was struck by how much smaller Monty looked compared with some of the other runners. Darkened sweat patches had broken out on his neck and Clem had already removed the exercise sheet and held it scrunched in her free hand.

'Don't want him overheating,' she explained, tossing it to Tom. 'He's a touch sweaty but he's coping OK, all things considered. They're doing a grand job of managing us.'

'Keep him walking, Clem, don't make him stop,' Fred snapped as they came alongside.

He legged Georgie up in the saddle. She landed light as a feather but as soon as her weight was on Monty's back he shot forwards, nearly rear-ending the mighty hindquarters of the tank that was Polecat, who swished his long dark brown tail in warning. Zane sensed his horse's change in mood and swivelled sharply in his saddle.

'Don't get so close,' he barked, 'the Cat will take out your tiny nag if you do that again.'

Georgie saw Tom clench his fists with rage and motioned to him to let it go. There was no point wasting precious energy. Fortunately, Tom seemed to agree although, as he walked off, he was shaking his head in frustration.

Clem led them into place in the parade. As number fourteen of the fifteen runners, they were near the rear.

Georgie studied the behaviour of the horses as the line snaked ahead. Some remained calm, walking smooth and straight, others were now het up and cantering sideways. She could see the jockey on Wings of Wonder, face creased with concentration as the grey bucked twice in quick succession, throwing him upwards, setting off a chain reaction. Horses bucked and plunged, turning the line into a rodeo with jockeys clinging on, until they regained control of their mounts. Deftly Georgie undid the plaits nearest Monty's withers, pulling the elastic bands free to release the soft black hairs back down his neck. As they turned onto the turf to begin the parade in front of the heaving grandstand, the racegoers spotted their favourite Polecat. The cheer that followed was filled with the hopes of thousands of yet unclaimed betting slips.

On the rails someone flapped a flag in the air and Monty flew sideways, yanking Clem off her feet. She clung on to the end of the lead rein attached to Monty's bit. Her naturally calm demeanour prevented her panicking as she found her balance. While Monty lowered, he threw his head back with force, making contact with Georgie's already damaged face again. With smarting eyes, she knew to play it down.

'Georgie. Are you OK? Is it broken?' Fred called in alarm, running forward, arm outstretched to grip the right rein.

Georgie shouted a warning. 'No … no … give him some space.'

Fred's eyes flashed with confusion, Georgie sensing his dilemma as he rocked on tiptoes, impetus halted by her command. He stayed put. Georgie touched her nose briefly with gloved fingers. They came away sticky. Her face maybe bloodstained, but there was no damage.

'I'm all right. Clem, unclip the lead rein. Let me ride him by myself,' she said gently, rubbing Monty's neck.

With fingers barely touching the reins, fighting the instinct to grab hold of him in case he should flee, Georgie breathed.

If Monty did an unplanned circuit of the course without her, it would be a disaster and probably result in being withdrawn.

'I don't think that's a good idea. We've to stay in line for the parade.' Clem was torn, glancing at Fred for guidance.

'Trust me, Monty feels trapped. Let him free. It's winding him up. I know him. Let me ride him unaccompanied. He'll settle down.'

Clem shot a look of uncertainty at Fred, who nodded consent. 'Georgie knows the horse best. Do as she says.'

As the lead rein fell away, Fred and Clem stepped aside. Georgie held her nerve as Monty continued to chafe at the bit and jog, swinging his hindquarters one way, then the other, in a dance. Uncertain, it took time before he calmed down, ears flickering at the crooning of Georgie's voice. The steadicam loomed up, streaming the parade around the globe. Monty flinched from the alien looking apparatus. Georgie kept her hands light and turned Monty's head away. Without three people trying to control him all at once, he regained composure.

34

As the leaders cantered off, Monty followed. Matty had secured a last-minute booking on a scruffy bay wearing blinkers, called Wonderland.

'Well done. You did a grand job back there,' he called over.

Surprised to receive praise from a rival, Georgie almost toppled out the saddle.

'Cheers,' she said. 'How'd you get on?'

'Ah, this one's easy enough to handle. The owners are convinced blinkers will make it run faster. I could've told them not to bother. Should've saved their money. If this wins the Derby, I'll eat the winning post.'

Chuckling conspiratorially, they slowed to a walk until they reached the starting stalls, where the other runners and riders were circling. A constant hum rose and fell from the stands, occasionally interspersed by booming announcements from the commentary team.

'Take care, Matty,' Georgie called, as Wonderland was led away for a girth check.

'You too. Go for it.'

While a stalls handler checked over Monty's tack, Georgie tried not to get annoyed at the flies buzzing around the colt's head. She kept in the shade and flapped her hand to shoo them away.

'You're good to go.' The stalls handler smiled, patting Georgie's ankle briefly before moving on to his next charge.

Amongst the group of milling runners and riders, Georgie found herself alone. Zane flicked a glance her way, Georgie ignored him. Polecat was coated in white lathered sweat and kept zooming backwards. The others steered their mounts clear, fearing a collision with the solid bulk of muscle.

A murmur of strain rippled through the throng.

'What is it?' Georgie asked the handler nearest to her.

'Just checking whether Stardust's got a loose shoe. Farrier on it now.'

Georgie empathised with the racecourse farrier, who had to check the shoe in record time watched impatiently by the eager crowd. His task was not made easier by Stardust being wound-up and refusing to stay still. Two handlers and the jockey held him, while the farrier confirmed all was fine, then sprinted away, ducking under the railings.

A loud cheer of anticipation erupted.

Georgie could hear the starter calling them in as the handlers began to load the horses into the stalls. Monty was drawn in the middle in stall ten. He stamped a hoof and pawed the ground, backing away first try, then allowing himself to be led in, the padded sides smooth against Georgie's legs. The rear doors clicked shut. Georgie wrenched her goggles down from their perch on her skull cap one-handed, securing them over her eyes. Skin prickling as the thunder rumble of expectation from the crowd rippled across the Downs, Georgie worked to remain poised and contain her nerves.

'Hey, hey. Steady now,' shouted a rattled jockey, whose leg

was almost trapped against the side as his horse was loaded into stall nine.

With only a couple left to load now, Georgie looked forward, through the grill of the starting stalls, at the wide green carpet before her. Monty shifted beneath her. She needed a good start, to gain a reasonable position. She could ease back if she found herself too near the lead, too early. Polecat was the last to be led in and that was it. There could be no turning back, no bottling out, no pausing for reconsideration. It was time. The next few minutes would see history made for some, broken for others. It was all down to Georgie and a quirky black colt who loved to run and dared to dream.

Above the din Georgie almost missed the starter's preparatory shout as he raised the flag. The runners revved, full of stored energy ready to charge. The jockeys roared, letting adrenaline loose at last. The cheer was stupendous as the starting stalls flew open. The race was on.

On both sides of Georgie, the thoroughbreds leaped from their stalls. Underneath her, nothing happened. Seconds ticked by like interminable years as Monty remained stationary. Georgie watched in horror as the fourteen other horses surged away. This was humiliation on a grand scale. Worse than falling at the first hurdle, the last hurdle when twenty lengths clear or two strides before the finish combined. They were sitting ducks.

Then, with no explanation whatsoever, Monty suddenly launched fiercely from the stall with the thrust of a rocket fired from Cape Canaveral, Georgie's stomach left behind, weightless. They were fifteen lengths off the last horse in the field. Panic stricken Georgie urged Monty on flat out to try and make up the lost ground. The colt willingly obliged, lowering his head, hooves a blur.

Now they were ten lengths behind. This was good, making

up ground. Monty was flying, the fastest Georgie had ever gone onboard a horse. Soon be caught up, Georgie thought, then it hit her. She tried to rein back; fearful Monty was running too free. He would never be able to maintain this pace, never last a mile and a half. Yet, she could not stop him. He would not listen. She crouched low, oblivious to the crowds on the rails cheering them on. What to do with no time to think or plan. They had already covered the half mile. Tick tock went the clock.

From nowhere Fred's voice spoke, as if he were there beside her: 'Trust your horse. He won't let you down.'

Georgie stayed still as she could. Her horse was brave and clever; she knew he would find a way if she did not interfere. He knew what he had to do, as he ran on, ears pricked as though pleased with himself. Georgie gave his damp neck a discrete pat, murmured praise. It seemed to bolster him. Coming down to Tattenham Corner they drew up to the last of the pack. Wonderland was already trailing. Matty glanced over and smiled.

'Oi, oi!' he yelled. 'Here she is. Go on, Georgie, my girl. All the way home.'

Monty was full of energy. He swept by the next two horses as they negotiated the sweeping bend. Into the straight they blazed and Georgie knew the moment had come, it was time to make their move. They were in among the stragglers and needed to be nearer the main action so no one could steal first run on them, getting so far clear they would be uncatchable. Georgie had to decide, risk the rail with the chance of being blocked in or take the wider route around the outside. Her lack of recent race rides was beginning to take its toll, arms and legs tired, a stitch of pain forming in Georgie's right side. She breathed deeply, filling her lungs with air that tasted of sweat, leather and soil. Clods of grass flew through the air, kicked loose by the numerous hooves flashing directly ahead.

One grazed her face and she raised a hand to brush it aside, gloves smearing mud across her face like war paint on a warrior. She was grateful for the tint of her goggles reducing the reflection of the sun from the windscreens of the open-top buses parked along the railings of the centre of the course.

A gap she was moving towards closed when Flippity Flop began to lean inwards, coming within inches of bumping Dragon's Fire, forcing Georgie to switch Monty to the outside. It cost a length or two but now they had a clear passage all the way up the straight. The leading group had fallen back and, with Monty still cruising, they were gaining ground. Unsure how many were still in contention, Georgie felt those behind were surely out of the race.

Through Monty's pointed ears, Georgie focused all her attention on keeping the colt straight, visualising a line into the distance. She must not waver and risk accidentally interfering with any of the others for a steward's enquiry would follow and to lose the race in that way would be heart-breaking. Determined not to be shaken off, Monty extended his stride and with two furlongs to go ranged upsides Aquarius. Side by side the horses galloped on with only Polecat to beat. The jockey on Aquarius chose to try and sneak through on the inside, Georgie went wide again as Polecat gradually got nearer. Zane looked back over his right shoulder with astonishment, clearly expecting to be ten lengths clear. In desperation, his arms pumped wildly, but having led for the entire race, Polecat was starting to run out of stamina. As Fred had predicted, Zane had ridden with too much confidence and belief there was nothing that could give his horse a run for its money. As Zane pushed for more, Polecat changed legs, swerving outwards, knocking Monty off his stride. It flashed through Georgie's mind that if they ceased galloping, their race was over, even as she found herself hauling on the reins to avoid a thump from the mighty Polecat. Winning no longer mattered as much as escaping potential disaster. Monty would not slow down. Agilely he chose his own way, dropping back, only to surge again.

With the big horse in the middle, Aquarius on the rail and Monty on the outside, the trio raced past the final furlong pole. It was time to dig deep for the uphill decider to the line, to an explosion of appreciation from the watching crowd who realised they were in for an exciting finish. It would be all the way to the post.

Stride for stride, breath for breath, dream for dream, the gallant horses lowered their heads. Georgie had never felt more at one with a horse than she did in those split seconds. She threw herself with Monty's action, desperate not to hinder or affect his balance. Half a furlong to go and the three noses were still in a line, nothing to choose between them.

Over the tannoy, the commentator was working themselves into a frenzy, animated tones relaying the action aloud for all to hear.

'The powerful Polecat's being challenged. The underdog won't be dismissed. What a race and it's not over yet … Aquarius is refusing to back down … we're running out of turf … who will prevail? The trophy's up for grabs.'

Georgie raised eyes which were stinging with sweat pouring from beneath her skull cap and saw the winning line tantalisingly close. Her head fuzzy, body reaching the end of its tether, knees straining with the effort of keeping her secure in the saddle, she must hold on. As though she and Monty were running down an invisible tunnel, the surrounding cacophony of sounds were muffled, far away, just them against the world.

Monty thundered on. Polecat wavered, bashing into Monty more heavily this time, causing the colt to shorten his stride. For a few paces Georgie thought she'd imagined it but then a collective gasp from the grandstand reached her ears.

The onlookers had seen it too. Monty was beginning to ease up. He changed legs and slowed his pace.

'No, no, no,' she shouted, shortening the reins. 'Monty, please don't give up. Not now.'

Polecat and Aquarius were ahead by half a length. She could cajole no more out of her horse. Monty had fought bravely to the end. She couldn't ask for anything more. Despair and disappointment engulfed Georgie as she realised all their efforts would amount to finishing second or third. Desperately she rattled the reins, but Monty was done. Runner-up would have to be enough. Everyone had seen what a valiant little horse he was. They might not be the winners, but they would be victors against the negativity from those who had said they did not deserve to be there.

As though sensing Georgie's resignation, Monty picked up the pace again with a renewed burst of energy. His ears flicked back up as he lowered his neck and drove for the line. Inch by miniscule inch they gained ground on Polecat and Aquarius, then somehow were a neck in front.

Three strides … two strides … one … the winning post was a blur, but Georgie knew they had passed it first.

The crowd loved it. Georgie could see racecards being waved in the air by the people gathered at the rails. She clutched at the pommel of the saddle, clinging to it as her head went blank, on the brink of passing out. The realisation she had won felt unreal and yet she had never felt more the person she was supposed to be. She hadn't failed, she'd prevailed.

Georgie rested her hands on Monty's neck as he dropped to a steady canter, then an extended trot. She sank gently into the saddle and fell forward into Monty's mane. Sitting back up, she was surrounded by the other jockeys patting her on the back, offering fist bumps, congratulating her. As she pulled down her goggles, Zane trotted over. Georgie braced for what was to come.

'Well done. I've never seen anything as gutsy as that before.'

Georgie dropped the reins and threw her arms around him, to the delight of the camera crew. Gina West held out a microphone on a long stick, peppering Georgie with silly questions. Monty put a stop to that by swinging his rump towards her, forcing her to fall back and almost into the *Racing News* cameraman.

Fred and Clem were running up the course, followed by Tom who held his mobile aloft. As he got nearer, Georgie could see Hamish and Amiyah on a video call, jumping up and down holding each other's arms, Boffy's head appearing intermittently between them as though on a trampoline, catching a whiff of the hysteria. Fred looked as dazed as someone who'd just discovered they've won a million pounds … which he had, in prizemoney.

Clem patted Monty's sweat strewn neck, then tried to compose herself into leading him to the winner's enclosure without the horse kicking any of the press forming a scrum around them.

'Where's Angie?' Georgie called out to Fred.

'Having a stiff drink. What happened at the start? We thought it was all over.'

Georgie held her hands up. 'I don't know.'

'It's not how you start, it's how you finish,' quoted Tom.

As she gazed out over the sea of top hats and feathered millinery gathering at the rails of the semi-circular winner's enclosure, cheering and applauding their return, Georgie couldn't agree more. No one should be defined by their starting place, she thought, and no one should ever feel defeated by the odds.

35

Down the walkway to the winner's enclosure they went, racegoers reaching out to pat a startled Monty on his hindquarters, causing him to almost trample Clem and a couple of racecourse officials, who flung themselves out the way. At the front of the rail, Georgie's parents were waving both hands as though washing windows. Georgie's dad threw his hat high into the air, losing it behind him.

Georgie dismounted to a flurry of hugs and handshakes, as Clem sponged Monty down and Tom offered him a bucket of water. Drinking deeply, the colt then sprayed the nearby cluster of journalists from his nostrils.

'It was the most nerve-wracking minutes of my life,' Fred was telling the press.

'You ought to have been beside him,' Angie interjected, face flushed from what looked suspiciously to have been more than one stiff drink. 'Thought I was going to have to take him to First Aid.'

With fingers shaking through tiredness, Georgie undid the buckles on Monty's girth and pulled the saddle off. She could feel the heat transferring from Monty's body through the sleeves of her silks. Clem poured a bucket of water over Monty's back and set to with a sweat scraper, before the light rug proclaiming him the winner of the Derby was thrown over him. Fred fastened the clasp around the colt's chest with a look of delight on his face. They all posed for photos, Monty taking pride of place in the middle.

'You did a grand job,' Fred told Georgie. 'You got the horse to such peak fitness. In my opinion he could go around again.'

'He might but I sure as hell cannot,' Georgie replied with feeling, 'my legs are wobbling as though I've just ridden a unicycle up Mount Everest.'

'A good soak in the bath later will see you right,' Fred teased, as a television presenter pushed between them and asked Georgie: 'Tell me, how does it feel to be the first woman ever to ride the winner of the Derby?'

'It feels great, I mean amazing, a real dream come true,' Georgie answered, her eyes roving, seeking Tom.

She wanted to speak to him. Only Tom and his reassuringly down-to-earth solidarity would understand. He was Georgie's metaphorical lighthouse; solid, dependable and a refuge through stormy times. She couldn't even begin to try and explain to anyone else.

'You'll be celebrating with champagne tonight then?'

'Yes, yes definitely —' Georgie was interrupted by a steward insisting she must go and weigh-in immediately so the result could be officially announced.

Through the ebbing throng, Georgie could see Tom chatting to a tall, elegant lady wearing an expensive looking indigo dress and jacket. Long dark curls tumbled from beneath an elaborate hat with feathers that rose in a fountain from a wide brim. Netting draped dramatically down to nose level, below which Georgie saw pillar box red lips moving over perfect white teeth. Wondering who she was, Georgie freed her right hand from under the saddle and waved, trying to get Tom's attention, but he was engrossed in conversation.

Impatient at the delays, the steward took charge. 'No more photos for now,' he called to the posse of photographers, then turned to Georgie. 'You must weigh-in at once or the next race will be delayed.'

They hurried off, the steward acting as Georgie's bodyguard, clearing a path back to the weighing room. Congratulations came at Georgie from all directions, with no time to stop and acknowledge them. As they reached the door, Bert Russell was loitering outside. Frowning, he struggled to speak.

Georgie knew only three words were necessary. 'I proved myself.'

Then she was through the door, the steward propelling her onwards.

As Georgie stepped up on the scales in front of the Clerk of the Scales, her heart fluttered. If the scales read the same as when she weighed out, what now felt a lifetime ago, she would officially be the first female jockey ever to ride the winner. She glanced up to find Fred leaning on the wall nearby, whirling his top hat with nervous hands. Their eyes met.

The numbers tallied. Moments later, Georgie heard the official confirmation given out over the tannoy.

'Weighed in. Weighed in.'

It took a few seconds for the significance of those words to sink in, as the weighing room erupted into spontaneous applause.

'You can get off the scales now,' the Clerk said kindly.

Georgie's legs began to give as she stepped down. Firm hands gripped both her forearms, holding her upright. To Georgie's surprise it was Brewster supporting her.

'Well done,' he nodded, taking the saddle from her and

passing it to a valet. 'Go outside and get your trophy. You deserve it. No one could have ridden the horse better today. I'll be honest, I thought we had you beat at the stalls.'

'So did I,' Georgie replied truthfully. 'All credit to The Misfit. I was merely the one who pointed him in the right direction.'

Brewster raised his eyebrows and gave a look that clearly signified he disagreed but passed no comment. Instead, he held out a hand to Fred. For the second time that afternoon, Fred looked utterly dazed as he reached out and shook Brewster's hand. Then together he and Georgie walked to the winner's podium, no longer the farmer and the failure, where the crowd hollered and chanted. Clem had returned Monty to the stables for a well-earned relax. She reappeared for the presentation. Georgie tried to catch Tom's eye but was steered to the farthest end of the podium, with the sponsor's representatives blocking her view of him.

Georgie accepted her trophy and posed with it held up above her head in celebration. She kissed it a few times, her distorted reflection grinning back from the golden surface. Corks popped from bottles of champagne, sprayed around amid much glee. With the formalities over, the racegoers drifted away to try and find a winner in the final race of the day.

Weariness surged through Georgie; a feeling so profound it overtook her.

'You look done in,' observed Clem, 'go and put your feet up in the changing room, then get something to eat and drink. You need an energy booster.'

'I will. Just as soon as I find Tom. Do you know where he is? I can't see him.'

'He's taking his mum back to her hotel so she can get changed for the party later.'

'His mum...?' Georgie was confused until realisation

dawned. 'You mean the glamorous lady in indigo is his mum? Doesn't she live in New York?'

'She does. She flew in especially for the race. Wanted to show support.'

'Wow, good thing I didn't know beforehand. I felt under enough pressure as it was. Imagine if I'd known she'd flown all that way only to witness Monty going to sleep in the starting stalls.'

With the race over, the intensity of it all hit Georgie with full force. The stress she'd carried alone for months without even realising it.

Clem gently propelled Georgie away. 'Go and take it easy but not for too long. You don't want to miss out on the celebrations. Eight o'clock in the Final Furlong. See you then.'

In the cool sanctuary of the changing room, Georgie placed the trophy on a table, then sat on the bench, admiring the way the lights glinted off its shiny newness. To her it represented not only weeks and months of hard work but years; perhaps all the way back to the first time she'd sat on a pony and felt an affinity that had lasted all her life.

She had done it. Shown them she could hold her own, a good feeling, although not in the ways she'd expected. Her mood wasn't one of bravado and smugness, more a sense of accomplishment at achieving what she had set out to do. All thanks to Monty, who'd proved no obstacle was insurmountable if you wanted to get over it enough. Were they misfits? Absolutely and it gave Georgie an indescribable feeling of joy.

Having showered, changed, then packed up, Georgie walked outside, where she was approached for her autograph, an experience she had never had before. The concourse was less busy, with the last race over people were wending their way to the exits. Having signed the proffered racecard, Georgie strode towards the Lester Piggott gates. She needed to get ready for the celebrations with those who meant the most to her, but before she could relax completely, there was an important visit to make.

'Excuse me, Miss. Can I have your autograph?'

The voice hailed from behind. Georgie recognised instantly who it was from the sarcastic tone. 'Sam.'

'Ha ha. The one and only. Huge congratulations, Gee-Gee. You always were a feisty one. A terrier that won't be shaken off. How you cajoled that horse of yours home, I'll never know.'

'I didn't know you were here,' Georgie said, moving away as Sam bent down in an attempt to kiss her. His lips missed her forehead but she still got the full force of the unpleasant mix of lager and strong cheese from his breath.

'Invited to lunch in a private box by an owner. Had rather a lot to drink.' Sam clapped a hand over his mouth as though it was meant to be a secret, then giggled. 'You'll be much in demand now you're a superstar. Should never have let you slip away, you wily fox. I'll have to hunt you down all over again.'

Georgie stepped briskly away in revulsion. 'Drunk or not, you've a nerve. You derided me, the Pengelly's, their horses, their team and now … now, it turns out they're bigger winners than you'll ever be, so you want to backtrack. Reclaim me because I'm of some value.'

Aware some of the departing racegoers had stopped to stare at the spectacle, Georgie paused. Sam stood, mouth agape, stunned and swaying.

'Gee-Gee,' he pleaded, 'it's so not like that. If truth be told, you always were too good for the likes of me.'

Georgie could see straight through Sam's vain attempt at flattery. No longer would she be the fool deluding herself underneath it all was a good guy. 'Goodbye, Sam. Don't contact me again.'

'Hey … er … wha —'

'Your chauffeur's here. I suggest you go sober up.'

She nodded to where Abi waited, teetering in a pair of gold strappy heeled sandals that were clearly killing her feet at the end of a long day. Sam tottered off and took Abi's hand while she removed her shoes, then they walked off together in the direction of the car park. Georgie couldn't help but grin. Whether Sam would remember much of his day when he woke up in the morning was debatable but, as she bid the staff member at the gate farewell, Georgie felt relief at finally regaining both her sense of worth and perspective. With a flourish she dropped her belongings back in the car boot, then jogged towards the racecourse stables, waving thanks to the passers-by who congratulated her on the way.

Inside the stable, Clem was brushing Monty's coat with a soft body brush, singing a lullaby, while the colt swayed in a sleepy trance.

'You're spoiling him,' Georgie said. 'He'll get too used to it.'

'Settling him in for the night,' Clem whispered. 'Fred says we're not leaving until the morning.'

Georgie slipped inside and stroked Monty's nose. The colt gave a satisfied sigh.

'Where next?' asked Clem.

'Bodmin, I assume.' Georgie thought it a rather daft question.

'No, I meant what race next. There's plenty of big ones still to be won.'

'That's up to Fred and Tom.' Georgie's mobile began to ring again for the umpteenth time. Requests for interviews were flooding in. She let it go to voicemail.

'Everything's changed, hasn't it?' Clem put down the brush. 'The price of success.'

'We're still the same people we were this morning. Don't lose sight of that,' Georgie reassured her. 'And next year there will be another Derby winner and the year after and the year after that, ad infinitum.'

Clem sighed too. 'Yeah, it's just … I'm fond of our little cosy corner of Cornwall.'

'Me too, Clem. Me too.'

By the time Georgie stood outside the Final Furlong, fearing she resembled a walking rainbow in a glittery mini dress with coloured stripes, hair pinned up in a loose bun, feet encased in nude stiletto heels, her muscles were protesting at their overuse. Her mobile was full of missed calls and messages. She'd favoured a quiet night in but recognised she couldn't be a party pooper when everyone was so pleased for her.

A corner section of the pub had been cordoned off. Everyone cheered loudly and clapped as Georgie walked in, embarrassed by the fuss. The gin and tonic went down easily, the glass cold, ice cubes bobbing in clear liquid, jostling for space with a slice of lemon.

Georgie's parents appeared to have invited half of Epsom, including the couple who'd been sitting at the adjacent table during lunch. Once more Georgie was waylaid by someone wanting a stride-by-stride playback of the race, thwarting her attempts to reach Tom, who was chatting with a couple of jockeys. Then during the meal, they were seated at opposite ends of the table. A few times Georgie glanced up to find Tom smiling at her. He raised his glass in salute, she raised hers in return.

At the coffee and mints stage, Georgie looked down the table again, intending to signal to Tom she wanted to chat afterwards, only to discover his chair was empty, his jacket gone. Rising from her seat, she slipped down the side of the table to Fred. 'Where's Tom? Is he coming back soon?'

Fred turned to her. 'He's heading back home. We agreed it wasn't fair to leave Hamish and Amiyah doing it all any longer. It's a mountain of work for two.'

Georgie lent back against the wall. 'I didn't know he was returning tonight. Guess it'll have to wait until I get back tomorrow. I'll leave early.'

'You can't because of the press call.'

'What press call?' Georgie didn't know what Fred was referring to.

'Don't you read your messages?' Fred tutted.

'Usually, but there's rather a lot of them.'

'Not surprised. There's a huge amount of interest in your win, which is why tomorrow morning at eleven-thirty, you and I are to be at the racecourse stables for photos and interviews. You made history today, Georgie. It's my round, let me get you a drink.'

Georgie collapsed into the vacant chair beside him. 'Well, I guess I could ask you, Fred. What's going to hap —'

Some impromptu dancing had broken out and before Georgie had completed her sentence, Angie swooped on Fred, insisting he join in. He blew Georgie a kiss as he shuffled off to the beat.

Impulsively, Georgie dashed back to grab her bag and rushed outside, shivering in the cool late-night air as she listened to Tom's phone ring for ages before diverting to voicemail. As he was on the road, she wasn't surprised and left a short message saying she was sorry she missed him.

Leaning against the pub's entrance porch, feeling shattered, Georgie considered retiring for the night. Amazing to think the race had only taken place six hours earlier. She could sneak back indoors and let her parents know she was booking a taxi home, then slope off. She found them having a great time chatting with Marcia, Tom's mum, now wearing a violet evening gown. Approaching the table where they sat, Georgie could just about hear snippets of the conversation over the music. It sounded as though Marcia was inviting her parents out to New York for a visit one day, a city she knew they would love to spend time in.

She never made it to the table for hands grabbed her waist and she was pulled into a conga line snaking its way through the pub, picking up locals from other tables as it grew. Georgie thought of Monty, tucked up snug in his stable. What he would make of the festivities in his honour, she couldn't imagine.

36

Even for someone used to being up before dawn, Georgie woke early the next morning. Strange to be awake at such an ungodly hour yet not on a horse, she thought, as she heard the smoke alarm in the kitchen, triggered by the temperamental toaster burning the bread someone was preparing for breakfast.

Downstairs, she discovered her dad had been up earlier still and out to get the daily papers from the local shop. They were fanned out over the lounge table in Rose Cottage, for Georgie and Monty's win had made the front pages of most. Georgie had only expected the *Racing Life* to run it as the main story, although judging by the headlines, Monty's win was being billed as one of the best performances in the history of the race. To come from so far behind and be victorious was a true achievement. Georgie reached out and touched the nearest paper, reassuring herself it was real. The sensation of viewing the photos from yesterday, seeing herself in the various stages of the day from bag of nerves to beaming in the winner's enclosure, was odd. Her day, captured forever in both photo and memory, was already in the past, before it was even twenty-four hours old. Where to next, Georgie asked herself, repeating Clem's question. She wanted to remain a part of Pennhalow's little world and hoped the Pengelly's did too. The opportunity to rekindle the conversation with Tom about life after the Derby had been lost with his departure. He had not yet called her back, but she understood he must be knackered after driving mostly through the night and was no doubt busy on the yard. Fred would want him to call in on the farm too.

Right now, Georgie wanted to check on Monty. Clem had called to let her know the colt was well rested after a good night. She had taken him for a lead out to stretch his legs. He appeared to have no stiffness. Unlike Georgie, who yawned and stretched as she unlocked her car. She placed her mobile, full of voicemails and texts she hadn't had time to follow up, on the passenger seat, then took a sip of strong black coffee which burnt her lips.

Dressed in her smartest jeans with a black shirt, Georgie drove around to the racecourse stables. After the deluge of visitors yesterday, the Downs seemed oddly deserted, just a few clusters of racehorses out for an easy Sunday walk in the sunshine. Georgie stopped at a traffic light, admiring the sleek thoroughbreds as they crossed the road. They really were a beautiful animal, she thought, with such grace and speed, the cheetah of the horse breeds.

Continuing the sleepy Sunday theme, the racecourse stables were also quiet. There were a few horseboxes loading up ready for long journeys back up north, the staff jovial, having been set up for the day with a hearty breakfast in the canteen. Georgie stopped to chat and by the time she was leaning over the bottom door of Monty's stable, Clem had the colt glistening. Every inch of him looked worth the million pounds he had won.

'Here's the top team,' Clem said, flicking a final non-existent particle of dust from Monty's spotless hide.

'He looks great.'

'Yeah, all ready for his big moment in front of the cameras. Then it's homeward bound and a holiday.'

'For you or him?' Georgie joked, for she knew how hard Clem had worked single-handed and without the glory or the headlines.

A small crowd of media were gathering in anticipation by the gates. Clem led Monty over to where Fred and Angie were already engrossed in answering questions, Georgie following. Monty looked smart in his winner's rug but wasn't impressed by the adoration. He stood in the centre with his ears back and a mulish expression on his face. Even the enormous trophy paraded in front of him had no effect. Eventually Fred asked someone to rattle a feed bucket from the side lines and he pricked up his ears for some decent photos.

'No wonder you get on so well, turns out his biggest motivator is food too,' Fred quipped.

Georgie kept smiling while she answered the same questions over and over.

'Yes, it feels wonderful.'

'Of course, Monty is without doubt the most talented horse I've ever ridden.'

'I'm so pleased I've been able to open doors for the jockeys of the future.'

'*Racing News* are desperate to know what's next for you?' purred Gina. 'I assume you're getting loads of requests for rides now, having struggled for many years. It must feel good to be in demand. What do you want to achieve next?'

Georgie hesitated. It was certainly true her phone had been ringing non-stop with offers to ride for trainers who would never have considered her before, which felt good. Yet she yearned to go home and home was now defined as Pennhalow. She glanced at Fred hopefully. He did not jump in with any indication of how he saw things panning out. Georgie fluffed a reply.

As the press pack began to clear away, Georgie tried to snatch a couple of minutes with Fred. She wondered how she could ever thank him for helping her achieve her dream. His faith in Georgie had never waned, even when she hadn't believed in herself. Aware he was salt of the earth and wouldn't appreciate a fuss or an emotional meltdown, she asked him for a quick word.

'Can it wait, Georgie? The priority is to get Monty and Clem on their way.'

'Sure. Here, I'll give you a hand.' Georgie picked up a crate of gear and carried it over to the horsebox, greeting the driver, who was leaning on the door eating a Mars bar.

With all hands on deck, in next to no time Monty was loaded, Clem was in the cab and the driver was shouting, 'All aboard for Bodmin.'

Keen to follow close behind, Fred and Angie jumped straight in the pick-up truck and with a brief wave to Georgie sped off after them, leaving her alone, watching a staff member sweeping the finally vacant yard clean.

'Grand few days, eh?' he commented, stopping to lean on the broom. 'Loads of work though, then it's all over for another year.'

Feeling rudderless, Georgie returned to Rose Cottage to see her parents off on the journey home. Finally, she had time to listen to all the voicemails and reply to the messages. Very quickly it became apparent she would not be travelling back to Cornwall that day. Four media companies wanted Georgie to feature on their programmes, which meant a trip to London. She booked herself into a hotel near Waterloo station.

Standing in the kitchen waiting for the kettle to boil, Georgie watched a squirrel darting around the back lawn and found she couldn't contain her emotions any longer. Georgie wept for all the moments of joy, sadness, elation, fear, loneliness and frustration. Precious moments that had gone and could never be again. She wondered how she would ever follow up all that had happened over the past eight months. She didn't think it was possible.

Georgie's phone continued to buzz with requests. Every time she heard the ring or message tone she flew to pick it up in the hope it was Tom finally responding to her numerous attempts to make contact. Every time she found it wasn't, she experienced a sense of disappointment but consoled herself with the thought he must be busy too. Still, she longed to hear how it was going and how Monty had settled back in. She wanted to know if Clem and Hamish were getting on better and what the locals thought of the Derby win. She hoped they'd all had a few pounds on in the local betting shop.

For a few days Georgie's time was filled travelling around London, squashed on the underground or trying to figure out where she was with an online map. All the city streets appeared the same. She was pushed and pulled by crowds along bustling streets. Often the peace and fresh air of Bodmin Moor would pop into her head as she stood, squashed against a train door, watching the platforms with their well-known names flash by.

She hadn't stopped for a second to catch her breath, inundated as she was. She pushed on. To complain seemed churlish. Self-care fell by the wayside while she tried to be all things to everyone.

It was on the third day, when Georgie found herself back in the dressing room of yet another television studio, having a thick layer of make-up applied so as not to appear shiny under the lights. Overtired and feeling removed from the life she actually wanted, Georgie hadn't seen a horse for days, let alone ridden one. Exercising in the hotel gym on a treadmill in an air-conditioned bubble simply could not compare to riding out in the early morning, the breeze on her face, the familiar rhythm of a horse beneath her legs. She wanted to escape from the city. Take some time to absorb what had happened. Let the future wait for a while. There was no rush.

The make-up artist selected two lipstick shades, one nude coloured, the other pink, holding them up simultaneously against Georgie's skin, when her mobile's shrill ring erupted from Georgie's bag. Reaching for it, she was delighted to see Tom's name flashing on the screen. Eagerly she pressed the green icon to answer.

'It's so good to hear from you at last.'

'Georgie, hi, sorry, I can't hear you very well.'

From the background noise, Georgie guessed Tom was in the porch of the Smuggler's Barrels. She grinned fondly at the picture that formed of him leaning against the wall, as Francois and Joe rushed by, keen to get to a pint.

'I'm sorry I didn't catch up with you at the Final Furlong, Tom. You were gone before I realised and it's been crazy ever since.'

'Yeah … tell me about it. Dad's even been invited to feature on an episode of *Cornwall's Heroes*. He's been trying to get on that since the nineteen-sixties! Seriously though, we're all good. Dad's battling with Angie over doing up the manor. He fears she's going to spend all the winnings turning it into a palace with heated floors and everything. He rues the day he told her how much we won.'

Georgie couldn't help laughing at poor Fred being dragged around the shops looking at fittings and furnishings, completely out of his comfort zone.

'And how's Monty doing? Has he recovered well? No unforeseen aftereffects?'

'He's brilliant. Having a few days out in the field, then

we'll take him to the beach. Give him a chance to splash about in the sea. That ought to do him good.'

The make-up artist indicated they needed to get on by pointing at the digital clock on the wall.

'I wanted to restart the conversation about the future. Me and Penn—' Feeling pressurised, Georgie gabbled. A delay on the line meant Tom began to speak too.

'Georgie, I've seen you on television, you're a natural. I bet your cottage will be full of big race trophies before long.'

'The thing is I don't …' Georgie began but stopped again as crackling filled her ear. 'Tom … are you still there?'

'Only just, the signal's bad tonight. Must be the mist. Listen, you deserve this happiness and success. I would never want to stand in the way of that.'

Georgie physically recoiled from the phone. Tom's words shocked her. She didn't understand what he was doing nor why the conversation had taken such an unexpected turn.

'Tom … I.'

The crackling intensified, then she could hear Tom talking again.

'I know we said we'd talk about the future after the Derby, but you won. You're going to be unbelievably busy and in demand all over the country. I don't want to be the one to hold you back —'

'Wait, Tom, you don't understand. I'm trying to tell you something,' Georgie interrupted urgently. She knew the call was still open, but Tom appeared not able to hear her. 'Tom, I'll call you back. I want to explain,' she yelled frantically into the handset. 'I want to talk to you.'

With no indication whether Tom had heard, Georgie disconnected. No sooner was the call ended, than an incoming call flashed up from a well-known trainer. Georgie tried to divert it straight to voicemail but in her flustered state accidentally answered instead.

'Ah, Georgie, pleased I caught you,' the trainer began, 'I want you to ride for me. I've a young horse called Fickle Friend, entered at Newbury at the end of the month. I think you'd be a good match. I'll book you in, shall I?'

Georgie's brain couldn't process what she was being asked as her sole focus was to get back to Tom.

'Thanks for the offer. I'll need to get back to you on that once I've had a chance to check my diary.'

Abruptly Georgie ended the conversation and redialled Tom immediately. The calls went to voicemail again and again. Tom must have assumed Georgie wasn't calling back and gone into the Smuggler's Barrels. If the signal was poor there it would be non-existent at Pennhalow and probably morning before she could get hold of him again.

Ignoring Georgie's phone conversations, the make-up artist tutted. 'Which do you prefer? Pink or nude? Both suit you so it's a tough choice. Still as my hubby always says if you've never made a tough decision in your life, you've never cared about something enough.' She hummed as she turned away to pick up a blusher brush.

Before she could continue, Georgie was out the chair. Conflicting thoughts chasing each other around her head. She had the career recognition she wanted, yet the horses were her reason for working in racing and desire to be a jockey. She needed to move forwards, but she also knew her destiny lay down a different path … a path that led to a Cornish manor house hidden deep on a moor and the man she now knew she didn't want to live without. She could be a jockey from a base anywhere. It didn't have to be Epsom, Lambourn, Newmarket or Middleham.

A lack of mobile signal wasn't going to stop her. There was only one place she needed to go. Georgie fled from the television studios, lips still bare, back to the hotel, where she chucked belongings haphazardly in a case, then checked out.

It was late evening; she had many miles to cover but there would be no stopping her. Georgie willed the train to get to Epsom faster. It stopped at so many stations the journey seemed to take an eternity. Back at Rose Cottage, she tore about throwing everything in the car, grabbing provisions for the journey, before trying Tom's number one final time. Voicemail again. As she pulled out of the drive and turned towards the motorway, Georgie was on the final leg of the most important race she'd ever entered.

37

The traffic was sparse. Georgie had reached Exeter by two o'clock in the morning but simply could not go any further. Her eyelids were weighed down with bricks and she knew she had to rest. Pulling into services where there was a hotel attached, despite the hour Georgie was able to check into a room. Crawling into bed still dressed, she was asleep in an instant, her dreams a jumble of confused images, from past and present.

Georgie woke with a jolt, unable to figure out where she was. The roar of a lorry starting its engine brought her into the present. Dawn was breaking, the sky in the grey transition between light and dark. She checked her watch. It was five o'clock and she ached all over. Her mobile phone battery had run out and in her tired state she hadn't thought to charge it while she slept. It didn't matter. On wobbly legs, Georgie showered and drank a strong coffee, then went in search of a sugar laden breakfast.

The commuter traffic around the city was heavy, annoying an impatient Georgie as she crawled ever closer to the border. By the time she reached it, the moor looked beautiful, the heather purple, the gorse blooming, the moorland ponies grazing, happy to have the sun warming their backs.

At the Smuggler's Barrels, Georgie's face broke into a spontaneous smile. A notice pinned to the closed door gave the date of the next pub quiz as the coming weekend. Cador's tractor was chugging towards her. She pulled over to let him by. He waved as he bounced in his seat, stopping to greet Georgie.

'It's good to see you again,' he said. 'I won quite a bit on you and The Misfit. Paid for a few bits around me farm. Good on you.'

The huge tyres of the tractor being almost the same height as the Peugeot, Georgie had to crane her head to acknowledge him.

She didn't stop long for her final destination was so close. As she drew up to the gates between the pillars, mixed emotions crept in. Georgie still had her set of keys. No one had thought about them in all the action of the Derby weekend. Could she just let herself in? She wasn't certain of her position anymore. Although she knew she'd be welcomed, simply turning up might be a step over the boundary. The answer could only be found at the end of Pennhalow's drive, which had been smartened up, the edges trimmed and the unruly trees shaped. Georgie jumped out and slotted the key into the lock, pushing the gates, then drove on. A yellow skip filled with rubbish and scaffolding waiting to be erected lay on the ground outside the manor. Parking up beside Tom's Golf and a van, Georgie saw the front door was propped open and could hear music from within, as though a radio were playing.

Feeling nervous, Georgie popped up the steps.

'Hello?'

She scolded her stupidity. The occupant, whoever it was, wouldn't be able to hear over the song, 'Dancing Queen' by Abba. Walking through the hall, the mirror covered by a huge protective white sheet, Georgie found a decorator in overalls painting the walls. Her sudden appearance caused him to almost drop his brush.

'Blimey, you gave me a fright. I thought you was a ghost.'

'I'm sorry. I was looking for Tom … Pengelly.'

'Think they're all down the yard, mate.'

Thanking him, Georgie left, amazed by how quickly Angie had set to transforming the manor. Even with only a fresh coat of paint so far, it spruced up nicely.

She found the rear of the manor was also undergoing a makeover. The fountain had been scrubbed clean, fresh water gushed into a pool in the basin, where a pair of doves were bathing. A blackbird ran across the lawn, Georgie amused as ever by how it appeared to be pedalling an invisible bike. Blue tits flew low in formation, flitting amongst each other, a magpie chattered as it hopped, bounty in its beak.

Stepping through the gate into the yard where stable doors stood open, Georgie saw a shiny wheelbarrow propped outside the barn and Boffy dozing in a patch of sunlight. Spying Georgie, he jumped up and ran over to greet her, tail wagging as fast as a windscreen wiper on top speed. No one else was about but Georgie knew with certainty the task she had to do first before all others. It was to thank the horse who had changed her life.

She slipped into Monty's stable. He was lying down, burrowed into his soft bed of shavings, forelegs tucked neatly under. She sat beside him; he rested his head in her lap with a whinny.

'Thank you,' she told him, stroking his face gently.

They stayed that way for a long time until the sound of the tack room door opening disturbed them.

'It's my turn and that's that,' thundered Hamish.

'Stop being such a cry baby just because I got to go to Epsom and you had to stay here,' Clem replied.

'And muck out all your … Clem, look, Monty's door's not shut properly.' The panic in Hamish's voice made Georgie feel guilty. As his lanky frame appeared, she called out.

'It's OK. It's me.'

'Georgie? It's Georgie!' Hamish sounded thrilled it was her and not an intruder.

They were all still on edge after the events of before.

'Hiya, Georgie. Thought you were off being a media star.' Clem picked up a tortoiseshell cat with a bushy tail. 'This is Phantom.' Clem waved the unamused cat's paw.

As hooves clattered, Georgie raced outside to the sight she'd been yearning for. Tom and Guido trotted into the yard, Tom holding the reins loose, legs dangling out of the stirrups.

'I see you found Phantom,' he observed.

'We've been introduced.' Georgie tried self-consciously to tidy her hair and crumpled clothes discretely. 'Hi, Amiyah.'

Amiyah greeted Georgie with delight. 'Are you staying?' she asked, as she dismounted from Rosey.

Georgie glanced at Tom, uncertain.

He handed Guido's reins to Hamish and said, 'Come on, Georgie. Now you're here, I know dad wants a word.'

Removing his skull cap, he led Georgie out through the farm gate, towards the outbuildings.

'The manor's looking good,' Georgie commented.

'It is. Angie's wasted no time rustling up all the tradespeople in the area. I'm in the annexe temporarily. Can't sleep for the smell of paint.'

Georgie grabbed hold of Tom's arm, forcing him to stop and look at her. 'I wanted to have that talk with you and I couldn't get through. We said we'd chat after the race. I don't know what's going on with … anything … most particularly us.' She tailed off.

'Your dreams came true,' Tom pointed out. 'You have the career you always wanted. Not many people ever get that.

Like I said before, I don't want to be the one keeping you here, holding you back from that. You'd resent me. Say I ruined your chances.'

A light bulb pinged on in Georgie's head. 'Is this to do with Julie? You think because she left to pursue her career, I'm going to do the same, then end it with you.'

Tom visibly staggered. 'What do you know about Julie?'

Georgie feared she'd said the wrong thing. 'Angie told me ages ago, when I first came here, one night in the Barrels.'

'Right … well, it's not the same.'

'It sounds exactly the same to me.'

'It's not the same, OK?' Tom pulled his arm free and walked off.

'You think I believe all this stuff?' Georgie was shouting now; she couldn't help it. 'I know what it's really about out there. All this attention will fade off and they'll move on to the next one. There'll always be someone hot on my heels and that's how it should be. But that's not real life. This is. And, you know what. You're right … reality is way better than the dream. So, tell me that's not the same.'

Tom turned round and walked furiously back to Georgie. His face set, his hands fists, his eyes wild. 'It's not the same,' he growled, 'because I never felt about Julie the way I feel about you.'

Instantly they were kissing, to cheers from Hamish, Clem and Amiyah, who, distracted by the commotion had climbed up on the farm gate for a better view.

'If you stay, you'll have to share the annexe with me,' said Tom, stroking Georgie's face.

'I can't think of anything better. Although I'm really only interested in you for your heated floors.'

Tom took hold of Georgie's hand. 'You're a minx. I know dad wants to speak to you. He wanted to before he left Epsom, but it was all a rush to get Monty back and resting. Then he didn't want to bother you with all the demands you were under. Let's go find him.'

They found Fred chatting to one of the farm hands, who was holding a cow while Fred ran his hands over it.

'Yep, it looks a case of foot rot to me,' he said despondently. 'Better get it treated.'

'Look who's here,' Tom trumpeted.

'If it isn't someone who knows how to banish foot rot for eternity, I'm not … oh, hello, Georgie. Thought you were off being —'

'A media star. Yeah, that seems to be the consensus around here.'

Fred gave the cow a final pat. 'I fancy a cup of tea. Join me in the annexe, both of you.'

They walked up the lawn, Georgie and Tom still holding hands. Inside the annexe was the same as before. The plant from Sam was thriving despite a lack of attention. It must be a hardy type, thought Georgie with amusement, the same qualities necessary to be his girlfriend.

While Tom was bustling in the kitchen, Georgie and Fred chatted about the last few days and their shared experiences of the sudden interest in them.

'We didn't expect to see you so soon. Assumed you'd be making hay while the sun shines, as they say,' Fred told her.

Georgie accepted her brimming mug from Tom with thanks. 'I missed you, all of you. You made me welcome and this place, I love it here. I don't want to leave.'

Having expected Tom to immediately confirm she could stay, Georgie's hopes sank at the lack of response from father or son. Driving down, she had been certain her old life was over. She would sell Rose Cottage and base herself permanently down here, in the annexe or manor, whichever Tom wanted. Could it be the new life she wanted to replace it with was out of her reach? Previously she had been reluctant to commit, too many uncertainties were in the mix, but now all was clear, to her at least. Perhaps in reality she and Tom had been reading different scripts.

Outside the open window the magpie chattered and the sound of a drill reverberated.

'Angie would raze the place to the ground and rebuild completely if I wasn't standing firm,' Fred complained. 'Nothing wrong with it except needing a few repairs.'

'And some heating that works in the winter,' Tom reminded him. 'If you recall, two years ago when it snowed, I had none for weeks.'

Puzzled, Georgie wondered if she should speak up, whether they hadn't heard what she said. She was waiting for an answer to her future not the heating system in the manor.

'We'd like you to stay, Georgie,' Fred said, 'as Pennhalow's stable jockey —'

'Really?' Georgie was ecstatic.

'However, it's on the proviso you understand, we can't give you Classic race winners every week. Mostly it'll be run of the mill rides with the horses we've already got. We may get an influx of quality horses, or we may be viewed as having been a fluke, Monty's performance merely a phenomenon. I've had a couple of provisional enquiries from owners yet nothing concrete. We could fade back into obscurity. I'm only saying all this because I don't want you to be disappointed.'

'I won't be. Besides who's to say what the future will bring. If you breed from Monty, his offspring could inherit his talent and I'd bet on them being successful.'

Tom reached and laid his hand over Georgie's. 'We want you to be sure as you can be that you won't look back at what's happening and view it as a missed opportunity. You're being given some amazing chances and we'll support you to take as many as you can. Still, you can't underestimate living here permanently will curtail some of them.'

For a minute, Georgie gave the impression she was deep in thought, but she couldn't keep up the pretence.

'I'd be delighted to accept,' she shrieked, clambering into Tom's lap and circling him in her arms.

'You'll stay?' he checked.

'Just you try and stop me,' Georgie taunted.

Fred rose to his feet with a groan. 'Between you and Angie, Tom and I are clear on who'll be wearing the jodhpurs around here then.'

The drone of the drill ceased long enough for them to hear a vehicle's horn beeping continuously.

'Got business to attend to. I'll leave you to it,' Fred announced, shiftily.

Lifting Georgie off his lap, Tom asked, 'What's going on?'

Pretending he hadn't heard the question, Fred was out the door. Intrigued, Georgie and Tom chased after him.

38

Georgie stood aside, watching as Tom lowered the ramp of the horsebox parked at an angle on the driveway, wedged between the skip and Georgie's Peugeot. Fred was hopping with anticipation.

'Got to keep schtum when Angie's about,' he prattled.

Georgie was in the process of asking what when Tom exited with a huge grey stallion, flowing mane and tail tumbling in a snowy waterfall, who waltzed down the ramp. Head raised high, the horse surveyed his surroundings as if he already owned them. Chest proudly puffed, he trumpeted a neigh while, in the distance, Jackson brayed a response. Whether in welcome or challenge, Georgie wasn't sure.

'What do you think?' Fred asked, patting the horse's muscular white neck.

'He's impressive. He must be, what, nearly seventeen hands high?'

'Yep, he is. Say hello to The Mighty, also known as Pluto.'

'The name suits him.' Georgie held out her hand, palm flat upwards, for Pluto to nuzzle.

'Be grateful if you didn't mention this in front of Angie.

He was rather, er, pricey.' Fred's eyes darted warily as though expecting Angie to materialise from the leylandii hedge and tell him off.

'Cost more than heated floors, did he?' Tom asked facetiously, beginning to walk with Pluto, whose ears were flickering but his demeanour calm, round towards the yard.

Fred had his case ready prepared. 'I'm sure he'll be a good addition. He's so big he'll practically step over the hurdles. Plus, he's a stayer. Got him off the owners for a bargain amount because they're moving abroad and wanted him to go to a good home. Also, I, er, promised them I'd fulfil their dream.'

'What dream?' Georgie's suspicions raised to red alert.

'They've entered him for the Melbourne Cup in November.'

'What? Are you crazy?' Tom yelped, screeching to a stop. 'We don't know anything about Australian racing. We've never even been there.'

Pluto lowered his head and began to munch on the lawn. Georgie thought how fortunate it was Angie wasn't around, for sure her plans for the garden wouldn't include grazing.

'We've plenty of time to rise to the challenge. Perk up, you two. The adventure is only just beginning.' Fred danced with glee.

Looking from him to Tom to Angie's freshly chomped lawn, Georgie realised the new life she'd chosen would never be boring and she was thrilled.

Later Georgie walked a little way out on the moor to take a few deep breaths and process everything. She was a stable jockey again and a Derby winning one at that; had she but known how things would work out when she walked out of Beech Tree Stables that morning and so nearly tried to return.

Sometimes a calculated risk paid off. It was nearing sunset and, as she looked across at the glow from the last rays of daylight beaming through the clouds, she knew she had made the right choices. She felt no fear.

Back at the fields, the team were bringing the horses in for the night. They had spotted Pluto, turned out in a field on his own to give them time to get used to his presence. Mostly unperturbed by his sudden arrival, the only one showing any interest was Jackson, trotting up and down the dividing fence, braying occasionally, always the troublemaker. Pluto ignored him with an air of superiority which only wound the donkey up more, as he refused to budge from his spot, nose aloft, peering over the fence into the adjacent horse's field.

'Honestly, he's like a nosey neighbour twitching the curtains. I'm sure I've put my back out lugging the great oaf around,' grumbled Clem, as she and Georgie finally heaved the donkey into his stable.

As evening fell, Georgie was sprawled on a rug outside the annexe while the dinner cooked. Tom came out and lay beside her. The stars were visible, the moon bright as a bulb.

'Funny how life twists and turns,' he said. 'It's tough to let go of the person you used to be, I know that. When my career as a jockey ended, I was sure the world had too. I had to rebuild not only my life but my idea of who I was if I wasn't a jockey. I wasn't built for a jockey's life but what then? I thought I'd never be happy. Now I realise life is more about being content with moments of happiness woven through it.'

'And are you?' Georgie asked, 'content, I mean.'

Tom slipped his fingers between Georgie's. 'I've been content from the minute you arrived and appeared in Jackson's doorway. Every second of every minute of every hour I've spent with you is precious, I remember them all and I hope there are many more ahead.'

'There will be,' said Georgie. 'Some of them in Australia if Fred goes through with this crazy Melbourne Cup promise.'

The next morning was bright and sunny.

'Perfect day for a beach ride,' Tom announced cheerily.

'Yeah, that's if we don't all freeze to death. The sea temperature round here never rises above icy cold below the top two inches,' Clem moaned.

'Praise be the air will be warm when we get out chilled to the core,' Hamish added.

'Good job you two don't work for the Tourist Board,' said Amiyah. 'Your brochure would be miserly.'

'It's all right for you, you're not coming,' Clem pointed out.

'Oh, come on you guys, it's not called Dead Man's Cove for nothing,' joked Tom. 'Besides how many other employers are there who would give their team a morning out at the beach.'

'It sounds sublime. I simply can't wait to visit.' Despite the murmurings of Clem and Hamish, Georgie was excited about the trip. As she prepared Monty, she was sure he would love it.

'It's not a well-known place and should be quiet,' Tom told her. 'Let's get ready, the horseboxes are due in ten minutes.'

Fred had decided beforehand that alongside Monty, the best companions would be Guido, Jump For Joy and Fiddy. All had previously been to the cove and no one was quite sure how Monty would react to the unknown, particularly the waves.

They wrapped the horses' legs in protective padded boots, the tops of their tails in guard bandages and put on their light travelling rugs to protect their sides from the horsebox. Although they would travel in headcollars, they piled up bridles to take, although not saddles. A spending spree might be underway at Pennhalow but Fred didn't want all the tack ruined by salt water. Once they were ready, Tom led the procession up the lawn.

Monty figured now he was dressed in travelling gear he must be going to the races. He jogged sideways, stretching Georgie's arm to the limit, snorting and tossing his head with excitement. Whereas Guido plodded along as the old professional he was, with an air of having seen it all before, Fiddy and Joy caught Monty's excitement. It nearly ended with Clem being pulled through the leylandii hedge backwards by an enthusiastic Fiddy, not helped by the decorator dropping his paint splattered wooden stepladder with a crash.

With calm sort of restored, Georgie became aware of a clattering and banging from the far end of the drive. The sound reminded her of a tractor and Monty twitched anxiously as it approached. Georgie wasn't sure what to expect but she'd pictured one of the square modern lorries with an integrated cab and room for all four horses. She was alarmed when what pulled up next to them was a traditional two horse trailer of the type that resembled an enclosed motorcycle sidecar. It had peeling paint, patches of rust and was in direct contrast to the new black Toyota four-by-four towing it. A middle-aged man wearing a cream colour fisherman's cable knit sweater and denim dungarees over black wellington boots jumped out and shook Tom's hand.

'You'll be heading for Dead Man's Cove then?' he stated in a thick Cornish accent, 'for a spot of beach riding.'

'Yeah, thanks for coming, Rog. Couldn't get any other transport. Is Morag following with the other trailer?'

Rog nodded. 'She'll be here soon. Had some bother starting the motor, is all.'

Tom and Rog opened the doors, while Monty fretted and Guido tried to eat the dried up remains of cyclamen hanging limply over the edge of an ornamental tub Angie hadn't chucked away yet. He was pulled away before he could get his lips around any of it. Tom led Guido into one side of the partition with no fuss, then Monty, now more intrigued than afraid, followed on. With the ramp secured, Rog and Tom climbed into the front seats, with Georgie in the back. Inside was warm and the motion of the car alongside the drone of a discussion about local issues, made Georgie doze off.

She woke as they were pulling into a cliff-top car park, empty apart from them. Ahead were the tops of sheer cliffs. Georgie doubted they were in the right place. She could not see a route down to any cove which would be suitable for two legs, never mind four. Tom seemed happy they were where they should be as he crawled through the tiny access door in the front of the trailer to fit the bridles. By the time he had reversed Guido out and handed him to Georgie, the others had arrived. Monty shot out the trailer with his eyes bulging, then stood taut, turning his head in all directions as though confused.

'I bet he's thinking this is the funniest looking racecourse he's ever been to,' Georgie said, as they fastened their skull caps.

Fiddy was spinning on hindlegs, making it difficult for Rog to give Clem a leg up. Riding bareback after not having done so for many years took getting used to. Georgie tried to let her legs relax down Monty's sides, the heat from his belly seeping through her calves.

Tom led the way, with Monty practically climbing over Guido's hindquarters in curiosity. The path was steep but wound its way down in a gradual descent. Glancing down to the horseshoe-shaped cove below, Georgie's stomach swooped. It was a long way down to the deserted sand.

'The cove's an old smuggling route,' Tom called back over his shoulder. 'Well concealed. They used to hide the booty in the caves then move it up by horse and cart in the middle of the night. It's really Campion Cove, but always known as Dead Man's Cove. It's meant to be haunted by the ghosts of the smugglers who drowned trying to retrieve the barrels of rum from a terrible shipwreck years ago. So much so the locals won't fish here alone at night. They say too many odd things happen. It's a scary place when the sun goes down.'

'Can't say I blame them. I wouldn't choose to spend an evening alone here.'

At the end of the path, it merged with the sand. Guido crossed to the beach without hesitation. Monty stopped abruptly and snorted uncertainly.

'Give him some rein so he can check it out,' suggested Tom.

Georgie let the reins slip through her fingers until the buckle at the end. Monty lowered his head and sniffed at the sand suspiciously. Then he held out his left foreleg, hovering it over the surface before retracting it in a flash to the safety of the path. This he repeated a few times with alternate forelegs while plucking up the courage to actually place a hoof on the sand.

'Any second now and fear of missing out will get the better of him,' advised Tom, watching from a dozing Guido. 'Clem and Hamish, if you go by, he'll follow.'

Monty pranced on the spot a few more times, as Fiddy and Joy joined Guido, then leaped onto the beach. Rushing towards Guido, seeking assurance from the older horse, who startled awake, Monty stuck close as they rode towards the sea. The others laughed at him lifting his legs up in a highly exaggerated fashion, as though he were a dressage horse performing the passage. Then Fiddy bucked Clem off into the soft sand and they laughed at that instead.

Sheltered by towering granite cliffs, with waves gently lapping the shore, Monty walked into the water without hesitation, trotting in the shallows of the surf, splashing up high on purpose. Georgie shrieked as her jodhpurs were spattered, the coldness seeping through to her skin.

'Clem, you were right. Icicles are being thrown at me.'

'Can you imagine what it would feel like if you were to fall in,' said Tom, riding alongside Georgie.

Without warning he reached out and grabbed at Georgie, pretending to try and topple her off into the swirling water below.

They tussled with each other playfully, riding around in circles, laughing and squealing, like knights trying to joust without lances. Monty tossed his head and kicked water upwards, chasing the spray, delighted with the game. Meanwhile Clem and Hamish had ventured just deep enough for Joy and Fiddy to swim.

Georgie rode back up to the beach, Monty's tail running with water, leaving a trail of droplets sparkling as diamonds across the sand. Hamish was swimming alongside Joy. Clem and Tom were racing Fiddy and Guido to the end of the cove. Georgie watched, cold despite the sunshine, soaked through and on a beach supposedly rife with the lost souls of ancient smugglers but she'd never felt so alive and so present. She wasn't stressed about where her next race ride would come from or how her relationship was going. She was simply enjoying being in a spectacular place alongside people who wanted nothing from her except her company.

'Hey, Rog and Morag won't be back to pick us up for an hour yet. There's a café not far along from the car park. Let's get a hot drink and warm up,' suggested Tom, when he returned.

'Sounds a good plan to me,' Georgie agreed.

Having dismounted and dried themselves off with towels, Tom collected the exercise blankets Rog had also left folded up on a boulder at the top end of the beach and threw one of the striped rugs over each of the four sets of hindquarters. Georgie pulled Monty's forward a little, so it covered her legs and was soon cosy beneath the pure wool.

At the top of the path, they took a small track weaving from the car park through the gorse along the edge of the headland for about half a mile until they came upon a green shed with wooden picnic benches outside. A couple of ramblers were sitting drinking frothy cappuccinos, their walking poles propped up beside them.

'What pretty horses,' Georgie heard one say to another, 'must be from a local riding school.'

Amused, Georgie wondered what they'd say if they knew one was a Derby winner. Jumping off, they pulled the reins over the horses' heads. Georgie and Clem sat at the bench furthest from the café, letting the horses graze while Tom and Hamish bought hot chocolates.

As she sat with Monty's reins in one hand, the other wrapped around a white china mug, the sweet smell of hot chocolate in the steam rising up her nose, gulls crying overhead spying out for stray crumbs, Georgie found herself grinning irrepressibly.

'What are you smiling about?' asked Tom.

'I was picturing Bert's face if he knew I was having so much fun.' Georgie chuckled. 'He'd never allow it. Bert was only happy when his staff were stressed out and miserable.'

'That doesn't sound a proper environment for the people or the horses,' Tom frowned. 'Dad's always saying the racing might be the horses' job, but they also need a break and some play time, same as we do. Their happiness comes before anything else.'

Georgie sipped her drink and watched the sun turning Monty's mane a glittering onyx. He was grazing contentedly, swishing away the flies with his long tail, utterly oblivious to the history he had just helped to create. Georgie watched him fondly. It seemed as though everyone wanted to involve themselves in his success story. Given time, this would pass. She knew the Pengelly's would protect him, as would she. He was more precious than stud fees, more important than race results.

Clem and Hamish were scooping the miniature marshmallows from the froth of their hot chocolates and throwing them at each other. Tom gave Georgie a look of resignation.

'You can't take them anywhere,' he sighed.

'It wouldn't feel right if they behaved themselves.'

'That's true.'

'What do you think will happen next with Monty. Will he race again or go to stud?'

'Not sure yet. We'll see what races there are which might suit him before making any decisions.' Tom checked his watch. 'Time to go.'

Quicky finishing their drinks, Hamish then gave the others a leg up before vaulting on Joy unaided. With his long legs it wasn't difficult.

As they wound their way along the track in single file, Georgie was mesmerised by the sway of Fiddy's hindquarters, feeling sleepy from the heat rising from the ground. A boat sailed on the horizon, shimmering in the haze. Georgie yawned just as Tom eased back to ride alongside her. Monty gave a playful bite in Guido's direction.

'Keeping you up?' asked Tom with a grin.

'Just relaxed and pondering. Perhaps we do have the power to change our lives for the better. After all, there are always other options, even when we can't see them for looking. Nothing is ever set in stone.'

Tom stretched his legs and pulled a face. 'Those are deep thoughts for a beach day. I was simply wondering whether I had time to go for another swim before we leave.'

'Let's all do it again,' Clem called from upfront.

'Hark who's changed their tune,' Hamish retorted.

As they swung down again towards the sea, Georgie patted the horse striding beneath her. Relaxed, happy and looking forward to another canter through the waves, their future secure, a pair of misfits for sure.

Printed in Great Britain
by Amazon

32725036R00199